PRAISE FOR
NORTHERN WRATH

"Packs a punch worthy of the Thunderer himself. It rocks!"
Joanne Harris, author of *The Gospel of Loki*

"Holdt wows in her Norse mythology–inspired debut...
an electrifying adventure."
***Publishers Weekly*, starred review**

"Ferocious, compelling, fiercely beautiful.
Fantasy at its very best."
Anna Smith Spark, author of the *Empires of Dust* series

"This is fantasy as it should be written:
savage, liminal, full of wonder and magic."
Gavin Smith, author of the *Bastard Legion* series

"A classic fantasy grounded in real-world history and myth."
SFX

"The author joins a somewhat exclusive club as having
provided me with one of my favorite stories."
Kris Larson

"A promising start for a series that will
gratify lovers of epic tales."
Aurealis

"When you're reading in the garden on the hottest day of the
year and can feel the cold of the Viking North..."
Ebookwyrm's Blog Cave

First published 2021 by Solaris
an imprint of Rebellion Publishing Ltd,
Riverside House, Osney Mead,
Oxford, OX2 0ES, UK

www.solarisbooks.com

ISBN: 978 1 78108 925 5

Designed & typeset by Rebellion Publishing

Printed in Denmark

SHACKLED
FATES

Part Two of The Hanged God Trilogy

THILDE KOLD HOLDT

SOLARIS

*To all who've escaped the shackles
of their lineage and past*

EINER

Chapter Sixty-Nine

EINER'S BREATHS WERE heavy. His left eye was swollen and beaten; most of him was. Blood trickled down his forearms, over his hands, ran the length of his two swords and dripped onto the snow. His northern wrath had left him.

A thick blanket of fresh snow covered the streets, stained red from blood where dead warriors lay beneath. There were too many corpses for Einer to count. Shields he knew, and shields he did not. Friends and foes, all dead at his hands. He must have raged through the whole of the southern city. His own sword was firm in his right grip, and his father's Ulfberht in his left.

He had not wanted to survive, but through his rage, he had.

The battle was over now, although he did not remember it; only remembered that she had died. Her body lain on top of her shield, at the back of the battle. The smile on her lips.

Black winged birds cawed above. The gods were watching. Odin's ravens called for him, applauding his rage.

There was no one left to fight. Perhaps that was why the rage had left him. Einer sheathed his own bloody sword, and then the Ulfberht. His arms were sore and his body was worn like he imagined an old man's might be after a night of rowing.

His eyes caught the helmet of a familiar shield from Frey's-fiord. He had killed everyone—anyone who had come near—without mercy or thought, and he did not regret it, even as he looked at Sigismund's kinsman lying there. Those who were worthy would feast in Valhalla with their families tonight. Hilda's proud bench-mates. He wished he could have been among them.

The ravens squawked at Einer. The town, however, was quiet as the dead. Up the street, Einer spotted movement through the falling snowflakes. Southerners, still alive; they watched him from a distance, bows and spears in hand, as if readying to kill a great white bear.

The gold bracteate hammered hot against Einer's chest, melting the snow off his shoulders so it trickled against his back. It washed blood off his skin and stung against his wounds. Arrows stuck from his lower back and the fronts of his thighs. He saw them, but his body hurt all over. He did not know one wound from another. His chest felt hot as Winter Night embers.

Einer struggled to move his injured legs. The southerners had gathered at the top of the road to watch him from afar. Behind him was the way to the gates. Not a single southerner stood in his way. The gates were wide open.

He forced himself to move down the road. The pain of the bracteate on his chest blurred his vision and he staggered. An arrow in his calf snapped in half. The wound stung, but nothing like the bracteate did. The heat of it tore the breath from him.

Einer dragged his feet through the snow. He stumbled over bodies, catching himself on all fours. Suddenly he understood that white bear from so long ago.

Ravens swished over his head, through the falling snow. The gods urged him along, and from their high houses, the southerners watched him. No one came to block his way or challenge him. No one bothered to shoot arrows. They cowered away from him. They wanted him to leave, and tried to guide him towards the gates, as one might herd reindeer.

Crawling, Einer emerged from Magadoborg. The gates creaked shut behind him.

His skin was red and blood flowed from all of his open wounds; more wounds than he knew to count, more than could be bound, and yet, if he had been meant to die there, he would have died already.

Einer pushed himself up. He wobbled towards the riverside, where the ships had been. He knew they had left—Sigismund would have given the order—but perhaps they were not far away, and he could catch up. Perhaps his crew had waited behind to fetch him. He was their chieftain, after all.

Something shone from down by the river and Einer sped up, ignoring the pain in his limbs.

'I'm here,' he yelled, or perhaps he only thought it. His head pounded like Thor's hammer strokes. 'I'm here...'

He limped closer.

It was still there: a dim light on the river. A ship drifted in the middle of the current. The fires that had raged onboard had long burned out. Einer recognised the ship instantly: it was his own. The *Northern Wrath* had smouldered to little more than floating embers, scattered among the corpses of old friends. The river was black with its ashes. As he watched the last remains of his ship and its corpses, all Einer could think about was that Hilda's corpse was among them.

Fate had always been kind to Einer, but it had not spun a long enough destiny for Hilda. He knew he had no say or choice, but he refused to believe in a destiny that did not include Hilda. If fate had claimed her, it should have claimed him too.

There were no more remains of her in Midgard. No traces of her life; her corpse had been consumed by fire, as had Ash-hill, with everything she had owned and known. All he had of her was his memories.

Tears trickled down his cheeks, and he forced a smile as he thought of her, because at least, in the end, Hilda had finally been happy.

In Valhalla, she would be waiting. Saving him a seat at Odin's high table.

Ravens cawed in agreement, but Einer could not accept it. The gods had claimed her, and with all the strength and anger left within him, he roared for the gods to give her back.

DARKNESS

DEATH, PAIN, AND fear.

The Darkness was not yet done with Ragnar. The cold wrapped around his shoulders and lulled him into forgetting the pain of dying.

His body was healed anew, but his mind bore the memories of the several dozen deaths he had suffered during his time in the Darkness. Ragnar knew nothing anymore but pain and darkness and silence.

Ragnar felt his heart pump blood to every fingertip and every toe. He sensed the beat rippling through his entire body; along the bridge of his nose, down his arms and legs. He heard spit forming in his mouth, and the stroke of his clothes on his skin. The urge to break the silence rose, but he would not give the Darkness a reason to kill him. In silence he needed to remain.

He needed to prove himself to the Darkness and to the gods so that he may be released into his rightful afterlife. He needed to find a way to save Odin on the battlefield of Ragnarok, where Ragnar had unknowingly doomed his god to death. If only he could return to the beginning and stop himself from making that fatal mistake.

With those thoughts in mind, Ragnar clasped the narwhal distaff tighter in his hand. Silently, he tapped it, making the sound only in his head. *Tap. Tap.*

The harsh scrape of knives against glass filled his ears. A white thread shot from the hollow part of his runic distaff and tore a wide veiled hole out of the Darkness. The hole widened with the shriek.

Ragnar passed through.

The air beyond the veil was damp and familiar, as was the accompanying smell of wet rocks. This was his beginning, exactly as he had requested it.

The very first time Ragnar had walked through the veil, he had arrived in this cave where the giant Loki was sentenced to eternal punishment, tied to a rock, with a snake hanging overhead.

Loki hummed his song. Enthralled by his memory of the scene, Ragnar strode towards the voice.

The bloody plains of Ragnarok had been the second place Ragnar had seen. When he went back into the Darkness, he would open a veil onto the plains of Ragnarok, and then, finally, he could undo it all. The thought made Ragnar gulp, for in order to open a veil to anywhere else, he first needed to die here.

His distaff pushed the Darkness away to reveal Loki's giant feet and then his legs, chained to the rock upon which he lay. Like this, Loki was destined to be punished for summers and winters long, until the wolf Garm, standing proud outside Helheim's gates, would howl, and Loki would be freed from his bonds.

Right then, the howl of a great beast rang through the cave.

Ragnar swirled back to stare out the way he had come. Nej, he could not have brought this on too. Not Ragnarok. He should not have thought about the wolf and such doom.

Ragnar stepped back, shaking his head in firm resolution. It wasn't his fault. Not this time. His hip bumped into Loki's foot. His distaff clanged against the chains. At the touch of the runic distaff, Loki's bonds shattered. The chains fell to the rocky ground; exactly as Ragnar had foretold it.

Loki was free. Ragnarok was upon them. The gods would die.

VEULVE

Chapter Seventy

To SEE EVERYTHING at once, yet nothing at all, such was the price to pay for the veulve's star-dotted eyes. The veulve had made the sacrifice voluntarily, centuries ago, when time had arrived in the nine worlds, and all had been subjected to the mercy of the past, present and future.

The veulve's eyes did not see the blood dripping from runes carved into the ceiling of her home. Her star-dotted eyes saw beyond; always beyond, to all there was, to all there is and to all there might be.

Ice will spread. Flames will dim. Bones are shattering. Songs forgotten. Chains are broken.

Her mind rushed through visions, and she struggled to order them into their proper place in time. Centuries of practice had shaped her, but the star-dotted eyes never stopped seeing, and time seemed irrelevant to her, although she knew that it was not.

Images of things past and things yet to pass flooded her mind but one image returned. Not a flash, but a lingering vision.

14

Chains broken. She saw the chains, watched them fall onto rock, opened not by keys or a hammer stroke, but on their own. They clanged onto the rocky floor of a cave. Venom ran down the rock, and giant feet splashed onto the wet floor. Bare feet, newly released from their bonds, chapped and bloodied at the ankles. The veulve guided her vision and looked up, from the feet to the calves to a bare torso half hidden behind a beard that had grown long and wild.

She knew this cave. Her visions often showed her the snake hanging from the ceiling, dripping its venom into the giant's mouth. A constant reminder that the end was near, for all beings, her alike.

She forced her vision up, past the long beard, to the face of the giant sitting on the rock, stretching his limbs. It had been long since she had seen him in present and not in past. Her star-dotted eyes flashed with memories of his future.

His black and red hair will slap in the wind, as his sun-coloured hand wraps the steering oar of a ship made from human nails. The wicked smile will spread on his blooded lips as he stands on a battlefield; the last of its kind. The god Heimdall will lie bloodied beneath the giant's foot.

Ragnarok had returned to the future; returned to the plan of the nine worlds.

'He is free,' the veulve muttered aloud, as she realised what she saw, and what was happening, in the present. 'Loki is free.'

She felt it in her chest. A heaviness had been building there, and finally it was taking over. Many relished that feeling. Only those who, like her, had been captured by the great Alfather, feared the heaviness, which was called 'hope.'

Few were those who knew what the veulve did, and who feared the word. Few were those who knew that Ragnarok was hope. The gods would die and giants would die, and to the veulve, that was the meaning of hope.

'Free them. Free them all,' the veulve muttered.

An old memory stirred.

Blood vows had been exchanged between Loki and the Alfather, and runes had been used. Not by the veulve or by her two visitors, but by a presence hiding in the dark. In the place of nowhere and in a time that never existed and never would.

Someone hidden in Darkness had been using her runes, and the veulve had addressed the presence. 'Free them. Free them all,' she had said, in the hope that fate had been listening. At last she knew. Centuries, since her request. She had been heard. It had begun. They were being freed, at last.

The invisible runic chains that Odin had once used to tie the veulve to Asgard, and to him, felt lighter as she watched Loki leave the confines of his cave. Her bones were sore from the pull of Odin's chain. Bones older than time. She longed to be free, as did beings all across the nine worlds.

Loki rubbed his sore wrists. He was not the first to have been punished by the Alfather, or have his future taken from him. He was not the only one, but he was the first whose future had been returned to him. Fate had freed him.

'Only fate can free them,' muttered the veulve. 'Only fate can free us all from the threads of destiny, spun and tied up by the Alfather's three nornir.'

Wolves howled all across the nine worlds. The veulve saw it with her star-dotted eyes. She was always seeing. Everything and nothing, all at once. *Loki rose from his chains and his rock of confinement.*

At last, the Story-maker had begun to spin their final tale. The veulve allowed hope to flood her. If Loki was free, there was hope. Her servitude was coming to an end.

HILDA

Chapter Seventy-One

IN THE RIVER *your corpse rots,* the Runes whispered to Hilda. *The Hanged God will abandon you.* They had repeated their horrid whispers since Magadoborg. The Runes were eager for her to leave Sigismund's ship, so she could deliver her axe to the gods.

In the river—

Suddenly, their voices stilled.

A wolf's howl echoed across the icy waters. Hilda snapped her attention to Jutland's shore, but there was nothing there. The distant echo came in the wind, like the Runes' whispers.

Hilda grabbed her axe. With her left hand on a tarred shroud, she pulled herself to stand. Another howl rang over the deck of the *Storm.* Her snow fox yelped a bark. No answer came from the coast of southern Jutland. There was nothing to see; no wolves and no people, just harvested fields.

Hilda tightened her grip on her axe.

The man behind her still bragged about his ale-brewing skills. He didn't pause at the sound of the howl. No one else worried.

None of them had heard the wolf.

Hilda glanced along the length of the ship to be sure. At the aft, Sigismund scoured the fields inland. Maybe he had also heard it. A few other sailors were looking inland as well. It hadn't been the Runes, then.

The sail flapped above Hilda, for the first time since they had left Magadoborg. At Hilda's orders, the Runes had blown a steady wind at their backs. For days, the sailors had joked that they were sailing on the god Frey's famed ship, which always found favourable wind.

Again, the sail flapped.

The talkative warrior behind Hilda fell silent in the middle of his bragging. Gaping, he watched the slapping sail. His friends watched too. They seemed to have forgotten that they were sailors—forgotten how to sail on a shifting wind.

The entire crew watched the whipping sail, terrified to act as sailors and adjust their ropes. Hilda, too, watched. The Runes had left. It wasn't like back in the forge when they had been shut out at the top of the passage grave. It was like when she had come back out, eyes burning, and they had left. It felt like that time when they had thought they could no longer use her.

'Going on half-wind. Move the tack pole!' Sigismund ordered. At his voice, the sailors darted to their positions, but they gaped up at the sail, hardly able to believe it. Their perfect wind had shifted.

Hilda held on to the tarred shrouds and leaned over the side of the ship, listening to the wind. No whispers came to her. Maybe the Runes no longer wanted her. Though she owed them a promise and they hadn't received what they wanted yet.

Or maybe they had. She didn't truly know what they had wanted.

Axe in hand, Hilda moved aft out toward Sigismund and his helmsmen. She shambled at warriors' backs, cornered past their fylgjur, and hopped from rowing bench to rowing bench.

The snow fox strutted at her side, and warriors moved out

of her way to let them pass. They were unsettled around her, and had been ever since the snow had begun to fall, as they had sailed away from Magadoborg. Ever since the battle.

Weeks of sailing through the cold and they had hardly spoken to Hilda. Sometimes, she heard warriors whisper praise about her when they talked of the battle and those they had lost.

The battle had changed them all. There was much that they rarely talked about anymore. What they had done had not been honourable deeds. Not all of the things they had done. Some nights, Hilda dreamt of the two children Einer and she had allowed to run into a night of slaughter. She dreamt of them returning to see their dead parents, and of the terrors they must have faced in the streets. Other times, she dreamt of those who had passed on in the fight. Most nights she dreamt of Einer, and when she woke from such dreams, Hilda was no longer as eager for battles as she had once been.

She understood better now why Einer had changed when he had begun to raid, all those summers ago. Magadoborg had been no raid. It had been worse, and it had changed every warrior who had survived the battle. Maybe even those who had died.

'The gods have abandoned us,' Sigismund's helmsman muttered as Hilda approached.

'Nej,' Sigismund responded. 'The gods guided us this far north. We never would have escaped without their help. Now we're in Norse waters. We can make our own way home.'

His helmsman nodded thoughtfully, mollified.

Sigismund's wisdom made him an easy leader to follow.

Hilda hopped over the heads of sleeping crew members at the aft who tried to fend the frost off under layers of blankets. She joined Sigismund and his helmsman at the stern. A wool blanket was wrapped around Sigismund's shoulders. He was covered in layers of wool and fur, even wore his fighting gloves. Compared to most, he was lightly dressed. Not compared to Hilda. She wore the same simple brown trousers and red tunic she had changed into after the battle. Both were a little large for her, but they were comfortable, and the snow had washed off the blood. She wasn't cold, though she knew she was supposed to be.

'Hei, Hilda,' Sigismund said and brought her out of her thoughts. He smiled, but not to her. He was staring at her fox. 'It's alright. We'll get you home.'

He didn't look at Hilda. Now that she thought of it, though he had spoken to her, he hadn't looked at her since Magadoborg. Somehow, she knew it wasn't because of what had happened when they had waged war, killed and raided and murdered. It wasn't because they had left Einer either.

Hilda herself was different, and she knew that.

None of the warriors dared address her. None of them acknowledged her. She hadn't been given a rowing position. She hadn't been given shifts. She had asked, but had been ignored. They didn't speak to her either. They only whispered her name at her back, as if afraid to look upon her.

'Look at me,' Hilda demanded. She stared straight into Sigismund's eyes, barely visible between his blue wool hat and his frosty beard.

Sigismund didn't look up at her, but his fylgja did; the wolf at his back who followed him in the same way the snow fox followed Hilda. It stared at her. The wolf that no one else could see and that Sigismund didn't know he had.

The wind shifted around them. The sail beat again.

'If you can hear me, you will acknowledge me,' Hilda said and her snow fox moaned in agreement.

'I hear you, I hear you,' said Sigismund, in a reassuring voice.

Entranced by the wind, he exchanged a concerned look with his helmsman. They nodded to each other.

'Move the tack,' Sigismund ordered the crew. 'Close hauled.' His orders were shouted the length of the ship and the crew reacted immediately. No one was sleeping any longer. They were all awake, enthralled by the shifting wind that they had not seen in over a week.

'If you can hear me, then you will look at me, when I speak,' Hilda demanded. 'At least give me that respect, Sigis.'

Sigismund crouched to pet her fox, instead. He should not be able to see the fox, the same way his wolf was invisible to him. While he petted the snow fox, he kept a wary eye on the sail.

'Look at me,' Hilda pleaded, but he did not comply. He looked straight through her chest where her heart beat warm.

She knew what it meant. Days of being ignored and she knew why. She had known from the beginning, but she had feared to face it, because this was not how it was supposed to be.

'If you can hear me, Sigis, then look at me,' she pleaded, one last time.

Her snow fox howled with sorrow. A sad song ringing out to sea. Sigismund sighed at the sound.

'You can't, can you?' Hilda muttered. 'You can't hear me. You can't even see me.'

She had died, she must have, but she hadn't passed on to see the gold ceiling of Valhalla. The Runes had been right. The Hanged God had abandoned her. The Alfather hadn't chosen her.

BUNTRUGG

Chapter Seventy-Two

A FIRE CACKLED nearby, and memories of fire demons in a forge flashed through Buntrugg's mind. The heat of their hiss had melted the skin off him. But Buntrugg welcomed the sound of the nearby fire, because no demons laughed any longer.

Muspelheim's furnace had been closed, and the more Buntrugg listened to the crackling wood from the fireplace, the happier it made him. His lips did not move, but his heart warmed with a smile all the same and his eyes teared up. He wanted to blink the tears away, but he could not. He had no eyelids to respond to his commands. His neck was stiff and his body did not listen to him.

Buntrugg's eyes were wide open, but his sight was blinded with light. His vision settled slowly as if he had walked out of a tunnel onto a snowy mountain top.

He heard a sticky sound of sweaty feet moving on the floor, and the merry clink of arm-rings touching. Someone was there with him, wherever this was.

Shapes and colours began to appear.

Far above him was a ceiling made of gold shields. Images were painted into the shields, but the bosses and rims were left unadorned and gleaming. Although there were many spectacular places in the nine worlds, there was only one hall with a ceiling such as this.

The short-lived fought their entire lives in the hope of waking up to this very sight in their afterlife; the gold-shielded ceiling of Valhalla. This was where lucky short-lived came to spend their afterlife, waiting for the last battle of the nine worlds.

But it was not Buntrugg's afterlife. Giants had no such luxuries to look forward to once they passed on from their life.

'How am I alive?' His voice scraped and burned.

His question was acknowledged with a grunt, and the sound of barefooted steps shuffled closer. Buntrugg tried to move his head and see who was there, but even the simplest movement was impossible.

'Your forefathers didn't want you to join them,' answered the husky voice of an older man.

The forefathers had refused Buntrugg. His own afterlife had cast him back.

'You should eat,' said the husky voice, and the man to whom it belonged placed a golden apple on the bed next to Buntrugg. His sleeve was of a rich blue. His wrist, spotted with old age, was decorated with three clinking silver arm-rings.

At the corner of his eye, Buntrugg stared at the golden apple of youth, plucked from Idun's apple tree. Many ambitious jotnar had attempted to acquire apples for themselves, but no one had ever succeeded, for under the Alfather's command, the aesir did not share their wealth with anyone, least of all giants.

Buntrugg kept the corner of his eye on the golden apple. He had seen Idun's tree before, on one of his first tasks for Surt, a long, long time ago. As few beings did, Buntrugg knew how the aesir's golden apples smelled. Newly plucked, they gave off a sharp scent of seawater and fresh beech leaves. He inhaled deep. This was not a painted apple, or some other trick. Offered to

Buntrugg was a true apple of youth, and only one man in the nine worlds had the authority to gift it to him.

It had to be a trick, for he could not lift his arms and grab the apple. Besides, what he needed was a healthy body, not a young one.

'Youth will help you heal,' said the old man in response to Buntrugg's loud thoughts.

Buntrugg struggled to turn and see the man. His body was stiff and he did not yet have full control over his limbs. Yet he knew that there was only one man it could be. This was Odin's hall; no one but Odin could have invited him inside. But the Alfather would not help a giant. Besides, the Alfather was a busy man, requested in all nine worlds, so if he was sacrificing his time to sit watch over Buntrugg, a giant, it was because he wanted something that only Buntrugg could provide.

'I'll share a secret with you,' said the great Alfather on cue. His voice was a whisper that tickled Buntrugg's ears. 'Since the beginning of ages, your forefathers have only ever refused the death of one other jotun.'

Buntrugg did not need to be told who it had been. 'Surt,' he said, although he had never heard the tale before. His mentor never would have shared such a past, yet Buntrugg was not in doubt, because everyone in the nine worlds feared Surt.

Everyone apart from Buntrugg's sister, but she was different.

'Did Surt ask them to save you?' Odin mused aloud, but his tone made it clear that he did not believe it, and neither did Buntrugg. The forefathers did not listen to anyone.

Thousands of faces of old had flashed before him on his way through the passage grave with the dwarf. They were faces from long before his time, but he knew them now. They had been his forefathers.

More eagerly, Buntrugg listened for their voices within himself. The more he listened to the individual voices of all past giants, the clearer they became. They were shouting something, all together, but Buntrugg could not hear what they said.

The longer he lay on his back in Odin's hall and listened to the voices of the forefathers, the more his senses began to return. His sight sharpened and control over his limbs slowly returned. It came with a stabbing pain, as if his entire body was one open wound that hurt and ached with every feeble motion.

The more Buntrugg thought about the time in the forge, when he had thought he was dying, the more questions arose. 'I was drowning,' he said.

'A frightened dwarf hauled your charred body out of the water,' the Alfather willingly answered. Odin's tongue was looser than Surt's, yet disciplined. He was a man who liked conversation.

Buntrugg was certain, now, that the Alfather wanted something from him, but he could not figure out what that might be.

He mustered the strength to ask another question: 'Why did you bring me here?'

Of all the places he might have expected to wake up, Valhalla was not among them. The aesir and vanir who called themselves gods had no compassion for giants, and Buntrugg could not comprehend why the Alfather would help a giant in this way.

The Alfather chuckled at the question, and Buntrugg felt strangely like a little boy again, being praised by his father for a perceptive observation.

'Geri and Freki brought you to me,' Odin said, and Buntrugg heard a wolfish moan. One of the Alfather's wolves sauntered into view and slumped down next to a chair by Buntrugg's bed.

The Alfather remained silent for a long while, apart from a musing grunt here and there.

'How did they find me?' Buntrugg asked, eyeing the grey wolf laying docile with its head on its paws. The forge of Alvis's kinsmen had not been easy for Buntrugg to find.

'There is this girl,' the Alfather began, at last. Every answer he gave seemed modelled like a famous skald story. His voice carried the tone and skill of a story-teller. 'There is a town.

Well, there used to be a town. Its name was Ash-hill, but now it's no more than ashes.'

Buntrugg's heart skipped a beat. Ash-hill was where his sister had lived these past many winters. Of all the places in Midgard the Alfather could have kept an eye on, he had chosen the village where Glumbruck lived. It could be no coincidence.

'This girl grew up in Ash-hill. I've watched the town for summers and winters. *We've* watched it,' Odin said, and Buntrugg did not know if the Alfather's use of "we" referred to him and his wolves or to all the aesir or some third thing, but it made him uneasy. 'That night, the girl from Ash-hill led Geri and Freki to you.'

As it often was with questions and answers, with every answer he gained, new questions arose in Buntrugg's mind, and not one could satisfy his curiosity. 'What is so special about this girl?'

'Glumbruck marked her,' the Alfather answered.

Buntrugg's heart raced at the mention of his sister's name. The Alfather named Glumbruck easily, knowing exactly how much Buntrugg looked up to her, although no one else did.

'Seven hundred and forty winters I searched for her, after her banishment from Jotunheim.'

So confidently Odin admitted that he knew Glumbruck. Buntrugg's own parents had always kept quiet about the past. Buntrugg had only ever heard the banishment mentioned once, in passing, and when he had enquired about it, everyone had pretended not to know anything. No one ever talked about his sister and her trial, nor the many centuries before the banishment, when she had left Jotunheim behind.

A desire burned to ask the Alfather what had happened back in the old days that no one wanted to talk about, because the Alfather was the key to it all.

'When, at last, I found Glumbruck, she was in Ash-hill, standing at the foot of a leaking ash tree,' Odin continued. 'Your sister has always had a good nose for these things. It's a shame she didn't fix the tree on her own. It had to be cut and burned to close the leak.'

Another leak in the nine worlds. Like the one Buntrugg had sensed in the passage grave leading to the forge. The power of Ginnungagap was leaking out of passage graves and ash-trees, and when there was no more Ginnungagap to leak, the nine worlds would fade and disappear.

'What does a leaking ash-tree have to do with your wolves finding me in that forge?'

The Alfather laughed then, a crow-like laughter, yet a fatherly one that Buntrugg wished would never end. 'That girl from Ash-hill, your sister put her inside the leak. She isn't just a short-lived girl. Not anymore.'

'She leaks Ginnungagap,' Buntrugg realised on his own. 'Like the tree did.'

Suddenly it all clicked for Buntrugg. A good nose for these things, the Alfather had said. Buntrugg, too, had met the girl who did not smell of Midgard, but of runes and creation. In the entrance to the passage grave, she had sensed Buntrugg's and Bafir's presence although no short-lived ought to have been able to see them in their Midgard capes. She had marked Buntrugg by name and she had known his sister's real name. She had even called herself Glumbruck's daughter.

Neither Buntrugg nor Bafir had mentioned the forge to her, but he supposed that Odin's two wolves could have seen them then, and followed.

The questions doubled. The thoughts eased Buntrugg's bodily pains and gave him somewhere to put his focus.

The nearby fire crackled away and reminded him of how he had been supposed to die and how the forefathers had rejected him. Once again, he listened to their voices. They were whispering a name. Buntrugg strained to hear. *Einer Glumbruckson.*

'Einer,' he mumbled aloud.

'Your sister's son refuses to die, like you, but soon he will be seated in my hall,' the Alfather said. It almost sounded like a threat. He leaned back in the armchair next to Buntrugg's bed. The wolf at his side nuzzled up against his leg.

'He won't be seated in this hall,' Buntrugg said aloud. At the corner of his eyes, he watched the muscles in Alfather's face tighten with anger at the contradiction. 'Not ever. He isn't the same as my sister's other sons.'

The Alfather's single eye widened with understanding and fear. To hide his expression, Odin rose. His long robe dragged across the floor behind him as he walked towards the snap of the fire, out of Buntrugg's field of vision.

'The forefathers are with him,' Buntrugg continued. The Alfather needed to know, for only the knowledge of what Glumbruck's son had become—and would become in death— could keep a man like the Alfather from killing Einer. 'The forefathers won't kill him. He has chosen them. Einer is more long-lived than short-lived now.'

'You sound certain of yourself.'

'I know the forefathers. Better than ever before. I hear them whisper his name inside me.' Their whispers grew to shouts as he said it. Thousands of thousands of forefathers shouted Einer's name.

'Even the forefathers can't change someone's fate,' the Alfather said in a strict voice. 'He was promised to me by the veulve and the three nornir. I have a seat prepared for him.'

The thought of Glumbruck's son sitting in the Alfather's hall and fighting for the cause of an aesir, made Buntrugg's empty stomach turn with disgrace. The forefathers continued their loud shouts.

'Whether you believe me or not, it's the truth. Einer is more jotun than short-lived,' Buntrugg said to ensure that the Alfather understood. 'He is no longer Einer Vigmerson, the mere son of a short-lived chieftain. He is my kin. My sister's son, in full right, and he is lost to you. Never can he be a warrior in this hall. The forefathers shake at this talk of him. At the sound of his true name. Einer Glumbruckson.'

'He can't be a jotun son,' the Alfather snapped, but he did not sound as certain as he had moments earlier. He no longer sounded convinced himself. Quietly, he recited the old words of the nine worlds, musing on their meaning: *'To begin with, the beginning had not begun. Because change changes and does not change back. And, in the end, the ending will not come to an end.'*

With those words of old, silence settled in the room. Buntrugg stared up at the gold-shield roof and with the forefathers shouting his nephew's name in unison, his thoughts wandered to his sister. Everyone of importance knew his sister. Surt knew her, the veulve had spoken of her; even the Alfather had willingly named her.

'What happened back then?' Buntrugg finally asked, after silence had settled between them for such a long while that he had nearly forgotten his own voice. 'Before my sister went to Midgard?'

For a few heartbeats the Alfather considered the question, before he answered. 'Much happened. Much still does.'

As ever, the answer was fickle. No one wanted to speak of Glumbruck's past, even the Alfather who was eager to speak about so many other things. Perhaps it was better that way. Glumbruck's life was hers to tell.

'Much still does happen,' the Alfather mumbled, and then he chuckled. 'Your sister's son *will* come into this hall. One way or another.'

'Even if the boy was to die at this moment, he will not be yours,' Buntrugg told the Alfather. 'He is a giant now. In the afterlife, he shall be ours.'

'You speak like a forefather.' The Alfather padded across the stone floor and settled back into the chair at Buntrugg's bedside. 'You sound like Surt.'

'We are the same, now.' Buntrugg felt it at his core. Despite the pain, he found a newfound calm in his heart that he recognised from Surt.

'But you are younger,' the Alfather said. 'More ambitious. You see the real way of the nine worlds.'

No flattery was free, and Buntrugg feared the cost of flattery from someone as calculating and powerful as the Alfather. Like all giants, Buntrugg had been taught to be wary of the Alfather and his tricks.

'Your forefathers once chose Surt. Now they have chosen you.' The Alfather looked at his own wrinkled hands as he spoke.

'You want me to replace Surt,' Buntrugg realised. That explained why Odin had sacrificed his precious time to wait for Buntrugg to wake, and why he, a giant, was gifted with a gold apple and a private room in Odin's great hall.

'The forefathers want you to replace Surt. It is why they rejected you from death. They fear you, as they once feared him.'

'They don't fear me,' Buntrugg said. He was their pet, like he was the Alfather's pet, and Surt's pet, and everyone's pet; someone obedient, who did as they asked. He was nothing like Surt. 'But they fear Surt. They always will.'

'You don't,' the Alfather said. 'Your sister and you are different from most giants.'

The Alfather wanted Buntrugg to challenge Surt. For a moment Buntrugg lay petrified, and stared up at the ceiling.

Buntrugg knew that he was the perfect candidate to replace Surt. He was young and strong and he had knowledge of the nine worlds, and of the fire demons. Now that the forefathers had cast him away from the afterlife, he possessed a different sort of strength too.

'Of course, no one can match Surt,' Odin said, just as Buntrugg had acknowledged his own worth.

That statement would have angered most giants. Buntrugg knew better. He would not respond to the provocation, but he had forgotten that he was not alone. Within him, the forefathers became louder. Their voices rose in protest, claiming their worth. Together they were stronger than Surt. Together they could overthrow him. All they lacked was a body to steer, and now they had someone who could hear all their voices. They called for Buntrugg and shouted for him to say it aloud. They responded to the Alfather's provocations, and although his eyes were open, Buntrugg could hardly see anything over their shouting.

Buntrugg focused on calming the forefathers who had long forgotten any emotion other than rage. Without eyelids to close, it was a more difficult task than usual.

'Even Surt chooses to give in to their rage,' the Alfather said. He had spoken as he had, knowing exactly how the forefathers' voices would overpower Buntrugg and force him to listen. 'You're not a regular giant, Buntrugg.'

'Neither are you, Odin.'

The forefathers were silenced. No one called the Alfather a giant and survived the encounter. No being in the nine worlds even viewed the Alfather as a giant, although that was what he was. Centuries and centuries ago, Odin and his two brothers had been birthed by a jotun mother by the name of Bestla. All beings knew it, yet no one ever said it aloud, and certainly never in the Alfather's presence.

At the corner of his eyes Buntrugg could see the old god. The Alfather's long beard trembled from rage. Buntrugg's forefathers remained silent. Their roles were reversed.

'Do you hear the forefathers?' Buntrugg asked, knowing full well that he was overstepping. No one was allowed to mention the Alfather's giant roots. 'Or are you from before their time, like Surt?'

Few giants were that old, but Surt was from a time without time and a place without place, before there were any forefathers. He heard them within him only by choice, so that he could someday unite all giants, past and present.

Without Surt, no giants would know how to fight together.

They spent their days fighting each other, but at Ragnarok they would unite under Surt's lead.

Everyone in the nine worlds knew of Surt. No one knew about Buntrugg. No giants would follow him to war, and if all giants did not unite and go to war at Ragnarok, then Odin would win by default. The jotnar would die and have won nothing. That was why the Alfather kept Buntrugg here, like another pet, trying to flatter him into overthrowing Surt and leave all giants without a leader to unite them.

'I—am—not—a—giant,' Odin hissed.

Far above them, the ceiling's gold shields clapped against each other with the sound of hundreds of warriors raging war. The walls began to shake and sway at Odin's anger. The earth rumbled at his fury. The rage of a giant.

'Nej, you're not,' Buntrugg replied, unafraid. He had experienced near-death by fire demons, he no longer feared death. In death, he would just be another forefather, and he knew the forefathers now.

'You're not a giant,' Buntrugg repeated, and Odin's rage calmed so the earth no longer shook, but the shields above them still tapped like hail fell on them.

'Us giants have rage that makes many of us rash, rude and impatient, but even the youngest of giants knows to respect old beings like Surt and the veulve. You are nothing like us, Odin, son of Borr and son of Bestla.'

HILDA

Chapter Seventy-Three

THE GODS HAD abandoned Ash-hill. Seeing the town burn in the night was not the same as seeing it blackened. Ashes had washed into the earth and the ash-tree was nothing but a stump.

Alone, Hilda approached her old home.

Since she had no ropes to coil, she had been the first off the ships. Instead of waiting for the others to finish, she had marched home from the harbour, following the stream inland.

She had thought the town would still feel like home. That she would look at it and remember what had used to be, but it didn't feel like home. Her once happy memories turned bitter at the sight of it.

The gods had allowed nothing to survive. Not even the sacred ash-tree. All of Ash-hill was burned.

Hilda stared at the frosted stump of the door to her house. Without thinking, her legs had brought her home, though there was nothing there anymore. Her house had collapsed; one of the pillars had cracked and the roof had caved. Hilda didn't dare go inside. It wasn't her house anymore. The colourful images her father had painted into the far wall were blackened from smoke. White frost crystals lined the black soot. Nothing was left that had once made this place home.

Hilda clasped her right hand around the back of her axe-head.

The Runes had warned her. They had told her that the Alfather had abandoned her and that the gods were angry. She didn't know why the gods had been angry enough to abandon all of Ash-hill and most of Jutland, but she knew how to turn their anger. The Runes had told her how to appease the gods.

She needed to deliver the godly axe. She alone could do it. All she needed was guidance to reach Asgard. She needed the Runes. If she returned to where the whispers in the wind had first become loud enough for her to hear, then perhaps there was hope. Maybe the runemistress in the woods could help her regain the attention of the Runes.

With that thought in mind, Hilda turned away from her burned home. She tried to ignore the sight of it and the tears that swelled in her eyes. She had nothing anymore but a task. She would beg for the gods' forgiveness so that her kinsmen could survive.

The warriors begun arriving from the harbour. They would stay the night, and then some of them would sail on, home to villages that had not been burned. This was the last time the ships that had raided Magadoborg would dock together. Tonight they would drink the last of their ale. They would keep warm around fires, and laugh and dance, and say their goodbyes.

In the morning the ships would continue through the Limsound. Some would sail to Odin's-gorge, some to Tyr's-lake. Most of Ash-hill's warriors would follow Sigismund and cross the Jutland Sea to reach Frey's-fiord, where they would winter. Only two crews had decided to stay in Ash-hill: the crews of the *Mermaid Scream* and the *Serpent's Fear*.

A silence swept over the warriors as they arrived up the hill.

They stood like draugar in the distance. The warriors from Frey's-fiord who Hilda had sailed with murmured in shock. The town wasn't theirs, but the surprise was clear on their faces from seeing what little remained of Ash-hill. They had heard of it, but they hadn't seen the abandoned town. A town cursed and condemned by the gods themselves.

Hilda had to lift the curse so Ash-hill could rise anew. Nothing like this would ever happen here again. Ignoring the knot in her heart, she proceeded down the hill towards the only building the southerners hadn't burned. The Christian church stood proud among ashes in all its bright colours.

Hilda's worn soles didn't make her slip, though they should have. Her steps left no marks in the frost either. She wasn't cold or hungry anymore. Her snow fox seemed to eat for the both of them, in the same way the Alfather's wolves ate for him.

Hilda passed the charred offering statues at the edge of town without leaving anything. She didn't have anything to offer and it seemed pointless. The gods weren't listening, anyways.

'Say goodbye before you leave,' Sigismund called after Hilda, as if he could see her.

He stood with the other ship commanders who would sail with him to Frey's-fiord tomorrow morning. No doubt he wanted to reassure them about the journey ahead of them. Most of them were young and inexperienced. Many warriors and sailors had passed on since summer.

The snow fox turned its head to look at Sigismund, and Hilda followed its stare. With her father gone, and her aunt and uncle and cousins, and Einer too, Sigismund was the closest she had to home. She would have liked to stay aboard his ship and sail up to Frey's-fiord with the others; her heart warmed at the thought of it. But there were more important things in the nine worlds. The godly axe needed to be delivered.

The snow fox twisted its ears and looked up at her. Hilda was glad to have it with her, for it acknowledged her as none of the warriors did.

Sigismund came right up to her. Though he had become taller and leaner and could grow a curly beard now, he hadn't changed much since they were children and she had used to call him Sigis.

'You're like Hilda.' He crouched by the fox and unfolded a piece of cloth to reveal a piece of meat from last night. 'For you,' he said, and left it on the frosted grass by the snow fox.

He gave it a pet as it dug into the red meat and rose to his feet, looking straight ahead, at Hilda. For a moment she thought he could see her, but he looked through her, and then he turned away.

'Won't you stop it and make it stay?' a warrior asked Sigis. 'We need all the luck we can get.'

'It has given us luck. Plenty of it,' was his reply. 'We need to let it go on its own journey now. If it wants to leave, then we need to let it.'

Sigismund always made everything easier. Even leaving.

Hilda smiled bitterly at Sigis' back. Being alone was better than being ignored. Besides, saving the future of Ash-hill from the wrath of the gods was a task that only she could accomplish, and to do it, she needed the Runes. She needed to go to the runemistress. Regain the interest of the Runes and go to Asgard to meet the gods, and deliver the axe.

Her hand was tight on the axe-head, her knuckles white where she clenched it, as she forced herself to leave. It had to be done. She had to leave, and so she did. Determined to succeed, she walked into the forest and left Ash-hill, knowing that there would be no coming back.

The snow fox clasped its meat and hopped along ahead of Hilda, straight towards the stables, where she had killed Pontius at the end of summer and had made her escape from Ash-hill's slaughter.

THE TREK TO the runemistress was longer than she remembered. The road east of Ash-hill wasn't as straight and well-paved as she remembered it, either. The last time she had come this way, she had been riding, and the wind's faint whispers had helped guide her. She hadn't walked it in summers. Not since her father had fallen seriously ill. Before then, they had used to come here the two of them—just her father and her—and spend a whole week of summer together. She missed those days.

Morning came and went as Hilda trailed up and down hills, across streams, through half-burned and half-harvested fields, and through broad-leaved forests.

Her snow fox liked to run off, but it always came back to check on her, with wet fur and a muddy snout.

The wind accompanied her but didn't speak. It was cold with silence. All her life the wind had whispered to her. Before she had first visited the runemistress, after the attack on Ash-hill. As a child, too, she had heard faint whispers in the gust.

Hilda walked up the hill that led to the runemistress' hut. She had no payment with her. Nothing of value she could exchange for answers. Her axe was the only worthy payment she had, but that belonged to the gods, and she would not part with it. Though she supposed that the first time she had paid for more than she had received. That's how she would phrase it to get her answers. If the runemistress could see her.

The runemistress's hut was hidden in shadows. Smoke rushed out the open door. The hut was small as a thrall home, hidden in the woods. Had Hilda not been there before, she wouldn't have known how to find it. The wind had led her this way after the battle. It had led her many places. She needed it back. Even if the runemistress couldn't see Hilda, this was her best chance to regain the trust of the Runes. She still didn't know why they had stopped whispering.

Outside the hut, the snow fox fell in at her side, close, as if it were still chained to her. She had truly tamed it and made it hers.

Runes had been carved along every tree trunk by the hut. When Hilda had last been there, she hadn't noticed them; it had been dark. Or maybe they hadn't been there at all. It seemed so long ago. She couldn't really recall.

Hilda cautiously moved towards the door. The snow fox stayed back. Showed its teeth.

Inside, a burning fire made shadows flicker across the rune-carved walls and furniture. There were runic staves everywhere. On the ceiling. On the wood burning in the fireplace.

The hut most definitely hadn't looked like this when Hilda had last been there. There had been coloured runes on a few of the walls and on the door, but nothing like this. There were so many that they overlapped. Some were upside down, and others formed obscure new shapes.

At the back of the small hut sat the runemistress, alone, on her sleeping bench. Her hands curled around a bowl of steaming stew on the table.

Had it not been for the runes all about, Hilda might have thought that she had entered the wrong home. The woman was changed. She looked many winters older, and worn. Her hair had not been combed in a long time, and she had a bald spot behind her left ear. Her eyes were sunken in so her eyeballs popped out of a skeleton face. She didn't look at Hilda.

'I've come back,' Hilda said to announce herself.

Unbothered by Hilda's entrance, the runemistress brought the bowl to her lips and sipped her stew.

Hilda recalled how it had happened the first time. The runemistress had reached for her, and touched her hand, an ice-cold touch. That was all. And then the whispers in the wind had been loud and clear.

Hilda stepped into the hut.

Her heart raced. She entered the sacred home without invitation, walked to the table. The silver arm ring Hilda had provided as payment at the end of summer hung from the woman's right wrist. Hilda reached for the runemistress' wrinkled, marked hands.

She took a few shallow battle breaths and touched the runemistress' wrist.

Immediately she retreated again, expecting the entire hut to collapse on her, or a demon to appear. But none of it happened. The runemistress merely looked up from her stew, as she may as well have done had Hilda not been there. Then, the woman's gaze froze. Hilda looked back over her shoulder.

The snow fox had gained enough courage to peer into the hut.

The runemistress' eyes were fixed on it. 'Finally here,' she whispered. 'The Skald's daughter.' She rose from her seat and reached for a basket full of things. Hurriedly she searched through it. Her movements slowed as she found what she must have been looking for.

Forth, she brought a small spinning distaff, barely the length of her forearm, clasped it between two hands and knocked it twice on the table.

A white thread appeared inside the hollow part of the distaff. It spun out, accompanied by a squeal of knives scraped against glass. The white thread tore a hole right in front of Hilda, a bright hole into another world. A quiet meadow lay on the other side, blurred by a white veil. The squeal of knives on glass became louder and louder with every racing heartbeat, and the veil opened wider and wider.

Hilda had seen runemistresses tap their distaff to look beyond, but she had never seen anyone actually open a door into another world.

'Step through into your afterlife,' the runemistress hissed.

'I'm not dead,' Hilda said, though she was well aware of the truth. 'I am not dead.'

The runemistress was shaking from the effort of holding the white veil open. She bared her yellow teeth in pain.

'I'm not dead.'

'Step through now, or be stuck here.'

Hilda knew that she ought to step through, but she couldn't make herself move. Outside, the snow fox started away from the hut and the veil. Reluctant to leave, like Hilda. She couldn't pass through into her afterlife. She had to deliver the axe. She couldn't leave before then.

The runemistress unclasped her sweaty grip from the small distaff. It clonked against the table. The veil disappeared, and with it the horrid squeal.

'You should have gone through,' the runemistress huffed.

Hilda stared at where the veil had been. That distant vision of a calm meadow. She knew the runemistress was right. It would be a better and easier path, but she was not ready for it.

'I am not dead,' she insisted instead.

It was exactly like talking to Sigismund. The runemistress couldn't see her either. At least she seemed to know that Hilda was there, listening.

'The wind has stopped speaking to you, hasn't it? You stopped using my runes.'

'Why have the whispers stopped?' Hilda asked, though she knew she wouldn't be heard.

'I've never heard the wind whisper. I know the runes. Yet, they have never addressed me.' The runemistress spoke like a mourning woman recalling her husband. 'That's a gift reserved for gods.'

'Then only gods can give it,' Hilda understood. 'And only gods can take it back.' She had been cursed, as Ash-hill had. Only an offering could free her.

Her sight fell on the axe that hung from her weapon belt. She needed to deliver the gift to the gods, but without the Runes she had no direction and nowhere to go.

'I can't help with the whispers,' the runemistress said.

Hilda had hoped that she would find her answers here. She had allowed herself to hope a lot, and her mind was weary at the realisation that it had been for nothing.

'But there is someone hiding in Midgard—not a god, but someone who may help,' said the runemistress in a dark tone as if a demon of sorts had entered her mind and possessed her. 'I think... I think someone was here to visit me, after you. A jotun.' She stared up at her runic ceiling and narrowed her eyes to remember a half-forgotten dream from many winters ago. 'Down by Jelling, you will find a familiar face.'

The snow fox barked. It had been a good decision to come after all. The runemistress was close to the Runes and spoke for them. To hear her speak was a little like regaining the Runes, even though it wasn't quite the same and the wind remained silent.

'I shall carve my runes for you, Hilda, daughter of Ash-hill's last skald,' the runemistress muttered before Hilda could leave. 'It's why I live. In this life and the next.'

Hilda felt the weight of responsibilities on her shoulders, as she had when her father had died. At least she knew where she was headed. She would travel back to Ash-hill and then south to Jelling along the Oxen Road. The Runes were not yet done with her, even if the gods had taken away her ability to hear them. She would travel to Jelling and regain the Runes. Together, they would seek out the gods and deliver the sacred axe.

SIV

Chapter Seventy-Four

THE RUNES WERE weaker than ever before. Siv played with a runic coin she had carved and blooded last full moon. She twisted it in her hand as she waited for Harald to return from his talk with Christian envoys arrived from the south.

Every day, the runes were weaker to Siv's touch. Runemistresses were being killed all over Harald's Dane lands. Fewer runes were carved than ever before. Every day, the nine worlds seemed further and further apart, and Siv could not let Midgard drift away; it was her home and had been for many centuries. But it was more than that. The nine worlds were only whole when there were nine of them. If Midgard drifted apart, soon the other worlds too would drift apart and be forgotten, and then no one would be able to regain their afterlife.

The door swung open. Harald entered with a sigh and a grumble, more vile than usual.

'How did it go?' asked Siv with only the hint of reproach at the fact that he had listened to Christian advice and not allowed her to stay in the hall.

'They've doomed us,' Harald grumbled as he removed his coat and hung it up to warm next to the oven. He positioned himself in front of the fire, warming his palms.

'The southern kings?' Siv asked, though she knew that was not who he meant.

'These Jutes... They sacked cities, Tove. They killed children in their sleep.'

'And you are going to have to answer for those actions,' said Siv. Harald ought to be held accountable for much more. The peril they were all in, all of the beings in the nine worlds, was worsened by Harald's every action and decision.

He was one of many reasons the runes were weakening. If runes were not carved and marked according to the old traditions, they could not be used, and if the passage ways were no longer respected, Midgard would drift apart from the other eight worlds.

For the nine worlds to stay together, traditions had to be honoured, and set as he was on his Christianity and on the power with which it came, Harald was banning them all.

'These are your lands,' Siv said.

She put the runic coin back into the leather pouch that hung from her belt, knowing it would anger Harald to see it, and walked to him, all the way to the burning hot oven, and hugged him from behind. She placed her chin on his shoulder and hugged him tight so he would sense her support and good intentions. 'You can't let them tell you what to do.'

'I don't have a choice,' he responded in a tone that suggested she knew nothing of his obligations, although Siv probably understood them better than Harald did himself. 'These Jutes have forced my hand.'

'What Jutes?' she asked, although somewhere deep down she knew that it had to be Ash-hill's warriors. They had lived next to a sacred ash-tree and their belief and understanding of the nine worlds were both great and strong. It was why people like Ragnar, and Siv herself, had gravitated towards Ash-hill; a place where anything and everything had been possible.

'I think I know who,' Harald said and clenched his fists.

'I hope you didn't admit to knowing who it was—or even that it happened,' she said, for that would condemn them all in the eyes of southerners.

'Of course I didn't,' he nearly yelled, and his tone made it clear that he had said exactly who he thought it had been and in doing so had agreed to take the blame as the king who ruled over the lands.

'Why don't you take me with you when you discuss their terms tomorrow?' Siv suggested, putting on a pleading voice.

'This is a man's job. A king's job,' Harald insisted again.

He was set on doing all of the negotiations alone, and he would fail to get the deal they needed. He was dooming himself and Jelling; and worst of all, he was dooming the nine worlds. He was too stubborn and too dangerous. He never listened anymore, but let his greed for power take over. Siv's influence over him lessened with every step away from the old traditions he took. Every day that the strength of the runes dwindled. Soon she would have no way to sway him convincingly anymore.

Yet, she could not kill him. Anyone in a position to take over the role of king at this point had already pledged to the same Christianity as Harald. At least Harald's greed guaranteed that he would fight, although he had already given the southerners too much control in Jutland.

It would take more than a strong chief rooted in the old traditions, to change anything. It would take an extraordinary chief with a true belief. Perhaps Harald's son Svend could achieve it, but there were many winters left before Svend was old enough to take over for his father. In the meantime, all Siv could do was try to minimise the damage.

'The chiefs and jarls have pledged to you, but you are asking a lot of your people,' she said. 'You're asking them to change their way of life, even their beliefs.'

'I'm not *asking*,' Harald hissed. 'I *demand* that they do as I say. We're a Christian Kingdom now.'

There was no arguing with him, not anymore, and the runes were too weak in Midgard to be used to change his mind.

It wasn't Harald who mattered, Siv reminded herself, as she stood there hugging his fat belly in front of the burning hot oven. All that mattered was his eldest son Svend and that he grew up knowing the value of the old traditions, and with a belief in the nine worlds; and that someday, someone would be there to convince him to overthrow his father's rule.

Harald didn't matter, she told herself and hugged him tighter. All that mattered was Svend and Tyra.

HUGIN & MUNIN

Chapter Seventy-Five

MY RAVEN BROTHER and I, Hugin, search for the half-giant as the snow drifts around us. Through it, I struggle to see where the giant might be. My black wings are wet and heavy. The snow weighs me down, and hinders our task to find the half-giant who refuses to die.

My brother carries our memories, but I, Hugin, carry our thoughts, and it is I who thinks for the both of us, so it falls to me to find what we have been sent looking for.

We glide out of the snow-shedding cloud, and my vision clears. The river below us is glazed with frost. On we fly, above towns, and fields, following the river north from Magadoborg, as the half-giant must be doing. He should be here, among the fields covered in white and brown snow.

In the distance, walks a man. Just another brown patch in the snow. A half-giant, it would seem, by his hefty steps and figure.

'At last,' I caw to Munin.

My brother shakes his feathers. He is away in thought and not searching for the half-giant. Munin remembers too much and too often for his own good. It is why he always gets into trouble with our Alfather; if he did like me and followed orders, I would never have to hear the Alfather yell.

We flap our wings with more effort. Then I close them up and plummet towards Einer Vigmerson. I open my wings in the last moment and stretch a claw into the snow.

My brother flaps down next to me. Not as elegantly, for he stumbles ahead a little.

Einer Vigmerson stops up in front of us. Despite the snow, he is red with blood. His bound wounds are green from treatment, or perhaps lack thereof. He is still alive, still walking. We did our best to act out the Alfather's wishes back in Magadoborg, but no matter how many arrows pierced his skull and rib cage, Einer roared on and hacked men to unflattering deaths.

'You are back, again,' the half-giant mumbles. 'Odin's two ravens, always following me.'

I cock my head at him and wonder how many pairs of ravens he has talked to before Munin and I. We have not seen him since he left Magadoborg.

Einer's movements are pained, but he forces himself ahead. He circles around us, and continues to trail through the snow. 'Leave me, I won't follow you,' he says with no conviction in his voice. 'I have a life to live.'

'Should we follow?' Munin asks me.

I hop around to look at Einer walk away from us. A few arrows stick out of him at his back. I count six, and one through the head.

My feet and feathers cool from the snow, and they were cold already. We have been flying all morning. I tilt my head as I watch the half-giant. 'We have found him,' I say. 'And such was our task.'

I look to my brother, and he does not disagree, so we push off from the slippery earth, flap our wings to gain heights, and fly through the clouds. We fly all the way up to a layer where the rainbow bridge to Asgard may open for us.

'Home, home!' we caw, and Heimdall must have heard us, for a circular rainbow greets us above the clouds. We glide through it, and pass into Asgard.

The green plains of Asgard's summer greet us. The seasons here are nothing like back in Midgard where they seem to change every second time we arrive. In Asgard, seasons, like people, stay and last. The end of summer is near, I sense it, but my wings greet the giant Sun, and she seems to circle closer with her star for me and dries my feathers. I tuck my feet up under me, and bask in her sunshine and heat.

My brother, Munin, is lost in memories as we fly above Ida's plain on our way to Valhalla. Oftentimes I think that he never quite sees what I see, always lost in thought, connecting all the sights we have seen in the centuries of our life. Sometimes I even think he pointlessly recalls a life from before we were bound to the Alfather, back when we were free to fly where we wished. Such a long time past, when we used to spread our wings only to explore for ourselves. I no longer recall what it was like, or how we filled our days. It does not feel important, not like flying for the Alfather does.

Valhalla's proud weapons and shields soar in the sunshine. We dart towards them and drop through the shield-leaves of Valhalla's oak tree, into the smoky hall filled with fires, fights and laughter. We glide up and down from the hot air of the fires, and make our way across the hall, searching for our Alfather.

I hear a loud bang. I make a skilful turn, with my brother at my back. At the far end of the hall, the door to one of Odin's private rooms is open, and there, in the light, stands the burned giant that our wolf brothers saved.

He looks at us, and smiles.

'What's he doing?' I hiss to my brother.

'Where are Geri and Freki?' my brother asks in return. It was the task of Odin's dear wolves to watch over the fire giant, and keep him from entering the main hall, yet he stands for all of Odin's warriors to behold.

I plummet towards the scarred giant, claws first, and screech at him. 'Get back, get back!'

He seems amused at my protest. I sink my claws into his new flesh, and pull away. I open my beak and hack at him. Tearing at his red flesh and the meat beneath. 'Back inside!'

'You can nip at me all you want,' says the giant in his earth-shaking voice. 'I am not going back inside. The warriors have already seen me.'

I halt my screeching, and my brother and I both circle above the giant, casting our glances down the great hall. At every table we can see, the warriors have gone quiet. They're all staring straight at the giant and us. It's too late to make him leave.

'Stay,' I tell my brother, and then I fly over the crowd of warriors to find my god.

MY BROTHER, HUGIN, is sometimes hasty to act. He doesn't carry all of our memories, like I, Munin, do. As I watch Hugin fly over benches full of warriors, on a quest to find our Alfather, I sense a sadness form at the sight of him. He does not know the world. Not like I do.

'Your brother doesn't need to fly to him,' the giant tells me and snorts with laughter at Hugin's behaviour.

I circle above the scarred giant. He does not look up at me as he talks, but it is me that he addresses, so I make certain that I fly high enough to be out of his reach.

'Odin is already on his way,' the giant mumbles.

'How could he be?' I ask, but I sense that he is, so I change my question. 'How do you know?'

'I know what you are,' replies the scarred giant.

'We are his servants.'

'You are so much more. You are bound to him by runes. He is you and you are him. What you see, he sees. What you hear, he hears. You are him, but you are also you.' He looks into my black eyes, and I feel him trying to stir something. 'A servant for now, but not forever.'

A feeling warms me, and I am shameful for it, for I am not supposed to feel. Yet the feeling is there, and becoming stronger. I do not know what to call it, but I do believe that it is the dire complication that the short-lived call hope.

I fear that his words shall forever stay at the top of my mind—*A servant for now, but not forever*—and I fear that given time, the feeling shall only become stronger.

The giant seems to know that he has doomed me, for as I circle above him, he smiles triumphantly. It's the kind of smile I have seen pass from mouth to mouth on battlefields, and it belongs to victors.

My thoughts are disrupted by the call of my brother. He sits perched on the Alfather's shoulder. Odin walks fast towards the giant and me. He doesn't use his spear as a walking stick, and even from this distance, I can see his scowl. He is angry, and I knew he would be.

His face, half-hidden by his beard, is red to match the dark red cloak he wears. The warriors are silenced at the thought of their god angry, and they take it upon themselves to glare at the giant, and make him know he is unwelcome.

I circle and circle above the giant as we wait for the Alfather to make the long way across the hall to us, and when finally he is here, his harsh stare makes me fearful to dash down and settle on his other shoulder, so I continue to circle.

The Alfather does not speak to the giant. 'Geri! Freki,' he calls. Our two wolf brothers will be in trouble for letting the giant leave the room.

I hear a whimper from inside.

'They tried their best,' says the giant.

Hugin screeches at the insult, but the giant does not so much as glance up to my brother. He is fully focused on Odin. 'They refused to fetch you, so I had to do it my own way.'

'What for?' is all the Alfather says.

'Lying in that room, I have had a lot of time to think about your proposal, Odin, and if you'll let me, I am ready to show my loyalty to you.'

The Alfather looks bored. He knows that the giant is trying to trick him, that it is too easy, yet he lets him speak. Odin always knows how to have the upper hand, and it is usually by letting his opponent think that they're winning. It is the same as all the times he has tricked his son Thor, and the same as all the times he has tricked much greater giants than this.

'How do you intend to prove your loyalty after kicking my wolves and ignoring my commands?'

The giant whispers his response. 'I know how you can bring Einer Glumbruckson into your hall.'

FINN

Chapter Seventy-Six

FINN HAD NOT thought that he would miss Einer, but the unwelcome realisation sneaked into his mind as he stood in Ash-hill's remains and watched two dozen warriors argue.

His hands were grey with soot. Blackened pillars showed where houses had once stood. The Ting stones had been blackened from flames. In the midst of it all, warriors were shouting. No one listened to anyone but themselves, no one took charge and no one was allowed to make the simplest of decisions for the lot of them. They lacked a lawmaker, but more than that, they lacked a chieftain.

They were sixty-eight warriors without a cause and without direction. They needed a chieftain to unite them, and Einer had been a good chief.

'We need to assert our claim on these lands,' Finn cut in loud and clear, as a chief would have. 'We have been gone for a long time, and Harald Gormsson is a Christian now. Jutland is not as it was when we left.'

They all turned to look at him, like they had forgotten that he was there, standing outside the Ting circle where he was no longer allowed to tread.

'You do that,' one of them told Finn, and suddenly they were in agreement.

All twenty-four ash-coloured warriors in the inner circle voiced their approval, each one busy to appear as though it had been their idea, but none of them had the authority, and their eyes flickered to the stump of the old ash tree.

Hormod rested his hip against the stump. He was the eldest warrior, and they listened to him with respect, but not as they might have listened to a chieftain.

'Finn will walk to Jelling and argue on our behalf,' Hormod decided.

'Alone?' Finn asked. That was not the sort of travel men came back from, certainly not if they went alone. 'Under whose authority?'

Hormod licked his lips and stared at the warriors. He had not been elected or chosen by them, and if he intended to become their leader, then this was not the time to force the issue.

'That of the village. A majority vote.' He pushed away from the ash stump and addressed the crowd. 'Who says that Finn shall be the one to argue with Harald Gormsson on our behalf?'

Two dozen arms darted up at once, and when Finn looked down the hill at the warriors who'd chosen to shovel through the remains of their old houses instead of arguing about what to do, he saw that even they raised their hands.

Sixty-eight warriors in agreement.

'Why me? Why not you?' Finn said and pointed to a warrior in the crowd. 'Or you?'

'The rest of us have better things to do,' said Solvig, a gruff shieldmaiden who had used to sail on the *Northern Wrath*.

The warriors waved Finn off with their final decision and resumed their endless discussions.

'You are not my master,' Finn hissed.

'Nej, your master is dead,' Hormod said in a grave tone, as

if Finn was to blame for that too, as if he was to blame for everything. 'And his only child was Ash-hill itself. You owe all of us now, debt-thrall. You better make a great impression and ensure that we get to keep our lands.'

Hormod did not look at Finn as he spoke, but the others did. Their stares made him feel marked, almost outlawed. The only fate worse than thraldom.

'You know there's no coming back from this,' Finn said.

They could talk down to him and order him around—he had begun to get used to that—but to make him march to his own death was too much.

Hormod rested with his back against the ash stump and closed his eyes to shut out the sound of Finn's voice.

'I am a thrall.' Finn hated the taste of the word, and yet he had to say it, had to remind them of it. 'I have rights.'

'And obligations,' someone said.

In their eyes, he was only a debt-thrall, and his master, the only person who could have freed him, was dead. Finn did not know to whom he belonged anymore. He supposed that Hormod was not entirely wrong, and that he did belong to the village now. Einer had been their chieftain, and a debt owed to a chief was a debt owed to the lands he ruled.

'If I belong to all of you now, as you say I do, then by law you need to guarantee that I am fed, clothed and sheltered.' Finn knew his rights better as a thrall than he ever had as a freeman. The law was all he had on his side.

'Not while travelling, and right now, your masters are ordering you to travel to Jelling,' Hormod said.

He could not escape this. None of them had the courage to go south with him to face Harald Gormsson. To claim responsibility for the attack on Magadoborg and plead for their lands. They would much rather stay up here in the ashes, and hope never to be discovered, but unless someone confronted Harald, they would always live in fear that someone would show up, some day, and rip their newly rebuilt lives from their hands.

'What will you pay me if I go?' If he had no choice, he might as well get the best deal he could.

Hormod thought about that for a little while and Finn could see that his question surprised them all. They had not expected him to bravely agree to go. They must have thought that they would need to send him away at spear-tip, like a coward.

Finn was no coward.

'I will reduce one arm-length of home-spun off your debt for every word you speak in the presence of the great Harald Gormsson of Jelling,' Hormod decided.

'That's hardly payment at all. You can't order me away without either giving me a choice or proper payment.'

'I *am* giving you a choice: You can walk to Jelling and appease Harald Gormsson, or you can stay here and let your skin taste friendly iron.'

Finn sighed and closed his eyes. All of the warriors from the *Mermaid Scream* and the *Serpent's Fear* were looking at him. They were shields that he had risked his life for, and fought alongside, and bench-mates he had drawn breath with, rowing through the night to escape bloodbaths in plenty. They were supposed to be his friends, but Finn had never felt more alone. Even when everyone had sided with Einer, against him, he had not felt this alone.

He stood at the very spot where he had found his wife's corpse when they had returned to Ash-hill after the summer raids. Her face had been crumbled in horror. Finn buried the thoughts. She was not there to speak for him, and never again would she be. He opened his eyes and settled a harsh stare on the old man who seemed to make decisions for them now.

'Your axe has never been friendly to me, Hormod,' Finn said. 'But my ears are sore from your yapping, and I will enjoy the silence as I walk south.'

He turned away without giving them time to answer. He did not look back as he walked down the slope from Ash-hill, cornering poles and half broken walls.

He followed the stream to the harbour and their two ships. The rest of Ash-hill's ships had sailed across the Jutland Sea to Frey's-fiord where their children waited for their return. Finn had no one who waited for him, not even in Valhalla. His wife had not been a warrior, though she had been strong.

Many friends had passed on in the battle at Magadoborg, while Finn had been forced to carry the dead to their final resting place. They would not think of him as an equal, thanks to his debt to Einer—and worse, unless he found a way to repay the debt in full before he passed on, he might not be allowed into Valhalla, even if he died honourably in battle.

Finn sighed as he found his bag of things, not that he owned much anymore. He dug through it for his shoulder bag, into which he packed a set of clothes that did not smell too bad, and his dried food reserve. It was indeed not much, but it would get him on his way. He took an axe, a dagger and a spoon too.

"Never travel without your own spoon and knife," his mother had used to tell him. "You never know when you will be invited to dine in the hall of a king." He would have loved to tell her that she had been right, although he supposed he would not be invited to dine.

He tried not to mind that he was packing for what would likely be his last journey. This was not a task for a man alone. The *Northern Wrath*'s trip to Normandy had taught them that Harald Gormsson was allied with those they had attacked in Magadoborg. Harald would be under pressure to answer to his Christian allies' demands for revenge; whoever went to Jelling and claimed responsibility for the attack would not come home.

Finn would need to be cunning, and he would need to use all of the flattery he knew, for Harald was a pretentious man, and that also meant that Finn could not arrive empty handed. He needed some sort of gift.

With that thought in mind, he walked back to Ash-hill and kicked his feet through the ashes to find something of value to bring with him.

'Why haven't you left?' Hormod shouted at him, from up by the ash stump that he still leaned against while warriors argued.

Finn addressed Hormod loudly. 'If I am going south, risking my life to solve all of your problems, then at the very least you shall give me a chance to save myself. No one goes to see a king without bringing a gift. There must be something of worth here.'

The warriors did not stop him, so Finn proceeded to kick through the burned remains near the inner circle. Suddenly, he understood Loki's bitterness from the stories. Loki who lived among the gods but was never treated as an equal; Loki who was always sent to do the gods' bidding and was blamed for every small failure. It had not ended well for Loki, tied up in a cave with a snake dripping venom onto his face in eternal punishment, but Finn refused to share the same fate. He would free himself, and he would show them all.

A small wooden figurine lay forgotten in ashes. Finn picked it up. His hands blackened at the touch of it, but the figure did not crumble under the strength of his touch. The figurine had long hair woven with flowers, and her belly was pregnant; vines curled up her arms. A representation of Freya, the Goddess of fertility. It had clearly been carved by a child, rough at the edges and left unfinished. It was too intricate to be completed with the carver's poor skills. As Finn looked upon Freya's face, he saw Ash-hill so clearly for what it had been and what it was now: it had used to be so full of hope and expectations, and now there were only ashes left.

When he went to see Harald, Finn would not only have to argue for his life, he would have to argue with a Christian. A burned idol could prove to be a strong symbol. He stuffed it into his bag. It was not enough. Finn did not want to reveal how vulnerable Ash-hill was to a self-proclaimed king who had tried to take over their lands last summer. That was what a burned figurine of a goddess would do. He needed a symbol of strength as well.

As if the gods themselves had heard his prayer, the roar of a bear echoed out from the forest. Something worthy of a chief and king.

Finn walked back to the arguing warriors. More of them had gathered now than earlier. There was three dozen of them, and still they had not made any decision, other than sending Finn away.

Finn found young Berg among the warriors, and addressed him loud enough for others to hear, but without interrupting the main speakers inside the Ting ring. 'Do you have nothing better to do than stand and listen to old men argue?'

Berg laughed at that, and several of the other warriors too. 'What do you propose?'

Even after Finn had become a debt-thrall, Berg and the other young warriors had treated him decently. They still respected the reputation Finn had earned after summers of raids.

'Become a hero worthy of tales,' Finn said. 'Help me capture that bear.'

The two tall warriors who'd been arguing in the stone circle had gone quiet.

'Kill it instead,' Hormod ordered, thinking that he was in charge simply because he was the eldest. 'You can take the hide to Harald. The smell of a dead bear may attract some wild hogs, and we could use some meat.'

It was not a terrible idea, but bringing the hide alone would not get Finn the respect he needed to argue for Ash-hill's safety: the hide of a bear could be bought, but a living bear had to be tamed. To arrive with a chained bear as a gift would immediately make him appear as a fearless warrior.

'It was Einer's. We can't kill it.' A reasoning that even Hormod could not argue with. 'It belongs to our chief, and he didn't raise it to be skinned.'

'Loyal beyond the end,' one of the young warriors commented, and Finn shrugged. He walked with pride and did not look back over his shoulder, but he heard several young warriors rush to catch up with him, to follow him to glory.

'Why was Einer raising a bear?' one of them asked as they fell in at Finn's side.

'Pride,' Finn guessed, although he really did not know.

'Nej,' Berg said, catching up as well. 'I asked him at Midsummer. I'm from up by the Mare's Tits, so I had never seen a tame bear cub before,' he explained, as though apologising for being such a farmer, as Finn might have done too in his early days. 'Einer told me that he found a lone cub without a mother, and he gave it four whole honeyed fish to give it a chance to survive. It followed him home, and he took it in.'

'As I said: pride,' Finn dismissed.

With Einer gone, defying his legacy had become more difficult. Everyone had a story about Einer. Usually when good men died, all the bad things they had done in life began to emerge as those who were left behind began to talk about all that which they had not dared to say, but that hadn't happened with Einer. He had been friendly to everyone, even Finn, although that was a long time ago.

At the edge of the forest they slowed their confident walk. The bear was somewhere out there, close, but finding it would not be enough.

'How do we capture it?' one of the young warriors thankfully asked before Finn was forced to admit that he had not thought that far ahead. They did not have a net to sacrifice, everything was in dire need. Finn would be able to procure a chain or rope to tie it, but not a net to trap it, and he could not think of any other way to catch a bear alive. Einer might have tamed it, but it was still a bear.

'Yesterday's rain has softened the earth,' Berg said. 'We could dig a ditch and lure it towards it.'

'Let's do that,' Finn decided at once.

The young warriors rushed off to fetch spades and get to work. They seemed delighted to finally follow someone who dared to make decisions.

Finn and Berg searched for the right place to dig, and together they gave the others tasks. Without Berg backing him up, Finn would not have been able to do it; no one else would have listened to a debt-thrall. They sent mud-haired Egger off to check the beehives for honey, to lure the bear, and began to dig their ditch. It was hard work, but considering the cool air of early winter, and the indecisiveness of the other warriors, it was welcome work.

'Do you think our wives are in Valhalla?' Berg asked. They had dug in silence for a long time.

Finn looked up at him. He had forgotten that Berg had married before they had left on their raids. It seemed such a long time ago. 'Should have asked Hilda that,' he responded.

'Just thinking about her and those bloody tears gives me goosebumps.'

Finn looked out of the ditch into the forest for any sign of the bear, and for a moment he thought he saw the white flicker of a snow fox, like the one that had boarded Sigismund's ship, but it couldn't possibly have been.

When the work was done, and Egger came back with honeycombs—and a swollen wrist and neck from beestings, where he had not protected himself properly—they set the trap. They covered the ditch with slim branches and leaves and carefully placed the honey on top, and then they climbed a nearby oak tree, took their positions with spears in hand, and waited.

The wait was long, and they had to stay silent so as not to give away their position, but there was excitement in the air. Sooner or later, the bear would come.

Finally, they heard a thumping sound near their tree and watched the large bear approach the ditch. It had been a cub when they had left for their summer raids, but it had grown large over the moons they had been away. It had a slim body that indicated how little food it had found while they had been away, but its little belly swayed majestically as it approached the ditch. It eyed the honeycomb with suspicion, and circled the branches that covered their ditch. It noticed their trap, but it was hungry, and the honey was too tempting to leave.

The bear reached a paw out to reach the honeycomb without walking on the branches, but it leaned too far. The branches snapped and the bear tumbled into their ditch.

They roared in victory as they climbed down from their tree, and Berg hopped around yelling: 'Jaaa, jaaa, jaaa,' over and over.

Again, Finn caught a glimpse of something white in the forest, and this time, it halted long enough for him to see it. It truly was the snow fox from Sigismund's ship; it had the same horrid scars and markings.

The bear roared and clawed at the sides of the ditch. Finn forced his gaze away from the snow fox. He watched the bear struggle, and his smile faded.

'How do we get it out?'

SIGISMUND

Chapter Seventy-Seven

THE SHIP ROCKED. They were losing their course, in the night, when they especially needed their heading to be true.

'The currents are shifting,' said Sigismund's tired helmsman, wide awake and shaking his head. 'First the winds left, then the snow fox, and now this. The gods have abandoned us.'

'Nej, they have not.' Sigismund leaned over the side of the *Storm*. The waters were calm. A slight breeze scurried over the surface and blurred the reflection of the winter lights. The northern lights flickered across the sky, with their green and yellow skirts, and their reflection danced in the waters. Barely any wind on the small waves, but they were losing their bearings, and speeding up.

'The currents beneath us are pushing against the steering oar,' the helmsman added.

There was hardly any wind in their sail, yet the *Storm* advanced at greater and greater speeds. Sigismund's helmsman grunted to keep the steering oar in place.

Five ships followed their course through the night. The other ships were visible only as shadows on the green-tinted night and they were far behind, barely moving in the night.

The *Storm* was pulling away from them, and it had not caught a wind that the other ships had not. The sail flapped and struggled to fill, but they sailed faster and faster ahead.

They were steering for the coast, straight for the sharp rocks that they called the Sea's Jaws.

'Throw the anchors,' Sigismund yelled.

Sailors scrambled to their feet to do as Sigismund asked. They fumbled for planks to get to the aft anchor. The anchor at the fore of the ship was cast first, and sailors at the aft were quick to cast their anchor after, but in such a hurry that they forgot to attach the anchor to the ship.

'Secure it!' Sigismund yelled and fumbled for the rope. The rope nipped his bare hands but he held on. 'For Valhalla's sake!' The anchor fell fast. His sailors struggled to secure the loose end of the rope to the ship.

'Done!' a sailor shouted.

Sigismund let go of the rope, and flexed his fingers. The sailors hurried to give apologies and show concern, but they were not yet safe. The anchors were not enough. Still they drew ahead, as if the anchors were nothing. The steering oar set their course straight for the Sea's Jaws.

'Twist the steering oar out of the waters,' Sigismund shouted.

'I can't,' his helmsman cried. 'It's going to break.'

Sigismund grabbed onto the steering oar and tried to twist it out, but he felt it as well; with two hands forcing it, it would break, and it was already trembling in the undercurrents.

'Get down from the bench.'

Sigismund tore off the helmsman's bench to reveal the tackle that attached the steering oar to the ship, writhing like a serpent. He grabbed the helmsman's axe and hacked. Twice he cut before the tackle came loose as an old rope. The steering oar plopped to the surface of the water.

They drifted a little further, then the aft anchor rope caught, at last, dragging them back.

'By the veulve's visions,' his helmsman breathed in relief. 'I thought Ran had cast her net to capture us into the afterlife.'

Sigismund looked back to where the five other ships ought to be, but he could not see them, for they were so far away, and the sky was less bright, so it was harder to see in the moonless night. The coast was visible, though they were a good way out and close to the danger of the Sea's Jaws. They needed to get further out at sea, somewhere safe where they could wait until morning to find the other ships.

They were barely drifting anymore. Their sail hung limp from the yard.

Sigismund moved to the mid-ship, where his most experienced steersman slept on the oars. With a soft shake he woke the large man, and explained what had happened. 'Wake everyone up,' he instructed, and made his way down the length of the ship, giving the ship's foremen the same explanations and orders.

Almost everyone at the fore of the ship was awake. They had lost many sailors and weren't enough for two full shifts, so most of them had been awake ever since they had crossed the Jutland Sea—almost two days.

'Get an oar and test for undercurrents and depth,' he asked of two of their warriors. Steinar and Eirik were eager to do as bid, and while Sigismund explained what had happened to the others as well as he could, he watched the two sailors bring forth an oar and position themselves by the shrouds at the mid of the ship. Steinar pushed the oar down, and Eirik held it steady. There was a snap and they both lost their balance; their crewmates jumped in to keep the two of them from falling into the water. Steinar let go of the oar, and it immediately floated away.

The warriors with their many questions fell silent.

'What happened?' Sigismund asked the two warriors, already knowing what their answer would be.

'I don't know what it was,' said Steinar.

'Undercurrents,' said Eirik.

Sigismund nodded to them and returned to the aft of the ship, where his helmsman was bent over the bench, unknotting the cut tackle to ready the old steering oar to be secured again.

'Don't attach the steering oar,' Sigismund immediately instructed. 'It's not safe. And that's our last tackle, we need it to get home.'

All of the sailors were awake by now, and the deck had been cleared so they could move without tripping. Sigismund ordered the sail down. They drifted around the anchors, but Sigismund did not trust the undercurrents. They would need to row away, back to safety, away from the Sea's Jaws.

The sailors worked well, alert to the unusual currents— although Sigismund suspected that it was more than just strange currents. He had never experienced such a thing.

'What did you mean when you said it isn't safe to attach the steering oar?' his helmsman finally dared to ask.

'You were right,' Sigismund breathed. 'The gods must have abandoned us to the Jotun sea.'

'Oh, gods. May the Midgard Worm be busy biting its own tail,' the helmsman prayed. 'I knew we shouldn't have sailed in winter, and not stayed out here at night either.'

'The Midgard Worm sleeps,' Sigismund assured. 'If we are careful and quiet, we will pass without waking it.'

'But the steering oar...'

'Just currents.' Sigismund rubbed his beard as he thought about it. 'Sailors before us have sailed far in winter and survived.'

'And they have the most frightening stories to tell.'

'And so do we,' Sigismund said. 'So do we.'

The crew murmured about what had happened. They seemed afraid to lean over the side of the ship and look at the waters. They needed reassurance and only Sigismund could give it to them.

'We too have frightening winter tales to tell,' he said for them all to hear. 'Of a draugar named Hilda, of a snow fox sent from the gods, of terror and berserkers in southern lands. Of fallen warriors and heroes of a new time, standing tall against kings. Of warriors with tears of blood, and of children killings. Terrible stories, we carry,' Sigismund said. 'We *shall* deliver them.'

In the dark of night, he could not see all their faces, but he hoped it gave them strength for it was winter and the nights were long, and this one had hardly begun.

'All sailors to oars!'

His steersman was fully awake by now, and while the crew busied themselves to ready their oars and find their places, Sigismund and the steersman found their bearings. They had been drifting around the anchors, so much so that land was aft out. They found shore, although it was difficult to see, and agreed, roughly, on where the Sea's Jaws would be, and where they needed to steer away from.

The rowers were ready at their positions. Sigismund's steersman took the rowing commands, and brought them away. Meanwhile Sigismund helped a few sailors to heave in the aft anchor.

The waters were so still, only disturbed by their oars. It was unsettling.

The warriors were too worried and they were rowing too fast for strong strokes.

'Pace,' they shouted to each other. 'Remember the pace!' They were all out of pace, those who were shouting as much as the others.

'Pull yourselves together, sailors,' Sigismund urged. 'We're on homebound waters. We know these shores.'

He peered at the few faces he could see in the dark, and knew that they were afraid precisely *because* they knew these waters. They knew how close they were to the Sea's Jaws, and they knew that their ship would shatter and be eaten up on those rocks. They knew that if they were to fall over the edge, the undercurrents would take them, or the Midgard Worm would tear them apart. They were afraid because they *knew*.

'Oar strokes at my command!' Sigismund could do nothing else but sound strong and certain in his commands. 'Three, two, row!'

He gave them the proper pace; counted for them and shouted for every stroke, and with his voice they settled and fell into habit. Their usual calm resurfaced, and the oars took them further away from shore and the Sea's Jaws, and then, Sigismund heard an oar creak and break.

'Man overboard!'

Sailors were shouting, but Sigismund shouted louder than them all: 'Oars in water!'

They did as asked and seemed to remember through their fear that they needed to stay quiet. With their oars in the water, the ship came to a gradual halt.

'Can anybody see him?' Sigismund asked.

No one answered.

'Can anybody hear him?'

They were quiet for a long while, but again, not a single sailor answered.

'What happened?'

Finally, there was an answer. 'His oar got caught in undercurrents, and then it just... flipped up and him with it. Over the side of the ship,' said Astrid. 'Right in front of me.'

'It's Bjarki,' Sigismund's steersman said. He knew all of the rowing positions. 'Bjarki sits in front of Astrid.'

'Was he conscious?'

'Ja!'

'Bjarki!' Sigismund roared louder than he ever had in his life. 'Shout as loud as you can! We *will* find you,' Sigismund said, though he did not expect that they would. It was dark, they could hardly see anything, and they had been rowing at a good pace when it had happened. They had drifted since, and even if they rowed back now, Sigismund was not certain that they would follow the same path, much less find a floating sailor in the night.

'There's something in the water,' the outlook exclaimed.

The crew was so quiet from the crisis that Sigismund heard the message all the way at the aft. 'Get him on board!'

'It's not Bjarki,' the outlook shouted.

A chill travelled up Sigismund's spine.

'I don't know what it is, but it's not Bjarki!'

'We woke it up,' the helmsman sobbed. 'The great beast of the Jotun Sea.'

EINER

Chapter Seventy-Eight

THE SLAP OF the gold bracteate against Einer's chest kept him steady. It blazed hot under his chainmail, and woke him when his mind was too weary to continue.

He did not know for how long he had trailed along the river, but he had noticed at least five nights come and go, and it was night again. Jutland was so far north. With his ship, it would not have been a difficult sail; but on foot, the way was steep and cold and lonely.

The snow had begun to melt, soaking his shoes, and he could no longer feel his feet. He could not feel much other than a loud banging in his head, and the heat of the bracteate against his chest. The world swayed before his eyes, and he trudged ahead, dragging his feet over melting ice.

Ahead of him was a figure in the night, outlined by the shining snow. Einer stopped his walk, and struggled to balance on both feet. No doubt, it was more ravens. There had been so many ravens cawing at him, and crows.

'I won't follow,' he said, as he had all the previous times.

Unexpectedly, he was not answered by the call of a bird or the swish of wings, but by a grim voice. 'Follow me to where?'

The man had a strange accent, but he spoke Norse. There were people who spoke Norse this far south, but the man did not sound as southerners usually did when they attempted to speak the tongue of the north. It sounded like his native tongue.

Einer blinked furiously to see through his pain. A tall man in thick winter clothes and a cloak stood by the river-side. His fists were clenched on the long shaft of a scythe, and reeds lay at his feet.

'Early to be harvesting river reeds,' Einer remarked.

'Winter was early too,' said the tall man. Even Einer, who was taller than all of his warriors, thought that the man looked tall.

On the flat field inland waited an ox, tied to an old cart loaded with river reeds.

'Where are you going?' asked the man.

'North,' Einer responded before he could think.

No one but ravens had approached him during his many days and nights of walking. Once or twice he had noticed someone in the distance, or heard the sound of hooves, but no one had come near him.

The man warily watched Einer, the same way the warriors had used to watch Hilda, but although the man had stopped his work, he was not afraid to speak. He should have been terrified.

'What do you want?' Einer hissed, to show that even hurt and worn, he was a warrior. He clasped his right hand around the hilt of the Ulfberht sword.

'I could kill you,' said the man with the scythe. 'Easily.'

'Others have tried.'

'I can see that,' the man responded. Einer imagined that this was what it would feel like to hear his father's voice again. He knew that gloomy voice, but he could not place it, and he tried to focus on the man's face, but his mind was muddled, and the man's hood was dark.

'*Many* have tried,' said the man after a pause. Then he lifted a gloved hand to his face. 'Someone should have succeeded.' With the hand, he tapped his forehead through the hood.

Einer reached a hand up to his face and glided a cold hand over his own forehead. His fingers grazed the feathered end of an arrow. He moved his hand to the back of his head, feeling for the metal tip.

All the while, he kept his eyes on the man with the scythe, who had moved a few steps away from the river, weapon firm in his grip.

Einer's fingers brushed over a sticky bump. The arrow-head must have struck his helmet and stopped. It had been stuck in his head for a week.

He reached for the fletching at his forehead and got a good hold of it to push the arrow through. His skin had begun to heal, and it would hurt, but better have the arrow out than risk an infection, or something worse.

'Wait! Don't do that,' yelled the man with the scythe, his grip looser, his stance no longer frozen. Perhaps he had only been startled at first, thinking that Einer was a hired guard from the north, come to capture him for stealing river reeds owned by some great king.

'You think I'll die if I pull it out?' Einer asked, for he could not see the damage it could do.

'Nej,' answered the man. 'You should be dead already.'

'Then why do you tell me to stop?'

'You can't know what it will do to your mind to pull it out.'

'It's just an arrow.' All the same, Einer let go of the fletching, and dried the fresh blood from his forehead into his trousers. The man was right, someone's head and mind were the most difficult to heal. If his luck was good it would not become infected—and his luck had been good so far, for normally the wound would already have begun to rot.

The tall man leaned on his scythe. 'If I were to take you somewhere and heal your wounds, what would give me in return?'

Einer considered it for a moment, he did not have much to give. The bracteate hammered against his chest, but since the time Finn had stabbed him in the stomach and Einer had nearly died, he knew not to gamble with the gold his mother had gifted him. 'What do you need?' he asked instead.

'A favour.'

'Favours are expensive.'

'As is healing a dying man.'

As the son of a chief, Einer had always been taught to be careful of favours, especially undefined ones, because nothing could undo a chiefdom quicker and more tragically than a favour owed to the wrong man. 'My wounds will heal eventually,' he decided.

'They may, but they would heal quicker if you were to come with me.'

Einer looked down at himself. His red chainmail was full of holes from spear and arrow wounds, and Einer knew that there were arrows and spear-heads stuck in the mail at his back, where he could not reach. Sometimes, when he walked, he thought that every step may be his last. He needed proper healing, and he needed rest. The heat of the bracteate kept him aware and awake, but he needed rest and care. Equally, he could not trust an utter stranger with a scythe in hand.

'You only offer so you can kill me on the way,' Einer decided. They had not exchanged names, and Einer did not trust a Norseman come this far south just for river reeds.

'What would I gain from killing you?' asked the man, as if to consider his options.

'Glory,' Einer responded. 'Revenge. For the blood my hands have soaked in.'

'If I *were* to kill you—for glory and revenge—would you care?'

He would not. Every part of him knew it. With Hilda's death something inside him was broken; a wheel that could not spin. Having lived his life trying to impress her, he no longer knew what he should do. All he knew was that he needed to continue living, and live well, and take a wife and have children, and explore Midgard. He had always wanted to be a father, and it is what he would have done, if she had not died but chosen another man. It was what he had been prepared for when he had thought she did not love him. And yet, in this moment, Einer did not care if the scythe man killed him. So he approached the tall man, bent to pick up the cut reeds, and walked to the cart.

The tall man followed, packed away his scythe with the reeds and gestured for Einer to get onto the back of the cart. After so many days of walking with the loud hammering in his head and the caw of birds, and the sensation of the bracteate heating his chest and keeping him alive, Einer struggled to move in a different way. His body was stiff, as he hoisted himself onto the back of the cart. His swords were in the way, as he was seated there, and his chainmail was so heavy, and his feet throbbed.

The reed cutter goaded the ox into moving. The cart bumped over the field, and Einer experienced pain in parts of his body he had never before known, but he welcomed the pain.

Out over the cold winter field they trailed, until they reached a little road, where the cart did not rattle as violently and the snow had already melted.

The cart driver walked at Einer's side. His face was hidden by his dark hood, and with Einer seated at the back of the cart, the man looked much taller.

Einer closed his eyes and enjoyed the soothing rumble of the cart. They travelled for a long time in silence before he asked: 'Where are you taking me?'

'Where I said I would.'

Einer thought to ask how far away this place of healing was, but he supposed that it did not matter, for he had already walked for so many days. Sitting on a cart was a welcome change.

'A place to heal…' Einer muttered. 'My heart will need more healing than my wounds.'

The reed man chuckled, as though he had heard Einer's quiet muttering, although it had not been loud enough to be heard over the noise of the cart. The tall man walked with difficulty, but at the same time he had the youthful sway of a young warrior hungry for what the day had to bring. A strange contradiction that made Einer stare.

'Is she a warrior, this girl of yours?' asked the man.

'She wasn't mine, I was hers.' Einer smiled at the thought. 'But ja, she was a warrior. A good one.'

'Then this place may heal your heart too.'

Only one place could heal his heart. Only in the afterlife could he hope to see Hilda again and mend the pain in his chest, not from the bracteate, but from the thought of her. There was only Valhalla—

—And then a thought struck him. The cart driver had not yet shown what lay in the shadow of his hood. And he talked like a wise man, and used tricky language like the Alfather was known to do.

Einer crouched to look under the hood of the tall cart driver who walked at his side. A scarred face and two eyes stared back at him, although he expected to see only one.

'I am not the Alfather,' said the man, as if he knew Einer's thoughts. 'But the Alfather's hall is a good place to heal.' He talked as though they were truly going to Valhalla.

'Am I dead?' Einer asked.

'If you were, don't you think the Alfather or one of his valkyries would have woken you up? Nej, you are very much alive.'

Einer had never heard of anyone going to Odin's hall before their time in Midgard was finished.

'Then, if I am not dead, I shall continue on my own way,' he said, though his mind craved to see Valhalla, with its gold-shielded roof and its thousands and thousands of warriors. Hilda would be seated amongst them, feasting on mead and meat.

'You do not need to come,' said the cart driver. 'It is an offer. You can hop off the cart, if you want, I won't chase you.'

Einer knew that he should leave now, slide off the cart and resume his trail north to Jutland. He knew that his place could not be in Valhalla until the afterlife claimed him. He imagined Hilda's disappointment at seeing him so soon, and he imagined the laughter and surprise of the other warriors in the hall. He imagined the shame of it. Everything he knew was wrong about the offer.

And yet, he did not jump off the cart.

Einer had an uncontrollable will to stay put, enjoy the rest he had been gifted, and allow fate to lead him elsewhere. A voice inside screamed to listen to this strange man, and to follow. He supposed that it was his destiny to follow. Some people had destinies that led them off their intended trail.

So, although he knew that he ought not to, he stayed on the cart, and listened to the voice within. The ancient forces, the ones he had welcomed at Magadoborg, grew stronger, feeding on an anger within Einer that he had not yet named.

'Are you angry with the gods because she is dead?' the tall man asked, again, as though he could hear Einer's thoughts. Perhaps he had been frowning.

Einer considered the question honestly. 'I am not angry with the gods,' he decided. 'I'm angry with the fate spinners, for not spinning a longer life for her.'

Being asked about it made the fury retreat, shrinking to a bearable tickle at the corner of his mind, no longer a scream.

'If you aren't angry at the gods, then why do you refuse Valhalla?'

'I don't refuse. There is no greater honour than Valhalla. I have no greater wish than to enter Odin's hall in my afterlife. But as you say, I am not yet in my afterlife.'

'You should be.' The cart rider sounded like he knew a thousand things about Einer that he himself did not know. 'Fate has freed you. There is no destiny planned for you any longer.'

No one but the gods or nornir could know that for certain. Einer did not even think a natural runemistress like Hilda would have known.

'It matters little,' he decided. If it had been Hilda, she would not have let such a detail keep her from pursuing life. 'I'm still here, and I am going home.'

'Do you even know where your home is?'

With every exchange, the cart driver revealed himself to know more about Einer. Regardless, it was a good question for with Ash-hill in ashes there was not much of a home left, especially now that Hilda was no longer there. 'Up north,' he answered.

'Home is a lot further north than you can imagine. I know who you are, Einer. Do *you?*'

SIGISMUND

Chapter Seventy-Nine

THE ROWERS WERE silent as the night as something stirred beneath the ship.

'Try again,' Sigismund whispered to the cook.

The cook bent back down by the ballast stones where they cooked meals. His hands were shaking as he blew on the moss to get flames. He set the wooden pins on top, hoping they would catch.

A sudden blow of wind extinguished the cook's fifth attempt to get flames. Shaking, he picked up his fire striker and another handful of dried moss to start anew.

Sigismund held his breath and watched over the cook's shoulder. They needed to get a fire started: if not to see others on the waters, then at least so they could be seen. The other ships were indistinguishable from the dark, and the night was yet long. Sigismund continued to look for the ships, hoping to glimpse the light of a cooking fire, but he saw nothing. Clouds had moved in, covering the green light of the winter night, leaving the waters obscure.

The rowers were careful with their strokes. They kept the oars close to the surface as Sigismund had instructed. No deep strokes.

Something whacked into the ship's starboard side, and Sigismund heard splashes. He leaned over the side. There was nothing to see. He'd known there would not be. He could barely see three arm-lengths ahead.

Fire snapped at his feet, and the bright light of flames welcomed him. The cook had started his fire at last, and was lighting torches with which they could signal the other ships. There was hope yet.

The two helmsmen and the steersman, gathered around the cook, were as excited as Sigismund. Their faces lit up at the sight of flames. Sigismund stood to address the sailors with newfound hope, but as he looked up into the night and listened for the sound of them, he knew that something else was amiss.

The warriors had stopped rowing. The steady splash of their oars had ceased, replaced by the soft clatter of oars floating free. As if there were no rowers to hold them. As if they had all left their benches.

Little by little, those sounds too gave way to silence.

Sigismund's heart beat all the way up in his throat, as he silently held a hand over the head of his steersman, demanding to be given the first torch. He secured his grip and carefully stepped behind the cook and other men by the cooking fire. His eyes were fixed on the first rowing bench. One slow step after another he approached, knuckles clenched white on his torch. The bench flickered into view: empty. No rower, and no oar.

Perhaps no one had rowed there. With a quickening heartbeat he legged over the rowing thwart to the next bench.

No one.

The third bench was equally empty. Sigismund turned back towards the cook, the steersman and two helmsmen. They were all too busy with the fire and their torches to notice.

Alone, Sigismund continued along the length of the ship and found empty benches with oars barely holding on through their oar holes. Each and every bench was empty, as if the gods had simply lifted the sailors and flown them away.

Sigismund's heart raced as he looked at the empty benches. Never in his life had he heard of anything like it. Not even in the old tales. His crew had vanished, and what frightened him more than anything was that not a single one of them had screamed. They had made no more sound than corpses.

The thought stuck with Sigismund. They would have screamed if they had seen or felt the Midgard Worm take them. They would have screamed if they had fallen overboard. They would have screamed, if they had been alive.

'Where are you?' Sigismund yelled to his warriors, and the sea and its creatures, and when he turned back to the aft where his two helmsmen and steersman and cook had been busy with the fire and torches, there was no one. The flames of the cooking fire flickered. A wind threatened to extinguish the fire, or worse, set flames to the tarred ship.

'Where did you take them?' Sigismund yelled to the gods, and although he expected no response, he received one.

Something scraped along the hull of the ship directly beneath his feet. Not the seabed, and not rocks. It sounded like a huge sword was slid across the hull.

The Midgard Worm.

Sigismund sped down the length of the ship to the shrouds. He found the spears, kept in a bundle with the remaining oars. He grabbed the first he found, jerked it free and pulled the safe-guard off the blade.

With the torch in one hand and the spear in the other, he stepped onto a rowing thwart and approached the edge of the ship. The waters were calm, no different from how they had been earlier in the night. There had been no splashes but there was nowhere else to go but into the deep.

None of the rowers had worn armour. They would not sink.

If they were unconscious, or dead, they would have floated. He should be able to see them.

'Where are you?' Sigismund bellowed.

The ship rocked, pushed from the outside. Sigismund staggered. His hands clenched onto the torch and spear, desperate not to let go of either. He lost his balance. Head first, he plummeted into the waters.

The cold engulfed him.

The torch was extinguished, and Sigismund let go. He tightened his grip on the spear, kicked and flailed to reach the surface. His head splashed into the cold night. He gasped for breath, and coughed up water. There were almost no waves, as if he was in an inlet and not at sea.

None of his sailors had come to the surface for air, or he would have heard them. Perhaps none of them had been conscious, but Sigismund knew nothing in all of Midgard that could make forty sailors unconscious in a heartbeat. They must have been dragged into the deep. The Midgard Worm had taken them, and Sigismund would not let them be taken to Ran's and Aegir's hall in the afterlife. Not when they belonged in Valhalla.

His tight clasp on the spear strengthened Sigismund's resolve. He would get them back. He inhaled deep, and dived.

He swam, as well as he could, despite the freezing waters. With each stroke, he stabbed the spear ahead of him. The waters were black. His eyes stung from the salt.

He dived and dived, deeper and deeper. The pressure was like a blow to the face. He kicked and struggled to go further. His lungs were nearly out of air. He stabbed the spear ahead with all of his might. Again and again he thrust, as he dived, and then, the spear caught something.

He was pulled along sideways in the water. Sigismund grabbed hold of the spear with both hands, and struggled to keep in the little air he had left. His hands were slipping off the handle.

He was cast away and twirled in the water. He swam after the spear, and what had taken it, but he had been pulled so fast that he knew it was impossible to catch.

He looked around, but could see nothing. Not even light above the water. He did not know what to do. He had dived far, and he would not make it back up, even if he tried. Besides, his warriors were still in the water, drowning with every slowed heartbeat.

Sigismund's foot kicked something: seaweed, or soft fabric. He dived after it. His hands were met with a strong fishing net, but that was not what the sole of his foot had felt. He groped at the net, and then his hands touched a woollen tunic.

One of his sailors was caught in the net. Sigismund shook the man, but there was no struggle or no resistance. He was dead, whoever he was.

Sigismund groped the net to find others. His hand got stuck in the sticky net. He could not see anything, but the net tightened and he heard others struggle. Every movement was muffled in the water, but some of his warriors were still alive.

He tried to wrestle free, to reach them. He twisted to move his left arm to his weapon belt and reach his dagger. His belt was stuck in the net, and the more he moved, the more stuck he too became. The net caught his clothes and fingernails, and his curly hair was caught in it too.

He could not free his warriors, but he struggled all the same. Water trickled into his throat and lungs. Every warrior on his ship deserved to go to Valhalla. They had fought for the Alfather, and they deserved to meet him in the afterlife.

A warm pain struck him at the top of his chest, and travelled through his entire body.

Ran had cast her net for his sailors, but not for Sigismund. He had been alone on the ship. Ran wanted his warriors but not him in her hall, but she would have to take him too. Sigismund left no sailor behind.

HILDA

Chapter Eighty

THE BEAR GROWLED at Hilda's snow fox. Hilda had expected the journey to Jelling to be lonely, but it hadn't been. Einer's bear cub Vigir and Finn had proven to be good travel companions. Neither said much. In the evenings Finn and Hilda sat by the fire, and stared at the flames in silence, while her snow fox played with Einer's bear cub.

The bear had grown over the past few months. It was not much of a cub anymore, and had it not been for Hilda's connection to Vigir, Finn never would have freed it from that pit into which he had trapped the bear. The others had thought he had managed it on his own, which made Hilda laugh.

Hilda tugged on her socks, which were wet from morning dew. At her side, Finn grumbled over the state of his own socks, while Vigir growled for them to hurry.

They were close to Jelling. Hilda had walked along the Oxen Road enough times to know that they would arrive at Harald's town before midday. Before the end of the day she would find the familiar face the runemistress had told her about, and then, she would get the Runes back. She could barely wait. The longer she spent without their voice, the more she missed them.

Finn stalled. From his bag, he brought out a blackened figurine, looked up at the sky as he held it and mumbled prayers to the gods. At the foot of the oak where he had slept, he placed the blackened figurine in offering to the gods. Then he grabbed his spear and the bear's chain. Vigir roared after Hilda's snow fox, but the fox had already run off into the forest on its own again.

Hilda knelt by Finn's offering. The half-burned figurine was almost finished, but not quite. The flowers in Freya's hair needed to be carved. Tears swelled up in Hilda's eyes as she recognised the carved figurine. It belonged to her. The morning before the battle she had caught Tyra making it for her, but Tyra hadn't lived long enough to finish it.

Hilda's hands reached for the figurine. Its body coloured her fingers black, but the face hadn't burned. It had been given in offering and she shouldn't take it, but it was a piece of home, so she did. Finn wouldn't notice it gone. If he did, he would assume that a beggar or a dog had found and taken it, as was usually the case with offerings to the gods.

Behind Freya's hair was a hole from which Hilda hung the figurine onto her belt. A piece of home to bring on her travels.

Her snow fox barked. It had come back. It let out another high-pitched bark and waited for Hilda to respond. It hadn't yelped the other mornings when she had let Vigir and Finn leave first. It could only mean one thing.

'Did you find it?' Hilda asked. 'The familiar face?'

Again, the snow fox yelped. Hilda strapped her shoes on properly and raced through the woods after her fylgja. The snow fox was eager. Hilda caught glimpses of its tail and followed as well as she could. Deer scurried away into the woods. A hare hopped along, chased by a snarling red fox, and then, finally, Hilda's snow fox stopped. By a clearing in the woods, it waited for Hilda to catch up.

There, the fox had found a man.

He was big and thick-boned, dressed in expensive robes. His hair was nearly black, but red locks grew from his temples and blended with his freshly cut hair.

He was in the midst of grooming himself. A mirror in one hand and shears in the other. Half of his beard was neat and cut into a form that suited his sharp chin. The other side, he hadn't yet reached.

All of his things lay at his feet next to an empty bag. He emptied the contents onto the dewy grass. Pincers, balms, clothes, gloves, hats, flasks of spices and dried foods. There was also a falcon skin, beautiful like those the gods were said to put on to gain wings and fly.

He hummed as he trimmed his beard. Sang, even. A song and tune that Hilda had never heard before. Her father had sung all the melodies in Midgard. She ought to know it. Unless it was a new creation, or unless, it wasn't from Midgard.

His features *did* feel familiar. As if Hilda had always known them, though she had never seen them. A falcon skin like the one Loki was said to fly. Loki, who looked sly and familiar and who would know songs that Hilda did not. A giant, not a god, but someone with great knowledge of godly gifts and runes.

DARKNESS

THE COLD DARKNESS buried Ragnar in worry.

He had freed Loki. He had not meant to, but he had. Despite his best efforts to set things right and save his gods, he had made everything worse. With another simple mistake, he had doomed his gods.

He needed to follow Loki and chain him back to the rock in the cave that the gods had destined for him. Ragnar thought of where Loki might have gone after leaving the cave with his chains undone, and silently, he tapped his distaff.

The bright thread burst from the hollow part of his distaff with a squeal that tore through worlds. So long had Ragnar spent in the Darkness that both the dark and the horrid screech had become comforts to him.

A veil tore through the Darkness, and Ragnar took a hopeful breath and passed through. The air was cold, and the grass at his feet too. The wild grass was not that of Asgard, he thought immediately. It was not lush green and evenly cut, but flawed as only the grass of home could be. He had arrived in Midgard.

Ragnar skipped ahead so his distaff pushed the Darkness far enough back to reveal Loki curled over himself. His hair had been trimmed and his beard too. He was plucking his eyebrows, and smiling at his own freedom.

Ragnar made his distaff push the Darkness further back. He needed to find some way to capture Loki and drag him back to the cave. The feat would be difficult to accomplish for Ragnar, who only had his thoughts and influence over Loki to help him. There had to be something he could do.

A woman with pale skin and blonde hair appeared at the edge of the Darkness. Marks stretched down her cheeks, like tears streaming from her blue eyes.

Ragnar froze at the sight of her. Her slim eyebrows were furrowed into a frown. Her square chin was sharp as if it had been cleaved. From her belt hung a new axe, better than any of the ones she had sneakily bought in the past. The handle was bloodied by battle. Now that Ragnar was gone, there was no one to prevent her from an early death, like that of Leif.

She did not look as she did in his memories. In the Darkness, he had forgotten the face of his own daughter, though his love for her had not been forgotten.

Hilda did not see him. It mattered little, for *he* saw her. And he had not expected to see her. Not in this life. Not in the afterlife. His heart seemed to crumble at the sight of her, and he took in every detail. The ragged end of her sleeve, on a tunic he had never seen before. The blood on the tunic had long dried into the thin fabric. Her strong arms barely fit inside the sleeves.

Hilda tiptoed towards him. Not towards Ragnar, of course— she could not see her father—but towards Loki. The giant was mumbling, singing his song, and had neither heard nor seen her approach.

He had emptied the contents of his bag onto the grass. His things lay in disarray around him. Among them was his famous falcon skin with which he flew through the nine worlds.

Ragnar was reminded of the horrid tale of Sigmund and Sinfjölte, who had put on two wolf skins, and been trapped inside because only gods and runemistresses had the necessary skill to use the skins.

Hilda, too, had noticed the falcon skin. Her eyes hungered for it.

As loud as he could, Ragnar thought hard about the stories to make Hilda remember them, and to warn her of what might happen if she put on the skin. He did all he could to urge her to leave the skin and Loki, like he had once made Odin abandon Ragnarok's battlefield. But Hilda was not a god. Her eyes were fixed on the skin. She stepped forward.

'Nej!' he yelled to keep her away and safe.

His voice echoed around him, alerting the Darkness to his presence.

He knew what came next.

'Keep awa—!'

A spear pierced his throat and kept him from screaming. Blood flooded down his throat and suffocated him.

Death, pain, and fear.

HILDA

Chapter Eighty-One

AN IDEA APPEARED in Hilda's mind, almost as if someone else had put it there. She remembered old tales her father had used to tell by the fireplace, of runemistresses and godly animal skins. Sigmund and Sinfjölte had not known how to escape their stolen wolf skins, but runemistresses often used skins. The warriors had called Hilda a runemistress.

She glanced to the back of Loki's well-combed hair. She didn't think she could trust him. That was why she had waited back as he had trimmed his beard. If she put on the skin, she wouldn't need to trust him. She could fly to Asgard, deliver the axe and get her Runes back all at once. All she needed was that falcon skin.

The snow fox looked up at her for commands. Loki might not be able to see her, but he would certainly be able to see her snow fox. Hilda pointed to the ground to make it stay back. Then, she crept closer to Loki. He didn't see her. No one saw Hilda: not Finn, not Sigismund, not the runemistress and not Loki. Maybe even the gods wouldn't be able to see her. Hilda didn't let the thought linger any longer than that.

She settled her sight on Loki's back. One step closer. He was focused on his eyebrows. Hilda watched her steps. There was no more than two arm-lengths between Loki and her. The falcon skin was exactly between the two of them. One more step and she would be able to reach it.

She glanced back to her snow fox. It paced behind her, opened its mouth with a sharp inhale. It was about to bark and alert Loki to her presence. She was too far away to stop it.

Hilda cast her head back towards the falcon skin. Loki had already turned around. The snow fox's yelps echoed in the clearing. It had wanted to warn her that she had been discovered.

Loki's thin lips pressed together and his eyes narrowed. He saw her, though no one did. Loki, giant among gods, cheater and swindler, saw her.

'You can see me?' asked Loki. Exactly what she wanted to ask *him*. He was as surprised as her.

This was her best chance.

Hilda lunged. Her hands groped greasy feathers and closed around them. She lifted the skin and ran. Away from Loki, out of the clearing. She hopped over grass patches and thickets and sped up into the forest. Deer watched her. A red fox stopped hunting a hare to stare at her. Or maybe it was her snow fox they saw.

Hilda heard a clatter behind. Her snow fox barked. Loki yelled and screamed. Hilda kept running and brought the skin to her face. She turned it in her hands as she ran, looking for the opening. It was so small. She would never fit inside.

The opening was laced closed across the back with a leather strap the length of her hands. Hilda kept running, eyes on the ground, as her fingers undid the lacing.

Loki was swearing and yelling behind her. Hilda glanced over her shoulder as she shot through the forest. She couldn't see him, but he knew which way she had run.

She took a sharp turn left, to throw him off her tracks. Her snow fox didn't run at her side, but she heard it bark. It was going after Loki, to give Hilda a chance to escape.

The last lacing came undone, Hilda felt the inside of the skin. It was rough leather, like any old skin, but when she put her fingers into the opening, they became smaller and longer— shrunk to fit the size of a falcon. Hilda opened the hole at the back of the skin and slid her feet inside. First her left, it barely fit as she pushed it in, but once inside there was so much room for more, so she inserted her right foot too and wriggled her toes to push inside. Her feet glided inside, and they seemed so small and lonely in there. Her calves were too large, and her thighs would never fit.

Loki's yelling came closer.

She had no time to worry about what was possible and what wasn't. She had to fly away, and now. Hilda grabbed the edges of the opening and slid it up her legs. It should have been impossible, but she lifted it all the way up to her hips. The opening stretched for her. She became shorter and smaller. Her legs were slim but strong. Her head shrank closer and closer to the ground, as she forced herself into the skin.

Hilda looked down at herself. She was standing on the twig-like legs of a falcon skin, and she stretched her claws. The skin fit her like a tight leather glove.

Her snow fox barked a warning. Loki was coming. She wriggled the skin up so it rested under her armpits and she only had her arms and head outside. She inhaled sharply, closed her eyes, shut out the voice inside her head that screamed not to do it, and pushed her head inside.

The leather wrapped onto her face, musty and sticky at first, and then it felt like her own. She twitched her cheeks and felt feathers flap against each other.

A twig crunched. Loki was coming.

Hilda opened her eyes and saw through the holes in the falcon skin, as if they were the eye holes on a helmet. She blinked to free her own eyelids of the bird skin.

Loki was racing through the forest towards her.

Hilda flapped her arms to fly away, but they simply knocked against the cold earth. Her arms hung limply outside the skin.

She hopped away on her small twig legs. They were strong but stiff, like she had never used her legs before. She stumbled. Her arms scraped behind her. They were heavy. Her shoulders were stuck outside. She tried to cock her head to the side, and free herself of the skin, but it didn't work.

Loki snickered as he grabbed onto her. His hand closed on her feathered belly, and she jumped away, but he gripped hard. She yelled. It came out a screech, and then she remembered that she didn't have a mouth but a hard beak, and she stretched her neck and hacked into Loki. She flayed her arms behind her, and pushed him away with her hands.

The snow fox snapped after Loki. The giant groaned, and grabbed Hilda's left hand. She flapped to get away, but she couldn't move her arm. His legs wrapped around her feathered stomach, and he pulled her arm back, to force her out of the falcon skin.

'Not—my—skin,' he grunted with each hard pull.

Hilda strained to stay inside, but the more Loki pulled on her left arm, the more her chest strained free of the leather.

As the feathered skin pulled free, the opening widened, and Hilda wriggled her right arm and shoulder inside. Her limbs shrank and stretched, her fingers spread into a long, feathered wing, and Hilda flung her one wing wide and lifted her twig feet from the ground. She pecked Loki's legs.

Loki squealed.

Hilda wriggled free and hopped off from the ground. She hit Loki's face with her wing, and went at it with her sharp claws.

He let go of her left arm. Hilda squirmed and forced it inside. She beat her new wing, to force the skin tight. She planted her claws into Loki's face, spread her wings and took flight. She felt heavy and light at the same time. Her wings kept her off the ground, and with three beats she flew free of Loki's reach.

On the ground, Loki set after her fox. He knew it belonged to her and that if he caught it, he may catch her too. The fox wailed for her as it ran; her fylgja was in trouble.

Hilda hovered above, and prepared to swoop down to the fox, as she had seen birds do, but she was not a skilled bird. Her wings opened too late. She plummeted to the ground, tumbled over moss towards the white fox. Quick, she opened her claws and clasped them around the snow fox's neck and body. She took flight, but the fox was so big. The weight of it pulled her down.

Loki hissed behind her. The fox ran along the forest bed as Hilda beat her wings and tried again. She struggled to hold on, but slowly she gained height.

A hand clutched Hilda before she reached the crown of the trees. She was so far from the ground, but the hand was giant. Two fingers closed around her. Hilda struggled to get free, and the snow fox whimpered. The hand squeezed them both, but Loki's giant hands were large. Hilda pushed against the fingers, and the snow fox clawed at them. The fingers parted slightly for a heartbeat, but Hilda only needed a heartbeat.

She rolled through the gap, fell from the height, but spread her wings and caught herself before they hit the ground. She glided over the grass, still struggling to keep the snow fox in her grip. Her toes were shaking from the strain.

But she found the strength and flew on, far and fast, down low among the tree trunks where Loki could not easily reach her in his giant size.

She didn't look back at him for fear of crashing; she was going so fast, faster than she had ever gone before, faster than a galloping horse. She swished between trees and along the ground. The forest thickened, and Hilda took to the sky, soaring to the tree tops and through.

The low clouds were thick with mist and dusted rain. Her feathers came out slick. She rose above into a gulf with clouds above and clouds below. She drew breath. The air was crisp and cold.

She had escaped Loki, and with her snow fox too. She had outsmarted a giant, and stolen a falcon skin. She could fly anywhere now.

The wind tickled the feathers on her tail and wings. Her stomach knotted from the feeling. The wind reminded her of the Runes. She missed their whispers. The wind swished past her ears. She listened and thought she heard whispers in its faint whistle, but it was just her own wishful thinking.

Her eyes were tearing from the wind. She wore a falcon skin, but her eyes were her own. They were not meant for flying.

The snow fox dangled below her. It did not strain or jerk, though it must have been scared. Even so, she needed to set it down soon. It was too heavy for her small falcon body. Her wings could barely carry them both.

Hilda wished herself far away, to Asgard. Claws full of snow fox fur, she screeched for it.

The gods heard.

They must have, because among the subtle rain, she saw a rainbow. Not the usual kind, which stretched to Midgard's ground; this rainbow was completely round, in a ring only three full wing spans wide.

Hilda flew to it, and through.

Suddenly the air was warmer than it had been and the clouds not as dark. Hilda folded up her wings, and glided down. She struggled to hold onto the snow fox.

There was no forest below the layer of clouds, as there had been, but a large plain. A river snaked across the plain and proud trees stood along it, and on the plain, bushy and old. Their leaves were dark red, and ready to fall, but they had not yet fallen as the leaves in Midgard had.

The grass was bright green, and over the plain were patches of sunlight.

Loki wasn't there.

She had done it. She had escaped to Asgard. She looked upon the plains where her gods walked. Flew over the lands where they lived.

Hilda struggled to keep her toes locked around the neck of the snow fox long enough to make her descent. A few feet off the ground, she unclasped her hold. The snow fox plopped down and darted away, happy to be free again.

Hilda plummeted onto the grassy ground. Not as elegant a landing as she had planned, but that mattered little. She was there. She was safe, and Loki was a world away.

The snow fox hopped around her, yelping loudly and chasing shadows on the bright green grasses. Hilda laughed, a loud shriek that rung over the plain. She wriggled to get her shoulders free and remove the falcon skin. Eager to get it off and stretch her limbs.

Her shoulder did not come out of the opening at the back.

Hilda squirmed from side to side, and tried to pull her hands out of the wings. They were stuck inside, as if the feathers and wings had been glued to her with hot tar.

The snow fox saw her distress and stopped its barking. Hilda puffed and wrestled with herself again. She couldn't reach the lacing at her back. She couldn't get out.

'Grab it,' she called to the snow fox, but only heard a falcon's screech.

The fox ran to her.

'Pull,' she screeched.

The fox was already pulling, tearing the leather strap from side to side. Hilda was being pulled this way and that by the force of it. Yet the falcon skin didn't come undone. The lacing didn't open. She couldn't tear the skin off.

She flapped her wings to reach, but she had no fingers to clasp the lacing, no hands to clench. Her long, feathered fingers could not grab anything and could not free her.

Her mind flooded with the stories her father had used to tell her. She could almost hear his warning in her mind. She remembered the story of Sigmund and Sinfjölte. He had not told it often, but she remembered it. She did not remember how they had been freed from their wolf hides.

There had to be way. Frantically, she rolled around to reach the lacing on her back and wriggle free of the skin.

Something clutched her twig-like legs, and clenched them tight.

Hilda screeched. She was lifted into the air, not by her own wings, but by a hand around her legs. Another hand grabbed her head and pinned her neck so she couldn't move.

'You thought you could escape,' hissed a voice.

Hilda flapped her wings to get free, but couldn't. Feathers were falling all around her. She was caught by the neck. This time, there was no escape.

MUSPELDÓTTIR

Chapter Eighty-Two

ONE, TWO, THREE, four, five, six, seven, eight, nine.

Muspeldóttir had found a warm host. This body was obedient too. Her last, the cold one, had trapped her flames. She had killed its snow fox, and escaped. It had required much heat and strength, but at last Muspeldóttir was free. At last she had a burning hot host. The perfect host body for her flames.

One, two, three, four, five, six, seven, eight, nine.

'I've always loved Jelling's winter songs,' said Muspeldóttir through her new host. A handsome man and important too. Styrbjorn the Strong, short-lived called her host. He had conquered Jomsborg and much more.

Now, with Muspeldóttir's strength inside, Styrbjorn would conquer all of Midgard.

One, two, three, four, five, six, seven, eight, nine.

This land was hers to take and to burn.

She would have to be careful and slow, but she would take one flame at a time. Muspeldóttir would burn Midgard whole, and free her brothers from Muspelheim. No one could stop her flames anymore.

SIV

Chapter Eighty-Three

'THAT'S WHO SHE will marry,' Harald told Siv as a slender chief walked into the busy longhouse. 'Styrbjorn the Strong of Jomsborg. He will be a good ally.'

Siv froze up at the sight of him. Styrbjorn had a definite presence about him. Heat oozed from his nostrils like a beast, and he was older, a lot older than Tyra. Although she was not certain why, Siv summoned the rune of ice to keep her skin and thoughts cool.

Styrbjorn's fiery eyes snapped to meet Siv's, as if he sensed her using the runes. He smiled, a frightening sight, and Siv armed herself with a perfect smile in return as she watched him enter her longhouse with other influential freemen who had arrived after the wedding to make alliances with Harald, unaware of the disastrous effects the recent attack on Magadoborg had on Jelling's influence.

'He is so much older than Tyra,' said Siv, trying once more to dissuade Harald from his quest of marrying Tyra off. 'There must be a better match.' The whole week she had attempted to change Harald's mind, but he was as set on marrying Tyra to Styrbjorn as he was steady in his Christian faith.

'There is no one better, or more suited.' Harald wrapped his arms over her although they were standing so close to the fireplace in the middle of the room that she hardly needed any more warmth. 'Styrbjorn the Strong of Jomsborg,' Harald mumbled, content with the match.

Styrbjorn's acquired calling name was accurate. There was strength in him. Not the usual sort of short-lived strength that made warriors skilled at fighting. This was runic strength. Abilities beyond those a short-lived ought to have, though he neither smelled nor looked like a long-lived, except for his eyes. His eyes were burning with strength and heat.

More freemen entered the house and shielded Styrbjorn from view, despite his stable posture. Talk rose and Siv sensed the waves of excitement pass from one rich freeman to another. Outside the longhouse, the bear everyone talked about roared, and stunned the crowd into an uneasy silence.

'It's real,' exclaimed Harald's eldest son, Svend, loud enough for all to hear. 'The bear.' He leaned in over his table at the back of the hall to see the bear through the open door. Tyra shouldered him back in his seat and whispered something that made them both laugh while Svend's younger brother demanded to know what was so funny.

'They shouldn't be here,' Harald grumbled at the sight of his three children. 'I didn't call upon them.'

'Let me,' Siv said, glad for an excuse to shoulder out of his warm hug.

He included her only in the smallest decisions, and there he was easy to sway and convince, but when it truly mattered, Harald was stubborn beyond repair. So stubborn that Siv no longer believed that she could sway him to reintroduce old traditions and beliefs. At most, she could push him away, into a corner, turn his allies against him and strike him down to make way for his son to take over.

There was hope yet for Svend, and he was smitten with Tyra. His long curls bounced as he laughed at something else Tyra had whispered to him.

'You know you aren't old enough to be here,' Siv told the kids. Their laughter stopped immediately.

They looked up at her with doe eyes, silently begging to be allowed to stay to see the huge bear and the man who had come with it. Tyra also knew whose bear it was. It had belonged to Einer, and only Einer could have brought it.

Svend, Hakon and Tyra waited for Siv's final decision to either send them away or allow them to stay. Outside, the bear roared again, forcing Siv make her decision. She could not tell Tyra to leave when they were finally going to receive news from Ash-hill, especially not when it was Einer coming to deliver it. 'I will allow you to stay if you are silent, do you understand?'

'Tak, Tove.' Svend turned to his brother and punched him in the shoulder. 'I told you she would get him to agree.'

The boys both told her that they would be quiet, but Siv had not decided to start another argument with Harald for their sake. Tyra smiled so much at the thought of seeing Einer that her freckled cheeks turned red.

Ash-hill's warriors had returned home, and now they were in Jelling. Siv struggled to keep her calm, but she had to play her role well, or she might risk ruining everything they had worked for these past months. Tyra and she would both need to pretend that they did not know about Ash-hill.

At the end of summer, a few warriors from Ash-hill had joined Harald's ranks. Siv had sealed their silence and locked away their memories of her and Tyra early upon their arrival in Jelling, but minds took a long time to change, and memories required calm to seal. She would not have that sort of time and quiet today.

Siv left the kids and walked back to the middle of the room to stand by her new husband, close to the fire where it was too warm for comfort. Harald hooked an arm on her waist and pulled her closer to him and the fire. She knew him well enough to know that he was nervous. He had combed his hair and beard, and changed his silver arm-rings for gold jewellery. He intended to intimidate Ash-hill into submitting to his rule, and Siv would do what was required to prevent him.

The door was open. The heat of the hall oozed out and reminded Siv of Styrbjorn sitting in the corner of the room, hot eyes glaring at her. The bear roared once more. It was Einer's cub, there was no doubt about it. Siv's heart tightened and raced at the thought of seeing her son again, and having to stand there and pretend not to be his mother.

While he had been off fighting their enemies, she had married a man who was not his father, and Christian to boot, and she had made a new life for herself. It would not be an easy truth to accept, and they needed to act accordingly.

Einer would understand. He was not a dumb warrior. He had her wits, and he would understand why she was there, and know that she would use her influence to his advantage.

The freemen muttered about her son. They talked about the big warrior from Ash-hill who had tamed a bear and brought it as a gift, about his scruffy beard, his hair, a little short for a freeman, and his foolish smile. Einer had always had a simple farmer's smile, exactly like his father. She so longed to see it, and to see how much he had grown over summer and early winter. She had not seen him since Midsummer.

As she stood and played with her thoughts, she sensed a presence near the longhouse. The freemen fell silent as he walked inside. His steps were confident, his posture proud, and she recognised his presence and knew that he was not who she expected him to be. He was not as tall as her son. He did not carry Einer's ease, but he wore her son's clothes, and he stared straight at her.

'Siv...' Finn muttered, before she could seal away her disappointment and stop him.

Her heart skipped a beat, and at the corner of the hall, she saw Tyra rise from her seat. The crowd fell silent and suddenly every last freeman followed Finn's stare to Siv. Harald around twisted to look at her. His smile faded as he did. His eyes examined her anew; almost for the first time.

Siv grasped for the forefathers, called them forth, let them tingle out of her hands and up the veins of her arms, felt them gather at her neck, ready to be let loose into her mind and kill everyone.

Harald stared at her from head to toe. 'Ja, ja, ja,' he said and laughed. 'My wife certainly is as beautiful as the golden-haired goddess Sif.' His hands grabbed a lock of her blonde hair and held it preciously. He had misheard.

Siv locked her fingers into a fist and forced the forefathers to retreat.

She kissed her husband for his kind praise. Their tongues intertwined in a long kiss for Finn to see, so he would understand her position. As she pulled away from Harald again, she glared at Finn.

Siv forced herself into Finn's mind to make him close his gaping mouth. His face was flushed red and shrugged his cloak onto his back. The heat of the hall bothered him the same as it bothered Siv and anyone else used to the cold. The hall was hot like only that of a rich man would be on a day of drizzle. Harald was indeed a rich man, and even in winter he dressed in summer tunics.

Finn looked different than how she remembered him. His hair was short. She did not think he had ever had short hair. Not as a young man when he had first begun to follow Vigmer, and certainly never since. His clothes she knew well. Three winters ago, she had stitched the light brown tunic he wore: a winter during which Einer had grown out of all his clothes, again. She wondered if he had grown more this summer too. All of her other sons had grown every summer they were away, up until Odin took them.

At Siv's side, Harald made his hands drift over the flames,

perhaps to look unbothered by Finn's arrival, although all of these influential farmers and freeman had gathered in his hall to watch Harald and Finn exchange words, and that was enough to bother anyone.

'You think a gift and flattery will persuade me to help you?' Harald said, no longer amused. He narrowed his eyes at Finn. 'You go on a murderous raid and cause trouble for all of us, and now that you're back home you expect me to help you?'

Outside, Einer's bear cub roared with hunger. Finn turned away from Harald and closed the door. He looked more composed than Harald, but Siv could hear on his heartbeat that he was nervous.

Finn faced Harald and her again and took a few more steps inside, assessing the situation. Harald had spoken without giving him a chance to introduce himself.

'Do you realise how much you have ruined for me?' Harald hissed. His spit landed in his beard and on the floor, and fizzled on the fire. 'I've had to promise free labour and gold, and I've had to allow more southern warriors into these lands than ever before, because of *your* stupidity!'

Siv eyed her new husband. The most stupid of all had been Harald's own decisions, yet Harald had every advantage over Ash-hill. In Jelling they had food to last the winter, warm shelter, farmhouses and sheep and cattle, and unburned lands ready for the next season. They had wealth to pay for berserkers and guards.

Finn's jaw visibly tightened, and Siv could hear his heart boil with anger and a will to retort, although he could not. Ash-hill did not have anything anymore, and Harald knew that as well as Siv. Finn had no choice but to take whatever Harald decided to throw at him.

'Vigmer should have come himself,' Harald continued. 'Or is he too much of a coward for that?'

Siv closed her eyes and took a deep breath at the mention of her old husband's name.

'Vigmer is dead,' Finn's voice announced.

A knot gathered in Siv's throat at the news. She had known—her visions had shown him dead—but it still hurt. She took a moment to swallow the knot of grief in her throat.

'Hiding even in death,' Harald grumbled at her side.

Dishonouring a dead man went against all of the Alfather's sacred advice, but Harald was no longer a man of Odin. He did not abide by the same code of honour.

'Clearly, you aren't his replacement,' Siv said, and opened her eyes to look at Finn. She made her eastern accent slightly thicker for Finn to notice it. 'Your clothes and posture are not those of an influential man,' she said. 'Besides, I doubt that chieftains travel alone.'

'I am not Ash-hill's chieftain,' Finn admitted, looking at Harald, not at Siv, who had asked. 'Although I should have been.'

His voice was filled with hatred at Einer for that, and Siv wondered why, of all the warriors in Ash-hill, Einer had decided to send Finn to Jelling and not another warrior who may have been more willing to take his side. She wondered, as Harald must, why he had not come himself.

'Then who is, and why is he not here?' Harald asked.

'We have not yet elected a new chieftain.'

Siv noticed Finn's desperation to avoid her gaze, as if he knew how easily she could change the minds of men who looked at her.

'Did Vigmer not have any sons to take over?' Siv asked.

Harald chuckled at her question and brushed the hair off her shoulder. 'Up here, in the north, we elect our chieftains,' he arrogantly explained to her. 'All freemen who own land in a chieftaincy cast their vote, and the one with most supporters becomes the chieftain.'

He talked as if it were the most obvious thing, although he was a chieftain like his father, and his father's father had been a chieftain and his father before him. They may have been elected by freemen, but they were still sons of chieftains.

Through the blurred heat from the fire, Siv watched Finn. He evaded her gaze and her true question. He knew who she was, and knew what she asked, but he would not tell her about Einer.

Finally, he matched her gaze. 'Not anymore,' Finn answered. 'He doesn't have any sons anymore.'

Siv's eyes fell on Tyra at the back of the hall. Sweet Tyra, crying silent tears. They had both expected Einer to show up. The tall build, the short hair, the tamed bear. Every description Jelling's villagers had given had screamed *Einer*.

But this was something different.

Einer had passed on, and she hadn't known. She always knew. During her long life, more than a dozen sons and husbands had been taken from her, and she had always known.

The forefathers stirred to ignite Siv's anger, but she did not let them. Their meddling gave her something else to focus on than her own thoughts. She tapped her fingers on her thigh and played with the forefathers, so they tingled up and down her arm. The forefathers pushed to be let loose. They urged the thought of all of her sons to the front of her mind, and called upon the rage she had always subdued and hidden away.

For centuries, Siv had travelled in the shadows to avoid Odin, but each and every time she tied herself to a family, he found her and claimed her sons. For centuries she had run from him, and never had she been able to save any of her children from Odin's call of death.

She had thought Einer would be the one to survive. With Surt's gold bracteate at his neck, he should have survived, but perhaps Odin had known, perhaps he had stripped Einer of the gold and left him to die, to claim him, as he had claimed everyone Siv had ever loved.

Einer should have survived, but if he had not, then there was only one person left in all of Midgard that Siv cared about. Across the room, she smiled at Tyra.

Shadows and sacred gold had not saved Einer. With every

son, Siv had tried more desperate measures. There was only one thing that she had not yet dared do to save her children. The time had come for Siv to leave the shadows and face the Alfather.

FINN

Chapter Eighty-Four

ALL HIS LIFE, Finn had been poor compared to most, and now he was the poorest man that he knew, yet the longer Finn stood in the presence of Harald Bluetan, the wealthier he felt. He had pride and honour, beliefs and convictions, and most of all he had the bravery of a true Norseman.

'I remember you,' Finn said, no longer willing to stay silent. 'For two days our ships sailed together on my first raid. You were so set on Christian revenge. Look at you now. A Christian coward.'

Harald was surrounded by wealth. His cup was adorned with gold. His arms were rich in jewellery, and a hawk screeched from a cage by his raised chair. The chair alone was a big enough statement. He thought himself raised above freemen, and not on equal footing as a Chief would have. Harald had amassed wealth instead of respect.

'Is that how you beg for an alliance?' Harald said, staring at Finn across the hot air from the fire by which he stood with Siv at his side. His hawk screeched in its cage.

'I have not come here to make an alliance with you,' Finn said, although that was exactly why he had been sent to Jelling.

Among Harald's followers in the hall were faces that Finn had fought with as recently as last summer. A few had abandoned Ash-hill and joined Harald before the winter raids on southern lands. Ketill, who had fought in the same shield-wall as Finn for four summers, was among them. The shame of having abandoned Ash-hill made Ketill hide himself in the shadows from Finn, and rightfully so. It was a shameful deed he had done, abandoning his town and bench-mates when they had all needed each other the most.

Everyone in this hall was more of a coward than anyone else Finn knew. None of them had come to Ash-hill's cry of help. None of them had the decency to stand up for their beliefs, except for Siv.

'If not to make an alliance, then why have you come with gifts to flatter?' Harald asked.

'I have not,' Finn answered, although he had. 'The bear is not a gift to flatter. To me it is a burden that I give to you. I can't afford to feed it. I can't afford to kill it. I gift you my burdens.'

The freemen in the hall moved in their seats to watch Harald's response. Einer's bear growled outside, and the fire snapped.

The only person in the entire hall who looked at Finn was Siv. She stared at him as if she saw straight through him and knew his thoughts. She could solve all of his problems.

Finn's debt was owed to Einer, whose sole heir was Siv. She could free Fin from thraldom, and she could use whatever influence she held here to benefit Ash-hill. It had been a clever move for a woman who had used to be married to a chieftain and was used to comforts of riches. Harald was the richest man in Jutland. Here she would live a life without worry, as she would have in Ash-hill as Vigmer's wife, had the southerners not attacked.

One thing was strange. The accent with which she spoke was not her own.

'And why would I help you by accepting your burdens?' Harald asked through gritted teeth. 'I'd rather have your head on a spike with your dick in your mouth and send it back up to Ash-hill.'

'You can choose to do so,' Finn said, for there was no denying that Harald Bluetan could do anything that he desired. 'But no one in Ash-hill would care if you showed them my mutilated corpse. I have no family there, no friends. Ash-hill is not as it was, nor am I the same man who sailed with you so many summers ago.'

Harald had not yet ordered Finn's killing. A simple execution would not benefit Harald, especially not if Finn was not a man who would be missed. For once, his thraldom served his interests.

'Then who are you?' Harald asked.

'I am Finn, debt-thrall of Einer Vigmerson.' he said and looked into Siv's grey eyes. She could free him. He belonged to her now. He had told her that Vigmer and Einer were both gone into the next life, so she had to understand that he belonged to her now. 'I owe Einer six marks of silver, and my life.'

Siv's eyes had a coldness that he did not recall. Her hair was brighter than he remembered. She was taller than Harald, but even if she had not been, her presence would have demanded more respect than that of the King of Jutland. Bluetan looked fiercer with her on his side.

'A mere thrall, and you dare address a king?' one of the freemen said. He sat at a table far from the entrance where Finn stood. An accusation easy to voice for a man sitting at the back of the hall.

'Of all the warriors who raided Magadoborg and gained glory, why did they send a thrall here?' Siv stood forward and took the floor. Harald smiled at her wit.

'I volunteered.' Finn was quick to answer, perhaps too quick, for Siv saw straight through him.

'You did not. They sent you here to die.'

Harald smiled brighter at his wife's smarts. Wealthy men who married for advantage revelled in a good opportunity to show off their clever wives.

'Then imagine their surprise when I return,' Finn replied with a playful smirk. If he were to return, they would likely believe he had never gone to Jelling.

Freemen in the hall laughed at him, but Finn welcomed their laughter. They might decide to keep him alive if they thought him funny or witty. At this point, all that could redeem him and save him was his own tongue.

'Why are you here?' Harald Bluetan's stare had hardened. He was not a man of patience.

'I come here because your wife—' Finn's voice was halted in his throat, and he coughed.

'What about my wife? Tove, do you know this man?'

Finn coughed and grabbed his throat. He needed to ask Siv to release him of his promises and debt, but his body would not let him. His throat felt clenched by an invisible hand. It forced him to stop his struggle, and give in to the silence imposed on him.

Siv took a long moment to answer. She examined Finn carefully, and then finally she shook her head. 'I don't know him.'

Her accent was foreign. She was not exactly as Finn remembered her. Her hair was a different tint, and her eyes truly were colder and they had changed shape too.

'He was not one of the men who attacked you, was he?' Harald asked, and rubbed her back. He was a different man when he looked at Siv. Most men were.

'He was not. I would have remembered a nose like that.'

To Harald, she was not Siv. The thought hit Finn suddenly. When Finn had entered and spoken her name, Harald had thought that he had referred to Thor's wife, golden-haired Sif. Harald did not know her true name. She was here under pretence, and in that case, Finn could not use their past and the thraldom that he owed to her to gain Harald's favour. He needed to find a new way.

His throat suddenly became light and he could speak. The gods themselves allowed him another attempt to convince Harald to help Ash-hill.

'I have come to wish you happiness in your new marriage,' Finn said, hoping to come up with a new plan.

He had no other plan.

'A thrall's well-wishing means nothing.'

'Then undo my thraldom and let it mean something.'

The freemen began to laugh at him, mocking Finn for what he had become and for daring to think of such a possibility. They did not know that Siv could free him from his promises, but Siv knew.

She made Harald turn away from Finn and the freemen, and whispered to him, glancing at Finn every now and again. She was talking about him, and Harald was listening.

All around the room, freemen laughed, and Finn refused to be intimidated by their mockery. He stared them in the eyes, and his fierce resolution made them laugh harder, but he could see that he also had their respect. A normal thrall would never have been allowed to talk for so long, nor stand and address so many freemen. He was no ordinary thrall, and every influential man in the room knew it.

Harald and Siv turned back to their warm fire. The laughter died as Harald looked over the crowd. 'Six marks, you said?'

'Six marks,' Finn confirmed.

'Owed to Einer Vigmerson,' Harald repeated. 'Who is dead, as you say.'

Finn nodded.

'Did you kill him?'

'His own bravery took his life in battle.' Finn praised Einer for Siv's sake. He needed her to be on his side and convince Harald to help him.

'How did you come to be indebted to him by as much as six entire marks?'

Whatever Siv had whispered to Harald, it had awoken his

curiosity, and curiosity was all Finn needed. As long as they listened to him and allowed him to speak, he had hope to survive and make it home to Ash-hill.

'I owed Einer not six marks, but fifteen,' Finn said.

Freemen gasped at the price. Despite their expensive clothes and jewellery, he doubted that many of them would have been able to pay a fine of fifteen marks of silver.

'I used my warship to pay the first nine marks, but with my home in ashes and cattle slaughtered, I had no means to pay the remaining six, so Einer removed my name and bound me to him by debt.'

Finn's story enthralled the crowd. They whispered about his achievements. The more he talked, the more obvious it would become to them that Finn was no ordinary debt-thrall. The more interested in him the crowd became, the more difficult it would be for Harald to kill him.

'When Einer's father, our chief, passed on, I fought at his side,' Finn continued. 'He had come into the possession of an Ulfberht blade. The perfect blade.' He had to be careful with how he told his tale, so as not to speak badly of Einer. He needed both to flatter Einer and Vigmer, so Siv would help him, and also flatter himself so Harald would want to help him.

'In the downpour of battle, when his fate was clear to him, Vigmer passed his sword onto me. He was honoured and sent into the afterlife the following day.' He looked at Siv as he said it. She may have married another man, but Finn had seen how she had reacted when he had announced Vigmer's death.

'By law of inheritance, the sword was said to rightfully belong to Einer, and since I had deprived his father from taking the blade to his afterlife, I was both to give up the sword and pay full price for what I had taken. A price of fifteen marks of silver.'

Harald nodded as Finn talked, and then he turned his back and walked away from the fire to sit in the raised chair. Siv stayed by the fire, and Finn walked closer to her.

'Who do you owe your debt to now?' she asked, although she knew. Her eyes seemed to want to tell him something, but that was all she said.

Every freeman in the hall held their breath, waiting for Finn's answer. He took another step closer to the fire and looked into Siv's cold eyes. He knew he should not say that it was her. She knew who she was and what she owned.

'I do not know,' he said instead. 'Einer had no known heirs. I suppose I owe it to Ash-hill.'

Siv smiled and Finn could not help but smile back. He must have said what she had hoped he would.

'Finn the Nameless. What you tell is a tale worthy of songs, but songs need names, and you have none,' said Siv as if she were a skald telling a story. 'So, let me ask you something else: what do you aspire to in this life?'

'I want my name back before the afterlife chains me.' His answer was obvious. Siv had called him Nameless, and the calling-name almost hurt his heart more than being called thrall. Being kinless was the worst punishment for debt-bound men.

His answer did not please.

'I did not take you for a man short of ambitions.'

Guided by Siv, Finn spoke of much higher ambitions. 'I shall be chief of Ash-hill, someday,' he said. 'And all those who laughed at me when my hair was cut and my name was taken, I shall make them crawl and beg to kiss my shoes.'

No one dared to speak before Harald, but the rich men in the hall nodded their agreement and approval. He had spoken well and they understood his rage and ambition. At last, Finn was among men as ambitious as himself.

'That's a man I understand,' Harald said, leaning back in his chair. Finn was not so certain that he wanted to be praised by the like of Harald Bluetan. He was not known to be a kind man, but in front of this crowd and inside this hall, he was the only one who mattered. Him, and anyone who could sway his mind, like Siv did.

'I'll help Ash-hill,' Bluetan decided. 'I'll buy you, Finn the Nameless.'

So that was what Siv had whispered into Harald's ear by the fire. A proposal to buy Finn and gain Ash-hill by providing favours instead of waging war. It was clever advice. The people left in Ash-hill were not merchants, but warriors who when met with axes and spears, grabbed their shields and fought harder. The only way Harald could gain control over northern Jutland was by showing kindness, and spending his wealth on something other than blue tunics.

'You'll buy my freedom?' Finn asked.

At last he would be free, and regain his father's name and lineage so he could die with honour and enter Valhalla in death. At last he would be free to follow his wildest ambitions that Siv had made him speak aloud; and at last, he would gain the glory he deserved.

'Who said anything about freedom?' Harald broke his hopes and dreams as easily as Vigmer had used to do. 'I'll buy you from Ash-hill. You'll be *my* thrall from now on.'

Finn could not think of anyone he was more reluctant to serve than Harald. He would rather serve Einer, or Richard of Normandy. Anyone was better than a traitor like Harald Bluetan. But Finn knew that he had no say in the matter. This was the only way for him to leave this hall alive.

'Six marks of silver,' Harald mused, and ruffled the little stubble of his beard. It did not grow evenly as the beards of most grown men did. 'Thorbjorn!' he called out. The freemen in the hall turned to look at the man named Thorbjorn. 'For half a mark of silver, how many workers can you find to work for two moons?' Harald asked, and then called another name. 'Magnus, how much timber can you deliver?'

Harald continued to call names and favours and discuss prices with his freemen and close friends while Finn stood and listened to all of the things his worth could buy, and for the first time, he felt grateful to Einer for the high price he had put on Finn's name.

It would be an expensive endeavour for Harald, and when Finn arrived back in Ash-hill with dozens of workers and timber for longhouses, and cattle and pigs and sheep, Hormod and the other warriors would not believe their eyes. That was if Harald decided to send Finn back north, and not keep him in Jelling as a house thrall.

Details of the purchases were arranged over the top of Finn's head, but it did not matter, for he would arrive home with more than anyone could have hoped. The warriors would not again doubt his worth.

Finn leaned equally on both feet and looked only at Siv and Harald, as they made decisions on his behalf and spent the price of his debt on goods for Ash-hill. He waited for them to finish and tell him what they had decided for him, but the longer he waited and listened to them address anyone else in the hall but him, the quicker the worry raced, and he could no longer wait.

In the middle of a negotiation over two goats, he interrupted Harald. 'What shall happen to me in your service, Harald son of Gorm?' he asked, although no thrall was allowed to interrupt a freeman—and least of all, he imagined, a Christian king.

Other price discussions ceased, and the hall became quiet once more. Everyone knew that Finn had overstepped the bounds of a thrall, but he could no longer bear to stand and wait to be handed his fate. Harald could still decide to kill him and feed him to Einer's bear.

'You'll serve me, as you once served Vigmer,' he said. 'You're my cattle now. You'll carry out my orders.'

'And what is your order?'

'Ash-hill will acknowledge my rule as King of the Danes, and you'll make it so. You'll manage the building of the new town. Henceforth one portion of all of Ash-hill's earnings shall be paid to me for my timely protection.'

They were good terms, considering that Ash-hill was only a town in name now, but Finn had accompanied Vigmer to enough negotiations to know that the more at a disadvantage he was, the more firmly he had to negotiate.

'Our allegiance to Jelling, I will give you,' Finn said, although he should have been in no position to negotiate. 'But Ash-hill's profits shall be managed in Ash-hill. We will not be treated the same as Angles paying Dane debt.'

Harald smirked at Finn, a mere thrall, standing up for his village. Loyalty was a matter of honour, and even in the hall of an honourless king, honour was respected.

'Building projects in northern Jutland under my rule will be managed by you, then, and paid by Ash-hill's village funds.'

'A yearly fund which shall not exceed the price of a longhouse.'

'Two longhouses,' Harald insisted.

'Agreed.' Finn knew that it was as favourable a deal as he could ever hope to gain. Had Ash-hill been in good standing, it would still have been a good deal to avoid war.

The smaller terms were easily agreed upon, and the crowd relaxed, and began talking prices again. Harald made his thralls, all apart from Finn, bring ale for them to drink. Finn was given a place among freemen, for the first time since the holmgang against Einer.

In Jelling, warriors sought his attention. Ash-hill's old warriors who had followed Harald at the end of summer came to greet Finn, one after the other. The last one was his old shield-mate Ketill.

'We were a man short in our shield wall over winter,' Finn told the dark-haired warrior.

'Perhaps someday we can fight side by side again,' Ketill said, and in that way, admitted his fault in leaving Ash-hill at the end of summer. 'How is Dan?'

'Dan is dead.'

Ketill struggled to keep his composure. Seeing Finn may have given him hope for his best friend as well. They had been inseparable, the two of them. People had used to call them *night and day*: with his flamed hair Dan had been the sun and with his dark face framed by curls from the south, Ketill had looked like the night.

'How did he die?' Ketill asked.

'Smiling.' He truly had, and they both grinned at the thought. Few warriors met the afterlife with such deaths.

'As shall you, my friend,' Ketill said and tapped Finn on the shoulder. Although Finn had raided for longer, their positions had changed since summer. As the freeman, it fell to Ketill to put their differences aside, and with those words, he had.

'A debt-thrall, yet you sway the minds of kings,' the warrior praised. Being praised filled Finn with warmth. Ketill may have made a wrong decision by leaving Ash-hill, but Finn knew his true worth, and he acknowledged Ketill for the warrior he was.

'If not before, then in death, you make sure we fight on the same side.' Finn looked into Ketill's dark eyes. The younger man served a Christian king, and if he died with a cross on his clothes and in his heart, they would not meet in the afterlife.

They stood in a Christian longhouse, surrounding by Christians, both at the mercy and command of a Christian king, but Ketill did not glance back to check if they had been overheard before he answered. 'In the afterlife we were never meant to meet. But I was glad to have met you in life, old shield-friend,' and as such they parted ways.

Finn enjoyed himself, feeling like an equal to freemen once more, and when the time was right, and Siv did not sit next to Harald, but travelled between tables and greeted freemen in the hall, Finn got to his feet and walked to her.

'Siv—'

'That is not my name,' she hissed and together they moved through the standing crowd, so as to pretend that they had not previously known each other.

Finn proceeded, leaving her name out. 'You have to come

with me up north,' he pleaded. 'To show the others that you are alive and that I speak the truth.'

'I shall not,' she decided without second thought. Her stare was harsh and decided. 'You shall not speak of having met me.'

Finn's voice was sealed away at her command.

'If you can't handle Ash-hill, I shall make alliances elsewhere,' she said.

Alliances elsewhere meant that Finn would end up decapitated by Harald's guards, exactly as he had feared he would, but he had entered Jelling regardless of that danger. Now, he would go home to Ash-hill's dangers, as Siv demanded. 'You have helped us enough,' Finn agreed. 'I'll pay you back.'

'You will pay your thanks not to me, but to the most important person in this hall.'

'Harald?' he asked. He had not thought that she had married Harald because she liked him or agreed with his actions, merely for the comforts of a good life and the influence with which it came.

'You see that curly-haired boy?' Siv discreetly gestured to the far corner of the hall where a few children were sitting. Two young boys and a girl, but only one boy with curly hair.

'That boy will come to look up to you after today, and someday, when the time is right, he will need you to convince him to wage war against Christian kings.'

Three children were in the hall where no children should have been allowed, and tales were already being sung about Svend, the eldest son of Harald who, someday, would rule these lands.

'You want him to wage war against his own father,' Finn understood.

'The gods demand it,' Siv said.

'The gods demand it,' Finn repeated. 'And their demands shall be answered.'

EINER

Chapter Eighty-Five

'DUCK!' THE CART driver pushed Einer back into the reeds.

Einer had fallen asleep to the rumbling of the cart, and at some point, while he had slept, reeds had been put over him, to conceal him at the back of the cart.

'Lie still.' The cart driver tossed some reeds over Einer to disguise him again.

He had not had time to see anything for the brief moment he had sat up after waking. His eyes had been adjusting to the light. Wherever they were, they were far from Magadoborg, because Einer felt warm under the reeds although the day had been clouded. For days, he had trailed through ice and snow, but they were far away from such things now.

The cart rumbled over fields. Einer lay still and tried to ignore how much his head pounded. The bracteate on his chest made him feverish.

In his dream, the cart driver's question had repeated over and over like a distant chant: *I know who you are, do you know who you are?* Right when Einer had been about to collapse from exhaustion, he had met the cart driver. The meeting almost seemed fated by the nornir.

'You were waiting for me,' Einer said to fight his own fever and the urge to close his eyes again. 'You weren't by the river to cut reeds, you were there to trick me into getting onto your cart.'

'I did not trick you, and you can still leave, if you so desire.'

Einer scoffed. 'I would not know how to find my way back to Midgard.'

The cart driver laughed at that. 'You live up to your lineage, Einer. Observant and careful.'

Einer should have known. That was how the cart driver knew who Einer was; his father must have talked of him in Valhalla and asked someone to look after his son.

'Is my father well?' Einer asked. Suddenly he was not afraid of the thumping in his head and his strength seeping away. In death, he would meet all the people he loved. He did not know how he could have forgotten. His father would be there.

'I assume that he is,' the reed cutter responded.

'My father didn't send you?'

'You have more than one proud kinsman in Odin's hall.'

'Was it Hilda?'

'Hilda,' the man slowly chewed on her name. His voice had the ring of danger.

Warm tears rolled down Einer's cheeks. He did not know when he had begun to cry, but the thought of Hilda sending for him from the afterlife made him smile and cry all at the same time, and suddenly everything was right in the nine worlds. 'Are we truly going to the Alfather's hall?' he asked. He so dreamed of seeing her again. It had not been long since their paths had parted, but he missed her more than he had ever missed anyone.

'I hope it will be everything you dreamed it would be,' the cart rider responded.

Einer closed his eyes again and resigned himself to the steady rumble of the cart. His chest was heavy with the burning from his bracteate, and he struggled to draw breath. Something else hung heavily on him, too: excitement at what was to come. He imagined her smile as he finally entered Valhalla and walked past the rows and rows of warriors, ready to fight. He imagined her hair lit up by fires reflected on the gold-shielded ceiling above.

'Is the ceiling really made of gold shields?' he asked.

'It is beautiful.'

As would she be. He imagined what she would say to him, but he could not. Sometimes, Hilda was unpredictable. But they had promised to meet in Valhalla, so Einer knew that he was welcome although he had never imagined that this was how that promise would be fulfilled. He had expected to have to die before he got a chance to see her again.

Perhaps if he had continued on, he would have died, like the reed cutter had told him he would by the icy river. Perhaps that would not have been close enough to battle to wake in Valhalla. This was better.

With dreams of Valhalla and Hilda, Einer dozed off beneath the reeds.

'GET UP,' THE tall man whispered and shook Einer's shoulder. 'This is it.' He helped Einer to his feet, and off the cart. All of Einer's limbs were sore, and his chest was burning more than ever before. He could hardly breathe. His head pounded as if he was beating it against a shield.

They had travelled across a plain of high grasses and red poppies and arrived at a wooden wall. It stretched as far either way as Einer could see. Each plank was thick and round like a tree trunk.

With the support of the tall reed cutter, Einer slumped against the wall. It was not merely made of big planks as Einer had thought. It was made of actual trees, with long roots that snaked into the poppy field.

'Is this?' he asked, tilting his head back as far as he could to see the top of the trees. They shot so far up that he could not see the top, but he thought he saw the shine of metal up there.

'Valhalla,' said the tall man at his side, and pulled Einer ahead, past two tree trunks that stood far enough apart from each other to allow a man through.

Einer struggled to slither though. The arrow in his head kept tapping against the tree trunks and sent shocks of pain through his entire body. The reed cutter pushed him the last way into the hall.

Valhalla was larger than Einer could have imagined any hall to be. The floor was made of a bright coloured stone that reflected the light from the fires. His steps echoed as he walked inside.

Tables lined the hall, rows and rows of them, as far as Einer could see. There were empty plates and dishes, clean and ready for food to be filled onto them. Drinking horns and cups, equally empty. The benches were empty too. The seats were worn where warriors usually sat, although not today.

'Where is everyone?' Einer asked in a whisper, scared to speak aloud. His voice echoed far into the large hall.

'Fighting on Ida's plain.' The reed-cutter entered the hall behind Einer. 'Same as every day.'

Einer knew the tales, of course he did, but he had never stopped to think how the Alfather's hall may look abandoned by its warriors. That was not the sight that the songs and tales told about, but it was how Einer first greeted Valhalla.

The tall man pulled his cloak tighter over his shoulders and guided Einer further into the hall past dozens and hundreds of tables and benches. Einer took in the full sight of Valhalla as they walked. Great pyres both warmed and lit the broad hall, and no matter which way Einer looked, he could not see the outer walls for the hall was so great. He tilted his head back and looked up, but where he expected to see gold shields align the ceiling, there was no ceiling at all, just branches and oak leaves. 'You said the ceiling was made of gold.'

'It is,' the tall cloaked man simply confirmed. 'But right now, there is no ceiling.'

'Why not?'

'You know the tales.'

'A ceiling made of gold shields…' he muttered. The tales definitely promised a gold-shielded roof. Although Valhalla was everything the tales said, it was not as he had expected it to be. Had he not seen it, he would never have been able to imagine so vast a hall. 'Do the warriors take the shields with them? Do they fight with gold shields?'

'They do.'

'Isn't that heavy to fight with?'

'They're not made of gold, they're painted in it. They're not any different from any shield you may have fought with in Midgard.'

Of course, now that he heard it, Einer could not imagine it to have been any other way. The Alfather too was a warrior, who knew the importance of a secure shield's grip and light weight.

Einer dragged himself ahead, holding onto the reed cutter's arm for support. He was so sore that the hot throbs of the bracteate had become soothing. His legs were ready to crumble.

'Where exactly are we going?' he strained to ask.

'We just need to cross the width of the hall.'

Einer glanced over his shoulder. He could no longer see the trees of the outer wall by which they had entered. Just the width, he thought, and wondered what the length of the hall was in comparison. It seemed they had walked for a rest already, and he could still not see the other wall ahead of them.

'We are about halfway there,' the tall man announced.

Einer sighed at the thought of that.

'I can carry you.'

'I can walk,' Einer insisted. No warrior was carried through Valhalla. Einer refused to be the first to show such weakness in a great hall such as this, ruled by none other than the Alfather.

Einer stumbled and was half dragged along the hall, but he still walked on his own two feet when they reached the other side. In front of them was a grand gate. Considering how the reed cutter had made Einer hide at the back of the cart, it was doubtful that the gate led outside, which meant that what lay beyond was Odin's private hall.

The cart driver urged Einer to take the last few steps to the door on his own. The door was twice his height, and large, as if made for giants. Einer pushed his shoulders painfully back to stand proud, and knocked.

The door came open. His knock had gently pushed it in. The door did not creak. Everything was perfect in Valhalla, even the doors were oiled.

Einer was thankful to see that although the room was large, it was not as vast as the hall. He could see the far wall, and exhaled with relief. It was a bedroom, but every chair, every table, and the bed too, were surrounded by emptiness. The room felt bare, and there was no one inside.

Einer looked over his shoulder and out the door to the reed cutter, but he was gone. Einer was entirely alone in Odin's great hall.

'I have waited for you,' said a smooth voice.

With his back to Einer stood a man by the fireplace at the far wall of the bedroom, although previously there had been no one. He was tall like Einer but not as much as the reed cutter, and unlike them both, this man was slender. His silver hair waved down his back and his robes twinkled in a hundred colours of blue. 'At last our fates have allowed us to meet.'

The voice soothed Einer's pains and made him focus on the hot throb in his chest from the bracteate and the itch of the arrow stuck in his forehead.

The Alfather's posture was not that of an old man. His shoulders rolled back and his head held high. He looked at the fireplace's flickering flames from above. He was exactly as

Einer had imagined, yet even from the back, he was so much more.

Einer licked his dry lips and his mind ran through all the words he had ever learned and knew, to find the right ones to speak aloud. Einer knew that it was his turn to break the silence, but no words seemed to be the right ones.

'Why not wait?' he asked at last. The question had nagged him before he had fallen asleep. 'Another few days and I would have walked to my death.'

'I wouldn't want to rob you of your life to seat you in my hall,' said the Alfather in his husky voice.

'You wouldn't have to rob me of anything. I would have died within days.'

'Enough of Ash-hill's warriors have died,' the Alfather said, acknowledging their worth. 'Come in and lie down.'

Einer did not budge, although his legs tired and his mind was weary. He would not lie down in the presence of his god.

'The healers are on their way,' the Alfather said. 'Although I don't know if they can remove that arrow from your head.'

The Alfather had neither faced Einer nor looked upon him, yet he knew about the arrow in Einer's forehead. As expected, the Alfather knew everything. After all, his ravens had often come to see Einer as he had walked from Magadoborg.

'Not as often as you think,' the Alfather said in response to Einer's thoughts. 'There are many ravens in the nine worlds, and all of them are not Hugin and Munin.'

Had he not been in so much pain, Einer may have felt embarrassed at that, for he had spoken to every raven he had seen, but his entire body trembled from heat and strain.

'It is an honour to stand in your presence,' Einer said to the Alfather's back. 'I have dreamt of it for a lifetime.'

'A lifetime of expectations.' The Alfather turned on his heels and faced Einer. Both his hair and beard were neatly brushed away from his face and looked like they had never been tangled.

Einer's eyes moved up Odin's face, from his beard and his slim lips to his crooked nose. Einer gaped when he saw the famous grey eye, and the missing one. Odin's eyelid was sunken in where his eye was supposed to be.

Some men—not warriors—might call it a defect, but Odin did not have defects. His missing eye proved his strength. What others did with both eyes, he did with one, and better.

As a child, Einer had used to argue with Hilda's brother, Leif, about which eye it was that Odin had sacrificed to quench his thirst from the well of wisdom. Einer had claimed that Odin must have given his left eye to Mimer, because that was the eye that archers closed anyways. In gifting it, he would have increased his precision and it was a decision that would have made Odin's aim better. Leif had laughed at him then, and insisted that Odin had given away his right eye because Mimer so demanded, and that it made no difference which eye it was for someone as powerful as the Alfather.

For half a moon, both of them had been stubborn and eager to prove that they were right. Einer had bound his left eye and practised archery every day to prove that his aim would be better. Naturally, his aim had improved quite simply because, for once, he practised every single day.

Tears trickled over Einer's cheeks at the distant memory.

'Leif was right.' The Alfather spoke Einer's thoughts aloud. 'He would have made a fine warrior for you.'

'He would have,' Odin confirmed, and thereby also implied that Leif did not fight with his warriors and did not sit among them in his hall. 'The manner in which he died... I had no claim over him.'

Although Hilda had repeatedly told him that it would not be so, Einer had always hoped to see Leif seated at his side in the afterlife. The next life was supposed to be a time to rekindle with old friends and drink with foes, and fight them again. It felt strange to realise that he would not get to meet everyone he loved. Hilda had known what fate awaited her in the afterlife, for she knew that her brother and father, and even her mother, were in Helheim and not Valhalla.

Einer chuckled at himself. Even now, barely able to stand any longer, with his head hammering, and the great Alfather in front of him, Hilda was all he could think about.

'Where is she?' he asked. 'Where is Hilda?'

HILDA

Chapter Eighty-Six

'YOU THOUGHT YOU could escape,' Hilda's captor hissed.

It wasn't Loki, but a woman's voice. Deep and smooth like a river.

Hilda's wings were locked away in a tight grip and her head was covered with a falcon mask.

'You thought you could come here. That I wouldn't be waiting,' her captor grumbled. Her hold on Hilda was so firm that she thought her bones might break.

Hilda tried to respond, but her beak was shut tight with a ribbon, and she couldn't get a screech out. She wished and wished that her snow fox had escaped so that it may come to rescue her.

The falcon skin was stuck to her own. She may be killed without having a say. That was usually how it went in her father's stories, when people put on animal skins that weren't destined for them. She never should have done it, but it had seemed like such a good idea. Loki would have talked her into some treachery.

Maybe her fox could distract this stranger long enough for Hilda to escape, as it had done with Loki. It was her only hope now.

Hilda's head slammed onto the floor. Her wings were released. She tried to flap away, but banged her head into metal. The mask was still on her head, blocking her sight, but Hilda was no longer afraid to move without sight. Again, she tried to take flight. Again, she banged her head.

She stretched her wings. The edges of her feathers swept against cold metal on either side of her. She was trapped in a cage. A bird in a cage, and all she could do was screech.

'I've got you now, Loki,' said her captor with a cheerful tone. 'You won't get away this time.'

Of course. All her captor saw was the falcon skin Loki had stolen from Freya and made his own. She had no idea that Hilda was the one inside, and not Loki.

Hilda tried to tell her, but all that came out were muffled screams. Her beak was still tied. There had to be a way to turn this around. Some sort of escape. Her snow fox wasn't in the cage with her. And she hadn't heard it as she had been taken; she would have heard its yelps if it had been captured. But her snow fox couldn't open a locked cage and set her free. Maybe her Runes wouldn't have been able to do it either, if they had been with her. They could have helped, though.

Nej, it mattered little. Everything she had ever achieved, Hilda had done on her own. With her Muspel sight she had found her own way, and when the Runes had left her, she had found Loki without their help, and had flown to Asgard.

Hilda made her own destiny, and she wouldn't let a cage stop her from meeting the gods.

She stretched her wings out to touch the edges of the cage. It was not much larger than her wingspan in any direction. Her claws scratched against wood beneath the metal. Everything smelled strange and different through the layer of the falcon skin. Her hearing was distorted too, by all the feathers.

Twigs snapped under someone's steps.

Hilda didn't know what her captor had intended. Whatever it was, if that woman thought that she was Loki, then it was not a pretty destiny that awaited.

Her worst fears were confirmed at once.

'You were lucky back then,' said the woman. Her voice was calm and decided. 'Odin convinced the others not to kill you. But he isn't here now.' The woman's twig-snapping steps neared. They stopped right in front of Hilda's cage. 'For centuries, I have wanted nothing more than to watch you bleed on my floor.'

The woman chuckled at the thought of that, like a crazed berserker.

'There won't be anything of you left for the forefathers to pick up when I'm finished,' hissed Hilda's captor. 'I will eradicate every slimy trail of you. I will rip off your nails, claw your eyes out, chop you up and feed you to your own wolf son. And I will enjoy your every screech.'

TYRA

Chapter Eighty-Seven

'WILL YOU TRAVEL with me?' Svend asked Tyra, lying at her side on the blanket they had brought to Gorm the Sleepy's gravemound to sit on. As if it were summer, and not a snowy winter day. 'When I get my own ship, and can go anywhere?'

'Where will we go?' she asked. Tyra had always wanted to explore the world. This world, with its mysterious souths of hot summers and grand statues, and people who spoke foreign tongues. She wanted to explore the other eight worlds too, but she suspected that Siv would show her those someday. At least she hoped so.

'Somewhere far away,' Svend decided. 'Somewhere no one has gone before.'

The wind howled and Tyra heaved the furs higher on her shoulders. 'Somewhere warm,' she said.

'Down south,' he added. 'Just you and me.'

'And thirty sweaty crewmembers,' Tyra added.

Svend laughed at that. He always laughed when they were together. And Tyra liked his laugh, and his smile too, like he said he liked hers. 'Armed and ready to wage war,' he said and then he leaned in and whispered: 'For Valhalla.'

'For Valhalla,' she agreed. It felt good to be alone and talk about the gods and the other worlds. Playing with Svend's younger siblings, Hakon and Sigrid, was fun, but they didn't talk about the gods, not like Svend did, or Siv.

Right then, Siv walked along a line of stones marking a ship's hull around the gravemound. She saw Tyra and Svend on top of the snowed mound, and waved for Tyra to come down.

Siv was alone. Finally, Harald had left. Tyra leaned away from Svend and rose from the wet blanket. 'I have to go,' she said.

'Do you *have* to?' Svend was looking up at her, and he seemed hurt. The long curls of his hair danced in front of his face, but he didn't brush them away.

'I do,' she replied, not knowing why he questioned it. 'It's Tove. She's asking for me.'

'You always run off when she tells you to.' Svend said it like it was a bad thing.

'It's usually important,' Tyra replied. In truth, it was always important. When Siv came to find her, it meant that they could be alone. And then Tyra could ask questions about the nine worlds and they could make their plans about how to save the runes and the nine worlds. She didn't feel like a young girl during those times, and it didn't matter that she had become the daughter of Harald the Cowardly King.

She took a few steps down the snowy slope of the gravemound, her eyes fixed on Svend. He smiled, but it was not his happy smile that she liked.

She turned away from him, and skipped down to Siv who was already walking towards their living quarters. Tyra had to rush to follow.

'We need to pack your things before Harald returns from his hunt,' Siv said.

'Pack?' They hadn't talked about that. 'Where are we going?'

Tyra ensured that no one was close enough to hear them talk. 'Into one of the other eight worlds?' she whispered.

'There's a village north of Odin's-gorge, I know a woman there who will take you in.'

'Take me in? What about you?'

'Where I am going you can't follow,' Siv said. 'It's too dangerous.'

Tyra knew better than to argue with that. 'I'll stay here then, in Jelling, and wait for your return.'

'You can't.'

'Why not?'

'We can't stay here,' Siv answered.

Suddenly Tyra didn't really want to rush anymore. 'So, we're not really going somewhere. We're just leaving.'

Siv did not deny it.

They walked the last few paces out of the ship of rocks and entered the warm longhouse where they slept. Tyra took off her gloves and coat and hung them up. Siv didn't remove hers. The snow on her shoulders melted and dripped onto the wooden floor, but she didn't seem to care.

'Hurry up and pack your things,' she told Tyra, handing her an empty skin bag. Her voice was strangely distant. She was in deep thought.

Two full bags sat next to the door. Tyra supposed they were what Siv had packed. Two entire bags were a lot; three, with Tyra's things. 'What should I pack?'

'Everything.'

They wouldn't come back to Jelling, then. It had finally begun to be a home to Tyra. It wasn't Ash-hill, but Svend made it a nice place to live nonetheless. 'We can't leave.'

'We have to. Hurry up.' Siv gave her a look that said not to argue, and Tyra knew there was no use in resisting, not with Siv who always had a reason for everything. If Siv said that they had to leave, then there was a good reason.

'Has Harald discovered who you really are?' Tyra guessed.

Siv looked at her with that frown on her face that meant that this was serious and that Tyra shouldn't argue or she would be silenced, but Tyra needed to know.

She fiddled with the bag opening. 'Siv, why are we leaving?' she asked again. She continued to fiddle with the bag, so she wouldn't be intimidated into silence by Siv's stare. 'I won't go until you tell me,' she finally found the courage to say. 'I thought you said that it was important that we were here. That we have to convert Harald back to the old way. That we have to make certain Svend trusts in the Alfather. You said that's how we can save the nine worlds and the runes. You said it was important.'

'It is,' Siv admitted. 'It *is* important. But some things are more important than the nine worlds and the runes.'

Even though Siv was the one saying it, Tyra couldn't imagine that to be true. Nothing was more important than the nine worlds. 'What things?'

'You.'

Siv's answer was straight and short, like only the truth could be.

Whatever it was, it had to be bad if Siv had decided that they needed to leave. Because when Tove's parents had arrived and Siv was about to be found out, they hadn't left. Siv had been calm, though she had not had a plan at the time. At least no plan Tyra knew about. She was calm now as well, but this felt different. It felt like a last resort, like Siv had tried everything and that all else had failed.

'Siv… what has happened?' Tyra looked straight into Siv's grey lynx eyes, to show that she needed to know what was going on and why they were leaving.

'Harald has found a man for you to marry,' Siv said. Without taking off her shoes, or her dripping cloak, Siv brought Tyra further into the hall and sat her down on the bench by the burning fire. The fire was always going in the longhouse. 'He told me the day Finn arrived,' she revealed in a calm and quiet voice. Only Siv could say bad things and make them feel like they weren't so bad at all.

The fire made Tyra's hands thaw, and the snow melted from her curly hair and dripped down her face. So that was why Siv wanted them to leave. Not because Harald had found out who they really were or because a flying lizard would come and burn Jelling or something equally grand and terrible. But because Harald had found a man for Tyra to marry.

She had never thought of marriage before. Only really last midsummer, back in Ash-hill, when she had gone to pluck the midnight flowers and put them under her pillow and had dreamt of three lovers. In the morning, her mother and sisters had teased her because most women dreamt of only one or two future husbands.

'He wants to marry me away, so I won't be here to ruin his perfect family,' Tyra said.

Siv and her had stayed together ever since the battle, and Tyra couldn't imagine what it would be like to not have Siv at her side. 'Then I won't be with you, or with Svend.'

Siv took Tyra's hands into her own, and matched her stare. 'And you're too young, Tyra, and I won't have it,' she said like only a mother could. 'I made a sacred promise to your father that I would protect you, so we're leaving.'

'But we can't just leave,' Tyra blurted.

'We have to. I can't talk Harald out of this, or anything important anymore. His mind is Christian and shut. If you stay, with or without me, Harald will have you married off to that man.'

'There has to be another way.' Siv could do so much. She had convinced Tove's parents that she was their daughter, and she had seduced Harald in a single evening, and she had killed those guards in the retinue on the Oxen Road, and she had fought a thousand warriors and survived, and she had saved Tyra. She had to be able to do something more. If nothing else, she could kill Harald, and end his rule and everything else.

'Killing him would do more harm than good, Tyra,' Siv said. She must have been listening to Tyra's thoughts again, as she sometimes did. 'Svend is still too young.'

'What about those beings from the other worlds who helped you make Tove's parents forget?' Tyra said aloud, not wanting her thoughts to be heard. 'Can't you do that again, and make him forget that he wants me to marry?'

'It doesn't work quite like that,' Siv calmly explained. 'Besides, their debt to me is paid.'

'Other debts, then. Someone must be able to help.' Tyra searched her mind for a solution, because there had to be one. There had to be something that Siv had not thought about, though she knew that Siv always thought of everything. And she knew almost everything. Almost.

'I know a dwarf who owes me a debt,' Tyra said.

Siv narrowed her eyes at Tyra. 'How do you know a dwarf?' Siv did not give Tyra time to come up with a clever answer, before she already had the truth. 'You went back to the passage grave. You gambled with a dwarf. You could have died, Tyra.'

'But I didn't, and now there's a dwarf who owes me.'

'A dwarf can't help us. Not to stay here.'

Then they really had no choice. Even knowing that, Tyra couldn't imagine leaving. She thought about what Svend had told her on top of the gravemound. She didn't want to leave him behind.

'I'm sorry Tyra, I know you care about Svend.'

'Can't we ask him to come with us?'

'He has a destiny here. He is the best hope the Danes have of reuniting with their gods, or at least of choosing their own gods. Svend is our best hope of overturning Harald's decisions. His brother, Hakon, can't do it.'

She was right about that, but Tyra didn't want to leave Svend.

'We have to stay,' she insisted. 'Otherwise, it was all pointless. Your efforts with Harald, and Tove's death and Tove's mother's death, and even Ash-hill's attack on Magadoborg.'

She didn't want to mention the warriors and Vigmer and Einer, but she couldn't help thinking about them either. They had died in Magadoborg. It had to have been for something.

'We can't let their efforts go to waste,' Tyra insisted. 'We can't leave.'

'Their efforts won't be wasted. The southerners will continue to put pressure on Harald. He will have to pay for the attack again and again. He will have to answer for it. When Svend takes over, he will allow the people to believe in their own gods. Runemistresses won't be killed anymore and the runes won't disappear and the nine worlds will be saved.'

Siv was being so patient, and Tyra didn't like it, because it meant that there really was no choice. Siv could force Tyra to be silent, and make her obey with a single look. Instead she had made Tyra sit by the fire, even though they were in a hurry, and let Tyra voice all her concerns and hopes, before she plucked each of them down.

'What if Svend doesn't do that? What if he carries on like his father?'

'Then we will find other ways to save the nine worlds, you and I,' Siv said, and rubbed Tyra's hands. 'There are other ways, Tyra.'

If there were other ways, then those ways were dangerous and bad, because Siv wouldn't have chosen to come here in the first place if it was not the best way to save the nine worlds. If there truly were other ways, then she would have considered them all. Siv had chosen this way for a reason.

'Will those other ways keep us together?' Tyra asked.

'They will keep you safe.'

'And what about you?'

Siv did not answer her this time, and Tyra knew she wouldn't. Sometimes Siv talked not about the end of the nine worlds, but the end of *her* time. Sometimes she talked as if she was about to die.

'Harald found a man for me to marry,' Tyra said. It sounded

daunting and strange. She tried to be brave and strong, like Siv. 'A husband for me. Me. It's my decision.'

'I'm your mother,' Siv said. 'It's *my* decision, and we're leaving.'

'You can't make decisions for me anymore,' Tyra argued, although she knew that Siv could. Siv could make decisions for anyone. Tyra shook her head. 'I can't leave Svend.' All the way down in the deepest part of her heart Tyra knew that. 'Not like this.'

It was wrong to leave Jelling, all wrong, and Tyra's heart hurt just at the mention of it. The thought of leaving everything she knew, again, and everyone she had come to trust and love hurt like a stab. And Tyra knew what it felt like to be stabbed, at least by arrows. Her skin had dark red scars from the battle at Ash-hill.

She wouldn't leave Jelling behind. She wouldn't abandon what she and Siv had begun together. That wasn't the action of a true Jute. And though no one else could know where she was from, Tyra knew in her heart and mind that she was a girl of Ash-hill.

'It's important that I stay,' she said. 'For the nine worlds.'

'Protecting the nine worlds is my burden as a long-lived, not yours.'

'It's mine too, now. When I die, I want to see my parents and my sisters. Even if I don't die in battle, and even if I can't sit at their table. Even if I go to Helheim in the afterlife. I just want to see them one last time. Be it in Valhalla or on the field of Ragnarok's battle.'

Siv looked at her like her mother had used to do. Tyra could not quite decide what it was that made her look that way. But her heart was warm as it had used to be when her mother praised her.

'The only way I can do that,' Tyra continued, 'is if we keep the nine worlds from drifting apart, like you said.'

'I can do this alone, Tyra.'

'You can't,' Tyra said, and she knew it was true. 'If you could save the nine worlds on your own, you wouldn't have told me about it all.'

Siv had nothing to say to that.

'So, it's important that I stay and that I marry this man Harald has chosen.' She would stand her ground and fight to save the nine worlds like Siv did. All she wanted was to be like Siv when she was older.

'His name is Styrbjorn,' said Siv. 'He is older than you. A lot older.' Every word was well placed, as it always was with Siv when she wanted to convince. 'You could have a different life. Marry someone you love.'

It was a pleasant thought. All the things Tyra could do if she didn't stay in Jelling as her mind and heart told her she had to do. But it was, and would be, no more than dreams. The same as when, sometimes, she dreamt and wished that her parents had not passed on and that her sisters were still alive.

'Do you love Harald?' Tyra asked in return and looked into Siv's grey lynx eyes. They curled into a smile. Siv's smiles always reached her eyes. At least if it wasn't a pretend smile. She was good at those too.

'Not Harald,' Siv admitted. 'But Harald is not my first husband.'

'What about Vigmer?'

They had not spoken of Vigmer and Einer and the rest of them since Finn had left Jelling. Siv didn't want to talk about it, and Tyra felt bad whenever she mentioned it.

This time, too, Siv did not respond.

'Well your first husband was not your last,' Tyra said. 'Perhaps Styrbjorn will not be mine either.'

'Perhaps he *will* be.' Siv sighed and looked down as if she was deciding whether to tell Tyra something really important, or not. 'There is something different and dangerous about him,' she said. 'He noticed me using the runes.' Tyra had never heard Siv talk that way about anyone or anything. She had never sounded scared before. 'No short-lived could sense that.'

'What does that mean? Is he like you?'

'I don't know what he is, but he is not from this world, and he is dangerous. There is fire and destruction in his eyes.'

'So we have to leave?'

'We can't stay. We don't know what he is.'

'Then I want to come with you,' Tyra decided. 'Don't leave me again.' Svend and Siv were all Tyra had. If she couldn't stay with Svend, then she wanted to go with Siv.

'Then we shall go together,' Siv said reassuringly, like only she could, so all of Tyra's worries melted away. Instead of telling Tyra that all would be well, or insisting that she had to pack and they had to leave, Siv simply leaned in and took Tyra in her arms. They hugged each other tight. Tyra had never hugged anyone so tight before.

'It's not just that he has found a husband for me, is it?' Tyra asked into Siv's shoulder. If it had been, Siv wouldn't need to leave Tyra somewhere to stay safe. They could go together and they wouldn't need to split up.

Tyra pushed away from Siv's embrace to get her last answers. 'Why can't we go to Odin's-gorge together? Why can't you stay there with me?'

'Einer is dead.' Siv's voice was cold and sharp as she said it. 'Odin has claimed my son's life. He shouldn't have been able to, but he did. I can't let him claim you too.'

'Odin?' Tyra asked. The thought of Einer being gone from Midgard made her want to cry, but in the next life they would meet. Tyra didn't understand what was so bad about being claimed by Odin. 'Won't I just go to Valhalla, then, if Odin chooses me?' In Valhalla she would meet her parents and Einer and everyone else. It was all she ever dreamed about.

'Being claimed and being chosen are two very different things, and if he finds you with me he won't choose you, he will claim you,' said Siv, and none of her answers made any sense. 'He won't bring you to Valhalla. Not if he smells you.'

'If he smells me?'

Every time Tyra had met someone from another world, they had smelled her, over and over. Siv's father had done it, and claimed that Tyra didn't come from Midgard, and Siv's brother too had smelled her. After smelling her, he had believed that she was Siv's daughter.

'Why won't he take me to Valhalla if he smells me?' Tyra asked.

'Because I hid you away in the ash-tree when Ash-hill was burning, and I shouldn't have.'

'You saved my life.'

Siv nodded. 'I kept my promise to your father. It was the only way I could save you, but I didn't think Odin was watching, and because of it, he won't let you survive.'

'Why?' Tyra asked. She didn't expect Siv to answer, but again, she did.

'Because now you smell of the great ash. You smell of new possibilities and hope, and if there is one thing that scares the Alfather, it's the thought of new possibilities that he did not envision and create himself.'

'Why?'

'I suppose it reminds him of Ragnarok, and the future, and perhaps even of me. All of that which he cannot control.'

SIGISMUND

Chapter Eighty-Eight

THE MIDGARD WORM. Ran's net. It felt like it had been a dream, but Sigismund knew that it had not been. His lungs stung from the truth. His throat hurt like someone had cut it open.

Sigismund gasped for breath but found none. He coughed and coughed but could not take a true breath. His clothes were heavy with water. It trickled out from his ears and mouth, even seemed to trickle out of his skin.

Coughs echoed around him, not just his own but that of other men and women; his warriors.

Sigismund blinked his eyes into focus. He lay on his back, awkward on top of the net in which he had been caught. Above him was the sea. The waters were lit from below. Fish swam by; bigger fish than Sigismund had ever seen before. The waters truly were above him, not below as they were supposed to be.

He pushed off from the sandy ground. He lay almost on a beach, although he did not. His arms were weak from his struggle in the water. He coughed. His lungs were full of salty water. He had drowned. The water stung as he coughed it up;

entered his nose from the back, and scratched like he had an open wound far up his nose and another in his throat.

'Cough it up,' his steersman urged with a whisper and rubbed Sigismund on the back. 'And while you do, help me think about something expensive with which we can buy passage into Ran's hall. Most of us lost our arm-rings in the water, and they're saying that what we have is not enough.'

Sigismund did not ask who *they* were. As he coughed, he glanced around. His warriors were mostly on their feet. Some were still coughing, but several of his drowned men had recovered from their awakening in the afterlife. They were yet bloated and pale, but they were walking about, sweeping their feet through the sand, looking for their valuables.

They were inside a huge bubble of air underneath the water. Sigismund coughed and turned to look over his shoulder. Nine mermaids stood on their scaled legs and blocked the way through an open gate. All nine of them were women, naked with long hair of seaweed that waved over their breasts, and the scales at their hips.

Still coughing, Sigismund turned his back to them. 'How much do they demand?'

'More than we have.'

'How much more?'

'They haven't said.'

'You haven't asked, or they haven't said?'

'They haven't said,' the steersman repeated.

Sigismund nodded his understanding, and ran through all the valuables he might have on him. His weapon belt was gone. It had been stuck in the net like the rest of him, but now it was gone. The mermaids must have taken it. They had taken his weapon belt, his warriors' arm-rings and left them bare of gold to buy their entrance into Ran's hall. He had been robbed before he had woken from death, as had all his warriors.

Tales always had some truth in them, so it was not just because Ran robbed sailors of their lives that she was called the Robber, but because she robbed them of their wealth before they could gain entrance to hers and Aegir's hall. She was also said to be a generous host. So, there had to be a way into her good graces, and into her halls.

Sigismund coughed up slime and spat it into the sand at his side. With his steersman's help, he untangled his legs from Ran's net. His clothes were damp but not wet, as he had expected them to be. With as confident a smile as he could muster, Sigismund rose to his feet.

His sailors glanced to him as he dusted the sand off his clothes. He saw hope in their gazes, and new confidence now that their ship commander was at their side, ready to argue on their behalf. In the worst of cases, they would have someone to blame for their misery.

None of them had anything of worth to buy safe passage into Ran's halls, and if they were not granted passage, they would be thrown out of the bubble, back into the sea for their corpses to rot and their afterlife to be taken.

In order to enter Valhalla, one had to show courage and be a fierce warrior. To enter Helheim one had to show value and worth, and to enter Ran's hall one had to drown and have wealth, and apparently also be able to outsmart mermaids.

Sigismund released a deep sigh. He would lead his warriors to a safe afterlife. It was his responsibility.

He turned to his steersman. A few other warriors had gathered at his back. He spoke to them all in a lowered voice. 'How much did you have before you woke to the afterlife? How much did they take?'

His crew was not stupid. Instead of immediately answering, they approached their bench-mates and gathered numbers for him, and with his warriors' final count, Sigismund approached the mermaids. They were three heads higher than Sigismund or any of his warriors, and their hair waved behind them, as if they were floating in water inside the air bubble.

The woman at the middle of the group had red seaweed hair,

which made her easy to identify. Only one among Ran's and Aegir's nine daughters had red hair. Bloodyhair, she was called, like the red foam of the seas. She was so easily recognisable that every sailor who was brought in by Ran's net was bound to address her. She would be used to dealing with drowned sailors.

Sigismund turned his eye to the other eight sisters. His eyes fell on the woman to the far right. Her hair and skin were fair, so much that her features seemed to blur, like the reflection of the sky in the waters.

'Skybright.' He named her aloud, and addressed her with confidence.

His warriors stood at his back, with their chins high, as he had instructed them to do.

'Your sisters and you have already gathered gold and silver from our corpses,' he announced, looking at Skybright, and only Skybright. 'Twenty-one silver arm-rings. Eight gold arm-rings. Thirty-seven silver finger-rings. Three gold finger-rings, and fifteen neck-rings you have taken, and that's excluding the decorated weapon belts and pouches.'

'Four gold finger-rings,' Skybright corrected. She almost looked shy to be noticed and addressed.

'So, passage has already been paid.'

'It is not enough,' she maintained.

Sigismund had expected that answer. 'You know about the gold,' he said, although his ship carried little gold. They had not raided Magadoborg, they had ravaged and killed. There had been no energy left to pillage.

'There is no gold on your ship,' Skybright said and smirked.

'My ship is precious as gold, and I intend to offer it to you, and your mother, for passage. These are my warriors,' he gestured to all of his sailors gathered at his back. 'On their behalf I would like to buy passage for us all into your halls with my ship, the *Storm*.'

'They may be your warriors, Sigismund Karson,' said a

muffled voice that was not that of Skybright. 'But I called upon *them*, not upon you.'

From the shadows of the gate that the nine sisters guarded came a woman larger than her nine daughters, with long black seaweed as hair. It trailed behind her, dragged on the sand, and disappeared into it. Unlike her daughters, she wore clothes; a dress of green seaweed sewn together at the bust. At the waist it parted into long slips of straight seaweed that showed the tops of her firm thighs.

'You followed them here.' She smiled a thin smile. 'You did not have to drown. But if you so desperately wish to, that is a fate I cannot save you from.'

Her daughters were not assured by their mother's presence. She had walked in and taken over a task that was supposed to be theirs and theirs alone.

'I shall take your offering,' Ran decided.

Sigismund heard the sighs of relief at his back.

'I shall take your ship, and invite your sailors into my halls. But you, Sigismund Karson; you do not belong here. I did not invite you.'

Sigismund felt a cough tickle in his throat again. Ran would take his sailors and warriors, and despite how he had launched into the sea after them, and despite how he had gotten caught in her net trying to free them, she would not take him.

'We have no claim over him. Throw him back out,' she declared and walked away.

Sigismund did not have time or strength to protest before nine pairs of giant, firm hands were on him. The sisters grabbed him and lifted him above their heads, out of the reach of his protesting crew. They kicked their way through the crowd, marched to the edge of the air bubble, and without a heartbeat of doubt or hesitation, threw him into the water.

The current took him. He was thrown about at the will of the sea. At the will of Ran's nine daughters.

Water foamed around him as the current cast him about, and

he could see nothing and feel nothing but the cold sea wrapping over him. His clothes pulled him down. He tried to swim and reach the surface, but he knew it was too far, and that he would drown. Again.

The voices of Ran's nine daughters were muffled in the water: 'Let him drown again. We have no claim. Let the Nornir not be angry. We did not rob them of a destiny. He robbed himself. Let him drift and be forgotten with the unworthy.'

HILDA

Chapter Eighty-Nine

ICE SPREAD ALONG Hilda's feathered fingers. The cold wrench into her. She howled in pain, but her beak was tied shut. She flapped to get away. The ice spread. She could hardly move her left wing, and then the ice reached her back and she was frozen in place.

Hilda wrapped herself in warrior courage. She had fought at Magadoborg. She had survived the slaughter in Ash-hill. Her captor was no different from any southerner, but Hilda couldn't fool herself. She was in Asgard and most likely, she had been captured by a goddess.

A hand clenched around Hilda's neck. From the neck, she was lifted out of the cage. Elegant fingers slid into the skin opening. They were warm on Hilda's back. Her captor tugged at the ribbon that bound the skin shut. Hilda's body was wrenched this way and that. The skin was stuck to her as if it were her own. Even at the command of a goddess, it didn't want to part with her.

'What did you do?' hissed the woman. 'Did you get yourself

pregnant again? How did you get stuck like this?' Finally, the skin lifted from Hilda's back, peeling away like red skin in the summer heat. The further out Hilda's arms and fingers it loosened, the more it hurt. Her own skin had as good as melted into the falcon skin. Her right arm was torn out of the skin, locked away by unyielding fingers. Next her left shoulder came free. Then a rope tied her wrists together. It cut into her skin and locked her arms behind her. Hilda wriggled to get free. Every shift made the rope cut sharper into her skin.

Her captor was not done. She forced one leg free and then the other and fastened them in the same way. Hilda lay wriggling on the ground. Flowers tickled at her neck and soft twigs crushed under her as she struggled against her bonds. Her head was still stuck inside the falcon skin. The mask over her eyes and her beak tied shut so she couldn't screech.

'A skin in a skin,' the goddess said. 'No wonder you were stuck.' She fully believed that Hilda was Loki, and tied up, there was nothing Hilda could do to prove otherwise. 'Sometimes you're as cunning as your blood-brother. Oh, stop flapping,' the goddess grumbled. 'You know it's useless.'

A warm hand moved up Hilda's thigh. Goosebumps popped along both her arms and legs. The hand lifted from Hilda's upper thigh. The Ulfberht axe was lifted from its belt clasp. At her other hip, her dagger was removed. Then, Hilda was kicked onto her stomach. She groaned, and her side stung with bruises to come.

Her captor sat on her back and pinned her down. Her tunic was sliced open at the back and a cold blade traced her spine. 'That bird skin took me a long time to make,' her captor hissed. 'How long did it take you to skin this young woman?'

The falcon skin had been made by her captor. The old tales said that Loki borrowed the falcon skin from the vanir goddess Freya. This was Freya, Hilda reasoned.

One of the vanir; a goddess of fertility taken captive by Odin hundreds of winters ago, back when the aesir and the vanir had been at war. It was Freya who held her captive now, but knowing that did not help to free Hilda from a terrible death.

She was lifted to her feet. Her tied legs wobbled under her. Freya held her up with a hand on her tunic, until Hilda managed to find her balance. As soon as she stood on her own a sharp blade was pressed against her throat: the blade of her own godly axe. Another pressed into her back.

'You cheese-stinking cunt,' Freya hissed into Hilda's ear. 'If there's no opening, Loki, I'll just have to make my own so I can slice off your balls and chop up your cock.'

Hilda controlled her breathing and tensed her muscles. The ropes dug into her skin. Blood dribbled down her hands. This goddess would skin her and kill her, thinking that she was Loki.

The blade was pressed harder against Hilda's neck. The one at her back pierced through her skin. Images of the past flashed before Hilda. It had always been *her* holding the knife. Back in Ash-hill with the priest. In Magadoborg, too. She didn't want to think about what she had done at that slaughter, but it had been *her* holding the axe. It didn't feel good to be at the sharp end.

The knife at Hilda's back withdrew. The axe was still at her neck, but maybe she could move away now, thrust her head back and hit Freya to make her escape. That's when she felt the stab.

Right as her mind flooded with hope, Hilda's own dagger was thrust into her back. It slashed through skin and muscle, drove between two of her ribs. Her insides twinged. She heaved for air. Her lungs were ready to collapse. The blood trickled warm down her back. Her body was colder for it.

She thought there could be no greater pain, but then Freya wrenched the dagger back out.

Blood splashed over Hilda's tunic and legs. The axe was lowered from her neck.

Hilda's head was light. Cool wind blew through her. Right through her. She couldn't die again. She didn't know what happened to people who died in the afterlife when the valkyries weren't there to wake them, but she didn't think that they went to Valhalla.

'I'll skin you if I have to.' The goddess's warm fingers fondled the wound, and Hilda gasped from pain. 'One layer of skin,' Freya hissed. 'Why only one…?'

Freya retreated from behind her. Hilda fell backwards. Her hands didn't catch her fall, but the grass softened it. She could barely catch a breath. Her lungs were out of air. Her insides spasmed. The pain in her chest stung all the way up to her temples. It hurt worse than a thousand arrow wounds.

Hilda opened her beak as wide as she could, but only wheezed. She couldn't get up. She would die here and then it would all be over. She would never see Valhalla and be seated with her rightful bench-mates.

A hand grabbed hold of Hilda's tunic. She was dragged across the ground. Flowers and grass tickled her wound. Slick blood soaked through her trousers and she panted. There was a hole through her lung. A hole that couldn't fill when she breathed.

Hilda's eyes pulsed. It hurt to die, she thought. It hadn't hurt the last time. Her body had been pumping with blood-lust, and she hadn't noticed death take her. This was different. Nothing shielded her from the pain of the wound that went from her back and all the way to the front of her chest.

Her wound was dragged along the ground as Freya hauled her inside. Her feet glided over the blood on the floor from her own wound. She couldn't find foot-hold. Her head was weary.

It was a worthy death, at least—killed by a goddess—but no one would tell stories of it. No one would sing songs of it.

Hilda was propped up against a wall as smooth as silk. Her breaths were shallow. Her weapons clanged to the floor next to her. Freya's hand reached for the falcon head. Two fingers wriggled off her falcon mask, and then let go. Head still stuck inside the falcon skin, Hilda blinked her eyes.

Freya was leaning close. Her eyes were lined with black kohl, as were her eyebrows. Her skin had been smoothed with colour and she smelled of raspberries. Her lips looked lush, as if she had eaten a handful of wild berries. She was handsome, and for a moment Hilda forgot that she was dying, and just marvelled at her goddess.

Freya leaned closer and looked into Hilda's eyes. They were her own, not those of a falcon. Hilda stared back at the woman without blinking. The pain pulsed all the way into her eyeballs.

'Who are you?' her captor asked in a whisper.

Hilda tried to speak her name, but her beak was tied, and the woman did not look about to untie her. Even if she did, all that would come out were screeches.

'A short-lived,' her goddess muttered and took a few steps back. 'You're just a short-lived... Trapped in my old falcon skin. How?'

Hilda didn't know how to explain. She wasn't sure that she understood it herself.

'I ought to burn you for stealing from a goddess.' Freya had a presence about her that demanded respect. The goddess removed the falcon skin from Hilda's head and threw it aside. 'Where did you get the skin?' she asked.

Hilda spat a feather from her mouth and wriggled her nose to be rid of the strange smell. Sweat rolled down her forehead and cheeks. Without the falcon skin on her head, she could breathe more easily. The room was heavy with the scent of flowers. Every wall lined with strips of expensive fabrics. Fluffy cats played with Freya's trailing cloak.

'How did you get it?' Freya asked, again. She was used to command, and Hilda was certain that she wouldn't ask a third time.

'I stole it,' Hilda wheezed. Her voice was raspy and her throat grated when she spoke. Switching skins was not an easy thing. She tried to wriggle to sit properly. 'From Loki.' Stealing was a crime, but she didn't think that stealing from Loki would be considered quite as bad.

'Where is he?' asked handsome Freya. The cats at her back mewled, demanding a response.

Hilda struggled to catch enough breath to speak. 'Meadow. Outside Jelling.'

'Jelling?' Freya's forehead furrowed in confusion. Blue flowers bloomed from the wooden floor under her feet. Flower and fresh leaves poked up between her toes. 'Where is Jelling?'

'Midgard,' Hilda wheezed.

At her answer, Freya pushed away the swaying fabric that lined the room and left Hilda, bleeding, alone in the corner. A few of the cats followed the goddess, but others stayed, clawing at the fabric that lined the wall and licking themselves. There were half a dozen of them.

Hilda stared around the room for an escape. Her arms were tied to her back and her legs beneath her, but she might be able to wriggle across the room. Focusing made the pain in her stomach bearable.

The room was twice as wide as Hilda's home had been and the ceiling was further up than any longhouse she had ever seen, but it reminded her of home. The walls were made not of wood, but of warm-coloured hangings, like the ones her father had painted.

Most of the images were not stories, merely scenes of Asgard in spring. The wall behind her was covered in a long red banner that shone unlike anything Hilda had ever seen before and on it was the image of Yggdrasil in jewels. One of the cats had crawled several feet up the fabric, and was now clawing at a jewel at the bottom of the tree. Hilda tilted her head back. The red cloth gradually shaded to dark blue, and gems twinkled at the ceiling—the distant stars that Odin and his brothers had cast from Muspelheim's flames over the nine worlds. The image of Yggdrasil was in bloom—everything in the room was—fresh twigs and small leaves grew from the old wooden floor-planks.

Her heartbeat had slowed as she looked around. Her eyelids

felt heavy. The fresh flowers sprouting from the floor around her were red with her blood. Hilda recognised the sensation of blood-loss. In Midgard she had often felt light-headed and tired from how much blood her eyes had needed.

Commotion rose from elsewhere in the hall and all of the cats began to meow.

Hilda strained to hear what was being said. 'An intruder?' Freya said. 'It has to be Loki.'

'Loki?' a man with a honeyed voice repeated. 'Why would you assume it's him?'

'He's free.'

There was a pause. Everything stopped; the footsteps, the voices, the panic. Even the cats were silent. 'He can't be,' said the man. 'That would mean—'

'He is,' Freya insisted. 'He's free. Ask the veulve.'

'It's not him,' the man insisted.

The footsteps resumed and the Yggdrasil fabric was swept aside by a wrinkled hand. A hand that had lived much, but a strong hand too. One that was acquainted with weapons and fights. For a while there was just the hand on the fabric, but then the man spoke. 'It has to be her,' he said.

'Her?' Freya echoed. 'Glumbruck?'

'Hugin and Munin tell me she disappeared in Midgard,' said the man, and suddenly Hilda knew who he was. He swept aside the fabric and entered the room. He was tall compared to Freya. His hair and beard mingled together in long silver locks. His forehead bore a frown, and beneath the frown was a single shining eye, and the sunken hole where the other should have been.

Hilda gasped for breath. Not because she was wounded and could hardly fill her lungs, but in sheer surprise. Her mind was bare and she couldn't remember why she was there or what she was supposed to do. All she knew was that the Alfather was standing in front of her. As if in a dream.

'You're not alone,' he said over his shoulder to Freya. His

voice was raspy and comfortable, like a warm fire on a cold winter night.

Freya pushed him aside as she entered. She hardly glanced at Hilda. 'A servant,' she dismissed with a back hand. Busily she made her way through her cats, across the room to pick up the falcon skin she had tossed aside earlier. 'You see? He is free.'

'Then we have two hunts to begin,' said the great Alfather, god of gods and creator of worlds, as he stared straight at Hilda.

Hilda's breath caught in her throat and gave her hiccups. Right there, in front of the Alfather. The great god and Alfather. She had spent her entire life hoping for this moment in the afterlife. This moment, standing in front of a being so wise and powerful, to profess her allegiance to him.

'Great Alfather,' Hilda wheezed. Freya shot her a quelling glare from across the room, but Hilda was already staring into the single eye of her god and professing her devotion to him. 'I declare my full allegiance to you. Allow me to fight on your battlefield.'

Freya stepped between Hilda and the Alfather. She faced mighty Odin, and hid him so that all Hilda could see was the goddess's back and the many cats crowding at Odin's feet. They were pretty feet. Or shoes, at least. Black leather. But they had trodden through dark red mud, which had since dried and settled. Even the Alfather's shoes looked different and godlike. Everything about him was *more*, and better, and more interesting than anything had ever been to Hilda.

She stretched to the side to look behind Freya and her cats to better see the grand Alfather. But Freya stepped in her way. Hilda stretched the other way, but again Freya was quicker.

'She's mine,' the goddess declared.

'What's your name?' the Alfather asked in a voice that carried. A voice that was meant for Hilda and demanded an answer.

She gladly obliged. 'I am Hilda, shieldmaiden among warriors, and daughter of Ragnar Erikson, late Skald of Ash-hill.'

Freya spun to face Hilda. Her hair slapped at her cheeks. 'How?' she hissed.

The Alfather muttered the same.

Hilda didn't know how to answer them. She was who she was and that was it. She had never thought to question how she had become Hilda Ragnardóttir. She just was.

'Hilda of Ash-hill. I expected you in Magadoborg,' said the Alfather.

The Alfather knew her name and lineage and where she had died. He had been expecting her. There was no greater honour in the nine worlds.

The Alfather had recognised her worth and he had chosen her and watched over her and waited for her, exactly as she had always dreamt it. All of her wishes came true at once.

'She is mine,' Freya repeated, standing between Hilda and her god.

'I thought you would have silenced her,' Odin spoke to Freya as a father to a disobedient child.

'I did,' she hissed back. 'And she is mine.'

'Why don't we ask her where she wants to go,' said the wise Alfather, knowing that Hilda would choose him. Any warrior would.

Hilda was about to open her mouth and declare that she was ready to assume her rightful place in Valhalla.

'Her choice doesn't matter,' said Freya, then. 'I have choosing rights.'

There was a long silence thereafter. All Hilda could see of Odin was the top of his head. Freya still blocked her view, and Odin's mudded shoes were shielded behind Freya's many cats. Finally, he spoke: 'Only on the battlefield.'

'I found her on Ida's plain,' Freya responded. Her voice had an ease that meant that she had won, and that she was right, after all.

'That can't be,' said the Alfather. 'She never entered my hall.'

'But she has entered mine. She belongs here, for now.' The

goddess stepped away so Hilda could stare up at her god again. His forehead creased with a deeper frown that complemented the wave of his silver hairline.

'I want to come with you to Valhalla,' Hilda panted. Her voice was shivering, and not by choice. She was really dying. It was exactly like it had been with her brother. The wheezing noises, the blood everywhere. The will to gag and throw up. That pounding nausea and headache.

Freya hissed at Hilda, but the Alfather did not react, and for a moment that felt like an eternity, the Alfather and Hilda stared at each other. Deadly holmgangs began like this. Not the sort her brother had prepared for, but the kind Einer and Finn had battled. Fought with honour and ambition. Hilda did her best to show the Alfather her ambition: how hard she would train and work to climb the ranks in Odin's army. While others were feasting, Hilda would train. Every day she would train as she waited for the fight to begin, until she was the best shieldmaiden in the entire hall.

The Alfather blinked and broke the connection. 'Freya, why is she here and not in my hall?' he asked, but his sight never quit Hilda. His single eye pierced through and saw the truth in her heart. 'What do you want?'

Hilda swelled with pride. She was not just wanted in Odin's sacred hall, she was needed. He needed her enough to strike a deal.

'You know what I want,' Freya mysteriously said. She fondled her jewelled necklace.

Skald stories often made Freya look like a young foolish woman, filled with greed and eyes for jewels. Hilda's father had never told the stories that way. In his versions, Freya was a woman who knew what she wanted and who went out and got it. She always got what she wanted. This time, Hilda was her leverage.

The Alfather nodded wisely. Some old men stroked their beard when they nodded, but the Alfather did not. His beard and hair were so perfect that a stroke might ruin their shine, and he did not need to stroke his beard to look wise. He *was* wise, and he looked it.

'What you want is not something I can give you,' the Alfather admitted. He removed his eyes from Hilda and studied Freya, from head to toe, as she stood and triumphantly fondled the jewels on the famed neck-ring called Brisingamen, with her cats circling around.

Hilda followed the Alfather's gaze and looked at Freya. Really looked at her. She was a woman who already had everything. She had power, strength. She had riches and a hall that warriors dreamt to be seated in. She had influence and beauty and her flowery steps of spring brought happiness to all. What could a goddess and woman like that possibly want more?

'You know what I want,' Freya repeated.

'I don't have time to waste with you, Freya.' Again, he spoke to her as to a child.

Freya wasn't fazed by his tone 'If you don't have time, then pay or leave my hall.' There was no room for compromise. Freya had made her decision.

So had Odin.

He stood for a moment, caught in Freya's unmoving stare. 'You know where to find me,' he said and his single eye moved away from Freya to rest on Hilda. 'Walk past Yggdrasil and Mimer's well, and you will find a modest hall where my warriors feast.' There was nothing modest about Valhalla. 'I will be waiting.'

Then he disappeared behind the Yggdrasil banner, and Hilda heard his footsteps get further and further away. With every step away that her god took, the pain in Hilda's chest seemed to double.

In her confusion and awe she had forgotten to present the Alfather with the axe and ask him to watch over Ash-hill and give her back her Runes. She supposed it wouldn't have moved him anyways. He wasn't ready to pay Freya's price. Whatever it was.

Her god was walking away from her, and there was nothing Hilda could do about it. Once again, the Runes had been right. The Alfather had abandoned her.

TYRA

Chapter Ninety

TYRA GASPED AT the realisation that they had arrived at Svend's favourite passage grave.

'Are we going to that snowy place again?' she asked in a whisper. She did not like to speak any louder so close to the passage grave. No animals dared approach it, but Tyra was drawn to it. The Darkness called her closer.

'Nej,' Siv answered. 'Not to the snowy place,' and she didn't say anything else.

High grasses protected the grave, but unlike the times Tyra had come to this grave with Svend, there was a trodden path through them. Siv had come here before, and more than once.

Siv went first through the trodden high grasses. Tyra followed, eyes on the grave ahead, not the ground. The sight of the dark hole into the passage brought on a sort of ring of silence in her head that seemed like it could swallow all the sounds in the nine worlds.

Their steps echoed against the stones as they stepped into the passage grave. Tyra made her steps light and careful. She wondered who had been buried inside, if there was a draugar living in it, and if that was why no animals ever approached, and why it felt so different to her from other graves.

'There is no corpse inside this grave,' Siv said in answer to Tyra's thoughts.

An empty gravemound. A fate much worse than what Tyra had imagined. She wondered how it had been emptied. Maybe grave robbers had opened it long ago. Maybe the corpse had walked out, or simply vanished—or maybe, just maybe, there never had been a corpse at all.

'That is why it demands your attention. It has been robbed of a guardian. There is only darkness down there.'

'Like in the ash-tree?' Tyra asked. The tree in Ash-hill where Siv had hidden her away during the battle had been filled with darkness.

'Like the ash-tree,' Siv confirmed.

'Does it smell like me, then?' Tyra asked, remembering what Siv had told her back in Jelling, before they had left.

'Nej,' Siv answered. 'But the Darkness it was made from does.' She crouched by the far wall of the passage. It was a large passage, and a large gravemound for an empty grave. Siv's hand reached for the dagger that hung at her belt. She didn't unsheathe it, but passed her palm along the sharp edge.

Tyra winced at the sight of Siv's bloody hand; she almost thought she could feel it herself. But Siv did not as much as twitch. Exactly like back in Ash-hill when Tyra had pulled an arrow out of Siv's shoulder.

'Don't you feel pain?' Tyra asked. She had been curious for so long. When it came to Siv, every detail made Tyra question everything she knew.

'Everyone feels pain,' Siv answered. 'But I know worse pains than cuts and arrow wounds.'

She touched her bloody hand to the far wall of the passage. The ground trembled, as if the world was coming apart. The stone at the far end of the passage rolled away, and Siv stepped into the dark.

The sunlight from outside did not shine into the passage. Tyra stepped through after Siv. She stumbled over the first step, and nearly tumbled, but Siv dug her fingers into Tyra's upper arm and held her steady as the stone rolled back into place behind them, and locked them into the damp passage grave.

The blackness was thick. It truly did remind Tyra of the Darkness inside the ash tree where Siv had hidden her away during the battle of Ash-hill. It reminded her of the scream she had heard.

'Kauna,' Siv whispered. Flames appeared out of nothing. They floated, above them, bound to nothing and burning nothing but darkness.

In the light from the flames, they began their descent through the grave. Though Tyra had walked along these steps before, she hadn't looked at them like this the last time. She had been so busy with excitement and questions then. The steps were worn and old. The middle of them was especially worn, as if a hundred thousand beings had walked up and down these steps before her.

Tyra looked at everything in detail. She wanted to remember everything, and never forget it, so that she could tell Svend about it if they ever met again. She would meet him again, she decided.

'Why couldn't we bring Svend?' Tyra asked, again.

'He has a destiny in Jelling,' Siv patiently said, as she had many times before. 'And besides, he is not like you, Tyra. Sights like the ones at the other side of this grave would frighten him.'

As ever, Siv was right. Tyra too knew that Svend and she were not alike in everything. When she had last been inside this passage grave, and had gambled with that dwarf, Svend had been terrified. He hadn't wanted to go back either. Tyra had. Despite Buntrugg's warnings, she had yearned to return to the grave. She yearned to see the other eight worlds and know everything about them.

Now, she finally would, though she supposed it wouldn't be for long. Tyra wished she and Siv would never be apart, but she knew that the time had come. That was why Siv answered all of Tyra's questions these days. Siv had used to keep secrets.

They walked on and on for such a long time that Tyra didn't care about looking around and remembering anything anymore. Every step was the same and the Darkness was so complete, and she kept thinking about that time in the tree when she had heard a scream in the dark.

Finally, they reached the other end of the passage. Siv stared at the far wall, but she did not blood her hand and open the passage grave.

'Sit on the steps,' Siv said. 'We need to eat something before we go through.'

'I'm not hungry.' Tyra could walk at least half a rest longer before she would need to ease her legs and eat. 'We can stop later,' she said, eyes fixed on the rock, eager to see what was on the other side of the passage, but Siv insisted that they sit, so they did.

'We can't stop later. Not where we're going,' Siv said and the way she answered Tyra's questions so easily felt wrong. It was as if her mind was elsewhere. As if she had half a hundred worries she was thinking about at the same time. 'Once we go through, they will be on our trails.'

'Who? Where are we going, Siv?'

'Asgard.'

Asgard where the gods lived and Tyra's parents and sisters feasted in Odin's hall. Asgard that Tyra had always dreamt about.

'But we can't,' Tyra said. Siv's serious tone made her remember the last time they had gone through that passage grave together, and what Siv's father had revealed. 'You can't go to Asgard. You said so yourself.'

Instead of answering, Siv handed Tyra a piece of flatbread filled with meat and a thick sauce. Tyra took it and nibbled on the edges. She really wasn't hungry, but she knew that if Siv said she had to eat, then she needed to eat something.

A question popped up at the back of Tyra's throat, and she could no longer keep it down. 'But why?'

'Why are we going to Asgard?' Siv guessed. She really wasn't herself, or she would have been listening to Tyra's thoughts and known exactly what Tyra was asking. Siv was so distracted that she couldn't focus. 'We're visiting the nornir.'

Tyra was half worried, half excited at the thought of that: Ragnar had often talked about the three nornir who spun fates. But she couldn't show real excitement, because Siv was acting so strange, and it made her uneasy and scared.

'Nej. I mean: why aren't you supposed to travel in Asgard?' Tyra said. 'Is it because your father is a giant? Is it because giants aren't allowed in Asgard?'

'Some giants are allowed in Asgard.' Siv answered without second thought. Talking seemed to help her. She found a flatbread for herself and settled down next to Tyra.

'Some giants are allowed, but not you,' Tyra concluded.

Siv smiled her usual mysterious smile. It felt good to see it again. 'I used to live there.'

'You used to live with the gods?' Tyra could hardly believe it. She saw Siv in a whole new light. She had always looked up to Siv and admired her, but now more than ever. Siv had lived with the gods. She was as good as a goddess.

'I'm not a goddess,' Siv modestly said.

She was listening to Tyra's thoughts again, and that was good. Not that Tyra liked having someone listen to her thoughts, but it meant that Siv wasn't as worried anymore, and Tyra felt less scared.

'I accept my fate, whatever it'll be,' Siv said. 'It's your fate we're here to change, and no matter if they catch up with us or not, we *will* change it for the better. I *will* convince them not to kill you.' She spoke as if she were trying to convince herself.

'Who?'

Siv was worried, and Tyra understood why. Asgard was not the same as Jutland. Everyone knew so much more in Asgard. Maybe they all had the same abilities as Siv. Her father had been powerful too, but Siv hadn't been afraid of him.

She was afraid now. Well not exactly afraid—Tyra didn't think that Siv could feel fear—but she wasn't calm as she had been. Her stare wasn't hard, and Tyra didn't like that. Seeing Siv like this made her more scared than anything.

'Siv, who will kill us?'

For a few heartbeats, Siv studied Tyra, and then she closed her eyes. She had a frown on her forehead. It looked painful to speak, but even so, she did. 'Odin and his valkyries,' she said. 'They will chase us from the moment we step through the passage, and when they find us, they *will* kill you.'

'Because I smell of the Darkness? And hope and possibilities?'

Siv nodded.

It sounded so dangerous, and suddenly Tyra understood why Siv wasn't herself. All the thoughts made Tyra really hungry. She gulped down her flatbread so the sauce dripped over her chin. 'If it's so dangerous, then why are we going to Asgard?' she asked, her mouth full of food.

Siv smiled at Tyra's impatience and wiped some sauce off her chin. 'If I had left you with my friend north of Odin's-gorge, would you have stayed there?'

Tyra wanted to say that she would have stayed, but she knew that she would have gone home to Jelling where Svend was. She shook her head and swallowed the last of her flatbread.

'I can't let you marry that man,' Siv said. 'Not without knowing what he is.'

'Because he could sense you using the runes?'

'Ja,' Siv answered. 'And while I don't know what he is, he *is* dangerous. Perhaps as dangerous as Odin. I couldn't leave you there.'

'But why go to Asgard?' Tyra asked. It was all so dangerous, and she didn't like how uneasy Siv was. Maybe this time they wouldn't survive. Maybe this was how they would truly die. It was starting to feel as hopeless as the battle in Ash-hill.

'I've had many sons,' Siv said, staring at the half-eaten flatbread in her hands. 'I tried to save them, but always Odin came and claimed them. I thought that Einer would be safe from harm, and out of Odin's reach, but I was wrong.' She sighed and her forehead frowned with pain. 'Einer passed on. Odin claimed him, and I didn't even know.'

She took another bite of food, and Tyra just stared at her and wondered why that meant she had to go to Asgard although she wasn't supposed to go there.

'I've tried everything to save my sons,' Siv said when she had swallowed the mouthful and wiped her lips. 'Nothing worked. There is only one thing I have yet to try. It's time that I confronted Odin. It's time for me to take my last stand against him, so that you may have a chance for a full life.'

'Your last stand?' Again, Siv talked as if she were dying.

'I can't wait for him to find me. I need to pick a place where I can have the high ground and fight him. I've been avoiding Odin for many centuries, but it's time I stopped and faced him.'

'But why? If it's so dangerous, why would you do it?'

Siv looked at her then, with her grey lynx eyes. 'Because to me, Tyra, you don't just smell of hope and possibilities; you *are* hope and possibilities. You are my only daughter and I would do anything to keep you safe.'

She finished her flatbread without looking at Tyra and packed it all away. Tyra felt full, but at the same time her stomach felt completely empty. She was terrified of what waited for them outside the passage grave.

'As soon as we walk out of this passage, Odin and his valkyries will come for us,' Siv said.

'And then you will face them?' Tyra asked.

'Nej. I need to face Odin somewhere I can have the advantage.

We will need to travel across Asgard to gain the high ground by the Hall of Fates.'

'The Hall of Fates?' Tyra didn't understand why that would be the high grounds for a battle. As far as she knew it wasn't at the top of a mountain. It was just a hall where the three old nornir spun fates day and night.

'In that place we will have a chance,' Siv said, and Tyra knew that if Siv believed it, then it was true and they had to get there, somehow.

'How will they know we're there?'

'As soon as we use the passage into Asgard, Heimdall will know, and he will blow his horn, and then they will come,' Siv willingly answered. 'They will search for us and track us until they find us.'

Tyra should have known that Heimdall would blow his horn. Heimdall controlled the rainbow bridge that led to Asgard, and she supposed he controlled all other passages too, and if he blew his horn then everyone in Asgard would hear it, as they would when he would blow it at the beginning of Ragnarok.

'Do you understand, Tyra?' Siv asked.

Tyra thought about it. She had to be certain that she understood it all before they went through, or it would be too dangerous. Finally, she nodded. 'We need to be quick.'

'Quick and careful,' Siv added. She crouched by the far wall and touched a bloody hand to it. The passage grave shook. The stone rolled aside. 'They will be coming now.'

BUNTRUGG

Chapter Ninety-One

THE VALKYRIES WERE leaving. Heimdall had blown his horn; it was not Ragnarok that had come for them, but some danger elsewhere in Asgard. Throughout the hall, the valkyries hurried out. The last one in Buntrugg's sight headed down the tables, pulling forth her crow skin. Buntrugg kept his eyes on her until she flew away and disappeared among the gold shields that made up the ceiling.

The Alfather had also left; there were only warriors in sight. Now was the time.

Buntrugg rose from the table where he had been seated. Since revealing himself in the Alfather's hall, he had been allowed a seat; he could hardly be hidden in a back room, as Einer was. His burns were healed enough for him to travel. Since he had brought his nephew into Odin's hall, he'd been ordered to leave within a week.

The warriors rarely spoke to him, terrified by his size, although he had shrunk to their height. They stared at his burned face and winced when they saw his scarred hands, so he kept his face hidden in the shadows of his hood, and his hands covered by gloves. The warriors at his table did not object as he stood up and left their company, although they were tasked to keep him there. Without a valkyrie to scold them, they let him slip away, relieved to see him leave so they could speak freely again.

He marched past tables and loud warriors to the doors that led into the room where Einer was being kept. He made his way inside before anyone of importance might notice, closed the door behind himself and turned to the bed.

Einer was not in it. He too had seen Odin's departure as a chance to act. He was standing with a hand on the wall, holding himself up and limping towards the door. He was weak, but he could walk, and he was not as pale as when Buntrugg had brought him into this hall, although he still had that arrow stuck in his forehead. The healers of Asgard had not dared to remove it, though they had secured it. His entire life, he would bear that arrow, until it left him dead. It was chance beyond the power of gods that it had not already forced him into the afterlife.

'You're off to find her?' Buntrugg asked.

Einer stood thunderstruck, clearly struggling to come up with a lie as to why he was standing up and not in bed. His straw hair had been washed and cut and he had been dressed in red trousers and a blue tunic, over which he had thrown his holed chainmail. It was a wonder he could stand with the armour weighing him down.

'I'm hungry,' he said, but he was not yet skilled at lying to long-lived. His thoughts were loud and his heartbeat betrayed him. He would learn.

'She isn't in Valhalla,' Buntrugg said. 'Your Hilda Ragnardóttir.'

Einer sighed with relief. He knew that he was a prisoner in Valhalla. He was not a stupid man, and despite his young age, he lived up to his lineage. There was no doubt that he was Glumbruck's son.

'Where is she, then?' he asked with a hardened stare. 'You were the one who told me that she was here. You said this place could also heal my heart.'

'I said it may,' Buntrugg responded. 'And I did not know that your heart longed for Hilda Ragnardóttir then, and I did not know that she was nowhere in this hall.'

Einer studied his face for the truth. He did not yet have the attuned ears of a long-lived, but he was more keen and able to see truth than a regular short-lived. 'Then where?' he asked.

Even if he could not yet hear it on Buntrugg's heart, he had to recognise the truth. 'No one knows.'

'But she should be here. She belongs here. The Alfather said so.' Einer spoke fast, and looked past Buntrugg at the door that led to the main hall. He was desperate to get out there and search.

None of the warriors knew that Einer was there, just as none of them had known that Buntrugg was there. Einer's entrance would stir a new wave of surprise, but that would make Buntrugg's plans easier, so Buntrugg stepped aside.

Dealings with short-lived required a lot of consideration. Einer could not hear the truth in Buntrugg's heart, so Buntrugg had to act with more care to show his true intentions. 'The Alfather says many things,' he said, and took another step away from the door. 'He will spin tales about where she is. If you find the table where she is supposed to be, but isn't, he will tell you that she must have made friends on the battlefield and have seated herself at another table. He will tell you that there are thousands of thousands of tables in this hall, and that searching them all would take days and she may seat herself elsewhere in the hall in the meantime. He will tell you anything that will make you stay.'

Buntrugg hoped that his intentions reached Einer, and were understood as he intended for them to be. The Alfather was not on their side, and the sooner Einer understood that, the sooner they could get on with their lives.

'You should go out and look for her. You won't believe me until you see the empty seat that she was destined for. You won't find her out there, but you should still look.'

Buntrugg's many truths made Einer stare blankly ahead, caught in his own loud thoughts. He leaned his shoulder against the wall to keep himself up. It seemed he was not finished with their conversation, and that he did not believe Buntrugg a liar, but was still ready to resume his march towards the door.

He was stubborn, like everyone in their family; and he was strong. No ordinary short-lived, or even long-lived, should have been able to walk so far with wounds like the ones Einer Glumbruckson carried. Buntrugg wondered if it were the forefathers who had sustained Einer all the way across the width of the hall when Buntrugg had first brought him here, but he had not sensed the forefathers stir, so it could not have been. It certainly wasn't the forefathers keeping Einer on his feet now. No giant would have been able to stand so soon after having such wounds bound.

'Why?' Einer asked. His eyes matched the shadow of Buntrugg's hood, and he narrowed them, as if in doing so he could see through the shadows. 'Why did he bring me here, though I'm not dead?'

Like most of Einer's questions, it was not an easy one to answer.

'You never asked my name and lineage,' said Buntrugg instead.

'What is it, then?' Einer asked in the exact same way Buntrugg's sister had when Buntrugg had first wished to introduce himself to her.

'My name you won't recognise.' No one knew or recognised Buntrugg by name, and he did not give it freely. 'But my lineage is the same as yours. I am the brother of the woman you know as Siv.'

Einer mused on that. It was a lot to learn all at once. He had not known that he had an uncle, he had not known that his mother's real name was not Siv, and he had not known that she came not from Midgard, but from another world.

Buntrugg heard Einer loudly grumble on those thoughts and considerations.

'You are my uncle?' he finally grasped.

'Ja. And I would like to show you your mother's home. *Your* home.'

'I know where my mother was born,' Einer said, but he neither looked nor sounded like he believed it anymore. 'I've been there, as a boy.'

'You think you've been there.'

'I remember my grandparents.'

'You think you remember them. Memories carefully placed. The way she talked to you; mentioned them and talked as if you were supposed to remember.'

'They weren't real?'

'You have a lot to learn about your mother, Einer.'

Einer looked at Buntrugg, not with mistrust or fear, but an expression that seemed to ask for help. His entire world was crumbling. Everything he thought he knew was changing and taken from him.

Buntrugg held out his hand, and offered an escape. 'Leave this place with me,' he said.

Einer looked like he barely had the strength and will to resist. 'Why?'

'Because your Hilda is not here, and if she is not here, after she has died, then do you truly believe that she ever will be?'

'She could be in Folkvang. Freya may have chosen her.'

It was no easy matter to tell the truths of the nine worlds to a man who thought he knew his gods. 'As Odin will surely tell you,' said Buntrugg. 'Freya may have chosen her every night. Spoken like a true follower of Odin.'

'I *am* a follower of the Alfather.'

'As are we all. He is not Midgard's father, he is the Alfather. We all wish to sit at his side and look out over the nine worlds.'

With a heavy sigh Einer closed his eyes and leaned his back against the wall. 'Why did you bring me here if you want me to leave?'

'Because you're family.'

One way or another, Einer would have ended up in the Alfather's halls. At least this way, it was in time for his wounds to not leave permanent damage; except for the arrow in his forehead. Besides, Buntrugg could offer an escape.

'It won't be easy. Outside this room there are eyes watching,' Buntrugg said. 'Even out there, in the big hall. When the warriors are there, others come too.' Everyone was watching the Alfather's moves, especially this close to the three-seasoned winter and the final battle of Ragnarok. The fire demons were already screaming for blood and terror. The end was near. All the beings in the nine worlds knew it, and all of their eyes fell on the great Alfather. He was watched, now more than ever.

'How?' Einer was so like his mother. He understood, and he wasn't afraid of anything, not even the Alfather, although perhaps he did not yet know that he needed to be afraid.

'You must fight your way out. During the daily battle on Ida's plain.'

'What will fighting do?'

'On the battlefield, there is a giant who can lead us away.'

'A giant on Odin's battlefield?'

'There are some who abandon their own and join the Alfather's masses in hope of better chances. Among these dishonoured giants, there is one who may help us escape.'

'How will I find him among all of those warriors?'

'When you see her, you will not be in doubt.'

'How will I find *you*?'

'I will leave tonight and I will be at her side.' Odin had asked Buntrugg to leave and return to Surt, so he would, but he fully intended to take Einer with him. 'You must fight your way to us. Fight your way to the giant ranks—without dying.'

'If I were to die, I would just try the following day. The

valkyries would simply wake me after the battle, as they wake all warriors who die on Ida's plain. And then I could try again.'

'You, Einer, are not all warriors.'

'A giant,' Einer mused. 'So that is the lineage you say I have. That is the home you want to show me.' He was quick for someone so young, and he was also not convinced, although he had to see that he was taller than most short-lived and that he had strength that most did not. He had to have felt the forefathers within him too, for Buntrugg could hear them whisper Einer's name.

The forefathers commanded him to take care of Einer, and Buntrugg would not fail them. They had saved him from early passage into their afterlife, and he had not forgotten that debt.

'The Alfather hasn't allowed me to leave this room,' Einer said. 'How am I to fight?'

He did not ask how he could be expected to fight while wounded and weak and weary, and he did not ask how to survive in battle, so he was confident in his abilities. Buntrugg hoped that Einer's confidence was justified, and that it did not rely on the forefathers, or they would all be doomed. No giant dared to release the forefathers in Asgard, out of fear of tearing the nine worlds apart.

'You must force the Alfather's hand and leave him no choice but to allow you into the big hall,' Buntrugg said. 'When I came in, you were about to leave, and so you shall. You will search for Hilda, as you had planned to do. You won't find her, but you will search, and then, when the Alfather and his valkyries come back, you will already be out of this room. He will own no arguments to keep you hidden any longer. You will have proven that you have healed enough to sit at his table and eat with his warriors. Then, you can convince him to let you watch the fight.'

'Why should I?'

'You owe me a favour,' said Buntrugg. 'When we met, in the snow, I told you that saving your life and bringing you to this place of healing would cost you a favour. This is it.'

Einer smiled a little at that.

Apart from the usual caution that all men ought to live with, Einer would have no reason not to trust Buntrugg. He had been brought to Valhalla before death; a chance given to none. He had been healed, mostly, and he would get to search for Hilda as he had meant to do. He had all the options, but he would follow Buntrugg's advice. Einer, too, knew to be wary of the Alfather who kept him hidden away in this room.

'Tomorrow, when you stand on Ida's plain and watch, join the battle. See what the Alfather does,' Buntrugg said. 'He will not stand by and watch you die. For, Einer, when you die, it is not your destiny to be seated in this hall and fight for the Alfather on those plains. That is not the afterlife that awaits you. The Alfather knows that as well as I do.'

'Of course it's my destiny,' Einer insisted, but his gaze was not as before, and they both knew that he was trying to convince himself that he truly would find Hilda in that hall. Although they both knew that he would not.

Einer limped towards the door, put a hand on the wood, ready to push it open, and stopped for a few heartbeats to address Buntrugg, one last time. 'See you on the battlefield, uncle.'

FINN

Chapter Ninety-Two

FINN'S HAIR HAD grown long enough to cover his ears and for him to feel like a freeman once more. He was a thrall and he ought to cut it, but he had no master nearby to tell him off, and he could serve Harald better if he did not look like a thrall. Although he was not eager to serve Bluetan, he was eager to no longer be treated like a thrall in the eyes of his shield-mates.

'I'll ride in first,' Finn told Thorbjorn.

Two dozen people had travelled north with him, and Thorbjorn was their overseer. He was in charge of all the men and all of the materials Harald had bought with the price of Finn's thraldom.

'You don't order me around.' Thorbjorn was a real freeman and land owner who thought himself above all others. But Finn was so much more.

'Harald put me in charge,' Finn reminded Thorbjorn. 'If I am to take charge of Ash-hill, this needs to happen on my terms. I know these people. If I arrive with all of you at my side, they will see it as their own success and not mine, and not that of

Harald. So I need to arrive first, and when you arrive, you are to put your men to work immediately exactly as we agreed upon yesterday.'

Thorbjorn grumbled at that, but he did not argue. Once, a grumble and lack of argument may have been enough for Finn, but in his current position, he could not be satisfied with so little. 'Do you understand, Thorbjorn?' he insisted. 'Can Harald count on your good word?'

'He can.' Thorbjorn matched Finn's gaze. His eyes were slim, as was his nose; all of his features were slim and sharp, and it gave him a mean look. He was not a man that others stood in the way of.

'I'll ride ahead, then,' Finn said.

He kicked his horse into trot and rode towards Ash-hill's cinders, clinging onto the horse.

Finn knew that the warriors who had wintered in Ash-hill would not welcome him kindly. They would disregard him, accuse him of never having gone to Jelling, of having stolen a horse, and of much worse things. He smiled at the thought of their surprise upon his return. He only wished that Einer had been among them.

The horse was reluctant, but Finn kicked it into gallop as they neared the end of the forest path, and prayed to the gods that he would not fall off. He raced to the path by the fields and up the way to Ash-hill.

There were warriors on the fields. They had not gotten far, but at least some of them had worked while Finn had been away. Now, with his help, they would be ready for spring when the children and other warriors could return home. They would be waiting in warm houses, with fields ready to farm, and animals to feed every household. Soon enough, they would be rich again, all thanks to Finn—and in a way, thanks to Einer, who had bound him as a debt-thrall.

The warriors on the fields yelled to each other and pointed at him. Finn rode on, pretending that he did not see them, as most rich men treated farmers. He was above them now, he told himself. He had left a thrall, but he returned as a chieftain.

He slowed the horse, relieved to be back to a manageable pace, and then he rode through the blackened gates and up the hill towards the ash stump.

There were more warriors inside the old village than on the fields. They had been busy after all, while Finn had been away. Most of the house pillars had been dragged away. Huge piles of ashes had been brought to the forest and laid at the tree roots around the town. A few more weeks and the old village would just be an empty hill with only the old stones in a circle by the ash-stump.

As expected, Hormod had assumed leadership. The old man did not work like the others, but instead rested in the inner circle, seated on one of the Ting stones. The one Vigmer had used to claim as his own; the chieftain stone.

'Why aren't you working when everyone else is?' Finn yelled to Hormod as he approached. His horse started at his loud voice. He tapped it on the neck for reassurance, as he had learned to do. Never before had he ridden so far on a horse. He had never been able to afford one. It was laughable that he was riding one now, when he owned nothing at all.

'Where did you steal a horse?' Hormod asked, exactly as Finn had expected him to do.

'I didn't steal it,' he replied and pulled back on the reins to halt the horse. 'I traded a bear for a horse. A fair trade.' He pulled back on the reins again. The horse didn't really listen to him, but it sort of stopped walking, and Finn glided off its back, relieved to stand on ground again. His legs were shaking with relief that he had survived another trip on horseback.

'No one could possibly be foolish enough for a trade like that in times like these,' said Hormod at his back. 'Tell us honestly: who did you rob?'

Finn fussed with the horse, tapped its neck as he had seen others do with their horses when they unmounted, and pretended that he was not terrified of the thought of riding it again.

'I didn't steal it,' Finn repeated. 'Although my tongue may have robbed the owner of his wealth.'

The warriors gathered at the top of Ash-hill to see Finn's return and hear what he had to tell about Jelling and Harald, and why he was here and not there. They expected excuses.

As he petted the horse's neck, he looked at the warriors at the corner of his eyes and he could see that they expected to have to kill him, or worse, condemn him to exile. No one would believe that Finn had escaped Jelling alive. Had it not been for Siv, he wouldn't have.

'You were supposed to go Jelling, and speak to Harald Gormsson,' Hormod said with the tone and air of a chieftain. He had waited for the warriors to assemble, as had Finn.

'You owe me seven-hundred-and-thirty-one arm-lengths of home-spun, Hormod.'

'What?'

'Seven-hundred-and-thirty-one arm-lengths of home-spun,' Finn repeated every word clearly. Then he turned to look at Hormod's shocked expression. 'You promised me one arm-length of home-spun for every word I spoke in the presence of Harald Gormsson.'

It was the proper count. During the travels up through Jutland to Ash-hill, Finn had been given plenty of time to re-live his conversations with Harald and count his own words. It had helped him to focus on something other than his fear of riding.

'So, you've been to Jelling? You've spoken to Harald?' Berg asked. Among all of them only the young ones who had helped Finn capture the bear seemed prepared to accept the truth and celebrate the victory. Young warriors were always ready to celebrate.

'I have, and Harald has granted me his support and sent me home to care for Ash-hill.'

'He did?' Hormod asked.

'He did.'

Finn had timed it all perfectly. He looked over the back of his horse to the forest, and right then, Thorbjorn and the others rode out of the forest. The men dismounted from their horses and began to empty the carts and release the oxen.

'He sent me back north with help,' Finn told the warriors who had not yet noticed Thorbjorn.

The clatter of Thorbjorn's men unpacking and unloading drew their gazes to the edge of the forest.

'You can start on the timber by the stables,' Finn yelled down to them, although they had already discussed the details earlier in the day. His voice echoed over the empty fields, and despite the distance, he thought he could hear Thorbjorn grumble over being given orders.

'You don't get to decide that,' Hormod was quick to say, and so were half a dozen other warriors who all thought they had more claim than Finn.

'I do,' Finn said. 'They're Harald's men, and Harald put me in charge.'

'Put you in charge?' they scoffed at him. 'In charge of what?'

'In charge of Ash-hill.'

They stared at him with blank faces.

'Quite simply, I am to be your chief from now on.'

'You will not!' Hormod decided at once, eager to defend his own claim to Ash-hill's chieftaincy.

'It won't be you either, Hormod. You aren't suited. You may be the eldest, but you haven't gained as much glory on the raids as half of the warriors who surround you.'

From the way the warriors looked at him, even Hormod had to know that he had lost his chance. 'Thora will be our chief,' he decided. 'We would have elected her if we hadn't chosen Einer.'

'And you think she will survive through the winter?' Finn said.

'She will live,' Hormod said aloud, as though to convince himself that it was true, but he wasn't convincing anyone else. 'She woke up back on the ship.'

'And blabbed about beavers for the three heartbeats that she was awake. She won't be able to walk again. And you want her to lead you? Do you truly want to put yourselves in the hands of a cripple who isn't here? I am here, and I am no cripple.'

Despite how Finn had survived the encounter with Harald, and despite how he had returned with hands and horses and pigs and sheep and half a hundred other things, and despite his convincing arguments, they did not want him as their chief. His reputation was stained by his lack of name.

Finn the Nameless, Siv had called him.

'You're as good as a cripple,' a shieldmaiden said and confirmed his thoughts. 'You're a thrall.'

'I may be, but that should only ensure my allegiance.'

'Your allegiance to whom? You couldn't have gotten all of that without giving Harald something.'

'I didn't gift him anything other than a bear.'

'Finn, what did you promise him?'

'He bought my thraldom from you all,' Finn shared, although he knew that the truth would not make it easier for them to trust him. 'That, down there, is his payment, if you choose to name me as your leader.'

'And if we don't?' Hormod asked.

'Well then you, Hormod, still owe me seven-hundred-and-thirty-one arm-lengths of home-spun, and I will take my services elsewhere. Ash-hill is not the only town in Jutland in need of help. If you judge that you do not need me, I will establish myself elsewhere.'

In a moment of silence the warriors stared over their lands to Thorbjorn and his men, who were already marching with their axes swung over their shoulders.

The pigs and sheep were tied up. The animals huddled together against the cold wind.

What Finn had arrived with was more than timber and men and animals. He had arrived with a chance at a new life, when all other hope had been churned to cinders, and he did not think it likely that Ash-hill's warriors would turn that down.

Out of the shade of the forest where Thorbjorn and his men had left the horses came a man in dark robes. Even seen from the Ting stones, he was clearly a Christian priest. No one else would be crazy enough to dress that way. The only stain on Finn's agreement with Harald had been that one Christian.

He had been given no choice. It had been part of Harald's final terms. As a Christian king, he had to ensure that Christianity was being practised in the lands he ruled over. Finn had been forced to agree, or there would have been no deal, and then, he certainly would not have escaped alive, despite Siv's help.

'You've brought a priest,' a small warrior remarked. 'I suppose you'll want us to keep the church and be Christian too.' The warrior spat at Finn's feet.

Others mumbled their mistrust, but Finn had known that they likely would.

'Do you truly know me so little?' Finn said. He did not like the presence of the priest either, but it was a condition that he could not change.

'Why else would you bring a priest?'

'The choice was between bringing a Christian or to be without shelter and food all winter, and starve all summer too. That's a choice I'll gladly make,' Finn told them.

He brought the horse closer to the Ting stones, and tied its reins to the stump of the ash-tree. None of the warriors watched him. They were all staring at Thorbjorn and his men, and in their ash-coloured clothes they looked like stone-cut statues from the south.

Finn marched back into their midst. 'Eh, you—Christian man, come up here,' he yelled to the priest who had stopped by Ash-hill's old church to examine the fine building.

The man startled at Finn's voice, but quickly made his way

up the hill towards them. No one spoke as he approached. No one but Finn. 'I mean to introduce you,' he said. 'What is your name?'

'Conrad,' said the man and he proudly joined Finn's side in the middle of the sacred Ting circle. He was unintimidated by the large crowd of northerners, although any foreigner ought to have been terrified. 'I am Father Conrad, sent here by the Bishop of...'

Finn gave Conrad a sharp tap on the chest to silence him before he could say any more. Finn was much larger than the priest, and his grip on the man's shoulder was firm and tight.

'This man is a fine priest. During these past few days of travelling I've had the full privilege of his preaching,' Finn loudly flattered. 'He has arrived to replace Pontius as priest and rule over that pretty Christian church down the road. From here on, he will be our priest and be allowed a seat at our Ting, as decided by King Harald.'

Conrad smiled shyly at the prospect, but the warriors had fallen silent and serious. The last thing they would have expected of Finn was to bring back a Christian to take part in their decisions. They knew him well, after all.

Finn smirked. 'And here is what I have to say to that.'

Quick as Thor's hammer, he removed his hand from Conrad's shoulder, clasped his old chopping knife and drew it. Before Conrad had time to realise what was happening, Finn plunged the blade into the priest's eye.

Conrad staggered backwards with a howl, screaming so horridly that Finn grimaced at the sound of it. With a kick, Finn made the man stumble and fall.

In a heartbeat, he straddled Conrad, planted a palm on the priest's face to keep it still and retrieved his knife. He rose to his feet again.

The priest rolled in the ashes, curled up and with his hands hovering over his face. Finn looked away to the many warriors. One by one they stopped gaping and focused on Finn. And when all of their eyes were on him and not the squealing priest anymore, he spoke again: 'Every last one of us will have to be sent to Valhalla before any Christian will be allowed to settle here again.'

He spat on the priest's face. Others did the same, and then Finn put a foot onto Conrad's chest, and with the knife sliced the priest's throat.

Conrad ceased squirming. His blood flowed hot over Finn's hands. Finn wet his hands in the blood, and then he took his hand to his face and marked his cheeks in offering to the gods.

'We are men of Odin,' he yelled. 'And for as long as we live, no Christian will have any say over our lands!'

EINER

Chapter Ninety-Three

EINER'S WEAPON BELT was heavy with its two swords and his chainmail rattled as he walked. He clasped a hand around the shaft of the Ulfberht blade. Finally, his father would regain his sword. Soon all wrongs would be righted, and Einer would be sitting at Hilda's side in Valhalla.

Friends, ship-mates and shield-mates waved to Einer from the last filled benches, at the far end of the Alfather's large hall.

'By Höd, Einer, who did you meet on Ida's plain today?' shouted his old friend Osvif with a teasing smile he had once learned from their mutual friend Leif. Osvif scooted over on the bench to make room for Einer to sit. His long red hair had been braided with beads. He must have found his wife in the afterlife. 'So you *were* up at the other end of the hall,' Osvif said. 'We thought you might be. The Alfather would be foolish not to invite you to sit at the high table.'

It was good to hear Osvif's voice again. Einer had not truly known how much he had missed it until he heard it. He sat down on the bench next to his friend. Osvif clapped him on the shoulder exactly as he had always used to do, and pulled Einer into a hug.

Despite the pain from the wounds under his chainmail and tunic, Einer smiled back without as much as a wince. 'It's good to see you.'

'You too, friend.' Osvif said and then he leaned over the table and yelled to a young warrior: 'I told you he wasn't too high and mighty to visit us, even if the Alfather had claimed him as his personal berserker.'

'I expected to see all of you up there,' Einer said. Instead they were here, at the far end of the hall. Rain dripped at their backs, over the last shields that made up the ceiling.

'It's not so bad. The mead is the same no matter where you sit in the hall. And the seats behind us will fill up soon.' Osvif was staring at Einer's forehead. Everyone always ended up staring at the arrow. 'Should we pull it out?'

'I'm told it might kill me, or worse.' The skin had healed around it, but the healers had refused to remove the arrow. All they could do was ensure that it would not kill him, unless someone pulled it out of his head.

'Suddenly afraid of death now that you know how much it hurts, eh, Einer?'

Death would be a welcome relief at this point, but Einer had more promises to live by. He leaned in and whispered so none of the others would hear. 'I'm not yet a warrior in this hall, Osvif.' He was not certain that it was an honourable deed to be in Valhalla without being dead.

'What? How?'

Einer shrugged. He did not really know why. 'The Alfather sent someone to fetch me and brought me here to heal my wounds.'

'Skál,' an old warrior yelled to Einer. Their talk interrupted, Osvif stuffed a mead horn into Einer's hand, and they drank. Every warrior at the table was smiling at Einer, eager to gain his attention. He had been their chief when they had died, he remembered. He straightened his back to look worthy of the title, despite his wounds.

Thus the drinking began. Einer moved along the bench, sat with each warrior and asked them one after another how they had been and what glory they had gained in Valhalla so far. And when he had been friendly enough to all, Einer asked the true question on his mind: 'Where has Hilda gone?'

Hilda was not among them, exactly as the reed cutter had warned him.

'Isn't she at the high table with you?' asked Arne who sat across from Osvif.

Einer shook his head. 'Freya's hall, perhaps?' he asked. 'She gets to choose first, right?'

'Each day,' Osvif confirmed, and kindly explained. 'She picks some lucky warriors at the end of each battle on Ida's plain to feast in her hall for a day or two, but everyone is led to Valhalla when they first arrive into this afterlife.'

The others looked confused as to why Einer did not know this, but they would not be suspicious. They would conclude that things were different at Odin's high table, and they probably were.

'Your father is there tonight,' Osvif said.

Einer removed his hand from the Ulfberht. He had hoped to deliver it, but it would not be tonight. There would be other nights, and he wanted to deliver it himself to let his father know that he had fulfilled his duties as a son and heir.

'Really, Einer, we need to do something about that arrow. I thought you were a narwhal when you walked towards us,' said Osvif, no doubt to make Einer think of other matters. 'Someone might pull it out during battle.'

Einer nodded. He had thought about that too. 'Can you chop the end off?'

'I guess so,' Osvif said and got to his feet. He tapped the table. Einer lay his head down onto it, cheek to the mead-sticky wooden surface.

'How in Asgard are you still alive?' Osvif mumbled as he saw the many fresh scars and more carefully examined the arrow through Einer's head.

Osvif grasped his axe by the axe-head. With a swift blow, he cut the arrow off, and then he placed the long, feathered bit on the table. Part of the fletching dangled off. It was strange to think that such a long arrow had been sticking out of his head all this time.

Einer groped his forehead and found the splintered arrow stump. It was impossible to get a solid grasp on it anymore. No one would be able to pull it during battle. One less thing to worry about on Ida's plain. He had already decided to fight his way across the battlefield. His uncle had been right about everything else. Hilda wasn't here.

'I suppose you won't stay, then,' Osvif said. He knew Einer well; from the mere look on his face, Osvif could tell what he was thinking about.

'Just for one more horn-full,' Einer replied and tapped Osvif on the shoulder.

Bald Arne frowned. 'But the horns have no bottom.'

The warrior's bench-mate elbowed him. 'That's what he means, Hammer-brain.'

Einer stayed to hear more about the glory they had gained in Valhalla, and their hopes and ambitions for the future. He laughed with them and drank so he could barely feel his feet or the bracteate hammering hot against his chest, or the pain in his body. He drank so much that he could no longer tell if Osvif sat on his right or to the left.

As Einer reached over the table for his sixth piece of meat, a hand clenched onto his shoulder so hard that even Einer noticed through his drunken haze.

A woman stood behind him. Not a shieldmaiden, but a valkyrie. The valkyries had left the hall, but there she was. Einer rubbed his eyes, but she was still there, staring at him, and her grip tightened.

'You are not here to feast,' she said without parting her teeth to speak. 'You are here to heal.'

'And I won't heal lying in bed.' His speech was not quite as clear as he intended for it to be, but he was proud that he could speak at all, so he continued in the hopes of being more convincing. 'I need conversation and movement if I am ever to heal well enough to fight again.'

Her stare was hard. He would not get her to budge, nor to remove her grip, unless he abided by her wishes.

'Those who passed on in the battle at Ash-hill are five tables in and two rows up,' Osvif told him as Einer got to his feet. 'Your father and the two dozen warriors who died with him moved up there before we arrived. We're still trying to strike a deal with the warriors at the next table to switch so we can sit with family.'

'I missed you,' Einer said, tapping Osvif on the shoulder, and he meant it. He missed Hilda too, but she was not the only one who had passed on in recent times. Had Einer been surrounded by friends, her passing may have been easier, because when he was alone, she was all he could think about.

The long walk back to the middle of the hall and the Alfather's high table sobered Einer, and by the end of it, he was almost able to walk without fear of tumbling over.

The high tables weren't really taller than the other tables, or raised in any way, but they had been arranged so that they crossed the width of the hall instead of the length like all of the other tables. There were no valkyries here either. There were so few of them left in the hall. During the long walk Einer had only seen two in addition to the one who forced him to march forward.

The Alfather was back. By the high tables, Einer could see him tower over the best of his warriors, and he looked at Einer as he spoke to them. Perhaps he was introducing Einer, or perhaps he was simply holding a speech. In any case, the Alfather looked cheerful and happy, quite unlike the valkyrie who urged Einer on; *she* looked ready to murder every last man in the hall, and then all of the shieldmaidens too.

'Come, Einer, come.' The Alfather's shout demanded as much respect as the best of skalds. 'Let me introduce you to your future bench-mates.'

Einer hastened his pace but the faster movements made his healing wounds hurt more. As the drink had unclasped its hold on his mind, and especially after he had filled up the piss pot about twenty tables down, the pain had snuck back.

The valkyrie who had hurried Einer's pace the entire way let him walk past the last few tables to the Alfather by himself. His feet were as heavy to lift as the chainmail that hung from his shoulders.

'This is Haskell.'

Einer had barely joined the crowd before the Alfather introduced him to the first man on the bench at the first high table. Haskell was handsome by any definition; a man carved from waves.

'And Frode,' the Alfather said, introducing the man who sat opposite handsome Haskell. Einer's heart warmed at the sight of Frode, who he liked immediately. Looking at Frode reminded Einer of his mother; he had the same eyes and nose, and his posture was straight like hers.

'Ove,' the Alfather continued, pointing to a man next to Haskell who bore long silky hair, and then continued on to 'Stig the Traveller,' who did indeed look like a sailor and traveller who had not seen land for a few weeks too many.

The Alfather skilfully balanced on the benches behind the men as he introduced them, to the sound of applause and laughter. He named them so quickly that Einer feared he would not remember a single name by the time they were finished.

'Tait. Viggo. Jary. Troels,' the Alfather continued without rest, and on he went, naming more warriors than Einer thought he could count.

Finally, the Alfather's long name recital ended. 'For many

summers now, a place has been reserved for you at this table.' It was the greatest honour one could hope for. 'Right here.'

The god showed Einer a place between handsome Haskell and silk-haired Ove. They both gestured for him to sit and assume his rightful position.

Einer edged along the side of the table. He lifted his weary legs over the bench to sit down on their chainmail. There was perfect room for him, as if they had always known that Einer would someday arrive to sit with them.

The chainmail-covered bench did not look it, but it was comfortable enough to sit on all day. Odin did not have a chair of his own, so he scooped behind the tables and positioned himself between warriors wherever he wanted to sit. Right now that was the seat directly in front of Einer.

The Alfather placed his elbows on the table and leaned in with a smirk, and somehow it felt like Einer and the Alfather had infiltrated an ongoing celebration at a local tavern somewhere. Only the two of them knew the secret that Einer was not yet supposed to be here. It felt like the first time Einer's father had taken him to a tavern over in Alebu, and they had entered and cheated their way to free drinks without his mother ever knowing that he had been in a tavern before he had taken his choice and become a freeman. It felt exactly like that to sit across from the Alfather at the high table.

It was all Einer had ever wanted, and yet it did not feel right. Because, unlike most warriors, Einer had never wanted a seat at this table for the glory it entailed, or for the riches, or fights, or feasts. He had dreamt of it because of the people who would sit at his side. It was Hilda's dream, and Einer would have followed her anywhere, even into her dreams.

'Where is she?'

'Who?' the Alfather asked back, although he knew exactly who Einer meant, for Einer had asked a dozen times already, when he had been lying in bed unable to move.

'I assume that you know of the battle in Magadoborg,' Einer

said. 'My warriors who fought at Magadoborg are seated in your hall. Among them there should be a shieldmaiden and runemistress who died at their side: Hilda of Ash-hill, daughter of Ragnar Erikson the late skald of Ash-hill.'

'Should be?' the Alfather asked.

'She gained more glory than many seated elsewhere in your hall.'

'She will be here soon,' said the Alfather.

Always fickle answers. The things Einer's uncle had told him gained more credibility with every word the Alfather spoke— or rather, with every word that he did not speak.

Einer knew that the Alfather was cunning, and he respected him for it, but this was more than that. These were the sort of tricks Einer had thought a prankster like Loki would play.

The answers Odin had provided were not good enough. The Alfather would not reveal Hilda's true whereabouts, exactly as his uncle had warned him would happen.

'She is with Freya,' said the Alfather then. He seemed to have guessed what Einer had been thinking, but it was the wrong kind of detail. The Alfather was lying to him, stalling him.

His uncle was right; he needed to get out of Valhalla.

HILDA

Chapter Ninety-Four

LAUGHTER WOKE HILDA. The laughter and talk of hundreds of warriors. Someone pounded on the table where her cheek rested. She lifted her head and rubbed her sore jaw.

It hurt to move, even to breathe. A bandage was bound around her ribs. Being impaled that way, she should not have been able to survive for long, but Freya was a goddess, and she had taken the time to heal her. So, it hadn't been a dream, then. She really had been stabbed and nearly killed by her goddess, and now she was seated in Freya's loud hall.

Like every room in Freya's great home, the walls and ceilings were draped in fabric. It was dark, too, lit only by fires. Hundreds and hundreds of people were inside. They were seated and walking between the countless tables, laughing and talking and singing. They were feasting, and among them sat Freya. The light shone perfectly on her. Everyone could see her. Men approached her from everywhere, complimented her and gifted her with their war riches. Freya accepted no gifts, but she basked in their compliments. She had a presence about her that made her feel superior. She didn't need to speak or point to get what she wanted. Everyone was eager to please.

She had killed Hilda. Or maybe she hadn't. It hadn't felt like dying. Not as it had in Magadoborg, and not just because it hurt this time. For a while Hilda sat to gather her wits. The table was filled with food and drink, but Hilda wasn't hungry. She hadn't eaten anything since Magadoborg.

Despite the pain, Hilda could no longer sit still. She had never been very patient.

Odin had abandoned her. The weight of the axe in her weapon belt reminded her what she needed to do. Leave this place, find her snow fox, find the Runes, deliver the axe, save Ash-hill, and join the ranks in Valhalla.

She began to walk along the hall and groaned in pain whenever she bumped shoulders with a warrior. The warriors noticed her, though in Midgard no one had. They stared at her as she passed them by. There were so many warriors, dressed for glory in chainmail and with expensive weapons, but there was something missing in the crowd. Something she couldn't quite place.

'Fetch me another one,' a short, drunk man shouted after Hilda. He could barely sit upright on the bench for he swayed so much.

Hilda snarled at him and he went quiet. Her eyes travelled over the crowd of Freya's selected warriors. The best warriors of Valhalla were chosen by the goddess to feast in this hall, but they were not perfect heroes as she had expected them to be.

Her eyes fell on a man standing by a table a few arm lengths ahead. She knew his bleached beard, and his eyes were so familiar that she could hardly believe them to be real. Einer's eyes. 'Vigmer,' she breathed.

Her old chieftain looked exactly as he had on his funeral pyre. His clothes were the ones Einer had chosen for him for the burial. His beard was combed in the same style, and he wore the healed scars of the battle wounds that had killed him.

'What are you doing here?' she asked. Immediately, she cursed herself for it. He was feasting, obviously. Chosen on the battlefield to feast in Freya's halls.

'So, you *are* here, after all.' He said it as if he had expected to see her earlier, elsewhere.

'Is Einer...?' she asked without really asking.

'Einer?' His eyes widened in horror at her unfinished questions. 'Is he...?'

'I don't know,' she hurried to say. She had thought that Vigmer would know. Einer was his son. If he had died in Magadoborg, he would know. He *should* know.

Vigmer's surprise settled at that. He took a drink from his horn, and with the drink, seemed to rediscover his old stance and confidence. He stood proud as the chief he had been and looked at her from above. When he straightened his back, he was still half a head taller than her.

'I didn't expect to see you here,' he admitted. 'So, you made it all the way to Magadoborg.'

So, these were the conversations of the afterlife. Tales about death and survival, and the worst of battles. 'Magadoborg, and beyond,' she corrected. 'You should have been there.'

'And now you're here,' said Vigmer. He looked her over with a gaze that seemed to suggest that there must have been a mistake. 'Magadoborg must have been glorious for you.'

'I don't have time for this, Vigmer,' said Hilda. Though she really meant to say that she had no *patience* for it. Einer's father had never acknowledged her like she deserved. She wouldn't allow him to dismiss her achievements. 'Freya is waiting for me.'

Vigmer laughed at that, but Hilda just strode past him. She pushed drinking warriors out of her way and marched on. She didn't need to walk all the way. Freya had already spotted her. To the surprise of all, the goddess swung her legs off the side of her chair and glided towards Hilda.

She was smiling. The goddess everyone wanted to be

acknowledged by was smiling at Hilda. She was larger than most of the warriors, but she had an elegance about her. She wore no under-gown, so her muscled thighs were visible from the side as she delicately put one foot in front of the other. Her toes were pointed towards the blooming floor. Every movement showed a warrior's control. Light of all colours shone on Freya's face from the jewelled ceiling. Her kohl-lined eyes made her look fierce.

Everyone was staring. Hilda hoped that Einer's father, too, was watching and would finally see that he should have let her come on the raids all those summers ago, when she had first asked, instead of conspiring with her father to keep her in Jutland.

'Awake at last,' Freya said as she reached Hilda. 'You look better. Come with me.'

Hilda had no time to answer before Freya had glided past her and out of earshot. She ran to catch up and together they walked through the hall. Freya's stride was fast as a man's, but Hilda followed easily. She looked over her shoulder, and noticed Vigmer gaping after them. His face was washed pale with horror. Hilda struggled not to laugh, and followed Freya through the loud hall.

'Don't gloat too much,' Freya warned. 'I assume you still care about this... Einer.'

'How do you know about Einer?' Hilda blurted.

'I hear every conversation in my hall,' Freya said quietly, for no one but Hilda to hear. 'Gossip is why I choose the warriors that I do. There is much to learn from Odin's warriors when their stomachs are filled with mead and they think you can't hear them.'

She seemed proud of it, though spying on Odin ought to be anything but a proud deed. Hilda had thought that the vanir and aesir were on the same side. There seemed to be no reason to listen to the gossip of Odin's hall, except... Maybe things were not as simple in Asgard as Hilda had assumed.

'What do you know of the snow fox?' asked Freya.

Her snow fox was there. Hilda knew it wouldn't have abandoned her. The thought made her chest warm. She peered around the hall to find it. Warriors were staring at her and Freya. Hilda searched through the tangle of their legs and in the shadow of the tables, and spotted brown fur. For a heartbeat, she thought it was her snow fox, but her fox had already shed its brown summer fur in favour of a white puffy coat. The brown fur belonged to a cat. Hilda's snow fox was nowhere. 'Where is it?'

'What is it to you?' Freya insisted.

'The snow fox is my fylgja.' Hilda revealed.

The surprise didn't easily show on the goddess' face, but her lined eyes narrowed, ever so slightly.

As Hilda followed Freya and searched through the thick crowd of dead warriors for her snow fox, the feeling that something was off came again, and suddenly Hilda knew what was missing. In a crowd such as this, she should have seen hundreds and thousands of fylgjur. Freya's hall was devoid of animal companions. A few cats lounged around the hall, but no fylgjur. Hilda knew that it was not because she had lost the ability to see the animals. It was because dead warriors had no fylgjur. That explained Freya's surprise.

Hilda followed her goddess into a hallway with a hundred and twenty doors without seeing as much as the flick of a white tail. Her snow fox wasn't in the hall, but the brown cat from earlier followed them out. They walked fast down the hallway. Muffled yells and music from the feast came from the hall, and then Freya pushed open a door that led outside into the night.

The fresh air cooled Hilda's skin, but the Runes didn't whisper to her in the wind.

'Where is my fox?' Hilda asked again. The snow fox had to be why Freya had brought her out here, but Freya was already walking across the plain away from her hall. The brown cat darted off into the night too.

Hilda skipped along to catch up, but buckled over with pain from her stomach, and settled for a crabbed jog with a hand pressed over her wound.

It was a moonless night. The stars shone bright. A thunderstorm raged in the distance.

'Do you know these stars, Hilda?' Freya asked, staring up at the sky as she walked away from her enormous hall, shaped like a ship flipped upside down.

Hilda trotted behind Freya and followed the goddess' gaze. She searched for the North Star and the Fisher star, but found neither. Maybe it was too late in the night, or maybe they hadn't come out yet, but they ought to be there. It was a moonless night, after all. She searched for other formations that she knew, but found none. These stars weren't the ones that Hilda knew. Sudden fear gripped her.

'Ja... Me too,' Freya whispered. 'These stars are strangers to me. Every night I look up at them, but I don't know their names. I never cared to learn. I wasn't going to stay here. We were just war prisoners, and when the war was over we would be sent home to Vanaheim. That's what I thought.'

'Why weren't you?'

'Oh, we were.' Freya sighed. She was still staring up at the stars. 'But by then our home was no longer our home. My best friend called me a spy of Odin's. So, we returned.' Freya slowed her fast walk so Hilda could catch up.

Even when she rushed along, Freya was so clearly a goddess. Her steps were elegant, and the touch of her bare feet on the cold grass left a trail of fresh flowers.

'That is why I'm here, in Asgard, although I don't belong,' Freya said. Her voice was strong but it had a ring to it that made it feel like a dream. 'Why are *you* here?'

'I've come to speak to the council of gods,' Hilda said.

'The council of gods?' Freya asked. 'What is that?'

'I come with an offering and a request for Ash-hill to regain the protection of the aesir.'

Freya scoffed. 'The aesir,' she muttered and sped away from Hilda again. 'Always the aesir.'

'And the vanir,' Hilda was quick to add, running to follow. Her wound hurt like it was bleeding again, but right now that didn't matter. Hilda couldn't afford to offend a goddess; least of all Freya. The aesir and vanir were both important, even if most folk back in Midgard knew more aesir names than vanir ones. 'We need your blessing to survive,' Hilda begged. 'And those of your brother.'

'And Odin, I suppose,' Freya said. She sounded angry.

'Anyone who will help us,' Hilda said. She had intended to seek the help of the Alfather, but here, in the presence of the almighty Freya, it struck her that any god or goddess might help Ash-hill.

Another thought, too, crept into her mind as she ran to catch up again. Freya was a goddess well acquainted with the Runes. Almost as well as Odin, almost as powerful, and she was right there, while the Alfather was a world away.

'What do you know of the Runes?' Hilda asked. Freya slowed her walk at her question. 'I used to hear them in the wind,' Hilda added. 'They whispered.'

The goddess spun back. Her darkly lined eyes stared straight into Hilda's. They looked shaped by ice, but her stare was warm like spring. 'The Runes,' she mused. 'Why do *you* hear the whispers?'

She didn't wait for Hilda to answer, which was good because Hilda had no answers to give. Freya's red robes swayed around her as she turned away. She moved quickly, yet every movement was calm. Somehow, with all of her contradictions and questions, Freya reminded Hilda of the Runes.

'The wind is silent now,' Hilda said, mimicking the nostalgic tone Freya had spoken in when they had examined the night-sky. 'Can you return the Runes to me?'

Freya brought them further and further across the field, but her pace had slowed considerably.

Absentmindedly, Hilda brought her right hand onto the hilt of the Ulfberht axe. She itched to blood her eyes again as she had in Midgard. Her eyes neither hurt nor needed it, but it was strange to not have blood run down her cheeks and to not feel it dry in the wind. Everything had changed. Her eyes no longer needed blood and the wind was silent. She needed to change things back to the way they had been.

Hilda freed the Ulfberht axe from her belt, held it so the sharp blade rested flat on her palm. As such, she presented it to her goddess. 'An offering, to you,' she said. She didn't want to be parted from the axe, but it had never been hers. It had always been meant as a gift for the gods.

'I have my own weapons,' said Freya without looking.

'If not a weapon, then what do you need?' Hilda sheathed the axe again, and her heart felt at ease. She wouldn't have to part with it. At least not now. A worry crept in too, because she had come so far following the Runes' instructions and wishes, and suddenly she didn't know what they wanted her to do anymore. They had known so much. They had to know that Freya would refuse the axe, so who had it been meant for? *South-forged will be a weapon offering to please*, they had said. But it hadn't pleased Freya.

The Runes had wanted her to cross Bifrost and come to Asgard. They must have had a specific plan for her. They wouldn't lead her astray.

'What do *I* want?' Freya repeated. 'I want the sun, the moon, and all the stars in the sky to tie onto a neck-ring.'

For a few heartbeats, Hilda thought that was all the goddess would say, and just as she was about to ask for a proper answer, Freya spoke again.

'I care about what happens to us after we die. After Ragnarok.'

'There is nothing after Ragnarok,' Hilda said, certain of herself. Everyone knew that the gods and many warriors who died at Ragnarok would never return, Freya included. 'At Ragnarok we die, and that is that.'

Freya did not dispute it, but there had to be more to it. She was a goddess, and she was not a stupid one. A stupid vanir, taken prisoner during the time of war between gods would not have survived for as long as Freya had. Not only had Freya survived, she had thrived. She was more famous than most aesir. She was respected and known, and Hilda knew better than to dismiss a goddess's warning.

'And you, Hilda, what do you really want? Is it the safety of your town, or your... Runes?'

'I just want things to go back to the way they were,'

Frey released an agreeing sigh. *'To begin with, the beginning had not begun,'* she recited.

Hilda had heard that verse before. In the runemistress's hut, moments before she had first been able to hear what the whispers in the wind said. On her own, Hilda continued the verse: *'Because change changes and does not change back.'*

Although they walked several steps apart, it felt as if there was no distance between them at all as they said the last verse together. Their voices mingled and their lips moved in the same heartbeat: *'And, in the end, the ending will not come to an end.'*

Hilda hardly dared to breathe. The verse must have been given to the runemistress by the gods themselves, or Freya would have no reason to know them. 'What does it mean?'

Freya was both cold and soothing. Like the calm, unmoving, yet frightening image of an iceberg that stretched into the depths of cold waters. Freya was like that.

'Hilda,' the goddess said. It was the first time she had uttered Hilda's name, and it felt right to hear her say it. 'We all have a past we would like to go back to, but that time is gone. *Change changes...*'

'*And does not change back,*' Hilda muttered.

Freya stopped in front of Hilda and bent down so their eyes were level, and their noses almost touched. So close that Hilda thought Freya might kiss her. Her breath smelled of a rye field in spring. Freya's lips twisted into a grin. 'What makes you think that the voices in the wind were the Runes?' Then she swept away and continued their march through the night.

If they weren't the Runes, she didn't know what they were. They had always been the Runes to her. The same ones that her father had said that he could see, near the end, when he had been dying.

Hilda hurried to catch up. What Freya had said turned in her head. If they weren't the Runes, then what could they be? And why weren't they with her anymore? Whatever they had been, she wanted them back. She felt naked without the Runes whispering to her.

'How can I get the Runes back?' Hilda demanded to know as she walked in Freya's flowery steps. Half of the field seemed to have bloomed with flowers and fresh leaves from the goddess' steps.

'I told you the whispers aren't the Runes,' Freya sighed. 'The whispers in the wind speak to you *through* runes, but they are not "the Runes." Runes don't speak. They obey.'

'Then what are they?' Hilda hissed through grit teeth.

'Hilda, daughter of the Skald of Ash-hill,' said Freya. 'In the river, your corpse rots,' said Freya in the exact words of the Runes. A chill travelled down Hilda's back. 'The Hanged God has abandoned you.'

Hilda's breath caught in her throat. The first words that the Runes had whispered to her in the wind. Some of their last ones too.

'It was you?' Hilda stammered. It had been Freya. Runemistress among goddesses.

'Why would I waste my time like that?' Freya dismissed.

'Then who?'

Hilda should have known she wouldn't gain a straight answer from Freya. Everything in Asgard was a clue, and everything was a riddle. Like one of her father's old stories. A day in Asgard was like a constant battle to stay ahead. To be cleverer than everyone else. And today, Hilda was losing.

Tomorrow was another day, Hilda decided, and today was still long. The sun hadn't even come up yet. 'Where are we going?'

'You said you're here to speak to a council of gods,' Freya said quite simply. 'That's where we're going.'

Hilda's father had always taught her that gods and goddesses respected clever conversation. And she knew that she needed Freya's respect to gain answers. Though she wasn't sure what a clever response would be.

'And my snow fox?' she asked.

'It's out there,' Freya said without pointing out where *there* was. 'Following us.'

Hilda stared through the night. She could see so much in the dark, more than she ever had when she had been alive. Freya's cat was following them, but Hilda saw no white tail.

Freya's robes trailed behind her flowery steps. Without thinking to do so, Hilda had begun to copy her, walking on the ball of her feet instead of her heels, but if anything it made her feel *less* elegant than her usual stomping.

Why Freya wanted her so much was a mystery to Hilda. She knew why the Alfather wanted her. She had fought her entire life to earn a place in his hall. He had to recognise her talent and skill. Freya, too, was a warrior, but that couldn't be why she had insisted on keeping Hilda. Something else was going on. 'Why did you fight with Odin over me?'

'I would stand up to Odin over a pair of socks,' Freya said, 'if it were the right pair.'

A pair of socks. That was all Hilda was to the mighty goddess Freya. A sock to hold her interest for a little while and then be discarded without second thought when something better came along.

'Then what do you want from me?'

Freya laughed a little—at least, Hilda thought it was laughter, though it sounded more like the purr of a cat. 'I want you to find your whispers again,' Freya said. 'So that you can bring me to Loki.'

'I already told you where he is.'

'You told me where he *was*,' Freya corrected. 'He could be anywhere in the nine worlds by now.'

'And you think the Runes know where he is,' Hilda realised. Suddenly she understood why she was valuable enough to Freya for the goddess to fight the Alfather. 'So you will give me back my Runes?'

Freya purred another laugh, and looked at Hilda over her shoulder. 'You have always heard the whispers, haven't you?' she asked. She could not have known it; Hilda had never told anyone. It wasn't something Hilda had ever wanted to say aloud or admit. Yet she nodded her head in response. 'My whole life,' she said.

'Then—if you were born with the ability to hear the wind whisper, why do you think that we, gods and goddesses, could possibly take it away from you, or give it back?'

The way Freya spoke reminded Hilda of her brother, Leif. She used the same tone he had. Amused, and keen to poke Hilda's interest. 'Come,' said Freya over her shoulder. 'We're nearly there.'

Hilda peered ahead. A hall was edged in shadows ahead of them. Freya's brown cat had settled in front of it. The hall seemed to have appeared out of nowhere, or out of mist. Behind them, Freya's feast hall was gone. Asgard truly was a strange place.

'If you didn't take the Runes from me, then why did they stop whispering?' Hilda asked, but received no answer. She was tired of the way gods and goddesses wrapped themselves in secrets instead of saying what they wanted or what they really meant. Hilda just wanted the truth, plain and simple. 'Can you help me hear them again or not?'

'Oh, we can help you,' Freya said without as much as glancing back to see that Hilda had stopped following her. They had arrived at the hall cloaked in mist. She pushed open a door and vapour from inside floated into the night, dripping like rain over Hilda.

The door swung back behind the goddess and her cat, and Hilda had to run to catch it with a foot. She entered the vapour-heavy room behind Freya. Women were giggling further into the hall. One step into the steamy hall and Hilda already felt the sweat bead on her forehead.

'Well, what did you think?' said a young woman somewhere. She could hardly stop her giggles. 'She certainly didn't marry him for Mjolnir's short shaft.'

Women whooped and howled with laughter. Freya chuckled in a cat-like purr with them as she gestured for Hilda to go further into the hall, ahead of her. Hilda proceeded carefully, towards the laughing women's voices.

'He is actually not,' another woman began. Her pleasant voice echoed out from further into the bathhouse, but she was quickly cut off by others.

'You don't have to pretend to save his honour, Sif.'

'We've all seen him.'

'Like Bragi is much better,' Sif retorted, her voice no longer as pleasant.

The girls fell quiet at that.

'Not that you need to know,' said the giggling goddess who had first spoken. The giggles were entirely gone now. 'But my husband has a runic tongue, and he knows how to use it.'

Again there was chaos as girls and women alike laughed and howled and splashed with water.

'Girls, girls, we better quiet down before Freya arrives and starts crying, again.'

'Why? I could use some gold for a new arm-ring,' said the giggling woman.

The stories Hilda's father had told seemed to come alive. Freya who cried gold tears over her husband's leaving. Sif defending the honour of her man. All the stories Hilda's father had told her, seemed to come to life in this bathhouse.

'Well, Idun, I'm not in the mood to gift you a new arm-ring,' Freya snarled into the vapour.

Sif and now Idun. The laughing women were the goddesses. All of them. Hilda froze. This was their bathhouse and though Freya had ushered her inside, Hilda didn't think that she was worthy to bathe with goddesses.

'I have news,' Freya called into the vapour, hugging her arms around Hilda's waist to unbuckle her weapon belt. The axe loudly clanged to the floor, and then Freya pushed Hilda forward.

'Well what is it?' asked an impatient goddess who was neither Sif nor Idun.

At last, Hilda came far enough into the bathhouse to see the women. They were robed in flowing silks, like Freya, but theirs were of lighter colours compared to Freya's deep red. Half of them were soaking in a steaming bath, large like the ones Hilda had heard stories about. The other half sat on the edge, playing with their feet at the surface of the water. Goddesses, all of them.

Freya's cat walked behind them, rubbing its fluffy tail along the goddess' backs, and there were other animals too. A great red deer was half hidden in mist, and a squirrel paddled through the water.

Hilda lifted her chin high, a warrior waiting to go into battle. She grabbed the edges of her tunic with her hands, and kept her jaw tight.

'Glumbruck left Midgard,' Freya announced to the audience.

'How do you know?' asked a woman seated at the edge of the water whose arms and fingers clinked of gold arm-rings. A viper snaked around her arms, like another gold ring.

'Your husband told me.'

Her husband. It was Odin who had told Freya, so the gold-rich woman with the viper had to be Frigg. Hilda could hardly think for the sight of goddesses. Most of them were watching her; she tried to keep her eyes lowered.

'The valkyries will be searching for her already.'

'I bring worse news,' Freya said, pushing Hilda forward. 'This one flew in wearing my falcon skin. Loki is free.'

'Then...' said the giggling woman who was Idun. She was young, round-faced.

Freya nodded before Idun could say anything more. 'Ragnarok is near. Soon we will die.'

'So you've just come to ruin a perfectly good bathing morning, then?' said a brown-haired woman who looked suspiciously like Freya.

'Nej, Hnoss,' Freya said in a scolding tone to her daughter. 'I brought entertainment.' She pushed Hilda further into the steam of the bath-house. 'A short-lived who hears whispers in the wind. With her, we will capture Loki before Ragnarok befalls us. With her on our side, we might just survive.'

SIV

Chapter Ninety-Five

THE SIGHT OF Asgard lulled Siv into a false sense of ease. Water gurgled in the creek to their left that Siv could no longer name. It had been centuries since she had last been here.

Asgard's beauty caught her off guard. The sunlight was so bright, and warm on her skin. The sound of running water and bees buzzing dazed her. Then she remembered their peril. All passageways to Asgard were guarded. Odin would know that she had come. His valkyries would be coming for them. Siv took Tyra's hand and made her hurry.

It was late summer in Asgard. Green grass full of blue flowers reached Siv's ankles. Her feet slid through the perfect grasses as she rushed along the plain towards the creek, dragging Tyra along.

Siv had used every passageway to Asgard at least once before. She had picked with care. The empty grave out of which they had arrived was far from everything, and the furthest from Valhalla. Out of all the passages into Asgard, this one gave them the biggest chance of disappearing into the eternal shade of Yggdrasil before Odin and his valkyries caught up.

When they reached the creek, Siv let go of Tyra's hand. The water was edged by a row of trees with dark red leaves. If they stuck to the cover of the trees, the valkyries would not spot them so easily when they came flying in their raven and crow skins.

Tyra was half-running to keep up with Siv's fast pace. It would not be an easy few days of travel for her. It would have been a difficult journey with or without Tyra, but at least with Tyra at her side, Siv knew that she would be more likely to keep going until the end and reach the Hall of Fates. Had she been alone she never would have taken the same route.

'Where exactly is the Hall of Fates?' Tyra asked. She was whispering, as if she were afraid that the bees and butterflies might hear, and rightly so.

'Do you see the mountains?' Siv asked and nodded to the horizon. There were many mountains and they were far away, casting long shadows over the lands this far into the evening. One of those mountains was not a mountain at all, but a vast tree, the top of which was buried in clouds. Yggdrasil.

'Is that really...?' Tyra couldn't even finish thinking her sentence, she just stared.

'It really is,' Siv confirmed. 'The tree of life.' Even from this far away, it was pretty. Sunshine painted the leaves golden, though it was impossible to see the leaves themselves this far away, just their shimmer. 'Come,' Siv said. 'We have a long way to go.'

Tyra had slowed to look at Yggdrasil in all its pride and beauty, but they could not waste a single heartbeat. Not until they were safe in the Hall of Fates.

Tyra half-ran, half-skipped after Siv. 'We need to go to Yggdrasil? But it's so far away.'

'Everything in Asgard is far away,' said Siv.

In Midgard, such a distance would have taken them weeks to cover—at least—but in Asgard, time and distances were different for those who knew the lands. When she had lived here, Siv had walked all the short-cuts in Asgard but one. She could get them to the Hall of Fates within days, though it would not be a pleasant few days. They would have to travel the only perilous way Siv had never travelled before. In the eternal shade of Yggdrasil they would walk, and there was no place darker or more dangerous in all of Asgard.

Alone she could never have taken that road, so the Alfather would not expect her to choose it. As long as they reached Yggdrasil's shade without being seen, they had a chance of disappearing from the Alfather's hawk eye until they were exactly where they needed to be.

They moved across the plain by the creek at a hasty pace. Ahead was the treeline of Star-given Woods. In a little while, the sun would descend far enough for Yggdrasil's shade to reach those woods. In the night, Siv and Tyra could more easily move towards Yggdrasil's eternal shadow, and reach it before morning bathed Asgard in sunlight again.

All they needed to do was reach the treeline of Star-given Woods without any trouble, and Siv had made certain they would have the time. The passage she had chosen was on the far side of Yggdrasil, so far from Valhalla, that it would take the Alfather and his valkyries a full day to travel the distance. By then, Siv and Tyra would be marching in Yggdrasil's shade.

The only thing that was close to Star-given Woods, and this passage grave, was Heimdall's home, but it was bath-day and Heimdall was at the high aesir bathhouse, so he would not be here in time to stop them either; not if they hurried.

Siv took Tyra's hand and rushed her along the plain. Once they were in the woods, they could take short cuts through it to reach Yggdrasil faster, but on the plain, they had to travel in a straight line, and any of the birds that flew overhead could be gods in disguise or valkyries—or worse, Odin. A bird in flight would be much faster than them.

'We will be safer once we reach the woods,' Siv told Tyra.

They raced through the high grasses, as fast as Tyra's legs would take her past the creek, and straight to the woods.

A strong wind blew in from the left. Immediately Siv let go of Tyra's hand. Tyra ran a few more paces ahead before she realised that Siv had stopped, but it was already too late.

It was bath-day in Asgard, Siv was certain of it. She had counted the days carefully. Yet here stood Heimdall, in his full strength and terror.

He must have been on his way to the bathhouse, for his beard was untrimmed, his clothes plain white, and in his belt he carried no weapon, but shears, clippers, and tweezers.

His skin was almost translucent, like that of an alf. He was nearly small enough to be mistaken for an alf, but he was round and had the lungs of the wind itself. He sucked in a deep breath, readying to scream and warn all of Asgard that Glumbruck was there, in front of him. Ready to compel every soul in Asgard to chase her, not just the valkyries and Odin.

'You shouldn't,' Siv told him, taking a battle stance without reaching for her weapon. 'Not if you intend to live until Ragnarok when Loki can kill you.'

She clenched her fists tight, feeling the forefathers stir within.

The breath went out of him. 'You wouldn't,' Heimdall said. His eyes darted to Siv's hands.

She opened and closed her fists, calling on the forefathers, although it was the last thing any giant would have thought to do. Even valley giants knew not to unleash the forefathers this close to the tree of life. The forefathers would tear her apart from the inside.

Heimdall took a step back as he examined Siv, and saw her resolve. All beings in the nine worlds were rightfully terrified of the forefathers. 'You wouldn't,' he repeated, hand slowly reaching for the shears in his belt.

'How well do you really know me? We've only met that once,' she reminded him. He looked exactly as he had then, centuries ago. Asgard, too, looked exactly as it had. Nothing ever changed here, for better or worse.

Heimdall's stance relaxed slightly, and he frowned trying to remember what he truly knew of her, and if she could be trusted. If he had been an alf, he would have used his ears instead, and listened to the truth on her heartbeat, but although Heimdall looked like an alf, he was not one.

'You danced with my mothers,' he recalled. 'They were fond of you.'

'They were good dancers,' Siv confirmed, well aware that Tyra was standing there committing every word to memory.

Tyra had retreated to stand behind Siv, out of Heimdall's way, and Siv could hear her quickening heartbeat. Heimdall too had noticed her, but he steered his sight back to Siv's fists.

'Why would you risk it?' he asked. His own hands were firm on his belt, edging towards the shears. 'You'll be lost to them, and then you will die.'

Siv did not answer, for no aesir would understand. Only those who had disobeyed Odin's wishes could understand that the alternative was worse than a painful death.

Heimdall stared at her for a moment. His heartbeat was steady and calm, and his eyes searched her face, as though trying to remember what she had looked like without her wrinkles. 'Of all the beings in the nine worlds, why you?' he finally asked.

'That's a question for him, not for me,' said Siv.

'Why are you here?' Heimdall asked, his voice grim as he circled closer. His hand fondled the shear clasps. 'I thought I wouldn't see you until you burned on a funeral pyre. After what you did...'

While Siv had not left Asgard on good terms with the Alfather or any of the aesir, she had done nothing to warrant this hatred—and then she realised what must have happened. 'I should have known Odin would blame it all on me,' she said aloud. 'It's always easier to blame a giant. Blame Loki. Blame Glumbruck. Let us pay for the deaths *you* all caused.'

'You haven't paid for anything.'

'I've paid. A hundred times over,' she hissed at him. Heimdall could tell her that he wished her dead, or attempt to kill her himself, but she would not allow him to dismiss the loss she had experienced at the Alfather's hand. 'Odin has killed and taken all of my children,' she told him. 'Every child. Killed them before their time, and claimed them as his.'

Her heart cried for her many children as she remembered their names and faces.

There had been Frode. Out of all of her sons, he had looked the most like her. His chin and eyebrows had been sharp, his hair had a red-brown glow and to hear him laugh had been like hearing herself. It had driven her father mad to never be able to tell which one of them had decided to mock him. And then he had died.

There was Ove with his long silken hair and a lust for axes and ladies. He had given her granddaughters who had made her wish for daughters of her own.

Haskell who had been outlawed, like her, but who had still known how to laugh and joke.

Viggo, Jary and Troels who had been taken each after the other during their first summers as warriors and freemen.

Stig who had travelled the world and hardly ever been home, until suddenly he had left and never come back and she had known that Odin had claimed him. His wife and children had searched for him for dozens of summers.

Tait who had given her grandsons like no other, and Thorbjörn's unnamed son who had been frail and delicate in her arms the days up to his passing. They had all passed on too soon, but Thorbjörn's son had never even been granted a name.

Finally, she thought of Einer's warm smile and how much she missed him. He had been so easy to raise. He had listened to advice and understood that Siv did not give warnings lightly. She supposed he was with his brothers now, in Odin's hall.

Anger and sorrow flooded Siv as she thought of them and

remembered the pain she always kept buried deep within. The forefathers surged forth and begged to be let out, to ruin all of Asgard, but Siv knew that she could not let them go, unless there was no other way out, so she kept them clenched tight in her fist, and swallowed her sorrow.

'He has killed every single one of my children. Except for her,' Siv gestured to Tyra, and if Heimdall had been looking for a chance to attack Siv before she could call on the forefathers, that had been it, but although she saw his muscles tighten, he never moved his shears.

'You married?' Heimdall asked instead, as if that was all that mattered. As if the deaths of her children meant nothing because she had loved more than one person in her life.

'Odin takes what he wants,' Siv said, focusing back on what was important, and watched Heimdall's response. She heard his heartbeat speed up, and knew that he was going to attack. 'You all do. Well, I won't let you take me, and I won't let you take her.' Siv unsheathed her seax.

As she had predicted, Heimdall was battle ready before her. His beard-shears were in hand before Siv had released the seax from her weapon belt. He lunged before she did. But she let him come. She was trained in the battles of Ragnarok and although she had never seen Heimdall fight, she knew his every move.

Siv's seax clanged against his shears. Heimdall deflected the attack, exactly as she expected him to do. Deep he breathed to fill his lungs as he pounced. His left hand reached for her neck. Siv ducked away from him. She did not dare to blink. To fight without the help of the forefathers was not the same, and it had been many centuries since she had fought a long-lived.

Siv evaded Heimdall's blow, and conjured the rune of ice on him. His breath became shallow. His teeth clattered. He wouldn't be able to use the wind to attack. His stare hardened and locked Siv's seax between the blades of his shears.

He pushed up to free his weapon from hers. He could have

pushed further and stabbed her as surely as she could have stabbed him, if she had tried. Heimdall could have killed her, but he had not.

It was not a mistake; aesir never hesitated. He had *chosen* not to go for a deadly blow. It had to mean that the Alfather wanted Siv alive, and that was her advantage.

'Are you certain of your move?' she asked him, not stepping away, although she could have. She retrieved her runes, and let the ice retreat from Heimdall's core where she had conjured it.

'I'm here. I'm already doomed.' He realised that coming to the edge of Star-given Woods had been a fatal mistake. He could not kill her, for the Alfather did not want her dead. He could not capture her alive either, and he could not say that he had arrived too late. The Alfather caught the best of lies.

Heimdall was in worse peril than Siv and Tyra, and he knew it. Perhaps he had rushed to Star-given Woods, precisely because he had been certain Siv would take another path from the passage grave.

'Let us go,' Siv requested.

Heimdall scoffed at the suggestion. 'No one lies to the Alfather.'

Indeed, the Alfather was not an easy man to lie to, but Siv knew how. She had grown up with giants.

'Tell him that you came, that our weapons clanged and that I left before you could capture me. All of it would be true. You know who I am, Heimdall,' Siv reminded him. Although he had never seen her fight, he knew her name and who she was. 'You know you can't capture me alive. You know that I would rather use the forefathers and kill us both than die at your hand. Even if you could kill me and keep your life, do you think Odin would forgive you?'

Heimdall relaxed his stance. He did not lower the shears, but Siv lowered her seax, and took a few steps away from him, gesturing for Tyra to continue on their road, and quickly.

'You look older,' Heimdall said, as he let them leave. Age was unknown in Asgard, where everyone ate gold apples to stay youthful and unchanged. Siv knew that she did not look as she had, but she cherished her fine wrinkles and her age. She had never understood why the gods ran from their age and from time.

'You don't,' Siv told Heimdall who looked exactly like he had when they last seen each other, and then she picked Tyra up and rushed into the forest.

Far and fast she carried them through Star-given Woods. Siv increased her height to carry Tyra with more ease and ensure that their pace was quick. They couldn't afford to slow down. Animals were following them at the edge of the forest. They needed to reach Yggdrasil's shade before Heimdall changed his mind, and before Odin's valkyries arrived.

The nearby forest stirred with the knowledge of her presence. Pheasants and deer peered at Siv. She returned their stares and sensed them hop along into the forest and warn others that Glumbruck had returned.

It would not be long before all of Asgard knew that she had come home.

The sun set and the woods darkened, but the stars lit the path for them, and early into the night, Siv spotted a thick tree root; one of Yggdrasil's. Following it would lead them straight to the tree trunk and from there it was a short hike in the sun to reach the Hall of Fates. If they timed it right, they might even find cover in the morning mist.

Yggdrasil's root disappeared quickly into a dark so complete that even the stars did not brighten the path. Siv looked up to the crown of trees. There were no stars directly above them anymore; the great ash's outer branches shielded them from above. This was where the eternal shade of the tree of life began.

At the edge of Yggdrasil's shade, Siv slowed her pace for the first time since they had met Heimdall. She set Tyra down and conjured a flame. It would not be easy to keep it lit in

Yggdrasil's shade, but a natural flame could be extinguished by a night breeze.

'Stay close to the flame, Tyra,' Siv warned as they walked into the dark woods. 'It will keep them away, at least a little.'

'Keep who away?'

'Your darkest fears.'

DARKNESS

Death, pain, and fear.

Ragnar silently sighed. His daughter had flown away in Loki's falcon skin and there was nothing he could do about it. He knew not where she was headed or what she had planned, and she had not listened to his warnings. But then, she never had listened to his warnings in life either.

And in all of the confusion Ragnar had forgotten that he had gone there to capture Loki and drag him back to the cave and stop Ragnarok.

He did not know how, but he *had* to save her. In the same way that he *had* to save his gods, although with Hilda it was different. She was his daughter, and her entire life he had aimed to keep her safe. No matter what happened with Loki and the gods, Hilda needed to be safe. Of course, with Loki free and Ragnarok about to happen, his daughter would not stay safe for long.

There had to be a way.

Once he had righted his wrongs and saved his daughter and

saved his gods, Ragnar would find a way out of the Darkness and into his rightful afterlife in Helheim, where his son and dear wife waited for him. He so missed them. He had gone so long without their presence, first in Midgard and then here, that he no longer remembered his wife's face, or which colour her eyes were, or her hair. He only remembered how warm he had used to feel when she smiled, how happy they had been, and that one night they had fought. The night before she had died in childbirth.

He missed her. He so wanted to see her again. Wherever she was, he hoped that she was well. Absentmindedly, Ragnar tapped his distaff. He was still caught in memories of his wife and barely flinched as the sound of daggers on glass pierced his skull. The bright thread from his distaff tore a hole into the Darkness. Ragnar passed through.

He had expected to arrive in the meadow where Loki had been chasing his daughter, but that was not where he had arrived. His eyes teared up at the sight that surrounded him. He was home. After all this time, he had finally returned home.

The longhouse was warm. The smell of curing pork mingled with the smell of wet sheep. Rain fell on the roof of the longhouse. The room was smoky; the hole in the ceiling was not enough to let out all of the smoke from the fire. Ragnar sat down on the sleeping bench at the far wall, in front of the image of Ragnar Lodbrog. The first image his wife and he had painted on these walls when they had moved into the house. The one they had made together. The other walls were yet bare.

From the backroom, through the smoke, came Signe. Young and beautiful as she had been. She was rounder than he remembered her. Her face was plump with pregnancy. She waddled to the warm fire with a big pot of water. She struggled to move far, and had to set the pot down three times before she reached the fire and was able to hang it up to cook. Her pregnancy was far along, and back then, that winter, they had not had means to pay for a thrall. It was before Signe's father had accepted Ragnar as his son-in-law, although they already had one child. It was before everything.

Her cheeks were rosy warm. She had a bright red zit on her forehead and dark circles under her eyes, yet, his gaze would not leave her. To Ragnar, who had seen gods and goddesses and marvelled at their beauty, Signe, with her puffy rosy cheeks and her zit and dark circles, was the most beautiful person he had ever laid eyes on.

Over time his memories of her had been washed of any imperfections, but to see her now, with his own eyes again, was enough of a marvel that even her imperfections, so visible to him by contrast of his memories, made her seem all the more perfect.

Ragnar shuddered at what he knew came next. The door swung open to rain and thunder. A much younger Ragnar limped over the threshold and slammed the door shut. He dragged his muddy boots over the newly cleaned floor.

Seeing himself from the outside was a strange experience. Ragnar knew and recognised his every movement, but it was like watching an impostor imitating him. Every movement was exaggerated as if to provoke laughter. He had not known that he had used to scratch his bad leg quite so often or dragged it along the floor behind him with his hips twisted to the side. He had not known until he saw it from afar.

His younger self reeked of ale.

Signe watched him tumble onto the sleeping bench. 'Where have you been?' she asked in a worried tone. She could smell on him exactly where he had been. Even Ragnar could smell it on himself, and see it on his greasy hair. But Signe still asked.

His younger self did not reply, and Ragnar wished, deep and strong, that he would not say the words he knew he had uttered back then.

Signe took a step away from the large pot of water she had dragged into the room. She tried to smile and her voice was cheerful. 'Where were you?' she asked a little louder.

'It isn't your concern,' Ragnar heard himself answer.

She tried to tell him that it was and she just wanted to know, but for some reason that he could no longer recall, Ragnar was too angry.

His younger self shook his head. 'You've never done anything for me!' he yelled at her. 'Never.'

He shouldn't have said it, but he had. He didn't know why he had, as he watched himself, a younger man, yell at his wife. He saw the shock on her face, and watched regret wash over his own. The same sort of regret that had stained the Alfather's face when Ragnar had told him to run from the battlefield.

Little Leif cried from the corner of the room, awoken by his parents fighting.

Everything suddenly made sense to Ragnar. He had not wanted to yell. He didn't know why he had said what he had. It had been as if someone else had inserted the words into his mind.

It was Ragnar. Right here and now, he was looking at himself, and thinking the words, like he had thought the word *Run* when he had seen the Alfather on the battlefield. By coming back here, he had doomed himself. He could have changed it, like he could have saved the Alfather, if only he had *not* interfered; but it was all too late.

Ragnar thought of all the things he could say to make it up to Signe, but nothing was enough. He knew that everything he came up with had been uttered back then, and none of them had been enough.

And like that, the moment passed. Signe lifted crying Leif and left Ragnar alone in the longhouse. He would not see her again, until she lay on the funeral pyre and he held crying Hilda in his hands. It was too late, like it had been too late to save the Alfather. He should not have interfered. He never should have interfered with anything. But Ragnar had meddled too much, and he had changed too many fates. It was time to make good and lasting change.

He needed to return to Ragnarok's battlefield. Back to the place where he had made the Alfather run. And this time, he needed to make Odin stay.

'I am ready,' he said aloud.

A cold, stabbing pain penetrated his skull. A dagger sliced off Ragnar's scalp. He knew only agony. He screamed for it to stop, and then it did.

Death, pain, and fear.

HILDA

Chapter Ninety-Six

HILDA GAPED AT her goddesses. They were all perfect, but each in their own way.

Frigg had a single waved wrinkle on her forehead. Her neck, arms and ankles were weighed with gold rings that her viper slithered across, and she moved her toes slowly through the water. The wrinkle, and her slow, controlled, movements, marked her as a wise woman, maybe even wiser than her husband, Odin.

Splashing in the water at Frigg's feet was Idun, with her plump rosy cheeks and a smile that made her seem like a kid. She looked the youngest of all of them, and everything from her giggle to her bright braided hair reinforced that. A squirrel swam around her, tail waving behind it.

Both of them were perfect, yet entirely different. The same went for every other goddess in the hall. There was half a dozen of them, and Hilda thought there might be more hiding in the mist.

Freya walked past Hilda and took the steps into the water,

soaking her red dress. The goddesses examined Hilda silently, waiting for her to do something, but she didn't know what. They couldn't expect her to join them.

'It's nice down here,' Idun called to Hilda through the mist. 'Watch your steps, though. It's slippery,'

Hilda looked at her shoes as she stepped closer to the steaming bath. The sand-coloured floor was polished like a blade.

'Isa,' someone whispered, and ice formed under Hilda's feet. Her worn leather shoes skidded across the wet surface, exactly as Idun had warned. Hilda landed flat on her bum. Water splashed up her trousers and the goddesses shrieked with laughter. The wound in her chest began to bleed again.

Hilda slipped into the water while the goddesses were laughing. Freya's twin daughters Hnoss and Gersemi, splashed water on her. Her wool tunic hung warm on her. Hilda looked down at herself. The tunic was so faded that she had to look like a beggar in a chief's hall—worse, a beggar in the presence of goddesses. It was no wonder that they were laughing at her.

She didn't know if she was supposed to remove her tunic and trousers, but with faded clothes such as those, she supposed that being naked could not be worse. First, she slipped off the worn leather shoes that had made her fall, then she lowered herself in the water and set her trousers and faded red tunic aside.

Though she was entirely hidden in the water, the girls whooped at her. Maybe it had been a bold thing to do. Hilda almost never changed her mind, but in the presence of goddesses, she was eager to please. She fumbled behind her to reach for the wool tunic, to slip that back on at least, but her clothes had already been carried away. She had been right; there were others in the bathhouse, hidden in the steam.

She lowered herself into the water and tried to look comfortable there. The wound dressing on her chest was soaked, but being in the warm waters soothed her pains.

'Who are you?' asked Idun. Even when she spoke, there was a slight giggle to her voice.

'I'm Hilda, daughter of Ragnar Erikson, the skald of Ash-hill.' Discreetly, Hilda lifted her gaze. All of the women were staring at her, waiting for more. 'I'm a warrior,' Hilda stammered. 'On Sigismund Karson's ship, the *Storm*.'

'A warrior,' brown-haired Hnoss said. Her sister and she were near mirror images of each other, and their mother Freya, save that Hnoss had brown hair and her sister Gersemi had hair so blonde that it was almost white. A spiky hedgehog sat on the blonde-haired sister's shoulder. The animals were the goddess' fylgjur, Hilda realised, and she wondered if the goddesses could see them, or if it was just Hilda, as it had been in Midgard.

The sisters waved Hilda towards them, and when she was within range, they pulled her arm to make her sit in front of them, facing away. Their slender fingers began to comb through her hair, and they parted it in two, each with their own thick lock. Hilda sat very still as they braided her hair. Their touch sent shivers through her.

'Tell us…' Idun began. It was always the young plump goddess making conversation. 'Are you in love, Hilda Ragnardóttir?'

Hnoss and Gersemi buckled over laughing at Hilda's back, pulling her hair a little as they did.

'You're not bringing her into this as well,' said golden-haired Sif. She kicked a wave of hot water over Idun, and then stroked her own gold hair, casually, as if to pretend that it hadn't been her at all. Her hair was not just golden, it was truly gold, but Sif didn't arch her neck to support its weight. Half-hidden in the mist behind her sat a proud wolf.

Sif's annoyance seemed to fuel Idun. 'So, Hilda. Are you?'

None of the goddesses seemed at all concerned about what Freya had announced when they had entered the bath-hall. None of them worried that their ends were near and that Loki was free and that only Hilda could save them. Even that seemed to be a laughing matter to them.

Again, they were all waiting for her. The goddesses would never stop staring at her with those hungry eyes unless she admitted something, but she didn't want to think about how she had left Einer behind in Magadoborg.

Hilda cleared her throat. 'There was someone, back in Midgard,' she admitted.

'His name is Einer,' Freya helpfully provided in a half-mocking voice. 'Son of a chief Vigmer.'

'Where is Einer Vigmerson, now?'

'Living his life,' Hilda said. She was doing her best not to think about Magadoborg.

Whenever the calm settled around her and Hilda felt safe, the thoughts came. Memories of the murders they had committed in Magadoborg. Innocent people had died at her hands, in the hopes of a future she would never live. Einer had been right. The scars of what they had done at Winter Night would never go away. Maybe they would dwindle someday, when she had worse scars to remember. For now, the thought of having left Einer alone, in that city, wouldn't leave her mind.

She didn't know where he was now, but his father seemed to think that he was alive. She hoped he had survived, but she tried not to think beyond that, to how he would live his life and grow old, and how she wouldn't be there for any of it. They had always been together. They had only spent their later summers apart, when he had been raiding and she hadn't. Hilda had assumed that Einer would always be there. Her family might have left, but Einer had always been there. She didn't like the thought that she wouldn't see him again until the day he died. It didn't feel right to hope for his death.

The goddesses were laughing about something. Hilda hadn't heard what. For a moment, thinking about Einer and the life they would never have, she had forgotten that she was in the presence of goddesses. She had forgotten that Loki was free, and that Ragnarok was drawing near.

Sif howled with laughter as deep as a man and Freya showed a toothy smile. They didn't seem concerned.

'Shouldn't you find Loki and capture him?' Hilda asked.

'Prevent Ragnarok.' Her question killed the laughter. A tense air settled in its stead.

'Well, aren't *you* supposed to help us with that?' asked gold-haired Sif. Her fylgja wolf had lain down at her side, its head resting on her lap.

The goddesses had just accepted that Hilda would help them and they were not in the least eager to see it done. They seemed to think that there was plenty of time to bathe and laugh and talk about love.

'I will, if I can,' Hilda said. Of course she would. 'But how do you know my Runes will tell you where Loki is?' Hilda asked.

The women looked to Freya for explanations. *Runes?* Idun and Sif both mouthed.

'It's what she calls the whispers in the wind,' Freya explained, and then she addressed Hilda. 'I told you, they aren't the Runes.'

'Then what are they?'

Freya swam close. Her skin was flawless and sun-coloured. Rosy cheeks and nose tip. Her dark red lips parted slowly. 'Only nornir whisper through the wind, with visions of past, present and future.'

'The nornir...?'

'You were born with the blood to listen to them,' Freya said as she swam away into mist again. 'You will lead us to Loki, I have no doubt about it.'

'But the wind doesn't whisper to me anymore,' she said. All she did in the company of her goddesses was stupidly repeat herself, but they also never provided clear answers.

'You just need to relax,' Idun said. Her voice carried a certain annoyance, and she turned to the other goddesses, ready to entertain again. 'Bragi started brewing again,' she announced.

Sif made a disgusted face, and Frigg let out a motherly laugh at the two of them arguing, again.

Hilda lowered herself into the water so it came up to her nose. The goddesses weren't concerned.

'There're always visions in the wind,' Hnoss whispered to her. The twin sisters still combed their fingers through her hair, braiding it and un-braiding it, again and again.

'You will learn to listen more carefully,' said Gersemi. 'In time.'

It seemed that the goddesses had all of the time in the nine worlds.

As Hilda sat there in the warm water having her hair braided by goddesses, she realised what had happened to Ash-hill. The gods hadn't been angry with her and Ash-hill. The gods and goddesses had been busy, feasting, bathing and laughing. They had been distracted from what really mattered.

The goddesses easily moved on to other matters. Idun was providing an account of her apples, and when the others grew tired of hearing that, she began to talk about how drunk Freya's twin brother, Frey, had gotten at the last feast.

Eventually Hnoss and Gersemi got bored of braiding Hilda's hair and moved over to sit across from their mother, submerged in the water, with Idun in the middle telling tales as her fylgja squirrel climbed on her head. Sif and Idun quarrelled more than once, and Freya and her daughters fuelled the conflict. The fights seemed to amuse them.

'What exactly *did* the wind whisper to you?'

Hilda started away from the whisper in her ear. While the others had been laughing and Hilda had watched, submerged in the hot water, Frigg had moved to sit close to Hilda.

'The wind... the wind whispered many things to me,' Hilda stammered.

Frigg was sitting so close to her, leaning forward with all of her rings clinking softly in tune to the splash of water. It sounded like a song. Her viper fylgja danced up her arm with a quiet hiss. 'What kind of things?' Frigg whispered in the same rhythm as the splash of water and the clink of gold. A chanter, singing along to soft drums.

Hilda closed her gaping mouth and tried to focus and not

think about how beautiful the goddess' voice was. 'It told me—I mean, it gave me instructions—sometimes. Other times it would tell me terrible things.'

Frigg's dark brown eyes were fixed on Hilda, waiting for her to conjure the exact words of the Runes. It was difficult to think. Frigg's breath was warm on Hilda's cheeks. The goddess smelled of a freshly split log. An odd smell to come from a person, but there was no mistaking it, and it made Hilda want to never leave Frigg's presence, despite the viper fylgja that slithered closer.

Hilda cleared her throat in hope to clear her thoughts. 'Uhm—they said: "In the river your corpse rots" and "The Hanged God has abandoned you." and—'

The goddesses gasped. Not Frigg, who remained as composed as ever, but Idun and Sif and Freya's daughters and the women hidden in the vapour. Despite how they had been talking on their own a heartbeat earlier, they had all heard what Hilda had told Frigg.

'I told you,' Freya said. 'She's going to solve our little problem.'

'For once, your luck is good, Freya,' said gold-haired Sif and as easily as that, the goddesses were back to their usual talk. They knew something that they weren't telling Hilda. It couldn't be that they could hear the whispers. If they could hear the whispers, they would have had no use for Hilda. There was something else.

Frigg was steadfast in her attention. She hadn't moved, hadn't gasped in surprise. Frigg still examined Hilda, and after another heartbeat, she moved forward, into the water, so she did not have to crouch, and sat next to Hilda. Their shoulders touched and the sleek viper's skin rubbed against Hilda. Frigg nudged her like they were old friends.

'We all know those phrases,' she said, though she didn't tell Hilda how or why the goddess knew what the Runes had said, if they couldn't hear the whispers in the wind. 'I have often wondered where those whispers ended up,' Frigg continued. 'It was you.'

Hilda's heart sped up at Frigg's cool tone. Even submerged in the hot water, goosebumps rose up her arms. There was a clear threat in Frigg's voice.

So these were the battles of goddesses. She never thought that she would, but after all of these winters and summers, Hilda finally understood why her father had used to say that words could also prove to be a worthy fight, a deadlier fight than those fought in blood with sharp blades. It felt, now, like every spoken word might end in death.

'Was it your mother or your father?' Frigg asked. Her singing voice was back, but the hairs still stood up on Hilda's arms and legs, and the viper slithered between the two of them. Her father's frequent warnings to discipline her tongue rang loud. She had to be careful with her words, especially in the presence of gods and goddesses.

'Which one of them had the noble blood?' Frigg pressed. 'How well did you know your father?'

Hilda didn't know how to answer. She knew her father, probably better than anyone else had. She had known him her entire life. It was her mother she only knew from stories. It was her mother who had the noble blood of a chieftain's daughter.

'My mother was noble, I think,' Hilda finally said. 'She was the daughter of a chieftain.'

'Why would the blood of a chieftain be noble?' Frigg asked.

Hilda shrugged. It meant a wealthier birth, but at the end of the day a chieftain's daughter was no more noble than the daughter of a farmer or merchant. Chieftaincy wasn't a title that passed from parent to child. Yet Hilda had always thought of her mother as noble. She remembered her grandfather. She had been young when he had passed, but she remembered his slender beauty, his curved back.

'And your father?' Frigg urged.

Maybe her father's father had been a great man, too, though

Hilda didn't really know. They had passed away when she was little, and she didn't really remember. Her father had been respected as a noble man, but Hilda knew how he was after a long day of telling stories. She remembered him snapping at her in the evenings when she wouldn't sleep. And how often he would get sad when he looked at her, and refuse to say anything; and Hilda had thought it was because he remembered her mother when he looked at her.

'He was a worthy skald,' Hilda said. 'A great storyteller.'

Frigg half leaned into Hilda's arm. She fondled the jewelled rings at her wrist, caught deep in thought. The viper continued to slither along her arms as they both watched Sif and Idun argue, this time about who would survive the longest if they left Asgard to travel through the other eight worlds.

Initially, when she had entered the bathhouse, the breath had been stolen from her at the sight of her goddesses. She had thought then that she would grow accustomed to their presence with time, but even now, she struggled not to gape at them, and frissons travelled through her every time Frigg nudged her shoulder.

Hilda let out a sigh and felt her chest. The wound Freya had inflicted ached, but it no longer hurt or bled. Whatever Freya had done to heal her, it had been more than simply wrapping the wound. The longer Hilda sat in the water, the stronger she felt.

Just when the water no longer felt boiling hot, but exactly the right temperature, and Hilda had settled in and become used to the goddesses' conversation, the women rose from the bath.

'See you in three days, girls,' Idun happily announced to the room. She strode into the vapour with her squirrel fylgja hopping after her.

Hilda was the last one out of the water. Naked, she fumbled through the vapour, looking for her tunic and trousers and shoes. A woman—not a goddess, but a thrall, eyes stuck to the floor—came out of the vapour. Hilda's tunic and trousers had been neatly folded. The clothes were no longer wet, and they seemed to have been washed. Her shoes and weapon belt lay atop the bundle. The soot carved statue of Freya from Ash-hill stained the faded red tunic slightly. Her throat clenched at the sight of it. The figurine reminded Hilda of everything she had lost in Ash-hill, but it also strengthened her resolve. She had used to dream of the goddesses, and now she was there, in their presence.

'Takka,' Hilda told the woman, and dressed. When she strapped on her weapon belt and felt the weight of the godly axe, the dream ended. She had been blinded in meeting the goddesses and forgotten what mattered. She had come to ask forgiveness from the gods, but they didn't seem to be angry with her or with Ash-hill.

Asgard was not as she had expected it to be.

Time had passed fast inside the bathhouse, for outside, it was already morning. The warriors of Valhalla would be about to fight on Ida's plain.

The goddesses were saying their goodbyes when Hilda came outside, their many fylgjur surrounding them. Freya and her brown cat were already heading off. Hilda trotted to catch up, and wondered if the goddess' grand hall was empty by now.

'Are you following me?' Freya unexpectedly asked.

They had arrived together, so Hilda had assumed that they would leave together. Freya had fought with Odin over Hilda, but she didn't seem to care anymore. Hilda was just another sock to her.

'You can come if you want,' Freya said, then, 'but you don't have to. You're free to go wherever you'd like. It's your afterlife.'

For a moment they examined each other, and Hilda didn't know what to do. She wanted to follow the Alfather, but Freya was the one who was known as a runemistress among the gods, and Hilda didn't think Odin would help her regain her Runes even if she followed his invitation to Valhalla. She was dead and she had the entire afterlife to live, but if Loki was free and Ragnarok was coming, that might not be a long time.

'Would you like to see Valhalla?' a warm voice offered at Hilda's back.

Frigg stood behind her, holding a hand out to Hilda. The viper was snaked along her arm.

A spider's web had been spun around Hilda without her noticing. She smirked. Even caught in a web, a stubborn fly could free itself, and Hilda was stubborn. Trap or not, she would go to Valhalla. It was every warrior's dream.

She took Frigg's warm hand and let herself be led through the vapour outside the bath-house. She remembered Frigg's cool tone from earlier and knew that it would be dangerous to follow. The soft hiss of the viper reminded her. Despite that, Hilda was certain that the worst was behind her.

After all, Freya had stabbed her. Frigg couldn't have a worse fate planned.

EINER

Chapter Ninety-Seven

UNDER THE ALFATHER'S watchful eye, Einer drank with his bench-mates, listened to their stories and jokes, and enjoyed their company, until the sun came up and the tall doors, so far away, opened wide for them to march onto Ida's plain and fight.

Horns were blown at every corner of the hall. From behind and above. The noise tore through Einer's ears, louder and louder as more horns joined in, and then, all at once, it stopped.

There was a loud bang overhead. Startled, Einer looked up. Thousands of thousands of gold shields were falling. The ceiling was coming down on them.

Einer's arms shot up to protect himself, but he knew there was nothing he could do. This was not the death he had envisioned, smashed to pieces by a gold ceiling.

In the last moment, Haskell stretched an arm in over Einer's head and caught the gold shield as he must have done thousands and tens of thousands of times before.

He laughed at Einer's surprise and rubbed him on the shoulders.

'You didn't scream,' Ove said, and he looked impressed.

'He didn't blink either,' Haskell added, and then, gold shields in hand, they resumed their drinking while warriors headed to the gates and the hall gradually emptied.

Haskell and Ove set their shields down at their backs and finished their plates in their own time. Einer followed their lead, gulping down his drink as he mused on his fate and Odin's motives. The Alfather did not rush them or complain that they were slow, although half of the warriors in the hall had already left.

When they finally brought forth the helmets under their seats and pulled on the chainmail that covered their bench, they made Einer join them on their march to their gates. Haskell and Ove were both as tall as him, and in their shadows Einer felt like a little brother. He had never before felt that way; even as a child he had been taller than most. He had looked up to Hilda's brother, but Leif had always felt more like a friend than an older brother.

As they walked, the hall was loud with excited chatter and battle shouts and teasing, but Einer was well aware of another sound behind him, of a sharp tap on the floor. A few steps behind Einer walked the mighty Alfather, using his famous spear as a walking stick. He was a head taller than everyone, and his single eye was focused on Einer's back, watching every step Einer took, and every direction in which he swung his head.

Einer knew how wide the hall was, but walking it alongside Haskell and Ove, it did not feel so endless. Haskell had good stories to tell and entertain with, about being outlawed back in Midgard and his rise to Valhalla's glory. He was among the Alfather's best warriors and proudly told of a time when he had almost reached the giant lines before he had been crushed by a shield some giant had thrown. Einer had asked for details, but even Haskell had not seemed to know how he had done it, for centuries later, he had yet to repeat the feat.

Meanwhile, Ove had the strange ability to name every shieldmaiden in the hall. No matter who Einer pointed to, Ove knew their name, and when they shouted to the shieldmaidens and asked for their names, the women's answers always matched what Ove had told them mere heartbeats earlier. It was a good trick that entertained them for a long time.

They reached the outer doors, larger than anything Einer had ever seen. It seemed as if there was no wall at all, although he knew that there was. The door was so wide that eight hundred warriors could walk through it at once without their shoulders touching. Einer marvelled at the sight as he walked down the steps outside the hall. He was cautious to keep his mouth shut so as not to look out of place in the midst of the warriors who had walked through this, one of the hall's other five-hundred-and-forty gates every morning of their afterlife. For most of Odin's warriors, their afterlife had been much longer than their life in Midgard had ever been.

The sounds of battle were already loud outside Valhalla. Clashes and storms, thunder, crazed screams, and laughter. Einer had fought many battles, even a war. He had fought with and against berserkers, but he had never heard such laughter on a blood-ridden battlefield.

Ove and Haskell looked at each other over Einer's head.

'Not today,' said Ove. 'Too much mead.'

'I only bet you two days, then,' Haskell said.

Einer looked from one to the other. 'What are you betting?'

Ove was eager to explain. 'Every second day we have to fight not on Odin's side, but that of the giants. It means leaving the hall early.' That had to be why neither Haskell nor Ove had been concerned about heading out of the hall early, and why the Alfather had not rushed anyone, merely observed them with a distant air.

'And what you betting on?'

Haskell straightened his back before he answered. 'Who can get furthest into the enemy lines today.'

'Well, nej. It's who can slay the biggest beast,' Ove corrected.

'Ja, but the bigger beasts are closer to the giants.'

'That's true,' Ove agreed, but still they continued to argue about which one of them was right.

Meanwhile, Einer reached for his own sword, and kept their brisk pace so he would not be left behind, and could attempt to fight to the giant lines as his uncle had instructed him to do. A task that seemed increasingly difficult, as neither Haskel nor Ove had ever succeeded and they had each fought for the Alfather for centuries.

Einer could neither see the giant lines nor the battle from outside Valhalla's gates, just the docile backs of warriors waiting to join the battle, and the bloody grass at their feet.

Ove and Haskell agreed on a deal and parted ways. Einer looked from one to the other, and decided to follow Ove, who seemed the most likely to take Einer under his wing and teach him the different ways of battle in Asgard, and the tricks to defeat beasts that Midgard would never know.

Einer glanced back to make certain that he could make it away with Ove and join the fight without being stopped by a valkyrie or the Alfather, and immediately he knew that he should not have looked.

The Alfather was standing ten rows back, towering over the heads of warriors. He stared directly at Einer and gave him a disapproving look that made Einer stop in his tracks. He wanted to join the fighting ranks, but he could not, and instead was compelled to walk against the crowd towards the Alfather. His arm moved to sheath his sword again, although he had not asked it to do so.

'Come with me, Einer,' the Alfather demanded.

'Won't the valkyries simply wake me if I die?' Einer asked Odin, as he had asked his uncle.

'If you die, you won't be able to return to Midgard,' the Alfather warned with an air that insinuated that he was simply looking out for Einer; and perhaps he was, but Einer was pretty certain that he would not be returning to Midgard either way.

With a decisive stare, Odin made Einer walk with him, away from the fight, across the perfectly trimmed grass towards a hilltop at a short distance from Valhalla and Ida's plain.

Thunder rumbled, and dark clouds gathered. Lightning struck at Einer's back. Odin's son, Thor, was fighting on the field. There were crashes and clangs.

Einer and the Alfather looked over the long fighting line that stretched as far as Einer could see. The warriors fought in unison. The sight of it was soothing, like watching the ocean from a longboat. From a distance, it looked like one great living animal. Growls, grunts and screams blended together in a formless roar that echoed out to the hill from which Einer and the Alfather watched.

Warriors were scrambling up the side of the Alfather's and Einer's hill to gain the high ground and see ahead. Spears and arrows pierced them one after the other when they finally gained the higher ground that they sought. That was why Einer's uncle had told him to fight through it, instead of telling him to go around. The battle was so wide, and lone warriors at the edge were easier pickings.

Odin seemed proud of the sight of it all. The great beast of war was his construction, and every day he got to admire it in its full glory and predict what the final battle between gods and giants might look like.

There were so many warriors at Odin's command that Einer found it hard to believe that anyone would dare to think about challenging it, nor did he understand what reason anyone would have to defy the Alfather, as someday all giants would. Although Einer supposed that he could be seen as defying Odin since he wanted to leave Valhalla without seeking permission, but that was only because he needed to find Hilda and knew that she was not in Valhalla.

'She's with Freya,' the Alfather maintained aloud. 'She will arrive soon.'

Einer found it hard to believe, and he had to find her. It was not betrayal, he decided. It was not like with the giants. The giants would not invade Asgard in search of their loved ones, and Einer could think of no other reason why someone would want to destroy the wonders of Asgard, knowing that they could never claim it for themselves either. All the prophecy guaranteed was the destruction of both gods and giants, brought on by the jotnar themselves.

Einer feared he would never understand why giants were so set on war. Even when the final battle came upon them and Einer assumed his rightful place between Haskell and Ove and they marched to war knowing that it would be their last march out of Valhalla, he did not think that he would come to understand why the giants were so angry.

A warrior climbed up the hill. She had come further than most and dodged arrow after arrow. Determined, she backed up the hill, glancing to Einer and the Alfather every few steps, and when she was far enough away from the enemy lines that she did not have to protect herself against incoming arrows, she turned and ran to them.

'We know where she is headed,' the woman said, puffing and short of breath. She wiped some blood off her cheeks with the back of her gloveless hand. Her armour was red with blood, and her helmet too. She reminded Einer of Hilda, and when she took off her helmet to speak to the Alfather, Einer realised that she was one of the valkyries. 'She's going to the Hall of Fates,' she told Odin. 'And the nornir owe her a favour.'

The Alfather sighed at that. 'Then we better go before she burns all of our fates.' He looked at Einer, then. A single look that Einer knew well from his own mother. A look that meant that he should not even dream of disobeying. Einer's limbs froze, and when he tried to take a step forward, his movements were blocked by an invisible force that held him back.

'Enjoy the view,' the Alfather told him and then he and the valkyrie walked down the backside of the hill, away from Einer and the battle. Einer took a few steps backwards to watch them leave. He could walk away from the fight, but not towards it. Odin had sealed his fate to keep him away, and safe. In a different situation, Einer might have been grateful, but he needed to find Hilda.

He listened to the Alfather and the valkyrie's quiet conversation as they walked away through the grass: 'How was Glumbruck?'

'Fearless,' the valkyrie responded.

Eventually, their voices faded and their footsteps disappeared. He waited a moment longer, despite how impatient he was; he only had until nightfall to fight his way to the other side of the battlefield where the giants were. He could not see them from up here, but Haskell, Ove and his uncle had all insinuated that they were at the very back of the battle.

The deep anger crawled up Einer's arms and spine as it had during the fight at Magadoborg, where he had allowed it to take over. The anger flooded his mind and his muscles. His legs strained as he tried to lift a foot and walk closer to the war at the foot of the hill.

Einer stumbled forward, as if he had won a game of tug-the-rope, and everyone else had suddenly let go of the rope that bound him in place. He was free to move. The anger retreated at his will, but Einer feared that in battle he would need to use it, as he had in Magadoborg. That terrible fight. He thought he heard children wail and scream at the mere thought of it. Families killed. Einer shook his head. They had been forced to attack. It had been a just cause, even if the fight had been neither just nor honourable.

He took a great, unhindered step forward. He truly was free from Odin's control. Wearily, he looked over the plains of fighting warriors. He was dizzy from his wounds and a little drunk from earlier. Nonetheless, he clasped his hands around the two swords at his hips. There would be no better chance; the Alfather was elsewhere. Besides, a promise was a promise, and his uncle was waiting at the other side of the battlefield.

Every warrior Einer advanced towards had been born into battle in their afterlife. Thousands of deaths had shaped them, and thousands more would strengthen them before the final battle against giants. Next to any of them, Einer was just a farmer in chainmail who did not have a shield to lift. He was no match for them. But not a single warrior on the battlefield could shake his resolve. That is what he told himself as he pulled his two swords from their scabbards and rushed onto the bloodied plain that claimed every warrior's life.

He tightened his grips on the swords to keep fear out of his mind. Someday, this plain would claim his life too, but not today.

Arrows hurled at him as he raced down the hill. Arrows as big as spears with deadly spiked heads. The air reeked of poison as the arrows shot past him. One was all it would take to claim his life on Ida's plain.

Einer's pace was quick. His eyes pulsed from the movement and sharpened his focus. He hadn't run in so long. His legs were sore from the walk through Valhalla and he needed rest, but the gold bracteate his mother had given him hammered against his chest at the smell of battle, and gave him strength.

An arrow clanged against his sword, knocking his blade to the grassy ground. Einer retrieved it quickly, scrambling not to stand still and become a target. With long strides he rushed towards the back row of the battle. A group of Odin's warriors had put up a shield roof at the very back. Under the protection of their shields they plotted. There were three dozen of them. A few were still drinking and eating some remains from Valhalla's feast that they had taken with them, while others were busy arguing and coming up with ideas.

Einer ducked under the shield of the last row, into safety. He had his chainmail and swords, but if he was going to make it across the battlefield and all the way to the giants without dying, then he needed a shield. He pressed in between two warriors at the back and didn't ask for forgiveness as he forced past them to the next row.

Ducking to hide from incoming attacks, he cornered his way through the three dozen warriors under the shadow of their shields. At the edge of the protection of the shield-roof, he formed his own battle strategy. This was unlike any battle he had ever seen before.

The ground was sleek with blood that trickled down the hill opposite them. The battle raged with clashes of swords and axes up there, and blood flowed down the hill from the corpses piled up under the feet of warriors. The corpses still had shields.

There was a gap between the plotting group and the real fight up the hill. The archers up there were ready. A warning arrow plunged into the ground at Einer's feet, and he stepped back into the shadow of the shields. He would be killed if he tried to run.

He turned to the crowd of men discussing their plan of action. 'We need to attack those archers first,' he said. 'Then we can talk.'

Their gazes turned to him. The group was small enough that they knew that he did not belong. They had fought together on this battlefield for maybe hundreds of summers, and Einer was pretty certain that they would not easily follow a new arrival, but he had to try.

'Who are you?' someone asked, ready to dismiss him.

'I saw him at the high table,' said a cautious voice before Einer could defend his warrior abilities.

'Really?' more than one warrior asked. They assessed him with new care, glancing over his outfit, eyes lingering a little longer on his two swords, especially his father's Ulfberht.

'Haskell and Ove are my bench-mates,' Einer said.

They knew those names.

'We have to attack those archers and spear throwers,' Einer explained again. 'Then we can move without worrying.'

The names of his bench-mates were enough to convince the

three dozen warriors. They gathered thick around Einer and followed his lead, eager to appeal to a warrior seated at Odin's high table who may help them gain rank, if they did well.

Einer hid in the middle of the crowd as they advanced up the slippery hill. Their shields protected him from the front and from above. Spear-like arrows hammered over them and scraped against the gold shields. The arrows were huge, but the arms that held up the shields were strong and trained to withstand even the blow of Thor's hammer.

Einer ducked every time the shield above him rang with the sound of another direct hit. He had never had to fear for his life in battle before. If he died, he had always thought that he would wake up in Valhalla. But what his uncle had told him had changed everything.

Every blow could be fatal. He had always known that, but it had never mattered, until now.

Yet, he had to find Hilda. The thought gave him strength. Wherever she was, on this battlefield or the next, he would find her, and if his uncle said that the giants at the back of the battle could help him, then Einer knew exactly where he needed to go.

His foot slipped over the bloody grass. The hill steepened, and blood flowed over his feet as it was raining over them. An arm rolled down the hill. Einer legged over heaps of intestines ripped from people's guts, and less-identifiable chunks of bodies that rolled like stones in the mud. The smell of death and sweat had a firm grip on his nostrils.

He had never seen such a battlefield before. The plain was alive.

Einer's group clashed against others on the hillside. Einer peered at the ground to find a corpse with a shield, but the corpses were stripped of their belongings like on any other battlefield. Was that why Haskell and Ove were so set on surviving the longest? Were items stolen in battle fair trade in the hall of Valhalla? Could a warrior's wealth pass from hand to hand when he died on Ida's plain?

A roar of thunder brought Einer out of his thoughts. Something clanged against the shields above.

'Nej, nej, nej. I knew we should have gone around,' a warrior breathed at Einer's back. 'He will peel us raw again.'

'Keep going,' Einer urged. He climbed his way up the slippery hill with one sword hand on the ground, and the other raised to attack.

Warriors who died every day, and ought to be afraid of nothing, hesitated to move forward.

'There are good ways to die,' whispered the warrior behind Einer. 'Bad ways to die, and painful ways to die. And then there is Thor's hammer.'

There was another loud rumble. A warrior ahead of them screamed. A short, loud scream soon replaced by a blow against their shields. Blood splashed over the edge of the shield roof and over them. It drenched Einer's tunic.

The man in front of Einer withdrew a step down the hill, not because he had slipped, but to escape the fate that awaited them ahead. Einer was desperate to push on, but he had no shield. Where the shielded crowd went, he had to follow.

The clashes of battle were deafening, and he needed to find the backlines where the giants fought before nightfall, when the battlefield would be swept clean. At nightfall it would be too late. Dead warriors would be woken, wounds would be healed, and the feast in the hall would start anew.

There was no time to waste on being polite.

Einer sheathed his own sword. The Ulfberht was a better battle sword and it hungered to be used. He turned to the scared man behind him, who held a shield above them both.

'You don't need to forgive, but I *am* sorry,' Einer told the bewildered mud-haired warrior. Then he thrust his head at the man. Their heads clashed at the forehead. Einer took the blow, but the mud-haired warrior stumbled backwards and fell over on the bloody ground.

Einer snatched the warrior's gold shield and pushed through the crowd. His uncle had been right; it was not heavier than any other shield he had carried, and it fit right into his hand. The smooth-worn handle marked its many summers in battle, but the face was bright, as if freshly made.

He shouldered his way out of the crowd of hesitating warriors, and continued up the hill on his own. Crashes of thunder and screams of pain drowned out the clatter of swords against helmets, and axes chopping through arms and legs.

Einer held his shield high, ready to brace for whatever came his way, and although he wanted to look ahead and see Thor's hammer blows that scared the crowd of warriors so much, he did not dare. A single glimpse might be fatal. So, he kept the shield up.

Drunk or not, Einer was determined to fight his way through the best warriors in the nine worlds, and somehow, he needed to do so without dying.

DARKNESS

THE TIME HAD come to right his wrongs, and Ragnar was ready. He closed his eyes and thought of the Alfather facing the great wolf Fenrir, and then tapped his distaff.

The sound of a thousand sharpened knives screeched against glass rung out. His distaff opened a bright veil into another world; onto the battlefield of Ragnarok where his god had died.

This time, he was ready, finally. On the battlefield, Odin could win against the big wolf, if Ragnar undid his own wrongs and let Odin fight, as the Alfather had wanted to do before Ragnar had interfered.

Ragnar stepped through the veil, out of the Darkness, into much worse.

Blood splashed under his feet. The grass was coloured black. The sky was dark. Sun had been eaten, and Moon too. Thor's lightning flashes lit the battlefield.

Spears and knives flew by Ragnar. None of them hit him. He did not think that any of them could. Only the shadowed warriors of the Darkness and the most perceptive beasts could kill him. No one else knew that he was there; no one could see him.

The smell of iron and rot was strong and made him gag. He tried to rid his nose of the foul smell, but it followed him with every step.

Ragnar kept his eyes off the ground, drowned in blood and body parts. He focused on the warriors. Through the dark, he struggled to see their faces. He waited for Thor's lightning to strike somewhere on the battlefield and give him enough light to see warriors and gods and goddesses and giants and beasts. He searched for the Alfather's long silver beard and single eye, or the face of the great wolf that would kill him, and who had already killed Ragnar once before.

His distaff did not push the Darkness far away. It pulsed with his heartbeat as he searched. Not seeing far made him focus on the little he could see, and that made it easier to ignore the horrors at every turn, until finally, he found what he searched for.

The Alfather fought like none other Ragnar had seen on the battlefield. Every part of him was a weapon in its own right. His beard slapped into the faces of his enemies; his eye pierced fear into less worthy opponents. His hands threw his famed spear through the crowd. The spear that never stopped and always came back to his hand. And while his spear flew around Asgard, unstoppable and mighty, the Alfather fought barehanded. He grabbed the weapons of his enemies and used those against them.

Ragnar marvelled at his god's force, and at his calm. As he watched on, Ragnar felt the truth deep within: the Alfather could win against Fenrir. There was nothing to fear.

So, as loud as he could, Ragnar thought the commanding words in his mind: find Fenrir, and kill him.

The Alfather caught his spear from behind, and stopped his fighting. He evaded the blows of enemies who had already launched themselves at him, and finished them off at spear point. He did not cast his famous spear this time, but kept it with him as he marched through the battlefield. The crowd split for him, as Ragnar had seen it happen last time he had come here. This was about the same time he had come last, for he had arrived in time to see the Alfather march determined towards the great wolf, and to make the Alfather run.

It would not happen the same this time. Ragnar would set it right.

A bird screeched.

Ragnar never saw it coming.

Death, pain, and fear.

HORRIFIED, RAGNAR OPENED his eyes to the Darkness. His time through the veil had ended, and instinctively he knew why. He could not go back to a place he had already visited. Everything he had seen and changed with his distaff would come to pass exactly as he had seen it. He could not change his own decisions.

No matter what he did, the Alfather would die at Ragnarok, exactly as Ragnar had made it happen.

EINER

Chapter Ninety-Eight

THE BATTLEFIELD STRETCHED as far as Einer could see. He clasped onto his sword and braced for the first blow. His eyes were on the horizon, black with arrows.

Heavy steps splashed towards Einer. He crouched, his shield covering all but his left foot and shin. Mud splashed up his leg.

He rose and thrust his Ulfberht sword up from under his shield. His sword hit chainmail, and Einer tried to drive it through, but the warrior was skilled. The bracteate hammered against Einer's chest and steadied him. He peered over the edge of his shield. An axe swung at his head. Einer ducked and the axe sliced through locks of his hair. It missed his face by no more than a fingertip.

Einer raised his shield again. He had caught a glimpse of his opponent. A bulky man, axe in his right hand, gold shield in his left, and chainmail that reached the knees.

Leaving no breath for his opponent to retrieve his axe and attack, Einer swung his sword at the man's legs. The Ulfberht blade cut through armour, flesh and bones.

Einer kicked the warrior's gold shield, knocking the man down, and proceeded up the hill. He had no time to show honour, to drive his sword through the man's throat as he screamed. He had to go on, up the bloody hill of Odin's battlefield.

One of Thor's hammer-blows struck. The earth trembled, and a shock flew through Einer's limbs, up from his right foot and down again. The noise drowned out all else.

Something struck against Einer's shield.

Half a body rolled down the hill at his side. The legs had been torn off, and the warrior's head hung loose. The body landed in the blood Einer waded through.

A sudden flash of light blinded him. Even hidden behind his gold shield, it stunned him, and then it was gone. He waited for the thunder. It clashed and roared above him. While everyone was stunned by the sound of Thor's hammer, Einer peered over his shield.

The clouds were black. Thunder crashed over the battlefield. Trained warriors were still fighting. Einer focused on his breathing and heartbeat. The thunder was so loud, and he wanted to look for Thor. The god so many warriors looked up to was nearby, but he could not risk it. Thor would kill him in a heartbeat, and Einer needed to survive.

The age-old anger made him move and act without thinking. Everything suddenly seemed so easy, like walking through the market place at midsummer. Einer rushed through the crowd of fighting men and women, avoiding every conflict like a coward running for his life.

He passed shieldmaidens cleaving heads, ducked under shields and sword swings. Axes flew above him. No battlefield he knew was as busy and crowded as Ida's plain. Arrows and spears constantly flew above. An axe was thrown at him. Einer evaded and it cleaved through the shoulder of a shieldmaiden behind him.

His feet slipped on torn ears and arms and other limbs that he could no longer identify. One gold shield was so sleek with blood that he could barely climb over it. He picked it up and fastened it to his back, and then climbed to the top of the second hill.

Feeling safe, with his back protected by one gold shield and his left hand holding another, Einer took a few heartbeats to watch Ida's plain. Lightning struck with Thor's loud thunder and clouds gathered dark above the battlefield. The plain below was as vast as half of Jutland. It stretched as far as Einer could see, and perhaps further, and at the back—at the entire other end of the battle—the giants were fighting, or so he hoped, for he could not see them. He searched the distant figures, but they were too far away and beyond the third hill he could no longer distinguish one warrior from another. They were all one big red mess.

Another lightning roar made Einer move along again, down the hill, into the hottest part of the battle, hoping for the best. He had to survive, he told himself over and over, silently at first but then mumbling the words aloud, as if he could somehow make his wish come true. He *had* to survive.

A spear swept under Einer's shield. his body reacted before he could think. Shield in hand, he dropped down. The spear was knocked to the ground and locked away by his shield. The warrior at the other end let go of the shaft, and the weapon splashed into the bloody mud. Einer raised his shield to protect himself from above. An axe hammered into the edge of his shield. It would have struck him in the neck had he been any slower.

Einer let his body react naturally, side-stepping as the warrior moved forward, and planted his sword into the man's left shin. The warrior stumbled back, exposing the top of his head, and Einer banged his sword against his helmet. The man was stunned from the blow; quickly, Einer moved in and finished him off with a pound in the chest.

He set down his shield, wrested off the warrior's helmet, and put it on. It was too large and the arrow stump at his forehead screeched along the metal, but it would protect him.

Again, he set off, avoiding every fight that found him. Dancing like a warrior, the familiar anger focused his movements and kept him alert. The mead and ale he had drunk in Odin's hall made it almost easy. His head and heart pounded in the same rhythm.

Einer cast away axes and spears with effortless sweeps of shield and sword. As if he were skiing down a snowy hill, pushing to go faster. His pace hastened. He hardly blinked. His sword arm moved quickly. A stab through the neck of a shieldmaiden. A blow to the back of a bulky warrior's knee. Never did he hesitate; exactly like Hilda. Lightning struck at his back.

The further he went, the fewer fighting warriors there were, but the more corpses piled up. They were piled on top of each other, making new hills. They were both warm and cold through his soles, and the smell of them enshrouded everything: a stink of shit and rot and a slight stench of puke.

Even with a lifetime of fighting, and summers of training on this very plain, Einer doubted that anyone could ever truly be at home on the battlefield of Ida's plain.

It wasn't anything like other battles. Despite having travelled far through it already, Einer could hardly fathom what he was seeing, and feeling, and fighting. The odour alone made him want to throw up the entire meal he had eaten inside the hall. Now that he was no longer drunk, it seemed like a really bad idea to eat and drink so much before a fight, and Odin's warriors did that every single night. Unlike him, they could allow themselves to be killed. A death was just another day to them. But to Einer, dying was not an option.

The clouds were still black as night above Einer, and Thor's hammer strokes sent shocks through the battlefield, demolishing mountains of corpses. The fewer warriors there were, the bigger the chance was that Thor's lightning would strike Einer next.

His head rung and his eyes pulsed. He wanted water, and he wanted rest, and there were no helpers in this kind of battle to bring him water, and rest would only come once he was through the other side—or dead.

An axe swung at him, and clanged against his large helmet. Einer thrust his shield forth, to clash with that of the other warrior. He moved his shield back, and attacked under it. The warrior in front stumbled from the wound to his shin. Einer pushed him back with another blow, and ran along the battlefield.

Light blinded him. A force trembled through him. And then came the thunder. A roar so intense that all the hair on Einer's body stood up.

Before him, where the lightning had struck, stood its maker. Red Thor, sculpted from muscles. His beard dripped red with blood and his laughter echoed as thunder on the battlefield. His arms were thick as tree trunks. His white tunic was red and black with blood, and his belt of strength was fastened with a magnificent gold buckle.

He threw his short-shafted hammer and Einer cast himself to the side. The hammer swished over his head, but Red Thor had not yet seen him; he had not been aiming at Einer.

Einer got up but he could not find it in himself to move away from his god. Red Thor was standing right there, in front of him, glorious and perfect, exactly as the tales told. The sheer honour of it petrified him in place. And then his god's eyes fell on Einer. Thor looked at him. His eyes were red, not blue, as Einer had always imagined. They were red as blood and as his hair and his beard. Eyes that craved blood and murder.

Einer knew he should run. The warriors he had met at the beginning of his journey had made it clear that there was no worse way to die than at Thor's hands. Yet Einer stood his ground. He was not certain why he did it; to prove that he was not afraid, or simply to look upon his god for a moment longer? But instead of running, Einer secured the grip on his shield.

Thor flashed a victorious smile at him, and that's when Einer remembered. Thor's hammer always came back to him, and it crushed everything in its way, even mountains.

Einer cast himself onto the corpse-covered ground.

A loud bang rumbled; not the sound of thunder this time. Einer wriggled onto his back, his shield covering his body. The clouds were black as night.

Thor's hammer flew over his head. It would have shattered Einer into a thousand pieces had he not cast himself to the ground. He knew that he had been seen, and he knew that he would not survive Thor's next strike.

A flash of light blinded Einer, followed by the roar of thunder. Einer looked up, expecting the last thing he saw to be Thor's hammer smashing his face, but Red Thor was gone. The god knew that Einer was there—their eyes had met—and Einer had not run away. Still, Thor had left.

Something hailed from the sky. A severed head plopped down to Einer's left. An eye splashed on his edge of his shield. A leg on his arm. A thousand corpses hailed down over him.

Thor's hammer had ploughed straight through a mountain of corpses, and now the carrion was falling to the ground. He would be buried by it. That was why Thor had left; he had known that Einer would be crushed by Valhalla's dead warriors.

Quick as a raven, Einer lifted his shield over his face. He held his arms strong in front of him, and curled his legs up. The shield was too small to cover all of him and a body clanged against his head. The arrow stub screeched inside his helmet and Einer clenched his teeth tight, bracing for the next blow. Another body hammered onto his shield.

He would never survive this. He had taken in no more than a glimpse before he had realised what was falling, but there had been thousands of corpses. He would never survive. But Hilda wouldn't have given up, and Einer owed it to her to not give up either.

He twisted his shield to the side to drop the two bulky corpses next to him. Another body slammed over him, and his helmet rung with the blow. His bracteate beat hot at his chest. Einer pushed away with his shield to make the body roll off, over his head. He kicked and pushed to lay the next bodies to the right of him. Heads, legs and whole bodies rained over him so he could no longer move them or hope to wriggle free. They crashed against his shield and on top of each other, and weighed him down so Einer feared he might never move again.

For what felt like half a day but could not have lasted more than twenty heartbeats, Einer lay entirely still and listened to the sound of dead bodies hailing over each other, of bones crushing and shields and weapons clattering against each other.

When at last the sounds stopped, and Einer dared to open his eyes, everything was black. He was walled in by dead corpses. Piling the first corpses up like walls had saved his life, but not for long. His breaths were already strained. Buried beneath a mountain of corpses, he would suffocate.

Einer breathed deeply to calm his racing heart. The bracteate blazed like a midsummer fire, and his breaths came back to him hot as well. He still had his father's Ulfberht sword in hand. There was no room for him to sheathe it in his weapon belt with his own sword.

The air already threatened to suffocate him. His head felt light. He could see no light. The cloud above had been so black earlier that even if there was a hole through the mountain of corpses, Einer did not expect to find it.

He needed to move. If he was to survive, he could not lie there and wait to be discovered. Never would he survive long enough for that, even with the bracteate at his neck. He would have to dig through the mountain, head first.

Einer relaxed the hand holding up his shield. The carcasses

weighed down on his body, but not as much as he had feared. He unclasped the shield attached to his back and rolled onto his side. Then he wriggled his right arm up. He forced his Ulfberht sword to cut through armour and corpses until his right arm was above his head, and then he turned onto his stomach.

The sweat already rolled off his forehead and trickled into his wounds and stung, but not as much as his bracteate stung with heat. Einer had only one possible escape from the depths of the corpse mountain. He needed to cut his way out.

Ulfberht blade first, he squirmed past corpses. His father's sword cut the way. He used his helmet to push pieces of warriors out of his path. His clothes got stuck, his weapon belt kept getting caught in the belts of others warriors, but Einer persisted.

Every time he was forced to stop, and thought there was no more hope, he thought of Hilda, and then his weapon arm slashed through dead warriors without hesitation and he pushed through.

At last he saw a glint of movement and light through the tight weave of corpses. He had once heard that in times of great peril, when people finally saw a sliver of hope at the end of their struggles, they gained strength to continue on, but just now he felt the opposite. Seeing the light made him sob, and not with hope. He was so close. It would be so easy to stay buried beneath the corpses and die, but if he sliced through perhaps no more than another dozen warriors, he would be back on Ida's plain. And there, he would still have to rush to the giant lines. What waited out there was much worse than suffocating beneath a mountain of corpses.

For Hilda, he told himself, and sliced through the last corpses.

Emerging at last, Einer panted for fresh air, but the air bore a heavy stench and gave no relief. Five deep breaths he took, then grabbed a new shield from the dead mass and sprinted for it. He scrambled up and down mounting piles of corpses. Angry lightning flashed at his back, but Thor was busy and there were many other warriors to kill. Einer kept running until he no longer had breath to run anymore, and then he crawled.

From the top of the tallest of corpse piles, Einer finally saw the back of the fight where the giants were battling. They towered over warriors and fought with rage and clamour. Their yells and angry voices carried all the way up to Einer, and made a strange hunger for blood roar within.

He had expected to see other creatures with the giants. More gods and goddesses, and alvar and svartalvar and dwarfs. He had expected everyone to gather and fight. But he supposed that they would have no reason to fight here, at least not until the final battle. Valhalla's warriors were the ones who needed to train, and Thor was merely there because he loved an excuse to blood his hammer.

Einer stared up at the sky. He was far enough away from Thor and his angry hammer that he could see beyond black clouds. The sun was high up in the sky. The day was halfway done, and there was far for him to go to reach the other end of the battlefield where the giants fought.

He climbed through the corpse hills. Crawling proved the easiest way to pass unnoticed and safely. No one cared about the bodies on the ground. He was half swimming through the blood of corpses. The smell was worse by the ground; the sweet iron of blood, but also the stench of puke and shit. Einer crawled through it all.

Many had died already, and the fighting warriors were few and easy to avoid. When he crawled, they did not notice him. They did not look at the bodies they stepped over. They did not care if their weight crushed the ribs of a warrior who was not yet dead and screaming of pain. They did not care if they stepped on a bench-mate or friend. Everyone here, dead or alive, would live to fight another day, so none of it mattered. Only to Einer.

He rolled down the side of another corpse hill, staying low, shield on his back and Ulfberht in hand. He evaded the fighting crowd although the old anger told him to join and fight and that it would not be dangerous, and that he was a better warrior than any of them. Perhaps he was, but most likely he was not, and then he would have to gamble with his life, and perhaps he would never get to see Hilda again. They had promised each other to fight side by side someday on this very plain, and Einer always kept his promises.

He crouched atop a corpse to see over the heads of fighting warriors, to the back line where the giants battled. One of them stood out. She had long red hair that slapped around her as she fought. She spun and slew anyone who came near. She held no shield, but wielded a large axe in both hands. Her size changed as she fought, becoming large and then small as she whirled and eradicated everyone on the field.

His uncle had said that Einer would not be in doubt when he saw the right giantess. It had to be her that he was looking for. Guided by the anger, Einer rose to his feet and moved straight ahead. A warrior came running at him, but he pushed the round man away with his shield and kept walking.

The giantess was far away, and Einer did not slow. He walked straight towards her, eyes fixed on her as the sun travelled across the sky and began to colour it red.

The giantess was still fighting, and she was good. Not a single worthy warrior cut her flesh or armour. No more than a handful clashed weapons with hers. Fewer survived long enough to block one of her axe blows. She was strong as the Midgard Worm, and as agile too, and she reminded Einer of Hilda.

Every strong shieldmaiden did, because Hilda had been the first strong shieldmaiden Einer had really known. Already as a four-summers-old child she had been a shieldmaiden and dreamt of fights and raids. He had taught her about Valhalla's battles and fights, but back then, neither of them had known that this was how it would be.

Einer was red from blood. He had bathed in it on his journey. The smell of iron was strong but not as much as that of vomit and rot. Flies gathered on the mountains of corpses. There was not much glory about a battlefield like this.

It looked and smelled and sounded like the end of all things, and some day, it would be.

The giantess knocked down another feeble warrior. Compared to her, they were all weak, although to have reached this far, they had to be among the best warriors in Valhalla. Perhaps some of them were Einer's bench-mates, although he mostly remembered Haskell and Ove. There had been so many.

The giantess planted her axe into a warrior's chest. The blood splashed up her arms. The sun was setting at her back. Einer continued the walk towards her. He hoped that he was right and that she was the one he was searching for, because he did not want to find out that he had been wrong. If he had to fight a shieldmaiden like her, that was an encounter he would not survive, even with ruses and tricks and anger and all of the luck in Midgard.

Another warrior approached her and was flung to the side with a kick to the shield. The giantess searched for her next target. Their eyes locked.

She knew that Einer was headed towards her, and she joined the march.

Her steps were wide and long. A few heartbeats longer and they would clash in the deadliest duel Einer had ever encountered.

He stared as the giantess launched into a run, and a terrifying thought rung through his helmet: he had no idea how to tell her who he was.

The giantess raised her axe, ready to strike him down. She leapt over corpses as if they were mere pebbles under her feet. Einer planted his left foot on the stomach of a dead warrior, digging his heel in above the belt buckle to keep himself steady. His right foot he placed on the face of the next corpse, pressing its head to one side; the warrior's nose guard supported his heel.

The giantess' red hair waved behind her as she ran.

Einer inhaled sharply. His shield was high, and the Ulfberht ready to strike.

The giantess swept Einer aside with a back swing of the axe. It rung loud and low against his gold shield and sent him flying. The air was kicked out of him. She ploughed right through him and he fell to the ground at her feet. Her axe rose above him, the blade as wide as Einer's head. Her red hair danced at her back like bloody waves. She stood above him with her axe drawn as once a white bear had stood on its hind legs over him, ready to strike, and exactly as the bear had, she looked at him, really *looked* at the face hidden in the shadow of his helmet.

Then, lowered her axe, and turned her head to the side as once the young white bear had done.

'The forefathers…' she said. 'It's you.'

Her eyes darted to somewhere behind him. She swung her great axe over him and cleaved off the head of a warrior at Einer's back.

Einer scrambled to his feet. She could have killed him easily, and she still could; that she had not had to mean that she was indeed the giant his uncle had sent him searching for.

'He is back here,' she shouted to the giants behind her.

She looked at him with awe, as fascinated to see him as he was to see her, and then she nodded at the ranks behind her. The hooded man who called himself Einer's uncle was there, standing back in the shadows of yet another mountain of corpses, clear of the fight and without armour or shield. His face and arms and body were hidden, as ever, and Einer could not shake the idea that this hooded man and the Alfather were the same person, and that this was all some grand scheme by the Alfather for Einer to prove his worth, and that he had failed by disobeying the Alfather's orders to stay at the other end of the battlefield.

For some reason, the thought of going against the wishes of a man as powerful as Odin made Einer tremble with excitement.

The heat of the fight rushed through his veins. 'Where to now?' he asked.

'Home' said the giantess, and smiled so her bloody teeth showed. 'The very place your mother spent a lifetime fleeing.'

TYRA

Chapter Ninety-Nine

Tyra started at every small sound. The valkyries were coming for them. They were going to kill her, exactly as Siv had said, and it was too dark for Tyra to see them. She would die there, in the dark of Yggdrasil's shade. She wouldn't get to fight so she could go to Valhalla in the afterlife, she would just die and never see her parents again.

'Don't be scared, it's just the dark,' said Siv, and clenched Tyra's hand, but her voice was shaking and she was scared too. Siv wasn't herself. Her eyes were not steady as they usually were.

'When will it be morning?' Tyra asked. It was so dark and terrifying and they had walked for so long that the sun should have come up.

'It *is* morning,' Siv answered. 'Maybe midday.'

There was no light to see anywhere. Not even when Tyra looked up. 'Then why is it so dark?'

'We're walking in Yggdrasil's eternal shade. No sunlight ever reaches these parts of the woods.'

'But how can there *be* woods, then?' Tyra's father had taught her that all growing things needed sunlight and love, and there was none of that here.

'They're night-clinging trees,' said Siv, but Tyra had never heard of night-clinging trees.

She supposed that there were different things in Asgard than in Midgard. There were no trees as large as Yggdrasil in Midgard either, and as for the blue flowers on the plain where Heimdall had arrived, Tyra had never seen anything like those before. She supposed that there could be such a thing as trees that didn't need sunlight and love to survive in Asgard, because everything in Asgard was different from what Tyra knew.

A low, flickering flame that Siv had conjured hung in front of them; they could see enough not to trip over the many tree roots on the ground and to see each other, just about. Tyra stared at the flame and wished and wished that it would never go out. She stared at it and was terrified that it would extinguish any moment. It was so weak and small.

Siv twisted to look back the way they had come, and then ahead and to the sides, staring into the woods. As if there was someone there. There probably was. Siv always knew when they were in danger.

Siv stopped walking and Tyra too, right behind her. For a moment they just stood there, Siv in front, and Tyra at her back. And then their roles were reversed. Suddenly Tyra was the one staring around wildly, thinking that maybe Siv had stopped because whoever was chasing them now had already found them. Like Heimdall had. But no matter which way she looked, they were alone in the pitch-black dark. Except for the birds she heard screech above, the fish in the stream she heard to their left, and the bugs at her feet. Maybe whoever was chasing them had put on an animal skin and was disguised as a bird or a fish or a bug, but Tyra didn't think it likely.

Finally, Siv turned to face Tyra. She looked into her eyes, and Tyra was almost certain that Siv could see straight into her and know all her truths and all of her secrets. 'Odin won't think to come here,' Siv said aloud, as if she struggled to believe it. 'We're safe in here. In these woods.'

That's what Siv said, but Tyra didn't think they were safe. Not at all. It didn't *feel* safe to walk here. It felt scarier than it had when Siv had put her inside the ash-tree and told her not to speak, and it had been all dark and Tyra had heard a scream and she hadn't been able to get out.

It felt much scarier even than that, and Tyra knew they weren't safe.

'We're safe,' Siv repeated, as if saying it would make it true, and then she began to walk again. 'Odin won't ever follow us in here. No one comes here.'

Then they could die here and no one would know. Tyra's parents would never know, and no one would ever find her, and Tyra would never be woken up in the next life and she would just disappear. Or worse. Maybe she and Siv would be separated in the dark, and Tyra would never find Siv again, because they walked in weird ways, not straight as she thought they should and Siv said that she knew the short routes, but what if she didn't and they were really walking around and around in circles? Maybe they would never escape the dark.

Her breath caught in her throat and she couldn't breathe. She puffed and puffed, but she was out of breath every time.

'Tyra, Tyra,' Siv called. 'It's fine. It's just your fears. They can't hurt you.'

But Tyra didn't think that was true, and she was crying now, and couldn't catch her breath. It seemed she had been running for days and hadn't taken a single breath.

'Calm down.' Siv clenched Tyra's hand, but Tyra couldn't stop thinking that they would never get out of here.

'We *will* get out,' Siv said, listening to Tyra's thoughts again. And for once, Tyra didn't mind at all. 'We will get out. And Odin won't find us. We will reach the nornir's cave and all will be well.'

Tyra managed to catch a breath. A proper breath. And then another. The fears swirled in her mind, and she didn't think she could keep them out anymore. 'How long?' she gasped. 'How long until we're out?'

'We're almost there,' Siv said, but she had been saying that for a long time, and Tyra didn't believe it anymore. 'We will be out soon. It's just your fears, Tyra. This place is a place of fears. But fears aren't real. They can't hurt you.'

Tyra breathed loudly until her mind wasn't screaming for her to run away anymore.

'We'll be there soon,' Siv repeated, and rubbed her back with a warm hand.

'Promise?'

'I promise,' Siv said, and Siv didn't make promises that she couldn't keep.

Again, they resumed their walk through the dark and through all of their fears, and Tyra tried to focus on the slim flame in front of them and on Siv's hand warm in hers. But she kept thinking about how she would never see Svend again, and how Siv and she would get separated and how she would be all alone then.

'Tell me something, Siv,' Tyra asked, because the silence made her think of the darkness inside the ash-tree at home and it made her all the more scared.

'What?' asked Siv.

Anything, Tyra wanted to say, but she didn't think she would like what Siv said if she said anything, so she thought for a moment and tried really hard not to be scared, and then she spoke again. 'Why did you first come to Asgard?'

'I was fleeing a marriage.'

'Like me,' Tyra said, and despite the dark and her scary thoughts, it made her giggle to think that Siv and she had both entered Asgard for the same reason.

'I had a good friend,' Siv continued. 'A great friend. He helped me. Brought me to Asgard where he said I would be safe... And for a while, I was.'

'Then what happened?'

'He had different priorities.'

'He was more than a friend, wasn't he?'

'He could have been,' said Siv. 'But he wanted more than I could give him.'

'Who was he?'

'He is famed all over Midgard,' said Siv and for a moment she didn't say anything anymore, so Tyra thought of all the famed aesir she could name. There was Tyr whom Tyra had been named after, and whom all warriors looked up to for his bravery and self-sacrifices. There was Heimdall, but Tyra already knew that it wasn't Heimdall because Siv had said that they had only met once before. Then there was the skald Bragi. Of course, Odin was the most famous, but it wasn't him, because he was the one chasing them. Maybe he was chasing them because Siv's friend was one of his sons. Thor, maybe, that could be why Siv called herself Siv although it wasn't her real name: because Siv sounded similar to the name of Thor's wife, Sif. But somehow Tyra didn't think that was right. Then there was Odin's dead sons Baldur and Höd. It could have been Baldur. Everyone loved Baldur and Odin would have done anything for his favourite son, even kill Siv.

'Although he will kill you in a heartbeat, the Alfather doesn't want *me* dead,' Siv said, and again she had been listening to Tyra's thoughts. Tyra didn't mind, because in all of her thinking, she forgot to be scared.

'Then what does he want?'

'He wants to take my freedom away,' she said. 'To relieve me of my choices and tie my destiny down. He has shackled others, and he intends to do it to me.'

'Why?'

'Because the Alfather wants to control everything. Especially that which cannot be controlled.'

'Like what?'

'The future,' Siv answered.

But it wasn't just the future that she meant. At least Tyra didn't think so. Siv had loved someone she shouldn't have, and that was why the Alfather was after her. Tyra was pretty certain of that.

'And love?' Tyra added.

'And love,' echoed Siv.

'Did you love him?'

'Who?'

'The Alfather.'

'The Alfather? Nej, not Odin, but I *was* in love.'

Tyra thought about that and who it was that Siv could have loved that had made the Alfather so angry and she had so much to think about that she hardly had any time to be scared anymore, and it all seemed a little silly. She didn't remember why she had been so scared earlier.

'I told you we were nearly there,' said Siv, bringing Tyra out of her thoughts.

Ahead, in the dark, dark woods were small patches of light that came through the crown of the trees. Finally, their long walk in the dark was over.

Siv extinguished the slim flame. Together, they walked to the edge of the woods. There was a huge wooden building outside the woods, but when they came closer, Tyra realised that it wasn't a building at all. It was Yggdrasil's trunk. It was so large and thick that it was all she could see when she looked straight ahead.

Tyra had often imagined Yggdrasil when Ragnar told stories of the large ash in the centre of Asgard where the gods lived, but she had never known that it would be *that* large. The tree-trunk was all she could see. And when they had looked at Yggdrasil from afar, the top of it had been buried in clouds. The ash-tree was much larger than any mountains Tyra had ever seen before. Not that she had travelled enough to see *many* mountains, but she had seen some large ones.

At the edge of the woods, in the last of the tree's shade, they slowed. Huge roots, taller than walls, shot out from Yggdrasil's trunk.

'This root, here,' Siv pointed to one of them. 'The first one in the sunlight. It leads to a small town where few people go.'

'Is that where you used to live?' asked Tyra, always eager to learn more.

'Nej,' Siv said. 'I lived elsewhere. But there is a dress shop there where you can exchange your dress.'

'That's why you asked me to put on my prettiest dress before we left?' Tyra knew that she was right, but it felt all wrong that Siv was telling her this.

'They will want to make an exchange for that dress. You need clothes from Asgard. It'll mask your smell, and make it difficult to find you.'

'I'm not leaving you,' said Tyra. 'Not when we're so close.'

'Nej. You're coming with me to the nornir, but I need you to know these things.'

They really would be separated. If Siv were expecting them to stay together, she wouldn't have to tell Tyra all of this. She was preparing Tyra for a life in Asgard without her—without Siv. 'Siv, promise me that you won't ever leave me.'

'I need you to know these things,' Siv said instead of promising. 'I need you to know that if anything happens, anything at all, I will be able to find you again, and now you know where to meet me.'

'But nothing will happen to you, right?' asked Tyra as they walked into the sunlight.

Siv didn't answer. She didn't make promises that she couldn't keep, and suddenly Tyra was much more scared than she had been in the woods.

HILDA

Chapter One Hundred

SUNLIGHT WARMED YGGDRASIL's outer leaves. The top of the tree was hidden in clouds. Frigg and Hilda followed one of the tree's large roots through Asgard. Already they had walked half the day. They had started among the fields, but now the root snaked through a forest, and judging from the sun, it had to be well past midday.

'What do you know of my Runes?' Hilda asked Frigg, goddess above all goddesses. Frigg seemed more eager to share than Freya had been. Walking in her presence, Hilda had convinced herself that she would finally gain answers to her questions, if she was sly enough.

'It's like... an arm-ring.' The goddess removed one of her many twisted gold arm-rings. Her viper fylgja hissed as she did, but the goddess didn't seem to see the snake that slithered along her arm.

She placed the arm-ring on her palm and showed it to Hilda. The arm-ring clasp was an intricate representation of the Midgard worm swallowing its own tail. Frigg had at least a dozen identical arm-rings. They reminded Hilda of her father's stories about Odin's gold arm-ring, which dripped eight identical rings every nine nights.

'Is that one of—?' Hilda began, but realised that she was being stupid and this was not how she would gain answers to her questions.

'One of Odin's copies,' Frigg confirmed. So, Hilda had been right.

As a child, the story of the dwarf smiths' gifts to the gods had been one of Hilda's favourites, although that was mainly because it ended with Loki's mouth being sewn shut so he couldn't spew any more treacherous words.

Hilda realised that she had been gaping at the ring. In Asgard and in the presence of one of her goddesses, it was difficult to stay composed and remember that she shouldn't be awe-struck at everything she saw. Hilda smoothened the frown on her forehead and glanced to Frigg as casually as she could. 'Like an arm-ring...?' she prompted.

'Imagine that you had never seen an arm-ring before,' Frigg said and licked her lips as she gazed at the ring. Her viper showed its long tongue too. 'Even if you've never seen an arm-ring before, you can see that it's round. You might touch it, and feel the cool metal. You can trace the ring with your fingers.'

Frigg was different from the other goddesses. She liked passing on knowledge as much as the Alfather liked to amass it. The explanation didn't make much sense to Hilda, though. She wasn't sure what it was the goddess meant. But she kept listening, hoping that maybe it would become clearer.

'You wouldn't truly know what it was unless you knew how to use it,' Frigg continued. 'It would just be some strange object. Like the whispers in the wind are to you. You only hear the outer edge. You don't see the core. You don't know how to use the arm-ring, yet.'

The goddess' explanation made no sense to Hilda, but she nodded as if it did. Her father had once taught her the importance of making people feel heard to keep them talking, so when Frigg looked to her to see if Hilda was following, she nodded slowly and repeated some of Frigg's words back to her. 'I only hear the outer edge...'

'Exactly,' Frigg said. 'Some norn children are taught to listen to the visions, but your bloodline is thinner. Neither of your parents was a norn, so you were never taught.' When the goddess saw that Hilda was nodding along thoughtfully, she continued. 'Sometimes, even those with thinner bloodlines in Midgard pass on the knowledge and become—'

'Runemistresses,' Hilda realised. The best runemistresses spoke of visions and could tell the past, the present and, more importantly, the future. Like the nornir could. 'They called me runemistress,' Hilda told her goddess. 'In Midgard. Towards the end, when the wind whispered to me.'

Right on cue, the wind whipped through the forest and birds took flight, but there were no whispers.

'The wind told you the future,' Frigg said. Her neck-rings clinked as her viper fylgja slithered around her neck and down her other arm.

'But it wasn't really... visions. Just whispers.'

'The outer edge,' Frigg said, but that made little sense to Hilda. This time, she didn't hide her confusion, and Frigg held out the gold ring again. She pointed to one of the wrought lines that snaked around the arm-ring. Some were smooth, but the one Frigg pointed to was a long, dotted line that looked like a chain of water droplets strung together. 'These are all on the outer edge,' Frigg explained. 'Only hanging on to the rest of the ring, because they are tied together.'

'So, what I heard was one of these other droplets,' Hilda guessed.

'Ja. Someone else on the outer edge whispered to you.' She offered Hilda the lavish gold arm-ring.

Hilda took the weighty ring and spun it in her hands. So, there were others like her, on the edge. Not full nornir, but able to hear the wind whisper anyways. 'Someone on the outer edge,' she muttered. 'But someone who has access to the visions.'

'You are perceptive,' Frigg said. 'For a warrior.'

Having turned the gold ring in her hands, Hilda offered it back to the goddess.

'Keep it,' Frigg said. 'I have others.' Her many arm-rings clinked in confirmation.

Hilda slipped the gold ring over her wrist. In Midgard she would have thought that giving away a gold ring like this was foolish and arrogant, but Frigg was neither of those things. Goddesses seemed to use everything they could and give away only that for which they no longer had any use.

The arm-ring knocked against the bones in Hilda's wrist, but it felt right hanging there. Her father had once given Hilda and Einer identical silver arm-rings. They had used to wear them always. After the slaughter in Ash-hill, Hilda had traded hers to a runemistress, and in exchange she had gained the Runes. It felt good to have a weight on her wrist again, and now, with the help of her goddesses, she would regain her Runes. Soon, all would be as it was supposed to be.

Yggdrasil's branches spread far over them, yet the trunk of the tree was at least the distance of three rests away. The ash bathed in sun, but clouds kept moving in. It would rain before nightfall, at least by Yggdrasil, which was still so very far away.

Centuries of centuries ago, the Alfather had walked to Yggdrasil to learn the runes. He had arrived seeking knowledge. The same knowledge Hilda sought now. She was on a quest for knowledge, as once the Alfather had been. To gain the power and truth of the runes, Odin had given the ultimate sacrifice, and Hilda was prepared to do the same.

Her father had often told the story of Odin's sacrifice. Thinking of the Runes had reminded Hilda. The Runes had always called the Alfather *the Hanged God*. This was why he had been given the calling name, once upon a time.

Pierced with a spear, Odin had hanged himself from the

tree of life. A sacrifice to the Alfather—a sacrifice to himself. For nine nights he hung there, thirsting for food and drink and knowledge, until the runes had come to him, and finally released him from the tree.

The Runes had already told Hilda how she could get them back. That had to be why they called him the Hanged God. They had known this would happen and they had given her a map to regain them.

All Hilda had to do was march to Yggdrasil's trunk, climb the tree and hang herself on it, and count the days and nights. Nine of each, muttering for the Runes all the while. Sacrifices were always rewarded, and Hilda would sacrifice anything to regain her Runes. She knew what sacrifices could do. A sacrifice had revived her snow fox, and another would reunite her with the Runes.

'Yggdrasil can return the Runes to me, can't it?' Hilda asked Frigg, though she already knew that it could. That had to be why they were walking towards the tree of life. They weren't going to Valhalla, after all.

Frigg looked at Hilda with a frown that deepened her single wrinkle and it made her look like she wondered how anyone could be so stupid. 'They're not the Runes,' she dismissed.

Again Hilda had forgotten. She kept feeling stupid in the presence of her gods and goddesses, and she didn't usually feel stupid. For once, she wished that her father was there and could talk on her behalf and outsmart them all. He had always been a skilled talker.

'So a sacrifice won't return them,' Hilda said.

Frigg laughed. Hers was not a youthful giggle like Idun's, but a chortle that bordered on a cough. 'Who would you sacrifice to?' asked the goddess, between stifled laughs.

Hilda hadn't thought about that. She supposed that since she was in Asgard, a sacrifice to the gods would be pointless. They hadn't wanted her axe, and she doubted they wanted anything else she had. When the Alfather had hung himself in

Yggdrasil, he had sacrificed himself to himself. Hilda nodded in resolution. 'I'll sacrifice myself to myself.'

Frigg rolled her eyes and shook her head softly so all of her neck-rings jingled. 'He was a foolish young man, my old husband,' she said with a sigh.

So that wouldn't work either. Hanging from Yggdrasil had worked for Odin because he was a god. Hilda released an exasperated sigh. All she wanted was for everything to go back as it had been. She wanted her Runes back and to be among warriors again.

'Then how will I regain the'—Hilda stopped before she could say *the Runes*— 'The whispers in the wind?'

'They never left you,' Frigg said, much the same as Freya had told her. So at least the goddesses agreed about that, although none of them had told her how to hear the Runes—the whispers—again. 'In time you will learn to conjure the visions.'

The longer Hilda spent in the presence of her goddesses, the more she thought that they didn't *know* how. They weren't nornir, so how could they know? She didn't understand why they needed her either.

'Why can't you ask the three nornir to tell you where Loki is?' Hilda asked. Her father would have told her not to be so direct, but she had already wasted enough time trying to follow his advice. She didn't have his patience for pretending and meaningless talk. 'I don't know how to see the visions,' Hilda freely admitted. 'Urd, Skuld and Verthandi would know where he is and where he will be.'

'The three nornir are tied to my husband,' Frigg said, smiling at Hilda's direct questions. At least she was no longer laughing. 'And he does not want the same thing we do.'

Hilda sighed. No real answer. Again. Frigg was an impressive woman, and so was Freya and the other goddesses, but none of them seemed to really care about Hilda, she was just a tool passed from hand to hand. Frigg was interested in Hilda for now, but there was no telling how quickly she would get bored.

Freya had not been interested in Hilda since the bathhouse, and the others hadn't been that bothered either. Before Frigg, too, decided to cast her aside, Hilda needed answers.

'What does he want that you don't?' Hilda asked, hoping that *this* time she might get proper answers.

'Odin likes... shackles more than he likes killings,' Frigg answered.

Now that she was thinking about it, it had always seemed strange to Hilda that a being as dangerous as Loki had been shackled in a cave instead of killed. The gods had chased him through the nine worlds after he had brought on the murder of the Alfather's beloved son, Baldur. They had killed Höd for the crime of shooting the deadly arrow, but not Loki for whispering in Höd's ear. 'Why wouldn't he want to kill Loki?' she wondered aloud.

'They're blood-brothers,' Frigg said. 'Bound together with blood vows.' She shook her head to dismiss it, as if Hilda didn't know what blood vows were, but she did.

'Kauna, may my heat be yours,' Hilda recited, as the Runes had made her recite in the cold of the night in Magadoborg, bent over the body of her dead snow fox. 'Naudir, you shall eat in my stead.' Five runic promises Hilda recited, as she stared at the gold arm-ring Frigg had given her.

At the corner of her eyes she saw Frigg's stance turn rigid and heard the agitated hiss of her viper. 'How do you know such words?' the goddess asked. Her walk had slowed.

'The Runes'—Hilda shook her head— 'the whispers in the wind taught me. They taught me many things.' She stared at the viper that wound over Frigg's many gold rings. In a cave, Loki had been tied up, with a snake hanging above him, dripping venom on him. It sounded like a terrible fate, but knowing that Ragnarok would someday come, provoked by Loki, it would have been more prudent to kill him. 'Why can't the Alfather kill his blood-brother?'

'They can't do each other harm. They share a fate,' Frigg said in a distant voice, like it hardly mattered, but to Hilda it did. Because suddenly the many stories Hilda had grown up with made sense.

She had never understood why the gods who were quick to decide on murder hadn't simply killed Loki for everything he had done. It had never made sense to her. Why they kept him tied up in a cave. Alive. At last she knew. Odin and Loki were linked. That was why they would both die at Ragnarok. When one of them passed on, the other would too.

The goddess twisted one of her finger-rings so it spun around her finger. 'Who did *you* exchange blood vows with, Hilda?' Frigg took on a superior tone, pretending that the answer wasn't important, but if a goddess as powerful as Frigg asked, it was definitely important.

'With my dead fylgja,' Hilda confessed.

The goddess ceased walking. Her eyes went wide and she turned to examine Hilda from the worn leather shoes to the top of her blonde hair. The viper leaned forward, off Frigg's shoulder to get closer to Hilda. 'That's why...' Frigg mused without sharing her epiphany.

'The Runes disappeared shortly after that happened,' Hilda said. 'They were with me for a while—'

'It's not about your whispers,' Frigg dismissed. Her eyes were far away, seeing something that wasn't there, or looking straight through Hilda, like Sigismund and the warriors had done. '*You're* the fylgja,' Frigg muttered. 'That's why...'

Hilda knew that reviving the snow fox had come at a great cost. It had meant her death, but it had also come at another cost. In a way, they must have switched places, the fox and her.

'Freya mentioned that she couldn't silence you,' Frigg said, though Hilda had been in the bathhouse and she hadn't heard Freya say anything like that. Nor had the goddess ever asked Hilda to stay silent. 'That's why your mind is shielded against influence.' Frigg cocked her head to the side like a bird, listening for something. 'You're like my husband.'

Hilda choked on her own spit in surprise. To be welcomed into Valhalla was a great honour, but to be compared to the Alfather... Hilda had never thought she would be honoured so. She coughed trying to catch her breath, but when she finally did, Frigg had walked far ahead of her, hand trailing along Yggdrasil's large root.

'How am I like the Alfather?' asked Hilda, but Frigg did not provide an answer this time.

The goddess almost walked as fast as Freya had. Hilda put a hand over her wounded chest. She wasn't in pain, but there was an ache in her chest as she walked in her goddess' footsteps.

Like the Alfather, Frigg had said. Frigg, who would know better than anyone what the Alfather was like. Hilda had noticed similarities too. She was never hungry anymore. Her snow fox ate in her stead, like the Alfather's two wolves ate off his plate. The Alfather was known as a runemaster too. Though the goddesses kept saying that the whispers in the wind weren't the Runes, the warriors at home hadn't been entirely wrong in calling Hilda a runemistress. Thanks to the whispers, Hilda had known things. Even if they were only whispers, and not the Runes, and not truly visions either.

Frigg didn't look like she was going to say any more. She made certain to always be a few steps in front of Hilda, and her viper fylgja had settled in a ball on her left wrist.

Yggdrasil's trunk never seemed any nearer. It was so tall that Hilda didn't think anyone would be able to crawl up it. The size of a mountain, it was, but a mountain too steep to hike. Yet the Alfather had done it, long ago. Maybe he hadn't climbed up. He was a god, after all.

'What's happened?' asked Frigg. She wasn't speaking to Hilda.

Cloaked in silence, another woman had arrived from the forest, seemingly out of nowhere. Long black hair, as black as a raven feather, was combed down her back. 'They found her,' said the woman. Her light green eyes moved from Frigg to Hilda. They seemed to pierce right through her. 'He left this morning.' A slick raven threw out its wings as it landed on the woman's shoulder.

'And you come now?' Frigg hissed.

'I thought you would fly home.' The woman's eyes bore through Hilda. 'Not walk the long way.' Her dress was dark blue, almost black like her hair. She was dressed for murder.

Frigg returned her attention to Hilda. 'Wait in Valhalla,' she commanded. 'Continue along the root until you reach the tunnel. Take it and continue straight.'

The goddess reached into a slim pouch hanging from her gold-decorated belt. From it she pulled an eagle beak and then the full skin, although the skin was much too large to fit inside such a slim pouch.

'Be careful,' Frigg warned Hilda as she set her feet into the skin. 'There are jotnar in Asgard.' In a heartbeat she had lifted the skin and an eagle with a viper slung over its shoulders took flight.

The dark-haired woman was gone too. Frigg's eagle drove up towards Yggdrasil's far-away branches and leaves. At its side dashed two ravens. Hilda watched them fly away, through Yggdrasil's branches and out of sight. Maybe that was how the Alfather had climbed Yggdrasil to hang himself. Maybe he hadn't climbed, but flown up into the tree.

Something rustled in the woods to her right.

Hilda freed the Ulfberht axe from her weapon belt and peered into the woods. Giants in Asgard, Frigg had said. The tree-trunks were so wide that a giant could easily hide behind one. They were nowhere near Yggdrasil's height, but they were larger than any trees Hilda had ever seen in Midgard.

Axe in hand, she stepped away from Yggdrasil's huge root. Shadows moved in the woods, but maybe it was just deer. After what Frigg had said, she couldn't take the chance. Hilda planted her feet firmly on the ground and took a warrior stance. With her left hand she reached for her dagger.

A loud yelp came from behind her. Hilda spun, axe ready to strike.

A white snow fox ran in behind her, blue eyes fixed on Hilda. Its puffy white fur bounced as it ran, its legs were scarred. And then it barked again. Her fylgja.

Hilda heard a branch snap by Yggdrasil's root, and saw movement at the corner of her eye. She spun and cast her axe before she had time to think. Before whoever was there had time to evade.

Her axe swung above the head of a red fox and slapped into Yggdrasil's root. The axe trembled from the blow. The red fox scurried away, laughing as it rushed into the woods. Had it been a giant, the jotun would have been whacked in the groin by her axe.

In a heartbeat Hilda had her dagger in her left hand. She turned slowly around herself. The snow fox was looking into the forest after the red fox. It didn't bark and Hilda couldn't see anyone. Just her snow fox. Its tongue hung out like that of a dog and it looked like it smiled at the sight of her.

Hilda too was smiling. 'I missed you,' she said and crouched down, holding a hand out to the snow fox. It ran towards her and hopped up to lick her face and then down to run around itself. 'I missed you, I missed you,' Hilda said, ruffling the fox's long coat as it bounced around her.

It had changed during the few days that they had been apart. Its coat was completely white and ready for winter. 'I'm glad you're alright,' Hilda muttered as she ruffled the snow fox's ears. She got up, set away her dagger and went to retrieve her axe.

It was planted firmly into Yggdrasil's root. The root was almost as strong as metal, but her axe had cut into it. The Ulfberht axe was worthy of a goddess. It could cut through everything, even Yggdrasil's hard root. Hilda rocked the axe back and forth to widen the gap, then set a foot against the thick root and pulled back, retrieving her weapon.

Where it had been was a hole into Yggdrasil's root. A hole into nothingness.

Petrified like a dwarf, Hilda stared into the darkness. The inside of the ash-tree revealed itself to her in all its silent complexity. The dark was so dense that she could not truly understand what it was she looked at. It was a hole, but it felt different, somehow. Strangely familiar. It felt like home.

The deep darkness seemed to call to her like a song and enthral her to look inside.

Her snow fox barked in warning. Hilda snapped free of the enchantment, and ran, but at the corner of her eyes, she thought that she saw a face longingly stare back at her, out of the darkness.

DARKNESS

RAGNAR STOOD, FOR a moment, and stared blankly through the Darkness, his mind searching for a solution. There had to be some way to save his gods, and chain Loki again. Somehow, he had to undo his own wishes.

He stared through the Darkness, full well knowing that there was nothing to see. It had begun to feel soothing to stare into the dark. No matter what changed when he went through the veil, everything in the Darkness was always the same.

Barely had Ragnar thought it before he noticed that all was not as it had always been.

There was light in the Darkness. He had never seen light in the dark before. It was no more than a white dot hidden away among endless black, but it was lighter than he had expected. Lighter than the Darkness was supposed to be.

He walked towards it. For an eternity he walked, and the dot of light barely became any larger. It was a welcome change and distraction from his worries. The dot came closer and closer, and soon he saw that it was a slit of light, not a dot. Ragnar could almost see through it.

He drew closer.

Shadows stood in front of the slit of light, scrambling to get to the front. The shadowed warriors who killed Ragnar at their own whim. They were the shadows who tortured him into keeping his silence. He could see the shape of faces and bodies, and outlines of helmets, shields and weapons. There were many of them, and they were silent, like him.

Ragnar tiptoed at a safe distance behind them. He peered out of the slit of light, which was not covered by veils, although every exit from this place he had known had been lined by a veil.

Ragnar nursed the courage to approach, despite his fear of the shadowed warriors. If he did not speak, they would not kill him. Or so he hoped and wished, as he took a few more steps into their midst.

There was someone in front of the opening. The hole opened to Asgard, no doubt about it: there were perfectly lush colours, and every leaf in the distance was evenly balanced and the mossy grass evenly cut.

Ragnar cornered all the way to the front and stared out of the Darkness.

The shadow warriors tried to push him away, but Ragnar did not budge.

There was no veil. This was not like his conjured dreams of other worlds. This was a real way out, and as Ragnar gawked through the opening, he clearly saw Hilda look at him. He stared into his daughter's blue eyes. As clearly as he saw her, she saw him.

A shadowed warrior elbowed Ragnar away. Weapons were drawn, as he continued to stare at his daughter's face. First through his veil and now here. He kept seeing Hilda, but Ragnar did not know how he could help her. He did not know how to help anyone.

He missed her. He missed home. His heart ached with longing at seeing her.

The shadow warriors shouldered him away. Ragnar released a surprised yelp. A sword was stabbed through his neck. Ragnar gulped up blood.

Death, pain, and fear.

EINER

Chapter One Hundred and One

EINER LEFT THE battlefield of Ida's plain amidst a large crowd of giants. He tried to catch one last glimpse of Valhalla and the bloody plains through their legs, but he could not. He was tightly masked, exactly as they intended for him to be. This was the only way he could escape.

The Alfather had not returned with the valkyries. The fields they walked across were littered with bodies. Everyone was dead. Only giants and beasts were alive and leaving, now that all others were finished.

'Why doesn't the Alfather wake them?' Einer asked the red-haired giantess who led them off the battlefield. He stared at the cold bodies at his feet. The sun had set, and the moonshine strangely made everything look as red as the giantess' hair and his own chainmail.

'Sometimes he leaves them for a day. Enjoys the quiet of a hall without warriors. Sometimes he doesn't wake them for a few days.'

That wasn't what the stories told. The stories said that every day the warriors in Odin's sacred hall went onto the field and fought until the last of them died, and every night they were woken up and brought back into the hall where they feasted the night away until sunrise when they would fight again.

'Why?' Einer asked.

'They're dead,' said the giantess. 'They don't know the difference. And it can all get a little tedious. The cleaning up especially. There are so many corpses to revive.'

Einer supposed that made sense; he had a lot to learn about Asgard and the nine worlds. Sometimes he even thought that there was a lot for him to learn about Midgard, too.

'At least you're willing to learn,' said the bulky giant who walked to Einer's right. 'That is a start.'

It was strange to feel small. Surrounded by giants on all sides, Einer felt small for the first time since he had turned thirteen winters old.

The giants were stealing glances at him when they thought he would not notice. He *did* notice, but he did not mind. He supposed that his presence among them was as mysterious to them as it was to him. The shadowed man who had brought him into Odin's hall and called himself Einer's uncle walked at the back of the giants. He was taller than Einer, but not like the giants. Perhaps he was a half-giant. Einer still did not know who his uncle truly was, or why he wanted Einer to leave Valhalla.

'Family help each other,' said the hooded figure at his back. 'Valhalla is not your rightful place. I'll lead you back to achieve your true destiny.'

'You know my destiny?'

'I have not seen your thread in the nornir's cave,' said his uncle. 'But I know what you need to become. What you need to learn if you are to survive long enough to accomplish whatever the nine worlds have planned for you.'

Under his chainmail the bracteate slapped against Einer's chest with every step he took, and it both steadied him and brought his attention to a nagging anger at the back of his mind that had been building for a while. It seemed to always be there; the rage that he had let loose in Magadoborg when Hilda had passed on.

'Where to?' asked the red-haired giantess. 'The tavern?'

'They are not here, watching. We can go straight home.' It was Einer's uncle who answered. The big giantess who had slain every last man and shieldmaiden on the battlefield listened to him, as if he was as powerful as the Alfather. Perhaps he *was* the Alfather. Einer did not think that he had ever seen the two of them in a room together, and Odin was known to deceive to get his way, whatever his way was.

'I told you that I'm not the Alfather,' said the hooded man, but Einer had yet to see definitive proof that he was indeed Einer's uncle and who he said he was. Except that he had caught a glimpse of the shadowed face a few times. So he knew that the tall man had two eyes and no beard.

Perhaps it was a trick of the eyes. The gods could do so many things, surely changing Einer's vision would be an easy task for someone as powerful as the Alfather.

'And what reason would the Alfather have to lead you off his battlefield, to create mistrust between you and him?'

It was a potent question and Einer did not have an answer.

'Because there is none,' said the hooded man in a final tone. His voice shook the ground beneath Einer's feet. All the giants listened to him, and although Einer did not know why, he was being swayed by the hooded man, and deep within himself, where the unknown anger that had once killed a white bear rested, Einer knew that his uncle spoke the truth.

He was so certain that he did not know how he could doubt it.

'The truth is often the most difficult to accept,' said the bulky giant to Einer's right side. The giants responded directly to his thoughts, and Einer did not enjoy the idea that they knew everything that went on in his mind.

'So, we are going directly to Jotunheim now,' Einer said aloud, to make the many giants focus on something other than his thoughts.

'Nej,' the red-haired giantess answered. 'None of us live in Jotunheim any longer. You are both coming home with me.'

Einer looked over his shoulder to his uncle. 'I thought you said that you would show me Jotunheim.'

'I will,' he answered. 'But these days rarely anyone goes there from Asgard. We will be caught if we go direct.'

That would not do. Hilda was not in Valhalla. That much was certain. No one had seen her. Those who had passed on in Magadoborg would have arrived together if she had been selected for the warrior life, as they all had, and that meant that she had to be in Helheim.

'Why does the Alfather want to keep me somewhere I don't belong?' he asked. His uncle had said that Einer's afterlife would look different, and that he would not be seated in Valhalla as the Alfather insisted. Einer had so many questions, and his uncle seemed to hold all of the answers.

'For the same reason he took your brothers before their times were up. He fears what you will become. He wants you on his side.'

'Do you mean my kinsmen?' Einer asked. He had always wanted a brother, especially an older brother, but he did not have any, and now his father was dead.

'Nej,' said his uncle. 'I mean what I say.'

'I don't have any brothers.'

'You do,' his uncle simply said.

Einer barely saw where he was walking as he thought about that. He knew that his parents had not had other children, and he had always thought and believed that his father had no bastard sons, but he must have been wrong. The hooded man had no reason to lie. At least no reason that Einer knew.

'You've met them,' said his uncle, and that confused Einer more than anything else in the nine worlds. Not only did he have an uncle that he had never heard about, he had brothers that he had never known about, and he had met them, too.

He wondered which one of the village children it had been. He wondered if he had sisters too, and how many. If his father had truly had so many other children, he wondered who it had been and most of all he wondered if his mother knew.

'Your brothers did not grow up with you,' the hooded man explained. 'You met them back at Odin's hall. So proudly he introduced you to each other, never telling you their full lineage.'

Back in the hall, the Alfather had introduced Einer to the warriors at his high tables. Einer's bench-mates, Haskell and Ove, and Frode, and half a hundred other names that he no longer recalled.

'Haskell and Ove?' Einer asked aloud. They had treated him like a brother and taken him in and told him about their bets and the battlefield. They had been like real brothers.

'Haskell and Ove. And Frode and Viggo, Jary and Troels. Many others too. I don't know all of their names.'

Einer liked the thought of them being his brothers. He had always wanted older brothers who would take care of him and show him the way of the worlds and introduce him to drinking and games and girls, and who would do whatever it was that brothers did. He had always wanted that, especially since Leif had passed on. Haskell and Ove would make the perfect brothers. And now it seemed they *were* his brothers. It was a difficult thought to accept.

They were so much older than him. They had been in Valhalla for so long. They knew all of the tricks in the hall and on the battlefield. They had spoken as if they had been there dozens of summers, perhaps hundreds of summers, but they could not have been.

'Liar.' Einer shook his head laughing. The air had been so serious, especially walking in this crowd of giants, that he had fallen for it. Such a blatant lie, and he had believed it. At this point he may start to believe anything.

The last few weeks had shown so many surprises that a crazy thought like that of his father having many other sons who feasted in Valhalla had simply seemed like another truth for him to accept.

'It's not a joke,' said the red-haired giantess.

Einer's laugh died out. No one else was laughing with him. 'It has to be.' They were too old. His father was not *that* old. Even if he had fathered a child at a very young age, they were too old, and there was much that it did not explain.

'They're not your father's children,' said the giantess. 'They were your mother's.'

Now he was certain that they were joking. He would have known if his mother had been pregnant before having him. He would know. Everyone would have known, and his mother most definitely was not old enough to have given birth to many sons before Einer was born.

'Oh, but she is,' said the shadowed man. 'You have much to learn about your mother. As I did, and still do.'

'Oh, I could tell you stories,' said the giantess. 'Of Glumbruck's young glory days.'

'What does Glumbruck mean?' Einer asked.

There was a moment of silence before the red-haired giantess answered. 'You probably know her under a different name, but it is your mother's true name.'

'You know my mother?'

'I knew her,' the giantess confirmed.

'We all did,' said the jotun who walked at Einer's side. 'Those of us who are old enough, at least.'

It was difficult to imagine his mother in company like this. She had a presence greater than any of these giants, but she was so young and she was just his mother who was caring and kind and watched out for the villagers and cooked an amazing rabbit stew.

'It's funny, isn't it?' said the giant at Einer's side, not to Einer, but to the other giants, over Einer's head. 'To him she is just a woman. A mother. Glumbruck, of all people.'

'It's like being the son of Odin, and never knowing,' said a giant that Einer could not see in the thick crowd of tall warriors that surrounded him.

'How do you all know her?' he asked.

They laughed at his question. They could hardly continue walking, they were laughing so hard.

'How do we *know* her?' a giant wheezed. 'Everyone in Asgard knows Glumbruck, and what she brought into the nine worlds.'

'She used to be one of us,' said the red-haired giantess. She wasn't laughing like the others. 'She was my first shieldmaiden, after I married and joined the beast ranks. Njord loved how it all ended. "I told you not to leave the Naust," he told me for a good dozen winters until I finally had enough and left for the mountains.'

Einer's mouth dropped open. He struggled to put the giantess' words together in his head. She had definitely said Njord and Naust in the same sentence. She talked as if she was married to the god Njord, and she was tall and beautiful and red haired, and he knew that she was a fiery huntress.

The longer he thought about it, the more certain he became. She had to be the wife of Njord, the noble god that every sailor and every fisher prayed to for fertility and prosperity, Father of Frey and Freya, the most famed of all vanir.

'You're Njord's wife?' Einer stammered. 'You're Skadi?'

'She is a lot more than Njord's wife,' his uncle warned from behind.

Einer knew that he should not have phrased it that way, but he was so thunderstruck by her mere presence that he had forgotten his words. 'I know,' he stuttered. 'She may be a giant, but in Midgard she is revered as a goddess. In winter, people pray to you. They offer to you to give them safe passage during snowy months and in the mountains of the north.'

Up north when he had visited Sigis as a kid, they had prayed a lot to Skadi. The white bear that Einer had killed had been offered in her name. No one had died on the snowy plains that winter.

'I received your offering,' said the giantess. 'I watched over you all winter and saw your safe return to Jutland.'

Einer's heart warmed, and not from the bracteate, but from knowing that his offerings had been accepted and his prayers heard, and that a giantess as famous and powerful as Skadi had watched over him for an entire winter.

'I thought you didn't get involved with matters in Midgard,' said a giant in the party.

'I don't,' she replied quite simply. 'I felt the forefathers call.'

She looked over her shoulder then, at Einer. Her eyes shone underneath her blooded helmet, and Einer struggled not to stare at her now that he knew who she was.

'As I do now,' she said.

The other giants turned their gaze to Einer who walked in their midst, a dwarf among them. They all watched him. They followed Skadi's every instruction. If Einer had been a giant, he would have followed her too.

'They call your name, short-lived,' she said. 'Do you hear them?'

Skadi stopped walking in the middle of the plain, and so did everyone else. The sun had set, and the stars were out. The grass at his feet was no longer slick with blood. They had left the battlefield but the crowd of giants surrounding Einer was so thick that he could not see through them and he did not know where they were. They could as well be standing in the middle of a plain as in a forest. All he could see was a patch of stars above, and the grass at his feet. He did not, however, think that they had arrived at Skadi's and Njord's home by the sea. He would have heard the sound of the waves hitting the coast, or the call of seagulls and other sea-life. At the very least he should have smelled it in the air.

'Do you hear them?' asked Skadi in a whisper.

Einer looked up at the faces of the many giants who stood over him. One after the other they closed their eyes as if they were listening to the wind. Einer did as they did. He closed his eyes and focused to hear the call that Skadi spoke about, but all he heard and smelled was the damp breath of giants.

'It's more of a feeling,' said his uncle from behind. 'The anger that you lock in your hand. The one that pounds on the inside of your chest.'

The beat of the bracteate against Einer's chest settled his focus, and beyond the heat, and beyond the hammering, deep within, was that familiar anger that he had always feared. The anger that had released itself in the stables and scared Hilda when they had been kids. The anger that had killed the white bear and ruined his friendship with Sigismund, the anger that had killed hundreds in Magadoborg and had brought him here. Nothing good ever happened when he listened to the anger. 'I don't hear anything,' he said.

All he had was that ominous feeling that he always carried with him. He closed his fist tight to stop thinking about it. Whatever Skadi and his uncle meant, Einer did not hear it, and they did not know what they asked of him.

Skadi had resumed her walk. The giants were following, but hesitantly, waiting for Einer to join as well so they could shield him from view as they walked.

Einer broke into a run to catch up. He wondered what Skadi meant, and what she had wanted, but he was glad that she did not press the matter. She had no idea what could happen if Einer released that anger. He knew it wanted to kill. It was all it ever did or wanted to do, and he would no longer let it. The anger was locked away securely in his fist as his mother had once taught him.

'We know,' said his uncle, as they walked. 'But the anger calls for you, as it calls us all.'

'You can't keep it inside forever,' said the giant walking on

Einer's left. It sounded like a threat. 'You don't belong with the Alfather. You chose the forefathers, and they chose you. You're a giant, now.'

TYRA

Chapter One Hundred and Two

SIV'S MARCH LEFT no room for hesitation. Tyra admired her for that. Someday, she wanted to be able to walk that way too. To lead someone this confidently when they both knew the danger that lay ahead. Siv and Tyra were being hunted, and gods and valkyries didn't give up.

'We're nearly there,' Siv said. She walked straight through the mist. It didn't in the least hinder her. Tyra had to walk fast to not lose sight of Siv and get lost. Strangely, she remembered the time in the snow storm when they had first walked through the passage grave.

Suddenly, Siv stopped walking.

Tyra tiptoed to the side so she stood next to Siv, and could see what Siv did. A woman was standing in front of them, half hidden in the morning mist.

'You cannot come here,' the woman said in a coarse voice that belonged to an old woman. 'Go back.' Her face was hidden in the shadows of a hood and a single lock of long blonde hair escaped. She was short, compared to Siv, but she had as much presence.

'Long time,' Siv said without the least bit of worry over the cold welcome the woman had given them. 'Where are your sisters, Verthandi?'

Tyra stared up at the hooded woman with new understanding. So, this was one of the three nornir who spun fates and destinies, and somehow Siv knew her. Siv knew everyone.

'They're working,' the norn replied. 'Always working.'

'To what end?' Siv casually asked.

'The same one as you.'

'I doubt it.'

'You can't be here,' the woman repeated. Her voice had softened, and she tilted her head slightly to the side. She seemed to speak out of concern, as if she and Siv had used to be friends and there was some sort of bond there that she wished to protect. 'You know that.'

The mist began to clear and Tyra was certain it did so on Siv's command.

'You look to the future too, sometimes,' Siv said. 'Don't you?'

The norn neither confirmed nor denied that, so Tyra supposed that it was the truth. Siv always knew what was true and what wasn't. Though the stories said that it was Skuld who saw the future, while Verthandi saw the present, and Urd saw the past.

'So you know what I will do if you do not lead me to your hall.'

The norn glanced to Tyra and then up at Siv again. 'Blood dripping over the threads, seeping out of the hall. Odin's servants flayed and stripped. You wouldn't... No one could...'

Siv smiled a wicked smile, and had Tyra not been standing at her side and had she not known Siv, she might have been scared. Standing there next to her, she almost felt scared of Siv. She was so superior, and so certain of herself.

'Your future doesn't show you what I *might* do,' Siv said. 'It shows you what I *will* do. Unless you change your mind and thereby change the future. What I ask of you is not a difficult task.' Siv's voice was like the gathering clouds above them.

The norn too was looking up at the darkening weather. 'It is not,' the norn agreed. Her sight settled back on Siv. 'It's an impossible one.'

'Lately I have seen many impossible deeds done,' Siv said. 'Do this for me, Verthandi, and I will forget what happened.'

Tyra stared from one to the other, hoping to understand and be included, but she didn't know what they were talking about, and she wasn't so certain that she wanted to know, either.

Siv reached down and took Tyra's hand in her own. She always knew how to reassure. 'I am not alone anymore,' Siv said and clenched Tyra's hand. 'Don't force me into the same corner twice.'

'I can't,' Verthandi said.

'Then we have both made our choices, and you know what happens next,' Siv said. Her hand reached for the seax at her belt.

Tyra took a step backwards, fearing what may come next. She remembered when Siv had launched at her on the Oxen Road back in Jutland, after she had killed the retinue. She remembered the look in Siv's eyes, the desperation as she had yelled for Tyra to run, and she remembered being as scared that night as she had been during the battle at Ash-hill. She didn't want to see Siv like that again.

'Glumbruck...' the norn muttered.

'I have nothing more to lose, Verthandi. You know that better than anyone.'

The norn looked like she wanted to protest, but she soon closed her mouth and nodded. 'Then I guess we have no choice but to help you.'

Siv let go of the seax again. She hadn't pulled the blade free from her belt yet. She hadn't needed to, and Tyra thought that Verthandi too must have known how Siv had been about to transform.

'Not an impossible task, after all,' said Siv as Verthandi

turned her back to them and disappeared into the thinning mist. Siv followed and Tyra trotted behind, worried about being left alone.

Tyra knew that she could trust Siv, but at the same time there was so much that she didn't know and that only Siv knew, and every time they met someone from one of the other eight worlds, Tyra uncovered yet another part of Siv's past and none of it made sense to her. Siv had so many secrets, and uncovering one led to the discovery of dozens more questions and mysteries.

'It'll be alright,' Siv told Tyra. She always knew when to say what.

Siv let Verthandi's heels disappear into the mist. Then she leaned in and whispered to Tyra. 'No matter what happens, make certain that you get away safe. This is the only hope for us.'

They began to walk up a hill, leaving the mist behind. Early morning sun washed over the front of a high rock formation with a huge gate opening into the depths of it. Yggdrasil's roots travelled over the rock, like the fingers of a hand trying to lift it.

Tyra marvelled at it. It was like something out of one of Ragnar's stories, and in a way, she supposed that it was. It was the nornir's cave of destiny threads, after all.

The huge gate was open, but Tyra couldn't see into the hall. They travelled up the hill, behind Verthandi, who huddled in her robes. She had to be old to have spun the fates of all the beings in the nine worlds, but although her voice was ragged and worn, her steps were light.

Tyra puffed on the way up. She had walked so much, and she didn't want to walk anymore. She didn't know why everything in Asgard had to be so far away. Siv would say that they were almost somewhere and then they would still have half a day of travel before they arrived. And there was no time to rest in Asgard either. Not with the valkyries chasing them.

The sunlight entered the open gate of the hall of spun threads of destiny. Verthandi paused at the entrance. Right so Tyra couldn't see anything in the shadows inside, though she tried her best.

'There is no other way,' Siv reminded the norn.

Verthandi nodded in understanding, and brought her hands up to her hood. She let it drop to reveal her face. From the voice and her age and all the stories, Tyra had expected Verthandi to be old and her face to be wrinkled. Her hair was so blonde as to be silvery grey, but she was young. Her face was that of a woman of no more than twenty. Her cheeks and lips were plump. She looked younger than Siv, though she couldn't possibly be and though her voice sounded like that of an old grandmother.

Tyra gaped at Verthandi. She hadn't expected the norn to be beautiful, either. She had expected an old woman, tired from spinning fates into eternity, but Verthandi was pretty.

'*You* can't go inside,' said Verthandi, looking at Tyra.

Tyra looked up at Siv. She didn't want to be left alone. She glanced back over her shoulder to the mist at the bottom of the hill, and with every breath she took, she worried that crows would fly out of the mist and that the valkyries would catch up to them.

'She comes with me,' Siv said.

Verthandi shook her head. 'I can't let a short-lived see her own destiny.'

'You either invite us inside, Verthandi, or we let ourselves inside.'

The norn understood what that meant, for she disappeared into the shadows of the hall and Tyra was certain they were expected to follow.

There was no light inside other than what little entered through the great gate. It wasn't much, and Tyra struggled to see where she walked. Siv made her walk in front. It felt safe with Siv at her back, watching over her, but she was scared to step out of the light and into the shadows of the hall.

Her eyes adjusted slowly. There were pillars throughout the hall. And around the pillars, ribbons and threads were bound. The threads wrapped over and under each other and as far into the vast hall as Tyra could see, though she couldn't really see that far. The ceiling was far up too. And when she looked up, she saw that there were threads wrapped around the pillars up there, too. The entire hall was full of them.

Tyra worried that she might trip on the threads at her feet, so she moved carefully. She didn't want to trip and maybe change someone's destiny, or ruin it, or break their thread and end their life.

The further into the hall they came, the more threads there were. Tyra had to duck under them and leap across. She felt her way with her hands before every single step that she took, because though some threads were thick and golden, others were thin and easy to miss, like spider webs.

'Keep walking,' Siv reassured her with a warm hand on her shoulder. Siv always made everything seem better and easier than it really was.

The hall was humid like a cave, and it kind of *was* a cave, since it had been carved into a rocky mountainside, but it looked like a great hall worthy of gods.

A little further along there was a light. It wasn't much, and it didn't shine far like the light that entered through the enormous gate, but it *did* shine. A simple candlelight that cast long shadows. A woman stood with the candle, and even from this far away, Tyra could see that the figure wasn't Verthandi. She wasn't bent over, like Verthandi, but stood proud.

'At last the day has come,' she said. 'I have waited for you to return ever since you left. I don't usually mind waiting, but this was a difficult wait.'

Without a response, they walked closer to the woman and her candle light. She looked as young as Verthandi, and maybe younger. Her hair was red, and she had the sort of face that was pleasant to look upon but difficult to remember.

'Then you can rest assured now,' said Siv in a grim voice. 'No more future predictions.'

If she looked to the future, then she was probably Skuld, Tyra guessed. Skuld was the one the tales said could look at the future, and Siv had talked differently to Verthandi who was said to see everything that happened in the present.

'Time is short,' said Verthandi's worn voice.

Tyra startled away. The blond norn walked up from behind her, and Tyra didn't know how she had arrived there, though she had walked into the hall first.

'Your fates have already been spun,' Skuld said. 'I don't understand what you hope to accomplish.'

'Take us to them,' Siv demanded.

With her flickering candlelight, Skuld led the way further into the hall. They reached a far wall, where a large set of carved doors lead into another hall. The doors were ajar and a few threads disappeared into the other hall. It was darker in there, and Tyra couldn't see anything, not with Skuld's candlelight bouncing off the carved doors.

Verthandi walked to stand at her sister's side. Without Tyra's knowledge, the third and last norn had joined them. Her hood was up, but she was the same height as Verthandi and her shoulders were straight and confident, much like Skuld.

Verthandi, Skuld, and Urd. In front of Tyra stood the three famous nornir who spun the fates of all living beings.

'Only those of short-lived and long-lived,' Verthandi said, correcting Tyra's thoughts.

Tyra gulped. She didn't like the idea that everyone knew what she was thinking. She knew that Siv did sometimes, but that was different. She trusted Siv, and Siv rarely corrected her thoughts or reacted to them unless it was to reassure her.

The nornir walked to stand by some threads intertwined between two pillars. There were many threads, but all three of them were staring at the middle. Tyra concentrated to see what they did.

There were so many threads that Tyra didn't know how the nornir could tell which was which. There were a lot of white and blue threads, but a few were different. There was a red thread that seemed to have been braided by four different red threads to form one. Most of the blue and white and grey and brown threads were wrapped around this one. From the red thread, they travelled away and came back. A bronze thread wound around the red one as if they were one and same, but sometimes they were separated for a little while, swirling together with other threads before they came together again.

Tyra didn't know if she was allowed to ask questions, but she wanted to. 'Are they ours?' she asked.

Skuld pointed to the thin bronze thread. 'This is yours, Tyra daughter of Gunna and Jarn of Ash-hill, future wife to Styrbjorn the Strong of Jomsborg, and...'

Siv cut her off. 'What is he?' she asked. 'Styrbjorn. You've spun his fate, you must know.'

'Why do you ask?' Skuld narrowed her eyes at Siv, and the candle light made her look wicked.

But Siv wasn't intimidated, and Tyra was proud to stand at her side. 'I'm here to ensure a good fate for my daughter.'

Colour prickled in Tyra's cheeks. Siv truly was her mother now. And though Tyra knew that her mother and her father were waiting for her in Valhalla, she felt such pride at being Siv's daughter too. She had so many parents.

For a brief moment, the nornir were flustered and exchanged looks. The nornir knew Siv's destiny. They had spun it. They knew that Tyra was not her daughter. But then Siv reached down and took Tyra's hand into her own. 'Give her the best odds to make destined choices,' said Siv.

Tyra didn't know if she liked the idea of having a destiny, but she supposed that it was alright, if there were some things that weren't fixed. She liked the idea of living up to the expectations the gods and nornir had set for her. She liked the thought of being able to surprise, too.

A destiny thread was a road of possibilities. Every choice she made still mattered and could change her future. That was why destines were spun in thread and not carved into stone.

'Who is Styrbjorn really?' Siv prompted again.

'He is fire,' Verthandi said and pointed to two slim threads intertwined.

Siv and Tyra stepped closer. One of the threads was brown and the other shone like embers. It enclosed around the first one, squeezing it.

'A fire demon,' Siv whispered.

'*The* fire demon,' Verthandi corrected.

'Escaped from Muspel,' said Urd who saw the past.

'Destined to release her brothers and burn Midgard,' said Skuld who looked at the future.

Their warnings didn't make Siv falter. 'All destinies can be changed.'

'What do we do?' Tyra found the courage to ask. It sounded bad, but Tyra didn't want to abandon Svend, because she was scared of Styrbjorn. And she didn't want Siv to leave her like her parents had. She didn't ever want to be left again. She liked having someone who cared about her and loved her and took care of her, and made sure that she had washed her hair well and asked her if she had eaten. She liked having someone who cared about her, and was not just a thrall. Thralls sometimes took care of things like that, but that was different. It wasn't like it was with Siv.

Tyra squeezed Siv's warm hand a little harder.

'We will have to change your destiny.' Siv was so calm and certain that Tyra too began to feel certain that all would be well.

She stared at the bronze thread that was hers. All the choices she had made could be read from it. And all future choices she would be presented with were there too, if one knew what the knots meant. There were many threads following hers. Many knots with hundreds of threads tied together.

Some threads followed hers for longer than a knot or two. Threads like the red one. It had to belong to Siv. It was so long and decisive, and it seemed to pull Tyra's thread along a lot of the time, judging from the way that they were intertwined and braided together. Other threads also followed Tyra's. A green one in particular caught her eye. It was both dark green like an ash, and bright green like spring leaves on a beech tree. Maybe it was her father, or maybe it was Svend. She didn't really know, but it reminded her of both of them.

She followed the threads back. They didn't follow each other all the way from what she supposed was her start, or perhaps it was her future. She didn't know which way the threads were spun, just that they were there, and that every thread that touched hers had destinies that were tied to Tyra's own.

'Some things can't be changed,' said Skuld.

'What?' Siv was as taken aback as Tyra.

Tyra squeezed her hand. 'Siv? What do they mean?' She tried to be as brave as Siv, but the nornir's stares made her tremble. They were so wise and they knew everything about her past, present and future. They knew every choice she had made and every choice she was destined to make.

'Some events have been tied too tightly to the destinies of others and cannot be unwrapped,' said Verthandi. Despite her youthful beauty, she sounded old.

Tyra examined her bronze thread again, and wondered what the unchangeable events were. She supposed it was where hundreds of threads were tied to hers in a big tangle. Her mother would have called such a tangle of threads a waste, but the threads of destinies were different. It was their *job* to get entangled.

Maybe she had no choice but to get married like Harald wanted. But then, maybe, she could find a way out of the marriage afterwards. Maybe she could run away with Siv and Svend and change all of their destinies. That's what she most wanted to do.

Tyra had always thought that knowing one's destiny was good. Knowing what would come could help one achieve one's true potential. Knowing what would come would make life's every challenge safe and secure. She'd used to discuss such things with her friends. They hadn't been supposed to talk about it until they came of age, because it was a little scary, but they still had. They'd discussed it in whispers, all of the kids, in the dark of Ragnar's longhouse on the stormy nights.

Once, she remembered, Ragnar had suddenly arrived out of the shadows, axe in hand. The light from the longhouse fire had glistened against the sharp end. 'It's best not to know,' he had said. 'If you knew what would come next, you wouldn't want to live.' Their skald had swung the axe above their heads to scare them, planting it in the wooden table. Laughing, he had walked off. It had been the shortest and scariest story he had ever told. Tyra had been so scared that she had hiccupped all night and hadn't been able to sleep until morning.

'What is this?' Siv touched a finger to a knot that tied Tyra's thread to the red one. On one side of the knot their destinies were braided together. On the other they were apart and Siv's red thread disappeared far into the dark of the next hall.

The knot had to be an event that tied them together. Probably it was the battle at Ash-hill, after which she and Siv had travelled together. They had hardly known each other before then. Siv had just been Einer's mother and the chief's wife and Tyra had been just one of many village kids. It was strange to think about.

'This knot,' Siv resumed. Her voice was shaking. 'It's...'

'It's today,' said the three nornir at the exact same heartbeat. 'You have until today.'

It wasn't their first meeting, then.

The threads parted after the knot. Tyra didn't want to know what it meant, anymore. It would have to change anyways. Everything that could be changed would have to change.

'And then?' Siv asked.

'You shouldn't have come, Glumbruck,' Skuld said with sorrow in her voice. 'This is a knot that cannot be undone. This is where your paths part. Your destinies do not cross again.'

'Today?' Tyra piped. Her voice cracked. Ragnar had been right. It was best not to know what one's destiny held. She clenched Siv's hand. 'Don't go,' she said. She was crying. The tears dripped over her cheeks. She was terrified. 'Change our fates,' she yelled to the nornir, but they didn't move.

'Some things can't be changed,' they replied, with one voice. 'Some days are unchangeable.'

'But this isn't one of them,' Tyra said, shaking her head. She refused to believe it.

She clenched Siv's hand even tighter. Siv clenched back. She wouldn't let go. They wouldn't be separated. Not like this. Not today. Not any day.

Tyra shook her head, and held onto Siv's hand. She couldn't give up. It wasn't what Siv did.

'I am not giving up,' Siv told her. She leaned down and gave Tyra a warm hug.

Tyra was still crying. She didn't like this. None of it. She wouldn't let Siv leave. There was no reason for her to leave. Just because their destinies had some stupid knot on them.

'I'll undo it,' Tyra cried. 'Let me undo it!'

She wrenched free from Siv's hug and rushed to the delicate threads, grabbed them and tugged. To untie the knot and braid them together again. But the knot was tight. She wrenched the threads to force them apart, but nothing happened.

The three nornir and Siv all stood and watched her. None of them opposed her, but none of them helped her either.

'They are not regular threads,' Siv said, trying to make it sound like it was fine, though it was anything but. 'They can't be undone.'

'Are you going to leave me?' Tyra cried. She didn't understand. They were just threads tied in a hall. They meant nothing. It hadn't come true yet.

'Tyra,' Siv said to calm her. She put a hand on Tyra's shoulder to make her stop the struggle with the two threads. 'Tyra.'

Tyra kept at it. They had to be undone. There had to be a way. She would cut them if she needed to. Anything to change what the nornir said was unchangeable. They had come all of this way, from Midgard, travelled through the passage grave, and run through the scary forests of Asgard so that they would not have to be separated. So that Tyra would not have to go far away when Harald decided to marry her to some scary wealthy man who knew that Siv was using the runes. That was why they had come. She refused to believe that in doing so, they had worsened their fates.

But the threads wouldn't come apart. She held them in her hands, but she no longer tugged on them. She couldn't get them free. Exactly as the nornir said. 'Siv, please don't leave me,' she said.

She didn't dare to look up at Siv. She didn't want to hear that there was no choice, and that the fates said that she and Siv had to go each their way.

'I would never leave you willingly.' Siv's hand was warm on Tyra's shoulder. Her grasp was firm, but then it gradually weakened. She let go. 'But you need to go. It's time.'

'You can't leave.' Tyra spun around. 'You can't!' She grabbed onto Siv's hand. She didn't want Siv to let go of her. Certainly not because of some threads three old ladies had spun and hung up in a hall.

'Some things are unchangeable,' Siv said in her wisest voice that left no room for compromise. 'Something else is coming. Our destinies part today. But I will find you again. I will have our fates spun and braided together once again. Until then, Tyra, remember what is important.'

Tyra stared up into Siv's grey lynx eyes. Nothing seemed important if Siv wasn't there with her.

'The nine worlds,' Siv said. She grabbed Tyra's wrist to wrench her own hand free from Tyra's grasp. 'We must save the nine worlds. Only then can we meet again. In your afterlife.'

'In the afterlife?' Tyra asked.

'The afterlife has no destinies,' Siv said. She was so certain; she always was. But she had been certain about coming here too, and about changing their destinies for the better.

Tyra no longer knew what the right thing to do was.

'Your heart will lead you true,' Siv said. 'Now you have to go. At the other end of the hall, there will be an exit,' Siv said. 'You have to go now.'

'Why?' Tyra didn't understand. But she heard the urgency in Siv's tone. And she felt Siv's insistence in her mind. She knew that she couldn't resist. She would have to go, or Siv would make her, and that would be worse.

'He is here,' Siv whispered.

Long shadows flickered across the hall. Tyra spun to face the entrance. Ravens and crows came flying in, and a slender figure stood in the illuminated doorway. The Alfather.

'Run,' Siv said, as she had so many times. 'Run, Tyra, and don't look back. I love you,' she said, although she never had. Not like this. Their time together was up. The nornir had said so.

'I love you too, Glumbruck,' Tyra yelled, and then she turned away from Siv, and ran past pillars and threads. She didn't want to move, but Siv made her.

Every instinct told Tyra to stay where she was. Where Siv was. But Siv forced her to run.

EINER

Chapter One Hundred and Three

THE WARM HAMMER of the bracteate reminded Einer of the smell of southern flowers that his mother had used to scent her hair with, and the warmth of her touch.

Most of the giants had left the party. Einer walked alone with his uncle and red-haired Skadi.

The air had a different smell, this far from the bloody plains of Ida. It smelled of home; of salty shores and strong winds, although the winds were stronger and the shores were saltier than the ones Einer knew. Seagulls shrieked and waves crashed against rocks and cliffs that Einer could hardly see from up where they walked.

Ahead was a stone house, built on the edge, extending over the cliff and down the rocks to the sea. The top of it was shaped like the fore-stern of a ship with a weather vane flying in the wind. The house was like a longship built upright on the side of a cliff.

'Is that where your husband lives?' Einer asked, still awed at the thought that he was walking with the most famous giantess of all.

'Oh don't call him that,' she replied. 'He might hear you and think that I finally accept the marriage terms.' Her voice carried a certain fondness as she looked at the ship house on the cliff.

'You hate him that much?' Einer asked. It was no secret that Skadi hated her husband's home in Asgard and that she spent most of her time trekking the snowed mountaintops of Jotunheim.

'Nej,' she said and sighed. 'He is the best of men. He is worthy and good. But he is a man of the Sea and I am a woman of the Mountain. We simply weren't destined to be, no matter what the aesir will have us believe.'

Her reasoning was good. No wonder she was the only giantess to be treated like a goddess in Midgard. She was worthy of all the tales spun about her, and she carried herself not in a proud manner like the Alfather, who was clearly superior to all, but in a gentle yet stern way that set her apart from others. She had her life figured out, and her death too, and everything in between and beyond. She knew exactly who she was, and she was content with her life arrangements, and somehow Einer could not help but think of his mother as he looked at her.

The stone ship house was strangely built. Crooked, as if it was someone's first house, or an old ruin that had been given a new roof and reinforced walls. It did not belong among Asgard's perfection. Einer supposed that this was why the great Njord, fertility god of the sea, was sometimes mentioned by other gods in a mocking tone. He might have lived most of his life in Asgard, but he was a vanir, a god of fertility, and he would never truly belong in Asgard. He had not adapted here like his two children Frey and Freya had. He had built a crooked ship-shaped house on a cliff far off in the distance and had never bothered to make it look perfect like everything else here. He was content in its lack of perfection. It fit the two of them well. Skadi and Njord, both residents in Asgard and both from other worlds.

'The boat will be at the bottom of the cliff,' Skadi said. They were a few paces away from the crooked stone house, but as Einer came closer to the cliff, he saw steps hacked into the cliff, slanting towards the sea. Stairs as crooked and charming as Njord's house.

'We're sailing?' Einer asked, turning to his uncle's hooded face. 'In this weather?'

It was not a bad day. There was no rain, no dark clouds anymore. The storm had raged and left, but an insistent wind blew towards the shore. A wind that would be near impossible to sail out on.

'Rowing,' his uncle said. He turned to Skadi. 'Is Njord home?' he asked.

'He is,' she said.

Einer's uncle fell silent and then, with a sigh, he pulled down the hood that covered his scarred face. He didn't explain.

Though Einer had looked upon it more than once, the sight of the scars that covered his uncle's face and hands sent a shiver through him. The scars were grotesque, but it was the thought of how it could have happened that got to him; of being burned to the core and surviving.

'A story for another time,' his uncle told him.

'A story for tonight,' Skadi said. She smiled warmly. 'A soup before you go.'

'But Njord...?'

'It's time that he decided where he will stand when the wolves howl. I know where I will be.'

She began to walk away from the crooked steps to the stone house instead. Einer's uncle followed, and Einer too. It felt strange to walk closer to the crooked house, like it was forbidden. A mere moment earlier it *had* been forbidden, at least to Einer and his uncle.

The wind howled up the side of the cliff and tugged at Einer's chainmail. The blood from the battlefield of Ida's plain had dried and his tunic and trousers were stiff from the blood. If he was lucky, he would be offered a bath as well as soup, although he had a feeling that perhaps he would not be. It would depend on the great fertility god that sailors and fishermen prayed to before they pushed away from port. It was Njord's house, and only he could decide what would be offered to the guests that Skadi brought home.

The back of the house had a crooked door. Every angle was skewed.

Skadi brought out her key and unlocked the door. It swung in and up, rising from the floor on its crooked hinges. 'Come inside.' She held the door open for them.

Einer took a cautious step over the worn threshold. The room was small and his uncle had to bend over so his head would not touch the ceiling, and Skadi had to crouch. They crammed inside and then Einer's uncle stepped down a swirling staircase that led into a room further into the ship-house. It was bright inside. The entire wall in front of the stairs was made of tiny glass-holes of different colours, through which Einer could see the blurred appearance of the rough sea.

The staircase steps were of different heights and Einer had to concentrate not to fall as he walked after his uncle. The steps swept around and down into a tall hall. It was not long, as Valhalla had been, and as everything in Asgard seemed to be, but it was tall and brightly lit by sunlight through the glass-holes on the far wall, which was shaped liked the keel of a ship.

Water washed against the glass wall with a loud clinking noise, so that Einer thought the glass might shatter. But it held; despite how it looked, the house was stable.

His uncle barely yielded enough room for Einer and Skadi to follow him into the hall.

An old ragged table that seemed to have been built from old ship planks had been placed in the middle of the room. Around it were chairs of the same construction, each different from each other, shaped to suit the wood from which it had been made. There were bowls on the table with fruits and nuts and bread. Skadi gestured for them to sit.

His uncle and Einer both moved towards the table as Skadi rushed to the back of the hall and down another set of stairs. Einer had thought that she would need to crouch to move through the crooked house, but while she had walked behind him down the first staircase, she had shrunk to be much smaller than Einer.

She rushed out of sight while Einer and his uncle awkwardly stood by the table. It did not feel right to sit, although they had been told to do so.

His uncle fondled the edge of the wooden table, although he seemed to not pay much attention to it.

'Have you met him?' Einer asked. 'Njord?'

His own heart was racing at the thought of meeting Njord. It was not as it had been with the Alfather. He had not truly realised that he was meeting the Alfather when he had. He had not been warned; not really. Although he had trekked through Valhalla, it had been such a long walk that he had begun to forget that it was a hall belonging to the Alfather, and he had been so weary from his wounds then that he had not been able to focus on anything other than survival. Now he only had sores, and the arrow stuck in his head. Everything else had healed. Even the wounds he had gained from the battlefield on Ida's plain.

'Njord and I have never been introduced,' his uncle answered. 'But I suppose the time has come.'

A wave slammed against the many small windows. Shouting rose up from downstairs, down where Skadi had disappeared. Another wave slapped against the windows. The sea rose with Njord's fury. His voice was deep like the sea itself, but Einer could not hear what they were shouting about, although he could guess.

He did not think that he would be invited for a bath.

'I wouldn't be so certain,' said his uncle, as if he could hear the conversation from downstairs. 'And keep your thoughts to yourself, Einer.'

Heavy steps were coming up the staircase. Skadi might be a giant, but her steps had been light and careful, like a trained warrior. These were the steps of a man who had never had to tip-toe on the way to a secret attack. Someone who perhaps had never been in a battle, although he must have been.

Einer's uncle swung around and shot Einer a harsh look.

His thoughts had been loud again, but perhaps Njord had not heard them.

'Oh, I heard,' rung the voice of the mighty vanir. 'My steps have become loud, but they are steady and my ears are sharp.' His tone was harsh and unforgiving.

He stepped up into the room. He was barefooted and his feet were wide and steady with his toes spread out. The true feet of a sailor who knew which way his boat would rock in the worst of storms. He had long waved hair and a similar beard. The ends of his hairs were ragged and white as if dipped in salt. His eyes and nose were big, all of his features were in plenty.

He looked at the two guests and gestured towards the table, as Skadi had done. 'Sit,' he said, although his tone was anything but welcoming. 'I insist.'

Einer slipped closer to the table, and with a wary glance to his uncle sat down. His uncle took the seat at the edge of the table, Einer the one next to him and Skadi grabbed a chair further down.

Alone, the great Njord sat at the other side of the table. He folded his callused hands on the table and stared at Einer. 'I have fought,' he gravely said. His wide eyes stared straight into Einer's and seemed to swallow him whole. 'In the worst of battles. Worse than what either of you have seen, or ever will. And I have no intention of fighting again.'

'You must choose sides before the time comes,' Skadi urged him.

He shifted his gaze to her, and his eyes turned soft at the sight of her, like he could hardly bear to contradict her and educate her in the way of the worlds, although still, he did.

'I have lived here, among the aesir, for more summers and winters than I can count,' Njord said. 'And for all of those winters, one thing has been clear to me: there are no sides but your own. Not here, not anywhere.'

'You're wrong,' said Einer's uncle. 'I don't know about the aesir, but the jotnar are all on one side.'

'And isn't that exactly why all must die?'

'Nej,' Skadi said in a resolute voice that certainly convinced Einer. 'The fates decree it. The forefathers pull us there, to that battlefield. Those murdered at Odin's hand pull us there.'

'Then don't let yourself be pulled,' Njord said, as if it were that simple. 'Don't let the draugar win.'

The longer Einer spent in the presence of his uncle and Skadi, the more he sensed the anger in him as a constant presence. It wasn't always roused, but it was always there, and he knew, and had always known, that nothing could make it go away and that nothing could sway its mind.

'You know perfectly well that nothing can change our fates,' Skadi said, not scornfully as Einer had thought she might—and as Hilda would have—but with kindness. 'Your fate is different from ours.'

'It is,' Njord admitted. 'But I wish it wasn't.'

'Wishing doesn't make it so,' said Einer's uncle.

Njord acknowledged the words with a long silence as he stroked his ragged beard. He was as filled with flaws as his house, yet somehow despite his untrimmed beard and hair, and his unplucked eyebrows, and his flawed and blushed skin, every little detail made him look all the more perfect. He was a god, but he was different from the Alfather. He was comfortable, like an old friend, and that made this conversation all the more difficult: no one wanted to hurt an old friend.

'So, what are you going to do?' Skadi finally asked.

Einer sat at the front of his seat, ready to leap out if Njord's answer was not favourable. His uncle and Skadi both sat back in their seats, but he had seen Skadi fight, and he knew that she was like Hilda. Even when she looked relaxed, she had the gaze of a warrior. She had to be as ready as he was. He suspected that his uncle was the same.

Perhaps Njord too was readying for the right time to reach for his fisher's knife. The one tied to the belt under his clothes where his woollen tunic bulged out.

Another wave crashed against the glass windows, making them sing.

Njord examined them all. His wife, the scarred face of Einer's uncle, and Einer. His eyes lingered at Einer's forehead, where the arrow in his head stuck out.

Then he sighed, deeply, as though breathing for the first time after nearly drowning. He reached his arms behind his back, and they all knew what he was reaching for, but his movement was so slow and carefree that none of them rose to stop him. As easily as that, Njord pulled out his fish-gutting knife. It had been freshly sharpened, and cleaned after its last use. The bone handle was worn and perfectly matched Njord's large hands.

From the corner of his eyes, Einer could see Skadi and his uncle reach for their weapons. They were ready. Einer's fingers fondled the pommel of the Ulfberht sword.

Njord brought the knife up to the table for them all to look at. Their eyes were fixed on him, not the weapon. All of them were blooded warriors; they knew that weapons revealed no emotions. Someone's eyes and facial tics could show what they were about to do, but as Einer studied Njord's both imperfect and perfect face, a frightening thought entered his mind: perhaps the same was not true of gods, and perhaps there would be no warning.

The great god of fertility looked over at his wife, still fondling his fishing knife. Skadi leaned forward in her seat and removed her hands from her weapon belt. She placed both hands flat on the table in front of her, and stared at Njord, waiting for his decision, accepting it, whatever it would be.

Njord smiled a little. He could not keep it in. So, the faces of the gods could reveal their thoughts, after all. At least Njord's did, and exactly as Einer thought it, Njord smiled all the brighter.

'He is a loud thinker,' the god said. He nodded towards Einer and laughed. Einer had never liked it when people laughed at him, but he did not mind it when it was Njord. It was not a bad sort of laughter, just amused. The laughter of an old friend.

'As are all short-lived,' Einer's uncle replied.

Njord's laughter stopped sharp. 'Nej,' he exclaimed and turned to Einer. 'He can't be.'

Skadi too was watching keenly. Her forehead wrinkled with concentration.

'Short-lived father,' said Einer's uncle.

'A giant mother, though,' Njord replied, entranced with Einer's features. 'But a mother... he doesn't look it...'

They were talking about Einer as if he were not there. It made him feel like a small child again, in a way that he had not felt in many summers, not since he had first joined the raids and sailed far south.

'In our eyes, you *are* a child,' said his uncle. 'Even in my young eyes.'

Einer looked into his uncle's burning eyes. They were green but not simply green, like some eyes were; they were a burning forest, and they had seen much. His skin was covered in scars, but there were no wrinkles. The scars were fresh, and despite how wise Einer thought him, his uncle did indeed look young beneath the scarred skin, and Skadi looked anything but old.

Njord was still fondling his fishing knife between his two large hands. He was weighing his choice, and none of them had forgotten. Although Skadi no longer had her hands on her weapon belt, Einer and his uncle were both ready.

Einer's right hand had moved from the pommel, to fondle the guard, ready to clasp the hilt.

'So...' Skadi said. 'What are you going to do, Njord?'

'Smoked fish,' Njord said. 'I'm going to prepare a smoked fish for us.'

Skadi chuckled, and Einer's uncle leaned back in his seat, and removed his hands from his weapons, but Einer stayed on the ready. He wanted to believe Njord, but he was no longer certain about who he could and should believe. He was not certain that he trusted his uncle either. Then, he remembered that they could all hear his loud thoughts, and he unclasped his hand from the hilt of his father's Ulfberht and leaned back in his chair.

His uncle and Skadi would have had no reason to hide Einer and smuggle him off Odin's battlefield if they merely wanted to kill him here. At least for now, he was safe.

'Oh, you are never safe,' Njord said as he rose from his seat with the decision to cook. 'You are never safe in the presence of your gods,' he said. 'We do not live to serve you, you live to serve *us*. Like cattle serve *you*, until the day you feast on their blood.'

TYRA

Chapter One Hundred and Four

TYRA HEARD THE flutter of crow wings behind her. The valkyries were following. She could no longer see where she was running. The hall was as black as the stables in the middle of the night. Her feet were getting tangled in threads. But she kept running, because Siv had told her to run, and Siv had made her.

Behind her, Tyra heard the clash of metal. People running and grunts and the scream of a norn or perhaps a valkyrie. It wasn't Siv's voice. Siv didn't scream.

Tyra wanted to turn back and look. She wanted to see that Siv was alright. She wanted to help and fight. But her feet brought her further into the dark of the hall, away from the entrance and the Alfather and his valkyries. Away from Siv, perhaps for the last time, like their fates had destined for them.

Tyra shook her head as she ran. It wouldn't be the last time. Destinies could be changed. Siv would find a way back to her again. And if nothing else, in the afterlife they would meet. They *had* to meet again.

The beating of wings came closer. Tyra tried to speed up but couldn't. Her feet were moving as fast as possible. Fast as if she raced downhill. She leapt across the floor—glided almost—like Siv always did.

Claws dug into Tyra's shoulder, and she tripped. The crow fell with her, claws stuck in her shoulder. Her hands broke her fall; her left wrist snapped and her shoulder knocked against the stone ground.

The crow squawked. It rose from her shoulder and went for her face. Tyra wrestled it away. The claws scratched the back of her hands. The valkyrie was coming out of the crow skin, to attack Tyra with swords and spears and kill her, like Siv said they would. They would kill her.

Tyra slapped the crow away. She shielded her eyes from the scratching and pushed herself up from the ground. Feathers were flying around her.

The crow was strong. Tyra slapped it away, but it kept attacking.

A loud slam made the scratching stop, and the bird plummeted to the ground. Tyra lowered her arms. Verthandi stood before her, a metal distaff in hand. The bird lay on its back on the floor, scarcely outlined by a fire that floated above Verthandi and followed her as she moved. Like the one Siv had conjured in the forest.

Tyra didn't know if the crow was dead or not, but it didn't move. She glanced over her back to where Siv was. Clashes of swords and iron rang through the hall, and voices so distant that Tyra could barely hear.

'More will come, you have to go,' said Verthandi.

'Why do they want me?' Tyra remained where she was, though she was ready to run. There was so much she didn't know, and Siv wasn't going to answer her questions anymore. Perhaps she never would.

The valkyries hadn't stopped to smell Tyra, like the giants had done.

The sounds of swords clashing echoed through the large hall.

'If you are important to her, then you are important to them.' Verthandi said. 'To us too. I owe Glumbruck. I shall arrange the fates in your favour. Svend will be at your side, I will make it so. But you have to find your own way back.'

Tyra didn't have time to ask anymore before the valkyrie's sharp claws were back, scratching at her arm.

Verthandi swung her distaff like a hammer and hit the bird's right wing, but it was persistent. 'Go,' Verthandi said, and not to the bird.

Tyra spun away and fled, further into the Hall of Fates. She felt scratches on her back, but then they were gone and so was the sound of wings.

Her feet scraped across the stone floor. She ran through threads and ruined them. She ran until she could no longer see anything; no threads, no valkyries, no nornir, no pillars, just pure darkness.

At this point, she no longer dared to sprint, not knowing when she would fall next, or what she might walk into. Her feet knocked into pillars, frequently, and she was slowed by tight threads that would not break when she tried to force her way past, but Tyra kept going. Siv had wanted her to leave and to keep her safe, and Tyra knew that the least she could do to repay the many times Siv had saved her was to do as she was asked this one last time.

'Save the nine worlds,' she whispered, and kept going.

When she looked back over her shoulder now, she couldn't see anything. Not a hint of light or a sign of movement. It was as dark as it had been inside the tree back in Ash-hill, but it didn't feel like that time. It wasn't quiet. Sometimes she heard screeches, and sometimes a wind swept through the hall and dishevelled all of the threads so they sounded like a pretty song. Inside the tree, she hadn't felt anything. She hadn't really been anywhere at all. Though it was dark in the Hall of Fates, Tyra knew that she was *somewhere*.

Tyra stopped her running. She was making too much noise

with her leather shoes sliding over the floor. She would be more difficult to hear and find if she walked slower, and it would be easier to move over and under the threaded fates.

There were no more clashes. Tyra didn't know when they had stopped. She just knew that they weren't there anymore. Maybe she was too far into the hall to hear the fighting and the voices, but she doubted it.

She kept walking through the dark, not knowing how much time had passed, although it felt like a long time. Siv had prepared her for such journeys. Tyra could walk for a long time without getting tired. It was a good skill to have in Asgard, where everything was far away.

A long time longer she walked, before she saw a light at the far end of the hall. The other exit.

It was not large like the one at the front; not at all like the one Siv and she had entered through. That had been a gate made for gods. This was more like a crack in the wall. The sort that a dog could walk through, or a small person might climb through.

The wall was thick. An entire arm-length thick. Tyra lay flat onto her stomach to crawl through the slim gap. She dragged herself through and out into the light.

The sun beamed over her and the flowery green grass. Birds were singing somewhere ahead. Tyra took in a large breath of fresh air, and then she sighed and a frown formed on her forehead. 'Where to now, Siv?' she mumbled.

She had been told to run, but she didn't know *where* to run to. The nornir had said they would tie Tyra's destiny in her favour, but if she couldn't get back home, it was of no use, and though Tyra knew many things, she didn't know how to get back home.

NORNIR

Chapter One Hundred and Five

THE THREE NORNIR huddled in the shadows of their hall. The fight raged around them. Urd looked back at what had been between these people as they fought. Verthandi looked on, knowing exactly who would strike whom and when, and Skuld looked ahead, knowing how the fight would end.

Valkyries scooped past them, grunting as their spears flew at the angry giant in the Hall of Fates. The Alfather stood back and watched. He was hesitant to join, and Urd, Verthandi and Skuld all knew why. The opponent was Glumbruck. There was a lot that no one but the Alfather, Glumbruck and the nornir knew about those two. A lot had happened, a lot was happening and a lot more was destined to happen. Their fates had been, were and would be intertwined again and again.

Glumbruck's skin was red from blood. She bore no armour. A valkyrie thrust another spear out of Glumbruck's chest. The blood splashed over the stone floor and soaked the destinies of short-lived.

The forefathers sustained Glumbruck, but she needed to

release them to win. Verthandi waited for it to happen, ready to escape as soon as it did, but Skuld knew that Glumbruck had no intention of letting the forefathers take over.

Urd too knew. She looked back at Glumbruck's life as Glumbruck evaded the valkyries' blows. A long time ago in Jotunheim, Glumbruck's uncle had been lost to the forefathers. Urd looked into the past and saw the little girl standing there, in the red snow, as her uncle's head rolled past her, and her father's axe dripped with a giant's precious blood.

Glumbruck would not let the forefathers take over as her uncle once had. She would rather die, Urd knew.

Skuld knew that Glumbruck's destiny thread was still long and she would not die here.

Verthandi watched from her shadows as Glumbruck stepped back to gain a stronger foothold. Blood flowed from her forehead and from her mouth. Her braided hair was red and black with blood.

'Come with me,' said the Alfather.

The valkyries halted their attacks. The Alfather's steps echoed down the Hall of Fates. He came dangerously close to Glumbruck.

Glumbruck's breaths were shallow. Her precious blood dripped onto the floor in spreading puddles. Her wounds needed to be bound soon or she would collapse never to wake.

Skuld looked behind Glumbruck, to the destiny thread that disappeared into the hall of long-lived where she was destined to go. With Odin, she was destined to leave. This was her last stand, and Glumbruck too knew it. Only the Alfather could save her from dying from the wounds his valkyries had inflicted upon her.

Yet she did not go to him when he asked. Glumbruck kept her resolve. She let her knee fall to the ground and gasped for breath. She could hardly stand anymore. Her entire body was shaking. Verthandi watched on as Glumbruck gathered the strength to speak. She did not have much left.

'You come with me, or you *will* die,' the Alfather threatened, for he no longer had any other way to convince her but deadly threats. Urd knew how many times he had tried to bring Glumbruck back to his side. Verthandi knew his resolve, and Skuld could see that there was nothing more for him to do.

Glumbruck shook her head, spraying blood around her. She knew her destiny, as the nornir did. She had seen her thread that had been spun into the hall of long-lived. And yet she did not follow Odin, as she was meant to do.

'I won't go with you. Kill me or let me live, on my own terms, far away from you.'

'I can't do either.' The great Alfather's voice was shaking. 'You know. I can't let you leave again, and I can't kill you.'

Neither could Glumbruck let the forefathers loose and kill the Alfather to escape. The nine worlds needed its Alfather. Glumbruck knew it. Never could she kill Odin, for love of the nine worlds and everyone living in them.

Urd knew how the knowledge had affected every decision Glumbruck had made. It was why she had run instead of killing the Alfather. It was why she had never returned to confront him.

Skuld knew that Glumbruck had no intention of killing him. They all knew that she never would. Skuld looked on, and then she saw it change. The future as she had predicted it, no longer was.

Her eyes shot to Glumbruck's gleaming destiny thread.

The thread flayed in a breeze. It was falling to the ground. It had been cut. Glumbruck's destiny was falling apart. Her carefully prepared future was fading.

Glumbruck's hand fell to the ground. The blade of her seax clanged against the floor. She had done it herself. She had cut her destiny thread, knowing what it meant. She would not go with the Alfather, as she had been destined to do.

I choose my own destiny, Glumbruck thought, barely loud enough for the three nornir to hear.

Skuld was the first to see and notice, and now that it had come to pass, Verthandi too could see what was upon them, and with Glumbruck's loud thoughts, even Urd let her eyes fall upon the destiny thread that danced in the breeze.

All of their efforts were gone. All of the Alfather's efforts were rendered pointless by Glumbruck's final decision.

'Why are you crying?' asked the Alfather. His eyes were no longer on Glumbruck, but on the three nornir.

Skuld had not noticed her own tears, caught up in all that could have been and should have been. Urd did not respond, trying to find reason in the past between the Alfather and Glumbruck. The past that only the two of them were supposed to look upon.

Verthandi brought up a backhand to dry her tears, but they continued to fall. The three nornir's proudest and most difficult work was dying in her hands and Verthandi could not save it, nor keep it from fading. A friend was bent over at her feet, dying, and no matter what any of the three nornir did, they could not prevent Glumbruck's new fate.

'All of you. Why are you crying?' the Alfather asked, his voice lower with each word. He did not really want the answer.

'Her thread...' Skuld's voice trembled at having to say it aloud. 'It's broken. It's cut.'

'Why are you crying?' he asked again. There was no leeway and no forgiveness in his voice. This time he demanded the truth; the simple indisputable present that only Verthandi could provide.

'These are her last moments.'

'We've all made our final choices,' Glumbruck hissed. Her eyes were no longer open. She no longer had the strength. Her voice was faint.

'I will *not* kill you,' the Alfather maintained.

'Fates don't lie,' Glumbruck whispered. 'Today, I die.'

The blade of her seax scraped through the blood puddles on the stone floor. Urd saw and knew now, that it was not a new decision. Glumbruck had already made her choice when she had seen her destiny thread. As a giant and long-lived, knowing what would become of her, she preferred death. The three nornir had chosen a long lifetime of servitude to the Alfather, but Glumbruck preferred death.

'My fate is settled. I would do it all again.'

They were the last words that the Alfather wanted to hear, Verthandi could see it on him, and Urd knew why. Even after leaving Asgard and living in Midgard's shadows for centuries, running from him, Glumbruck did not regret her actions. She did not regret fleeing from his offers.

'Come with me.' He no longer threatened, but begged. 'Let me save you.'

'Nej,' she answered.

'Listen to the forefathers,' the Alfather told her. He was raising his voice, although he rarely ever did. He never needed to raise his voice. Everyone always listened to the great Alfather. Always had and always would. Everyone except for Glumbruck. 'Call forth the forefathers! Release their rage.'

He would rather see her go mad than die, but the three nornir and Glumbruck all knew that she would never allow herself to go mad to the forefathers, as her uncle once had.

'Nej,' was her answer, once more.

The Alfather's full wrath turned on the three nornir. 'Spin her fate longer!' he yelled.

The Hall of Fates shook with his rage. Verthandi watched hundreds of thousands of threaded fates tremble.

'Repair it,' he ordered. 'Join the threads and spin it long like mine again.'

'We can't,' the three nornir cried as one.

Verthandi took Glumbruck's precious thread in her hands. 'It is already fading,' she observed. It was too late. The thread was still tied up in the hall of long-lived fates. Glumbruck's fate was the node that tangled so many others. The nine worlds needed her.

Urd recalled the care with which they had spun Glumbruck's thread. Once her fate had been free, but after she had arrived in Asgard and the Alfather had taken notice of her, they had tied it up with knots and braided it through their halls at his commands.

As for Skuld, she knew what grim destiny awaited them all if Glumbruck were to die in this hall. It had not been destined, and with Glumbruck's thread gone and faded, everyone's destinies had changed. Knots would have to be untied, and destined meetings would never happen. With her dead, the future was uncertain. Glumbruck's thread was woven so tightly through the nine worlds.

'You told me she had long,' The Alfather yelled so the hall shook. 'You told me she would survive until Ragnarok, like us all!'

'That *was* her fate,' Urd replied, for it *had* been.

'But not anymore,' said Skuld.

'She is dying,' said Verthandi.

All three of them let their tears fall freely as they looked upon Glumbruck's fading life thread. It had been so perfect and full of promises, but it had been spun into corners of the hall where Glumbruck no longer wanted to go. It had been long, like that of the Alfather, but it no longer was.

What had been was all there ever would be.

'Finish it,' Glumbruck said. Her eyes were open again. She stared up at the Alfather.

All the memories of the past circled loud in her mind. They could all hear her thoughts: the Alfather, the valkyries and the three nornir. Perhaps she thought so loudly in an attempt to soothe the Alfather by giving him old memories on which he could dwell. The same memories that Urd searched through. Perhaps she simply no longer had the strength and control to keep her thoughts to herself.

'I'm dying anyway,' she said, both answering the three nornir's thoughts and urging the Alfather to act and kill her.

The Alfather clenched his thin lips together and breathed deeply through his nose so that the long hairs of his beard quivered from his breath. 'It won't be by my hand,' he said.

'It already is.' Glumbruck's voice was faint but they all heard it. 'I wouldn't have died if you hadn't chased me.'

Urd searched the past and knew it to be true. Skuld searched all there could have been and she too knew. Verthandi did not need to search, neither the past nor the future, for she knew that giants who died in the present had no reasons to lie.

'And you wouldn't still be alive if I hadn't.' The Alfather's voice trembled with his breath.

'I know.' Her forces were weakening. Verthandi felt the destiny thread in her hands lose its last strength. 'I always knew. What did you have to sacrifice to the ice?'

'It doesn't matter,' the Alfather replied.

He took a step closer to her. Skuld saw the possibilities. Glumbruck could kill him, even wounded and hurt. If she just lifted her seax, she could kill him and be done.

The valkyries saw it too. Their knuckles were white from clenching their weapons. Their muscles were tense, and they were ready to defend.

Glumbruck made a move, but not to strike. Her elbow banged against the floor and then she lay down on the cold red ground.

Her wounds went deep. All the way up her back, spears and axes had pierced through and left great gaping wounds. Verthandi cried at the sight. Skuld cried with the knowledge of what it meant. It was too late, nothing could save Glumbruck anymore. She would bleed out within half a hundred breaths.

'Can I hold your hand... one last time?' the Alfather asked.

Glumbruck did not look capable of answering. Nevertheless, she moved. She rolled onto her side so that she could look up at the Alfather again and the three nornir standing at his back, and the valkyries that surrounded her and were ready to deliver the last blow, and with a hindered but steady voice, she spoke words that even Skuld could not have predicted.

'Let her go,' Glumbruck panted without giving an answer.

Every breath was a wheeze. Her eyes were closed, but her eyelids flicked with activity and a will to stay awake and alive.

'Who?' the Alfather asked, although he knew. 'The girl?' His stare hardened. Even in the end, Glumbruck did not do what he requested of her or as he wanted. Even as she was dying, she was set on defying him. 'I can't.'

'Forget...' Glumbruck coughed up blood. It blended with the already black pool on the floor around her. For all of her pains and fading strength, Glumbruck was determined to speak. 'Forget you ever saw her.'

Urd wept with the memories Glumbruck had shared with little Tyra, Verthandi wept at Glumbruck's devotion, lying there, moments from death, and Skuld wept with the knowledge of what would become of that young girl if the Alfather did not change his mind.

'You know I can't,' said the Alfather.

'Just a girl. No threat to you.'

'You know that's not true.'

The Alfather took another step closer to Glumbruck. He stood over her, trying to decide what to do now that it was the end. Now that even Verthandi saw Glumbruck's inevitable death, breaths away.

Finally, he decided to crouch at her side, and even squatting with his long coat and the end of his white beard soaking up the pool of Glumbruck's blood, he looked elegant and composed.

'She is not a simple girl,' he told Glumbruck in a lowered voice, meant only for her. 'I can't let her leave. Even for you.'

'Let her go.'

Even in death, Glumbruck's will could not be bent. She was harder than iron and more fickle than water. She was unlike anyone else in the nine worlds. The nornir knew it, for they had spun her fate, had seen her past, watched her present and knew her unachieved future, and the Alfather knew it, for he had discovered her so many centuries ago.

'You should have come with me, Glumbruck.'

'Nej,' she wheezed in such a weak voice that it could hardly be heard.

'You should never have left. We would have found a way.'

She wheezed. She was at an end. No more than a breath or two was left of her life. Urd began to sense it. Death passed from future to present and lay on the threshold between present and past.

'Nej,' Glumbruck breathed.

Her fingers uncurled from the seax. Her hand grew limp. Her eyelids stopped flickering. Her eyes closed for the last time.

And at her side sat the Alfather, in tears. Perfect tears rolled down his reddening cheeks as he looked at Glumbruck.

In death, she looked peaceful. As peaceful and composed as she had in life. Beyond all else, she was strong, all drenched in blood and covered in wounds that would have killed a lesser giant a dozen times over. Even now that she no longer had a voice with which to speak and protest, her will rung in the heads of all those who looked upon her.

The nornir, who had known her as well as all of their spun destinies and better than anyone, heard her protests and requests to change her own destiny. Their refusal had forced her to cut her own thread short.

Urd remembered holding in her hands the gold that had been spindled into Glumbruck's long destiny thread. When it had first been spun and hung, Glumbruck's destiny had been like any other. Until the Alfather had seen her, and her thread had been blooded and untied to be hung in new patterns; intertwined and braided with those of gods and beasts.

Verthandi observed her corpse. No light beamed from it anymore. Her strength was evident; it almost looked as if she were a dwarf turned to stone by the sunrise, for her muscles strained even in death.

Skuld looked at the destiny thread that had been cut. It was so long. There had been so much left for her to do. Thousands and thousands of destinies hinged on Glumbruck's choices. No one else could replace her and restore order to the nine worlds. With such care her destiny had been chosen and decided, yet so quickly had it been cut.

The Alfather's valkyries remembered the steady hand of Glumbruck's seax cuts, as they clenched the wounds she had inflicted upon them. Wounds that Skuld knew would sting and never quite heal, for Glumbruck's hand was steady and her grasp on the runes was strong.

Finally, the Alfather looked upon Glumbruck and remembered every shared moment, and every moment he had longed for her. The sheer memory of her had been enough to chase her for centuries, and now she was gone. His tears dripped onto her dead body as he rose from her side.

In the end, he did not touch her. She had not given her permission, and above all else, the Alfather had chased her because he respected her. Even in death, her words were his law.

His valkyries were shocked and trembling with fear. Never before had they seen their god cry, and never again would they. Urd, Verthandi and Skuld all knew that such a moment had never before come and would never come again.

Words that had been spoken and sung by nornir for centuries dawned.

Urd, Verthandi and Skuld all thought the verses together and sung them aloud to their crying Alfather and their dead friend.

A giant lays dead
In the Hall of Fates.
Now let the word spread,
And open the gates.

The battle begins.
So the crow cries.
Cut short all the strings.
Never shall they rise.

The song brought the Alfather out of his grief long enough to become aware of his own tears and sorrow. He did not sniff. Instead he let the last tears in his eyes trickle down his red cheeks and into his curling beard.

He watched Glumbruck as his tears dried out.

No one dared to move. Not the valkyries in the hall, not the three nornir; not even the wind dared blow through the open gates into the Hall of Fates.

The Alfather swallowed his tears and spoke in a steady voice without looking at anyone other than Glumbruck's fresh corpse. 'The others will want to confirm her death, and I will give her a worthy funeral.'

Verthandi hesitated to speak, but now, with the Alfather vulnerable and grieving, was the only chance she might get at an honest reply. 'Will you tell her sons?' she asked.

More than a dozen times the three nornir had cut the shimmering destiny threads of Siv's sons at the Alfather's commands. She had escaped the Alfather's grasp, but he controlled the afterlives. One by one he had pulled Glumbruck's sons and husbands away from her into the afterlife so she had been alone. The three nornir had done the destiny cutting at their Alfather's demands. They owed Glumbruck a great debt for what they had done to her, and now they would never repay it. At least, if her sons knew, it would be solace.

'It's time they knew,' the Alfather decided.

As one the three nornir looked at him in surprise. Not one of them had expected him to agree to share the truth with all of Glumbruck's sons, least of all the living one. The Alfather had taken such care to bring Einer into his hall without severing his fate. He had healed the boy's wounds, as he had done countless of times before to shackle the long-lived. The three Nornir had been instructed to tie Einer's fate in the Alfather's favour, but with their friend dead at their feet and only one living son, the task seemed wrong.

'You will tell them?' Verthandi asked, allowing herself to hope that her sisters and she might redeem themselves to Glumbruck's kinsmen a little, after all they had done. 'Everything?'

'No one knows everything,' the Alfather replied, killing her hope. 'Not even me. Not even you.'

EINER

Chapter One Hundred and Six

THE SEAS TO Jotunheim were rough like none Einer had ever seen.

'You have a strong stomach,' his uncle praised, and pulled in his two oars. Although Einer too had rowed, it had mainly been his uncle who had taken the shifts through the rough weather, while Einer had been fighting the urge to throw up.

The small rowing boat rocked on the huge waves like driftwood caught in the tide. His chainmail rustled against the stone ballast. The contents of Einer's stomach were cast around, and for the twentieth time since they had set off from Skadi and Njord's home, his mouth tasted the salty fish that Njord had prepared for them before their departure. A fish no doubt intended for this sort of weather and sailing, for it tasted the same every time he swallowed it again, if a little warmer and mushier than the last time.

Their boat swung up onto the top of a big wave, and Einer saw an icy coast. Finally, after they had rowed through an eternity of seasickness, they had arrived. His uncle pulled the oars into the boat so that their movement halted. It did not help Einer's unusual seasickness. Now he understood the pained expressions on his warriors' faces when he announced that they would not set foot on land at night, although half of the crew was seasick.

'Is it my turn to row?' Einer asked his uncle, although he knew that was not why the giant had stopped rowing. His uncle cast down his hood and looked at Einer with a serious tone.

'We can't row in,' he said. 'No boats can. You'll have to swim.'

Einer looked into shore. He had to wait for their boat to be propelled to the top of another wave to see it. The shore was not far away, in a row-boat, but he could not imagine swimming there. The waters were so cold that he thought the only reason they had not turned to ice was that they were too turbulent. Besides, the waves would drown him or crush him and he would never make it. Even if he survived the swim, he would die from the cold, on the coast. He had not fought as fiercely as a berserker to get through Ida's plain alive only to freeze to the death on a beach.

'You won't die,' said his uncle Buntrugg. 'They're waiting for you.'

'For me,' Einer repeated. 'You're not coming with me?'

'I have an appointment elsewhere.'

'Then what am I doing here? I followed you, thinking that you could get me to where I need to be. To Hilda.'

'I told you, then, as I am telling you now, no one knows where Hilda Ragnardóttir is. I only told you that I wanted to show you where you are truly from.'

His uncle waited for a time, and let Einer acknowledge the facts. Although his age was difficult to tell from all the burns and he called himself young, his uncle had the tired and superior eyes of an old man. Einer nodded.

His uncle cast his eyes to the shore. 'That coast, over there, is Niflheim, and beyond Niflheim is a passage through to the edge of Jotunheim, where your mother and I grew up.'

'How will I find it?'

'They will be waiting for you,' his uncle said, although he did not say who *they* were. Whoever they were, Einer was not certain that he could trust them. It was strange to imagine that his mother had come from a place such as this; had known so much and always kept it a secret from him. It had not sunk in that she was a giant.

Although Buntrugg acted like an uncle to him, in the way in which he took care of Einer with a rough and honest hand, Einer still could not quite believe that his mother was a giant. She had always been elegant and although she had been tall, she had not been tall like Skadi. Einer had been taller than his mother.

'We aren't tall all the time,' his uncle Buntrugg said in answer to Einer's thoughts. 'Not if we don't want to be. And your mother has always been... unique.'

'You're always listening to my thoughts,' Einer mumbled.

There was a moment of silence before his uncle answered. 'I thought you had spoken aloud...'

Einer tried not to laugh. Great peril awaited him, and he would have to go alone from now on, in a foreign land that he knew nothing about, other than it was filled with giants and that his mother had once lived there, or so his uncle said.

It was difficult to understand and believe, when she was not there to show him. It seemed like someone else's story.

Although Einer knew, and perhaps always had known that this was a road he had to take on his own, and that his uncle would not come with him the entire way, he was reluctant to part ways. He looked back at his uncle's scorched face that no longer frightened him.

'I thought you said you don't leave family behind,' Einer said.

'I don't. You are among family, always, and on your path now. Soon, we shall be joined again,' replied his uncle Buntrugg.

'Why not now?'

'I have work to do, and you are not yet ready. You may be a jotun, but there is much for you to learn before we can travel on equal foot. The forefathers will keep you safe. Your mother's golden gift too. It'll burn a fire in your chest.'

Einer knew that his uncle was right. The gold bracteate made him focus on the pain at his chest. Thanks to it, he had survived when others never would. The tip of the arrow that stuck out from his forehead was a reminder of that.

However, that knowledge did not make him want to jump into the freezing waters and ride the enormous waves towards the shore.

'It was a pleasure meeting you, Einer,' said his uncle Buntrugg, in a final tone that meant that Einer had to get up and jump into the waters now. 'Your mother will be glad to know that you are safe.'

'Where is she?' Einer asked. It had been so long since he had seen her. He missed her. Not in the same way that he missed his father; he knew that his father had gone into the afterlife and was happily feasting in Freya's and Odin's halls. But he did not know where his mother was, other than the fact that she was alive, out there, somewhere.

'I don't know,' his uncle answered. 'The last time I saw her, she was in Jelling. She was well.'

Einer smiled. She was well. The thought made him miss her as much as he had when he had been away all summer on his first raid. It had been so long since he had leaned into her embrace and listened to her voice telling him that all would be well, over and over until he believed it.

'Now I can tell her that you are well too.'

Einer nodded. His eyes were fixed on the freezing water, and he brought his hands into the waves to prepare for the cold. His stomach had begun to wave in the same rhythm as the ocean, and Einer had grown accustomed to the swing of the waves. He knew exactly when he had to jump; right before the top of the wave, where he could ride it long enough to get further in towards the shore before he was slammed into the sand. It would be a rough swim.

'Next time you see her, tell her that I miss her,' Einer said.

He took one last deep breath, and stood up in the rocking boat. He filled his lungs, as the boat ascended up the hill of a wave, and then he jumped in, head first. The water froze his scalp, and made his hair strangely warm, and his beard too. The will of the ocean whipped him ahead. The wave lifted him to the surface.

Einer gasped for air. The cold slapped him across the face and chilled his ears. He saw nothing other than water. The boat and his uncle were gone beyond the waves. He didn't know where he was. The cold was all he knew.

The waves would take him into land. All he had to do was survive long enough.

He rode the top of the wave. His stomach was in knots. The wave rushed him forward and then pulled back. Einer swam to get away from the pull of the wave. The ocean lifted him in its next wave. His head emerged and he sucked in air, while he could. Water rushed below him and above him.

The next wave took him further. His fingers and arms were so cold that he could hardly move. His legs felt as stiff as his two iron swords. His neck was frozen in place. The bracteate began to hammer at his chest. Heat blazed through him. He could no longer move his extremities, but the waves of the ocean moved them for him.

His forehead ached where the arrow stuck out. His entire head hurt from the cold and his vision throbbed to his slowing heartbeat. He refused to close his eyes. He could no longer move at his own will, but the ocean carried him towards the shore, commanded by the Midgard Worm's thrashing tail.

Einer let his body be taken by the waves. He no longer resisted when the waves took him, not that he could. The cold had taken him entirely, and for a moment he thought that his uncle had been wrong and that the heat of the bracteate would not be enough to save him. He was convinced that this really was how he would die, although even the plains of Ida had not succeeded in claiming him, but then his body broke with the reality.

The foamed wave that had taken him broke away. His shoulder was slammed onto an ice shore. His head clanged against it and his hip too. The water retreated and tried to take him away with it.

The bracteate sent heat through him and the hidden anger reached out through Einer. It unfroze his fingers and made him grapple for the freezing sand. The last water trickled away back to the ocean, and Einer thought himself safe on the beach. He lifted his head to see where he was and where he needed to be.

Another wave crashed into his back, driving the air out of him. He tried to hold his breath in, but the shock of it was great and his mouth already opened wide. Water flooded in.

The wave was lifting him from the sand and pulling him back to the sea. He coughed. Salty water trickled into his lungs. His limbs were frozen again.

Something grabbed his tunic and lifted him from the water. Einer gasped for breath. He coughed up water and wheezed. The water retreated below him. He was dangled above the sand, as if he floated, and then, right as he found the strength to look up, he was dumped onto hard, frosty sand. His nose crunched from the impact.

'Kauna,' said a voice. Einer's fingers heated like his chest did from the touch of the bracteate. Only this was the pleasant touch of a heat, which came from within. He began to feel it in his toes, and the heat travelled up his arms and legs.

His body warmed. The sand felt cold against his cheek. Einer coughed to get the last salt out of his lungs. It stung all the way into his core, where the anger rested.

'Get up,' said a woman in a stern voice that Einer did not dare contradict, although he did not possess the strength to rise on his own.

They had waited for his arrival, exactly as his uncle said they would, whoever *they* were.

The woman grabbed his arm with iron fingers, lifted him from the ground and placed him on his feet. It took a few attempts for Einer's feet to hold him up after being placed on the frozen sand. It took longer for his vision to settle from the motion of the sea, and for him to see who had lifted him.

She was a giantess as large as Skadi, but not as elegant. Her long hair was frozen at the tips, and her speech was muffled by a scarf that she had wrapped up high to cover her nose. Her cloak was not elegant, like cloaks Einer had seen the giants and the Alfather wear in Asgard, it was ragged and old, and partly frozen. Everything was white and frozen here, except Einer's body that was starting to come alive again with prickles of heat.

Einer sniffed to keep his nose from running. The snot was already freezing on his upper lip. He rubbed it off with a sandy back hand and looked at the giantess.

'Who are you?' he asked.

The giantess watched him for a long moment, as the waves crashed behind Einer with thunder slams, and the wind blew and threatened to freeze him again.

'Do you truly not know who you are, Einer Glumbruckson?' asked the giantess in an earthly voice.

Glumbruck. It was what Skadi and the other giants too had called his mother, although it tasted strange on his lips. At the back of his mind was the nagging voice which said they were all wrong and there was no way that his mother could be a giantess.

'Skadi and her giants,' the giantess grumbled and spat on the snow.

Again Einer's thoughts had been loud, but he did not know how to think quietly. It was not a skill he had ever thought that he would need to practise.

'Who are you?' Einer asked again. 'Why should I trust you?'

'I'm your grandmother,' said the giant. 'Your mother's mother.'

He should have known. His uncle had said that he would be with family, but he still wasn't sure that he truly believed that his mother was a giant and had grown up here.

'You will come to know the truth,' said the woman who called herself his grandmother. 'We will teach you.'

'And why should I trust you?' Einer asked again.

'Because I haven't crushed you... yet.' She began to walk away from him. 'And that would also be the reason that you would be wise to hurry up and follow me.'

Her steps were fast and her legs were so much longer than his. Einer tried to run after her. His legs were freezing, and unsteady. The sand was frozen and tough to run through. Einer slipped, but continued to run.

The giant did not slow her walk to accommodate him. She was far ahead into the mist of the frozen world of Niflheim. For a long while, Einer struggled to run and catch up, and when he finally did, he still had to run every few steps so as not to be left behind.

Although the cold of Niflheim made his skin tight and froze his hair and beard and ears, Einer felt warmth on his chest where the bracteate hung.

Nothing grew in Niflheim, or if it did, it was covered by mountains of ice. There was ice everywhere. Einer stared at it as he ran. It was so complete and perfect. It had never been touched. The ice shone so bright that he almost thought that he could see his own reflection in it.

'That's not your reflection,' said his grandmother, and as she said it and Einer sprinted to catch up with her again, he looked back over his shoulder, and saw that she was right. The reflection was still there, like a person trapped in ice.

'Not *like* a person. It *is* a person.' His grandmother's voiced was hushed, with the conviction of an old knowing woman. 'Trapped in ice for all eternity.'

Einer looked into the ice as she talked. There were more shadows in there. More people, trapped in ice for all eternity.

'They drift here and get caught in the ice. All those abandoned by the other worlds, with nowhere to go. The unworthy.'

'Does no one come to collect them? To free them?'

'Why would we? They were expelled from their own afterlives.'

'Where do they come from?'

'Mostly over there,' she said and pointed back to the shore. 'Right over there, across the waters, is yet another of the nine worlds. Helheim. You can sort of see it from here, through the veil. On a good day. A passage, like Bifrost, only less elegant, of much older design. Sturdier, though.'

The old giantess continued speaking. It was a welcoming change for Einer after having been surrounded by giants and gods who did not reveal anything of importance.

'Corpseshore, they call that shore and its house of snakes. The venom flows along the beach and burns everything. Drifts through the veil into Niflheim. Burns our beaches here.' She paused for a moment. 'Not that anyone comes here anyways.'

She looked down at him like a teacher or parent who could not wait to tell him something that she was certain he would like.

'It's why the Midgard Worm bites its own tail,' she said. 'You short-lived think that it's all because the Midgard Worm is so long and keeps growing, but it's more than that. When he patrols the waters out here, his tail gets scorched in venom from Corpseshore. Burns like that itch, so some thousand summers ago he began biting his own tail, and he hasn't stopped.'

Einer thought about his uncle and his many burns. He couldn't imagine having his entire body covered in burns. The giantess was right, it must itch, but he had never seen his uncle peel a scab.

The giantess stopped walking. 'What has happened to him? To Buntrugg?' she asked. Her tone was as cold as the ice that surrounded them.

'I... I don't know,' Einer answered.

'Burns?'

For a moment he had forgotten that if she were his grandmother, she was not only his mother's mother but also his uncle Buntrugg's. 'His face,' Einer explained. 'And his hands. Everything is covered in burn scars.'

The giantess began to walk again. 'Surt promised,' she said it like a curse and kicked a shard of ice along the side of the bare road they walked along, away from the beach. 'Promised he would never get caught in flames of fury.'

They walked through the blazing wind of Niflheim's cold as she grumbled to herself, until finally, her anger settled.

'Still,' she mumbled quietly behind her scarf. 'A preferable fate to the one that awaits us, forefathers permit.'

Einer saw his chance and grabbed it. She liked to speak, perhaps she would also tell him something useful. 'You all keep talking about the forefathers,' he said. 'Who are they?'

'Has Glumbruck taught you nothing?' His grandmother shook her head and sighed. 'They are your forefathers. My forefathers. Can't you hear them inside you? Can't you feel them?'

'The anger?'

'Ja, the anger. They are often angry, the forefathers. We all are. It runs in our blood and lineage. As you will soon come to learn.'

FOREFATHERS

Chapter One Hundred and Seven

No noise, no sight disturbs us. Our concentration is complete. The rage flows through us, and between us, and binds us together. Our closed eyes are focused on the minds of giants.

The descendants are getting angrier. Our chanting thoughts draw their fury out, and with their fury we can see. Up under their skin we travel and take over their sight and thought and body.

A descendant is close to the fury. He struggles with it and we feel the warmth of his skin on ours. Soon he will open enough for us to rush in and overwhelm him. A little push is all he needs.

'Where are we?' says a voice, disturbing our calm. 'Where am I?'

An individual voice where there ought to be none. Where there ought to be only us.

The descendant's fury fades and disappears and he is lost to us. Our concentration has shifted to the individual. The one voice in this place that is no place, where there ought to be no one but us.

As one, we attack. Our swords are drawn. Our axes. Our spears. Our shields. Our daggers. Our bare hands. We strangle the voice of thoughts and lash out as one great wave.

The individual resists, although no one should be able to resist. Our strikes and battle techniques of old do not surprise them. Every move is evaded, in the same way as we evade the moves of warriors through the hands of our descendants.

The individual speaks again. 'I didn't think this was how we would meet.'

The voice of the individual is female.

She knows us. She is not an unwelcome visitor. She is supposed to be one of us.

We flock to her with a new plan. If weapons cannot eradicate her, then we shall change her mind. In anger we shall bind her to us, as *we* are bound together. In anger we shall become one. She shall become us and we shall become her.

'I'm not angry,' says the individual, rebuffing our plan. 'I have nothing to be angry over. Not now, not ever.'

Our minds are one with confusion. Every being in the nine worlds has anger inside them. Our thoughts target their anger and bring it to the front.

'I have none,' repeats the individual.

We *will* break her. As we have broken many voices before hers. She shall be one of the whole, or none at all.

No individuality shall survive in the eternal afterlife of forefathers. The fault of her voice shall be eradicated.

'I shall not be silenced,' says she.

With her voice she makes us acknowledge her. She makes us focus on her and see her. We have travelled up her arms before. We have flooded her mind and taken over. We have fought with her limbs, and we know her name. We say it.

Glumbruck.

We know who she is, and we know her name and everything else about her. We see her for who she is. Never can she disappear into the united voice. Not anymore. Not now that we acknowledge and speak her name. We have one name. The forefathers. We cannot have two.

'Then what shall become of me?' she asks, listening to our collective thoughts.

We search for her anger. We search for unease, for fear, for any emotion that we can use, but Glumbruck has only serenity.

'If this is a place for only you to exist, Forefathers, and if I am not to become one of you, then what shall happen to us?'

We have no answers.

Our anger has turned to fear. Rarely do we know such fear, but we do now. Together, we fear this new voice and the peril her stubborn individuality brings upon us.

After centuries of anger, Glumbruck has been unleashed on us. Our end is near.

FINN

Chapter One Hundred and Eight

'YOU PUT ME in a difficult situation, Finn,' said Thorbjorn.

Since the death of the Christian priest, he had shown respect for Finn, and Finn was certain that it was because Thorbjorn wished that he possessed the strength to go against Harald, but it was too late for men like Thorbjorn. They had sworn their allegiance to Harald and his Christianity.

'I will have to tell him what I saw,' said Thorbjorn.

Finn nodded his understanding. 'Ja. You will have to tell Harald that his faithful thrall couldn't save his priest Conrad, although I tried with my life at stake.'

'That is what *I* saw,' Thorbjorn agreed with a dry laugh, and mounted his horse. 'But I don't know what my men saw.'

'I hope they saw the tragedy as clearly as you did,' Finn told him. 'The Jutes just aren't ready to accept another Christian priest among them so soon after the summer's slaughter.'

'No matter what we say, he *will* send another one.'

'He will,' Finn agreed. 'And hopefully before winter ends. There is nothing quite like a funeral pyre to heat your bones on a cold winter night.'

Thorbjorn laughed at that. 'I wish you luck, Finn the Nameless.' He kicked his horse into a light trot, to catch up with his men who had already left. At the edge of the forest, right before the shadows of the beech trees took over, Thorbjorn turned in his saddle to address Finn one last time. 'May your gods protect you from the wrath of rich men like me.'

'And may your riches wipe away your fears at night, now that the gods no longer can,' Finn yelled back, loud enough for the warriors who were inside the stable, tending to the new animals, to hear.

Finn watched Thorbjorn ride off into the shadows of the woods, and then he popped his head back into the stables. 'Do you need help?' he asked the two young men, so they wouldn't feel left out.

'We're nearly done,' said the red-haired one. 'We'll be there shortly.'

Finn lingered a moment longer. 'See you there, then,' he said and left the two warriors alone to talk about him and what he had said to Thorbjorn.

Yuletide had snuck up on them as they had worked, but thanks to Finn's dealings with Harald Gormsson, they had plenty of food for a good Yule feast. A few of the warriors had begun brewing as well.

Finn walked across the burned fields by the old beehives and out to the new settlements that Thorbjorn and his men had helped them built.

The resources Finn had brought with him from Jelling had been used well. They had built new houses, away from old Ash-hill and its grey earth. It felt wrong to build on the graves of so many old memories. Besides, when the remaining warriors came home they would need to re-divide all of the land, regardless of where they build the new houses. Nothing could ever be as it had been. It was better to start afresh.

Four longhouses they had built, and they were well on the way with the fifth. At least now they had warm rooms to sleep in at night, and they no longer had to sleep shoulder to shoulder to keep warm as if they were still on ship-deck. Getting good sleep had lifted morale significantly and tending to the animals and preparing the land for a new farming season helped to shape their days and made it easy to forget that anything had changed, although it had.

Finn skipped across the last of the field, wiped the mud off his soles on the stone outside and entered the warm longhouse. Despite the wide-open doors, the room was warm. Finn found a place at the back of the hall where he could lean against the wall. He was apart from the others and he knew it. It was both his weakness and his strength. A strength that he fully intended to use.

Since his return, they had almost begun to treat him like a freeman again. His hair had grown long enough for it to be easier to forget that he was nameless, although Old Hormod insisted that he be treated as no more than the servant he was.

Einer was gone. Vigmer too. No one stood in Finn's way anymore. No one but Old Hormod, who was unworthy of the place he had claimed, and Finn intended to prove that, before nightfall.

The chatter was timid as they waited for everyone to gather. The past few weeks while they had been building the longhouses with Thorbjorn and his men, they had been thinking about choosing a new leader. Most of Ash-hill's warriors were in Frey's-fiord and couldn't cast their vote, but they would be gone until summer, and they couldn't wait any longer. They needed direction and leadership, especially with Thorbjorn gone.

Finn knew that he was the right choice. The problem was how to make everyone else see it.

They had refused him as their chief once, but Einer's berserker death in Magadoborg ought to make it clear that they had been wrong. There was still time to right those wrongs. They could choose him now. They would. The time Finn had always dreamt about had finally arrived.

The door closed as the warriors from the stable came inside. They were the last to arrive.

Hormod had as good as claimed the middle of the room, and presented himself as the leader of the Ting, and the most likely candidate to become their chief, at least over winter.

'We have five moons, at least, before the others return,' Hormod told them as if they did not already know. 'And I see no reason why we should change anything. Let us work as we do now, building more longhouses and preparing the land for the season while we wait for them to return.'

Naturally, Hormod saw no harm in continuing exactly as they had; as the eldest, that would mean that he was in charge. Finn may have controlled the building works through his arrangement with Thorbjorn, but Hormod had delegated the work among Ash-hill's own.

'You're forgetting something,' Finn said from the back of the hall. He was still leaning against the wall, and although he was a thrall, no one complained that he spoke.

The warriors turned to look at him, and parted so that Hormod too could see who had spoken.

'Harald will send another priest,' Finn said.

The warriors' stares were hard. They blamed him for that death, although if he had allowed the priest to stay, they would have blamed him for that too.

'Harald will not be happy that his priest is dead,' Finn continued unbothered. 'The only thing that may ease his mind is a visit from our chief and a proper report.'

'This is a problem you created,' Hormod accused, exactly as Finn had hoped he would. 'You go.'

Finn nodded and pushed away from the wall. Slowly, he walked along the open passage the warriors had cleared for him to the middle of the room where Hormod stood.

'Every time I go to Jelling, I risk losing my head,' Finn said.

'Every time I leave this gods-protected town, there is a chance that I will not come back. But in order for us to survive and resist a Christian rule, someone needs to go, and you are right: it needs to be me.'

Gladly he offered himself up for certain defeat. In Jelling he had Siv on his side to protect him and give him second chances. And in order to ensure her help, he needed to live up to his part of the promise and form a bond with Harald's eldest son, something that was impossible to do unless he went back.

In time, through the young boy, Finn might regain his name and much more than a chieftaincy, as long as he was not hasty and as long as he calculated every action as carefully as the Alfather would have done.

'I have Harald's trust,' Finn said. 'And I hope that by now I also have yours.'

He looked over the crowd, and found Berg standing in the inner ring behind Hormod. His eyes stayed on the young warrior a little longer to indicate that it was time.

Berg stepped forward, and although Finn had expected him to be nervous to speak to the large crowd, despite his young age and inexperience, Berg's voice was strong and did not falter.

'There is no greater sacrifice than that of your own life,' said Berg. 'We would still be sleeping in the cold ship naust, if it wasn't for Finn. We wouldn't have made it out of Magadoborg if he hadn't called the retreat when Einer went berserk. We wouldn't have any lands if he hadn't sacrificed himself and gone to Jelling to argue on our behalf, and we won't have anything to our names if he doesn't go back to Jelling now.'

When he had been a freeman, Finn had not cared much about Berg and the other younger warriors. He had used to see them more as servants who would do his work if he showed them a little kindness from time to time, but now that he had no name and lineage, it was thanks to Berg and the other young warriors that he had a chance to rise again.

'I can think of no one more capable to lead us over winter,' Berg finished.

'He is a thrall,' said an older shieldmaiden. Half a moon ago she would have said it with reproach and disdain, but now it was said with a certain amount of regret.

Finn wanted to speak up, but he knew that he could not defend himself. That would seem petty and desperate.

'He is not a born thrall,' Berg said on Finn's behalf. For a youngster he was a good spokesman. He would have made a handsome law-man, if their fates had been different. 'We have already disregarded traditions. We have held Tings without a lawmaker, and raided in winter. These are unusual times. He might be a debt-thrall, but Finn has proven himself worthy.' At that, Berg stepped away. He had pushed enough. If the crowd was not convinced by that speech, then they wouldn't ever be convinced, not until Finn regained his freedom.

'You're worthy, Finn,' said the shieldmaiden Gudrun. 'You have my vote.'

Her vote was all he needed. Others looked to Gudrun for guidance where before they had looked to Thora. The two of them had fought shield to shield for many summers, and people respected her. Women wanted to lay with her or fight like her, and men wanted to *be* her. Few were those who did not like Gudrun or trust her advice.

'You have my full support,' chimed a shieldmaiden next to Gudrun, eager to agree. More people gave their backing, and they were no longer timid about it.

Finn looked at each one and nodded. He kept a serious tone and expression, but he was jumping for joy on the inside. Finally, he would go from having nothing to being a chieftain, and having everything he had ever wished for. If only Einer had been there to witness his rise.

Yet, everyone was not convinced. There was still Hormod. 'He is nameless. He has no kin or lineage,' said the old man. 'He can't possibly lead us.'

The time for Finn to speak had come. 'The reason we need a leader is because we need someone strong to represent us outwardly, so that others will fear to come here and ruin what we have. So that our lands will be safe.'

Finn addressed the crowd without looking at them. He stared at the new wooden floor as if noticing it for the first time. The less attention he paid to the gathered warriors, the less it would seem like he had planned every move, and the more likely they would be to show him their support. If he looked like he neither needed it nor wanted it, as Einer had before the holmgang, they would be more likely to push him to take on the role he so desired.

'I am nameless, yet I gained the favour of Harald Bluetan. I left with nothing and returned with the tools for us to rebuild our new life. Let me do it again. Let us rebuild Ash-hill as a place where success isn't determined by age or riches, but by abilities.'

Hormod was quick to react. 'So many of our traditions have been broken this summer and winter, and that is precisely why we should hold on to the few that we have left. We should hold onto our pride, as freemen.'

'Pride won't get us good reputations and invitations to Valhalla,' Finn retorted. 'But let others know that you picked a debt-thrall to steer the town, and the rumours will spread. They will whisper about the townsfolk from northern Jutland who were fair and brave enough to not rely on a wealthy man to lead them, but on ambition and abilities. That is how our names should be spoken in Valhalla, and how the mighty Alfather should come to know us. As those who stood up for him with everything they had, even when they had nothing.'

From the far corner of the room a man began to clap. Then another, and another. Soon they were all clapping at Finn, and it made him feel like a war hero returned home after a harsh winter abroad. Finally, they acknowledged him for his true worth.

'How can we know for certain that your word is true?' Hormod loudly asked, silencing the claps and the clamour. 'How can we know that you will do anything, even sacrifice your own life to keep Harald and his Christianity in Jelling?'

No more than a moon earlier, Finn would have sighed at the mistrust. He had slain a Christian priest in front of their eyes. He had brought back wealth to put them on the right path again, and he had overcome every obstacle in his way to be here. Yet, in their eyes, he was a debt-thrall, and if he was ever to become a chief, he would need to go much further to prove his worth than any freeman ever would have.

'How do you wish me to prove my loyalties, Hormod? I have given everything to this town and all of you. I have gifted you with wealth I did not possess. I have sacrificed my blood, tears and sweat for you. Always, I have acted with the interests of this town in mind.'

Every villager knew it to be true. Finn had done everything for the sake of the town.

'Tell me,' Finn insisted. 'If all of my proof is not enough. If my dealings with Harald do not prove my abilities, and my execution of the priest does not prove my loyalty to Odin, then how can I prove anything?'

Hormod smiled as if he had waited for Finn to say exactly that, like a fox lying in wait for its prey, and strangely Finn recognised that smile. A few moons earlier Finn had carried it in front of a crowd, back before his holmgang with Einer, when he had first thought that he would be chief.

Despite the smile, Hormod did not offer a suggestion. Perhaps he did not have one. Perhaps he thought that simply questioning Finn's worth would be enough to dissuade the others. Perhaps it could have been, but Finn was not about to allow Hormod to win.

He licked his teeth and spat a thick clump of spit onto the wooden floor. The room was pretty, and well decorated. The rough edges had been polished and filed and sawed to transform the new building into a real longhouse that might someday feel like home.

Every last warrior watched Finn as he examined the carved beam above him. They acknowledged Finn, although they did not dare to pick him as their chief. At least not yet. He had not expected it to be easy.

'Thorgal,' Finn called.

Thorgal looked up from his warm cup of herbs. His eyes shot up to the carved beam, as if to see if there was a carving fault there that he had made and no one else had noticed, but there was not. Thorgal was a skilled carver.

'Do you carry a file?' Finn asked.

'A nail file?' Thorgal asked, already searching his pockets.

'The one you use for wood. For bone.'

Absentmindedly Thorgal reached a hand up to his belt and grabbed his wood file. 'Why?' he questioned, before he presented it to the crowd and to Finn.

'I intend to prove to Hormod exactly why you can trust that my word is true.'

Thorgal and half a hundred warriors frowned back at Finn, trying to understand how a wood file would prove that he was worthy to be their chief.

Still with a frown on his forehead, Thorgal presented the file to Finn in an outstretched hand, but Finn did not move to get it. He stayed exactly where he was. He kept his distance from the crowd of freeman to show that he was different from them. Not because he was a debt-thrall, but because he could be their chief, if they dared to choose him.

Reluctantly, Thorgal walked to him.

'I'll need your help,' Finn said. 'And Stein and Ingolf to hold me down.'

Thorgal's eyes widened in sudden realisation of what Finn meant. Thorgal's wood file was the slimmest of its kind, made for fine details and bone carving.

Finn licked his teeth smooth again. His heart raced and he

tried to keep himself steady, but his hands were shaking in fear of the pain to come. He knew the ancient stories. On countless nights, he had winced at the mere thought of them, but Finn had come so far already and there was no step too great for him to take. He would become the chieftain of Ash-hill, whatever it took. He *would* prove his worth.

Stein and Ingolf forced him to his knees, grabbed his arms and shoulders and held him still.

Thorgal winced as he looked at Finn's face. 'You're sure?' he asked.

Finn was anything but sure, but he would never admit to it. He was shaking at the thought of it and repressing tears. He did not think himself capable of speaking in a clear voice, so he simply nodded.

Thorgal gave Finn a piece of wood to bite down on. It was big enough so that Finn could not easily spit it out. Two more men arrived to help Thorgal. They grabbed Finn's upper lip and slid it up to reveal his yellowed teeth.

Instinct made Finn want to wrench away, but he was held in place from all sides.

Thorgal brought the file down and looked away from Finn. 'Should we say something?' he asked, not to Finn, but the gathered warriors. He seemed reluctant to start, as if it was him who would be in pain and not Finn.

Finn bit onto the wood and breathed loudly through both mouth and nose. He kept his breathing steady, but he just wanted it to be over because he was already beginning to regret thinking of it, although he knew that he needed to go further to prove his worth. This would prove his resolution. It was the only way.

That is what he told himself, but his hands would not steady and his vision was shaking and his nostrils flared.

Worthy you have become,
Known by those who came before,

The crowd sang for him, but Finn found no strength in their song.

Thorgal lifted the wood file. It was big and bulky, seen so close, and Finn did not want it anywhere near him. But he was trapped as a thrall on a funeral pyre. It was too late to pull back.

His teeth hurt already from how tightly he bit into the piece of wood. Splinters drove into his gums, but Finn did not attempt to spit them out. He clenched down harder. His teeth sunk into the wood. What was to come would hurt more than splinters. Both his teeth and lips were dry.

Thorgal brought the file closer and closer to Finn's face. The cold metal touched his teeth. It made him shiver.

Finn clenched his eyes shut. Thorgal's bone file rested against his teeth, waiting for the moment. His lips were pulled up and out of the way. The file scraped across his teeth. His skull felt like it was being squeezed by a giant.

Bone dust from his teeth fell onto his lower lip. Thorgal lifted the file from Finn's mouth and prepared for the second round.

Finn clenched his teeth into the wood, embracing the blood in his mouth from the splinters in his gums. He opened his eyes to appear strong and resolute, and wondered how many rounds it would take. How many times would Thorgal slide his file along Finn's teeth before the marks would show and be satisfying enough?

His entire body was cold from the first stroke, and all of the bones in his face and even in his arms and the rest of his body shook and shivered as Thorgal placed the file back onto Finn's teeth.

A splinter from the piece of wood in Finn's mouth dug into his gums directly behind his front teeth. Finn focused on that pain, and the stinging of the blood, and on Thorgal's brown eyes, but as soon as Thorgal's cold file touched his teeth again, he lost all of his concentration.

The file scraped. Finn's teeth rocked and his skull sounded

like it was full of thunder, shaking from the power of lightning. As if Thor struck his head with every scrape of Thorgal's vile file.

The pain burned so clearly through Finn that he thought and felt nothing else. It pulsed through him; it screeched through his head and pinched his temples. It doubled in force. He clenched his teeth harder in agony, and then his eyes rolled back.

BUNTRUGG

Chapter One Hundred and Nine

BUNTRUGG'S SKIN ITCHED from the cold of Surt's house. He sat on Surt's stone-hard bed where he had slept often as a younger giant. Muspelheim was so close that Buntrugg almost thought he could hear the fire demons cackle. He had grown up with their cackles, but the sound of fire was no longer nostalgic; not since Muspel's demons had torched him.

The cold of Surt's stone home helped him ignore the distant shouts of fire demons from inside the mountain. Surt's home was always cold when Surt was elsewhere. The house had no oven and no fireplace; with Surt as master, it did not need either. Few beings could live in this way—in a home so bare, with so few comforts—but Surt was rarely home. Buntrugg had probably spent more evenings here than Surt ever had.

Steps crunched outside. The snow fizzled and whistled as it melted from the touch of Surt's hot feet.

Buntrugg held his breath. He prepared his mind to tell the truth and only the truth, and calmed his heart. Truth was always rewarded, he told himself over and over until he knew it to be true.

The door swung open.

Vapour and heat streamed into the room as Surt's heavy feet stepped inside. His long black coat swept the floor. His back was turned to Buntrugg as he swung the door closed. The long sleeves of his coat were folded up, revealing his strong forearms.

His skin was like embers, black and scorched into a thick crust on the outside, but from the cracks came the deep red gleam of fire and heat. Although he was a giant, he did not look it. Every part of him seemed made and conjured from embers. His muscles tightened as he locked the door; the embers cracked open and the heat and light of fires shone from his straining muscles.

Surt sighed. His stone house trembled and breathed with him. It heated at his presence. Buntrugg no longer needed to huddle in his hood.

Without a single acknowledgement that Buntrugg was in his home, returned from the dead, Surt made his way to his favourite stone chair. He plopped into the hard chair so his ember skin sputtered smoke. His coat was open to his bare embered chest. His eyes, black where they had been burned by fire demons, looked down at his own hands. Flames flickered from his chest with every breath.

Finally, Surt acknowledged Buntrugg sitting on the bed across from Surt's chair.

Buntrugg. Loudly Surt thought, so that Buntrugg could hear.

'You did well,' Surt said, aloud this time. His voice of fire and terror scraped Buntrugg's ears, like the sharp end of a burning hot dagger. His tongue clicked at the end and sent a slap of fire across the room like Muspel's own whipping flames.

Our destinies were not spun to meet again.

The last time they had met, Surt had knowingly sent Buntrugg to his death. He had known that they had not been destined to meet again, and still he had sent Buntrugg to die.

The forefathers should have been furious and trying to feed

his anger at the knowledge that Surt had sent him to his death, but they did not. The forefathers were calm and quiet, and Buntrugg too felt no anger at the fact. To be burned to death by fire demons had been Buntrugg's destiny.

Not death, Surt thought. *You didn't die.*

'I did,' Buntrugg said. 'The forefathers refused to welcome me into the afterlife, but I died.'

Did Odin convince you of that nonsense? Only Surt could think the Alfather's name like the god was a naughty child who needed to be reprimanded.

Suddenly Buntrugg felt like a stupid valley giant. He had been warned of the Alfather's tricks, but weary from his burns, he had listened to Odin and trusted him. Buntrugg hadn't used his ears to listen to the truth of Odin's heartbeat. He hadn't doubted what he had been told, until now. 'I didn't die?'

A long sigh of dark smoke puffed out of Surt's body. It was all the answer Buntrugg needed.

'He told me the forefathers had once refused your death,' Buntrugg said.

Surt's chest quivered with the cackle of a demon's laughter. *I never died*, Surt thought loud enough to be heard without halting his crisp laugher. *The forefathers refusing death,* he repeated like it were the dumbest thing he had ever heard. When his laughter died he examined his hands with his blackened eyes. *So, he shackled you too,* he sighed in thought.

'Shackled me?'

Surt released another puffed sigh. He stared at his hands. Heat oozed from his joints. *It's how he shackled me.* He rubbed his wrists as if there were invisible chains around them. *He catches us when we are dying. When our fates are malleable.*

Once Buntrugg recalled being in the Hall of Fates and watching a short-lived's destiny vane. The thread became limp, and instead of cutting it and ending the life of the suffering short-lived, the three nornir had been busy untying tight knots and freeing the fate from future obligations. He had watched as the fate regained strength, and they had tied it up in new patterns. So that had been the Alfather's way. That was how he reigned over Midgard, and over the long-lived. Aesir, vanir, nornir and jotnar who could not otherwise be convinced to follow the Alfather.

Buntrugg had been healed in Odin's hall while the nornir had bound a new destiny for him. He had been tricked under the pretence of being healed, and it was worse than that, for Buntrugg had also brought his sister's son into Odin's hall to be healed. Half-dead, Einer had been, when Buntrugg had wheeled him into Odin's hall. Einer's fate too must have been meddled with as he had healed in Valhalla.

'So, the Alfather has decided our fates,' Buntrugg said aloud.

His three nornir tied them. Perhaps they were merciful, Surt did not sound like that was likely.

Buntrugg wondered what destiny the Alfather had doomed him to follow. Odin had clearly wanted Buntrugg to take over for Surt in some way, and someday, and he shuddered at the thought of how that might come about. Destinies could not be evaded.

Destinies are marked in thread and not in stone, Surt wisely reminded Buntrugg. There was hope.

'I will fight the destiny he has prepared.' Buntrugg's heart beat with the truth.

Surt heard it and nodded slowly. Since entering the house, Surt had not yet looked at Buntrugg.

Hearing Buntrugg's quietest thoughts, Surt finally looked up at Buntrugg's charred face. It was not like Surt's own, which had slowly turned to fire and embers from his work within Muspelheim. It was the face of a valley giant who had played with fire.

'You are not a valley giant,' Surt grumbled aloud, so the stone floor shook and Buntrugg's ears bled.

The pain of Surt's voice made Buntrugg recognise the truth. A valley giant would not have survived a single night in Surt's barren home. A valley giant would not have survived frequent visits to Muspelheim. A valley giant would not have been able to learn the language of demons, and most of all, a valley giant could never have accomplished a single task for the great Surt.

You have accomplished many, Surt thought as he leaned back further in his stone chair.

Surt was in a good mood. He was speaking a lot tonight. Usually, he barely said three words in a week, and Buntrugg did not know how to respond to Surt's sudden cascade of loud thoughts.

My thoughts are not loud, thought Surt, and despite Surt's red blazing presence, his smile could chill worlds. *They are the same as always. It is your ears that have been sharpened, by fire and the blades of shadow warriors.*

Buntrugg gaped at the realisation. The forefathers felt different since he had seen them in the forge, but he had not realised that many other things too had changed. He had always had keen ears, and heard more than most, but Surt thought in the language of demons, and it was a quiet language, impossible to understand even if a little muffled, as thoughts usually were, unless they were meant to be heard.

The Alfather is not wrong, Surt thought, and Buntrugg was no longer certain if he was meant to hear it or not. *You could replace me. You could replace any of us.*

Surt thought him capable of replacing any of the old beings. Beings who were so old and knowledgeable that not even the Alfather could come close to their reach.

Surt rummaged in his chair. *What other worrisome truths did you bring?* he asked.

Buntrugg sighed and organised his thoughts. He was not certain how he should start or tell the great Surt of his discovery. 'As I travelled to complete my task and lock Muspel's sons back into their furnace, I was brought through many passage graves,' Buntrugg carefully began. 'The last one, the one that led us from Midgard into a dwarf's forge... It was leaking. A lot.'

Surt listened to Buntrugg speak with closed eyes. He did not interrupt. He was a patient being.

'The forge opened up to two worlds and they both leaked into the passage grave. I thought it was just the one, but it's not. I think they're all leaking. All the passage graves.'

At Buntrugg finished report, Surt neither opened his eyes, nor responded.

'What shall we do?' Buntrugg asked, to get an answer to his worries. He knew that leaking passage graves could not be good. Surt had sent him abroad to close leaks before, but never something quite as large and important as the leak Buntrugg had felt in the passage graves.

If the passages continue to leak… we will be doomed. Surt responded. *There is only one thing to do.*

'What?'

Collapse them.

'But the Alfather…'

Was foolish to have built them.

If Buntrugg was right, then it wasn't just one or two passages, but all of them. They were all leaking a little Ginnungagap, like the ash tree in Ash-hill had been.

'What about us? How shall we travel between the worlds? We don't have a rainbow bridge.'

We…? Giants, you mean.

'Nej. I mean *all* of the common beings. All of us use the passage graves to travel.' Jotnar, alvar, svartalvar, dwarfs, and all sorts of beasts travelled through passage graves.

Then we will have to use the old veils.

'Travel will be longer. Anger will rise.'

It rises already. Don't you feel the forefathers stir underneath your skin?

Buntrugg did feel it. There was something different and strange about the forefathers these days. They surged with anger, suddenly, without warning, and then other times, they were quiet, almost as if they weren't there. Though when they did flare, it was more powerful than ever before. The forefathers were growing in strength. All the nine worlds were. The last war was coming.

'And Midgard?' Buntrugg asked. There were no veils to the Alfather's Midgard.

Will be closed off.

'Only aesir and vanir care about Midgard, anyways,' Buntrugg decided. Even so, it seemed like a drastic measure to take, and besides, the Alfather would not take kindly to it, nor would any of the other beings in the common worlds.

His sister might still be in Midgard too, but there would be time to urge her to come home before the last passage was shut.

Your sister isn't in Midgard. Surt opened his black eyes. His brow flickered uncertainly.

'Then... where is she?' Buntrugg asked, almost afraid to do so.

Surt stared at his hands again. He opened and closed his embered fist. As a simple giant feeling for the forefathers. Buntrugg looked down at his own hands and clenched his fist. The forefathers were loud, not with their usual anger, but a mixture of emotions.

She is with them, Surt thought in response to Buntrugg's unspoken thoughts.

Panic washed over Buntrugg as he glared at his own hands. A panic full of questions. How could she have passed on? Why and at whose hand? The questions flooded him, but one by one they trickled out of his mind, for he knew the answers.

'My sister was always running from his shackles.' The Alfather must have abandoned his quest to shackle her, knowing that he couldn't control her. He had saved Buntrugg from near death, but it ought to have been Glumbruck who he had saved. In the grand scheme of the nine worlds, she was much more important than him.

The passage graves need to be closed, Surt thought. *That is important, in the grand scheme of the nine worlds.*

'The passage graves?' Buntrugg forced a laugh. He was still staring at his fists, trying to hear the forefathers' voices and his sister's among them. 'What does it matter now? Why is it more important than her?' He knew that he should not ask. No one ever questioned Surt's commands.

You are no longer a young jotun, thought Surt, proudly, as if he had been waiting for the day when Buntrugg would dare to speak back.

'My youth ended when I first took a bite of an apple of youth, as offered by the Alfather,' said Buntrugg. 'And I fear my appetite will never recover.'

Your appetite would not have had long anyways, Surt thought in consolation, although coming from Surt nothing was, nor could be a consolation. *The long winter is coming. Soon her wolves will howl.*

A chill travelled through Buntrugg. The wolves would howl and the end would come. The veulve, too, had spoken of the end. By Yggdrasil's roots, she had told Buntrugg that he would not live to see another Asgard spring. Perhaps that meant that this winter would be Asgard's last.

Asgard will stand even after the end, even if we will not. In red blood it shall stand. Flooded in corpses. There are worse things in the nine worlds than Ragnarok. It was the longest phrase Surt had ever spoken. That was how important this was.

Vapours rose from Surt's skin from exhaustion. He was an old being, ready for the end to come.

Why are we doomed if the passage graves continue to leak? He had not forgotten Buntrugg's question about the passage graves. Old beings like Surt and the veulve never forgot and never strayed far from the matter at hand. *Time will spin differently in the nine worlds, until all of time is undone. Then Ragnarok will never come. None of us will be freed. Our shackles will never be severed. Ragnarok must come. We have to sever the bond and ensure Ragnarok. Before we cease to exist. Before everything ceases to exist.*

FINN

Chapter One Hundred and Ten

FINN'S ENTIRE FACE ached and pulsed. He tasted blood in his mouth. He had been laid onto some pillows at the back of the hall. People were arguing. Their voices rung in Finn's head so he couldn't hear what they were saying.

Everything was spinning. He lay at a far corner of the hall. People were standing at his side, their backs turned to him.

Finn came to his senses. His head pounded and he heard a screech in his ears, still. The screech of his teeth being filed. He brought his tongue to his front teeth. They ached at the soft touch of his tongue, but he licked them smooth. There was a thick line across his teeth.

The conversation was getting louder, although he could hardly make it out from the ringing in his head. Finn's vision settled. A red face popped out in front of his.

'He's awake,' yelled Berg into Finn's ears. The shout brought the ringing back.

Finn grimaced and swallowed his bloody spit. 'What's happening?' His voice was rough and coarse, as if he had slept for half a day.

Berg whispered something back; he had to be whispering because Finn could not hear. He saw Berg's lips part and move but like the loud debate that came from elsewhere in the hall, Finn could not make out what was being said.

'This should prove it,' Finn said.

Berg and another warrior helped Finn to his feet. His legs were sore. His entire body was, but most of all his face and his teeth. His gums and eyes pulsed with blood.

Finn thanked Berg for helping him and nodded his thanks to Thorgal as he regained the inner circle where all could see him. Hormod was standing close, guarding his position as the eldest warrior.

Once more, he ran his tongue over his newly filed teeth. They felt strange, but good. He spat out blood. Then he waited for the blood to gather in his mouth again and displayed a bloody smile for them all to see. 'I am marked now. All who look upon me will know that my loyalties lie with Odin.'

And what sort of pain he had sustained to show his loyalty.

'And how are you going to gain Harald Gormsson's favour now?' Hormod asked. His arms were folded over his chest and he looked pleased.

Harald Gormsson had no choice. Besides, Siv was there to help as she had the last time. Finn knew that as long as Siv was there, he did not have to fear. Together, they would come up with a plan.

'I don't need to gain Harald's favour,' Finn said. 'I already have it. For him to change his loyalties would be too great a loss now. I will tell him beautiful tales about how this is the only way that I can make his words known in a land that is not ready for Christianity, and he shall believe me.'

'And how do we know that you aren't just telling *us* beautiful tales?'

Finn had gone so far already, even having his teeth filed to prove his loyalty, but it was never enough for Hormod and the few who supported the old warrior. As a thrall, Finn needed the support of every single villager to rise to the position of chieftain.

'It doesn't matter if they're just beautiful tales,' Finn said. 'It doesn't matter to Harald Gormsson and it shouldn't matter to you.'

The crowd had not expected that response. To say that it should not matter was almost as good as admitting that it was true. Hormod thought himself a winner already. He was ready to address the crowd and claim the warriors as his own, but Finn was not done.

'If my words are merely beautifully spun tales, it will not matter to Harald. All Harald wants is an increased reputation and to give the appearance that he rules all of the Jute and Dane lands. As long as I—as long as we—make him believe that he does rule, and that his orders are being followed, then he has no reason to waste his war efforts on us. Southern kings are undoubtedly pressuring him. Christian demands flood his court louder since our strike on Magadoborg, and he would rather believe our tales than launch an army to reclaim what he openly considers his own lands.'

The warriors did not care about Harald Bluetan and whatever nonsense faraway kings were planning. They were staring at him, waiting for him to get to the part about spinning beautiful tales for them. They were waiting for him to admit that everything he was saying was lies. To take a wrong turn, so they could oust him as the thrall that he was and forget that they had ever considered him as a possible chieftain.

'Whether I spin beautiful tales to Harald or to you or to anyone else, should not matter to you either,' he told them, and before the protests at the back of the room could rise, and before they all collectively decided to throw him into the mud, Finn continued: 'You know me, so you know that I do not speak without purpose. I am not a man of many words, except when words are needed. My hard-spun tales gained you this hall. They gained you pigs and horses and sheep and goats. They even gained you two cows. I did what any good chieftain would have done. I cared more about the honour and survival of our village than I cared about my own life or my own reputation. The day that my reputation outside of this town is no longer favourable— the day that warriors no longer fear Finn the Nameless and the townsmen who chose him—is the day that you can execute me as the thrall I am and throw me onto the funeral pyre to burn in agony. But right now, my tales give you profit. They have given you this hall, and I promise you that they will give you much more. They will give you honour and battles worthy of the eyes of gods and they will seat you in Valhalla.'

Women and men were nodding along to his speech as if they were the ones who had thought of it, and as if Finn's own words were not enough to convince, Thorgal took it upon himself to speak. Perhaps better than anyone, Thorgal knew the pain that Finn had suffered as his teeth had been filed, and perhaps better than anyone he knew what sort of courage it had taken.

'As the Alfather says,' Thorgal begun. '"If an idiot is with other kinsmen, he should hold his tongue, for none will know that he is useless, if all he says is silence." Finn's tongue proves his smarts. If he had no smarts to speak of, his tongue would speak him into trouble, but every time he opens his mouth I am more and more convinced that we could find no better chief, even if Thora was among us.'

Thorgal was met with roaring applause, accompanied by stomps that demanded a vote.

Finn stepped away from the inner circle that had naturally formed inside the longhouse, and found his spot at the back of the hall. By walking away, he suggested that he was merely offering himself as an option. By not pushing forward, he showed them that it was their choice and that he did not mind whatever choice they made, although he did.

His head ached and his gums were bleeding. And although he wanted to hear what they said in the middle of the room, his head was too weary to follow the conversation. He hoped that his teeth filing would be enough. His teeth ached so. All of them, not the just the ones Thorgal had filed. Even the ones at the back of his mouth.

Finn leaned against the back wall of the longhouse. The wood was cold, but he did not mind. His forehead was burning with heat. He crossed his arms and closed his eyes. His head rung and his gums throbbed as blood mixed with spit.

The longhouse was loud with noise and Finn just wanted to lie down and sleep and heal up. The pain was a lot worse than he had thought it would be. Worse than when his skin had been hammered with colour. He swallowed the bloody spit in his mouth, but he had hardly swallowed before his tongue was swimming in blood again. His gums had torn on the splinters he had bit, and he also thought that his lips had been scraped by Thorgal's filing after Finn had fainted. He knew that they had not stopped when he had fainted. The depth of the marks proved that they had continued, and rightly so.

At least now it was done, and as with all actions, it could not be undone. No matter what the villagers chose tonight, Finn knew that they would decide to send him south to deal with Harald Bluetan, because none of them dared to go, and that was a day that Finn did not look forward to.

Someone tapped Finn on the shoulder and brought him out of his thoughts. Someone else was shaking his hands and arms. People were touching him from everywhere and dragging him away from the wall.

The commotion had returned. They were cheering his name, and while he had been standing in the shadows, swallowing his own bloody spit, they had chosen him, and they had given him a new name.

'Finn the Nameless, chieftain of Ash-hill!' they bellowed.

Finn was brought through the crowd, back into the middle of the room, by the fireplace, where only a freeman and a chieftain ought to stand.

Hormod was nowhere to be seen anymore. He no longer belonged here, not like Finn did. They had chosen him. Finally, after all of this time. After Vigmer's insults, and the humiliation of the holmgang with Einer. After Einer's disappearance and the long journey home, after all of this time, Finn had finally been chosen.

His life was complete.

All his life, since he was nothing more than a barefooted farmer boy spinning wool in the stables, he had dreamt of this day. He had wished for it and he had worked for it and he had dreamt of it. Every single night in his sleep, he had seen himself walk to stand in this exact spot, with people shouting his name and cheering for him, and looking at him as they looked at rich men. They wanted to be his friend, they wanted to look good to him, so that he would choose them to stand at his side.

A hornful of ale was shoved into his hand and freemen no longer looked at him as a thrall or a mere farmer, they looked at him as they had before he had lost his name: with respect. They looked at him as he had never imagined they ever would, as they looked not at an equal, but at someone they wanted to become. As children looked at their fathers, or men looked at their gods.

Finally, Finn had become a man of influence.

He had no name and no lineage, but he had more than he had ever owned in his entire life, and nothing could take his title away now.

At that, the realisation hit him. Something *could* take his title away, or rather *someone*. When Finn next stood in Harald's court, he would not be able to hide the fresh riles on his front teeth that meant that he would follow no Christian into battle. But at least, in Jelling, there was Siv, and she would protect him against the retaliation of the greedy king Harald Bluetan.

TYRA

Chapter One Hundred and Eleven

Siv HAD TOLD Tyra exactly where to go and how to survive in Asgard, though it took her a full night to remember. It had been before they had arrived at the nornir's cave. But Tyra hadn't forgotten.

The town was small and reminded her of Midgard.

There were so many aesir in town. So many gods and goddesses that Tyra had never seen and whose names she didn't know. And the aesir were all better dressed than her. Their dresses twinkled and flowed elegantly. Though Siv had assured her that they would, Tyra didn't at all think they would be interested in exchanging clothes or buying her dress.

But Siv had told her to try. Siv had told her to follow the first root in the sun and get some new clothes that didn't come from Midgard, so that the valkyries would not be able to find her.

Aesir whose names Tyra didn't know looked at her as she walked along the street. They examined and admired her clothes, as Siv had promised that they would.

Perhaps if there was a dress stall somewhere, she might be

lucky, but she saw no market and she didn't know what was inside all the houses. A lot of people were coming and going. And she didn't want to ask, because someone might recognise her as being from Midgard, or reveal her whereabouts to the valkyries. But she had to do something.

Siv would have done something.

Two aesir were walking towards her. Two men with nicely trimmed beards.

'Excuse me,' Tyra said in her prettiest voice.

They stopped in front of her and one of them smiled.

'I came with my sisters to buy new clothes,' she said, so as not to arouse suspicion about who she was or why she was here. 'But I'm lost.'

Thankfully, she didn't need to say anything else. The two aesir were already looking around the street, trying to spot her imaginary siblings. One of them pointed at a house far down the road. 'They will probably be at the Nine Dresses,' he said.

She thanked them and rushed past them. She tried to seem eager to see her sisters, but she was only really eager to get away, so that she could find a way home to Midgard and to Svend. Back where Siv would be able to find her again.

Tyra was almost at the end of the road when she spotted the Nine Dresses shop. It was packed inside, with goddesses standing shoulder to shoulder. Tyra was smaller than most of them, so she pressed through to the front of the store, until she saw a seller.

Tyra's heart pounded loud with worry, but she thought of Siv, and how good she was at pretending. 'I have a question,' Tyra said, lifting her arms high to be seen and heard.

People pressed at her back and shoved to get to the front, and they were yelling orders over her head, and no one listened.

Tyra tried not to think about it, but it felt like the battle in Ash-hill—like the night her parents and sisters had died. It reminded her of fire and blood and shouting, of the sweat that had run down her calves and mixed with blood. The arrow stings and the pressure of the helmet on her head. It reminded her of stumbling over her mother's body as the town was in flames.

She shut her eyes tight and raised her hands properly and shouted with more conviction. The sooner she was done, the sooner she could get out of there. It wasn't a fight, she told herself. It was not Ash-hill.

The worker was busy and didn't stop to chat. She fetched dresses left and right to bidders and buyers, and Tyra watched her with hawk eyes. She focused all of her energy on the worker without as much as blinking, like Hilda would have done. Finally, the worker passed right in front of her; fast and quick.

'I want to trade my dress for one of yours,' Tyra quickly said and did her best to smile, despite how she was being pushed from behind. She tried and tried not to think about the battle at Ash-hill.

'We don't trade,' said the busy worker, and was about to leave, but then she glanced to Tyra, and examined her from her muddy shoes up to her uncombed hair. Tyra blinked away her worries. She flattened her hair with her hands to make it look nice and so that she would look more trustworthy.

'What would you want to trade?' asked the worker with narrowed eyes as she examined Tyra's dress a little closer.

'This dress,' Tyra said. 'The one I'm wearing.'

The woman tugged at the fabric. Her hands combed over the embroidery on the skirt and her eyes examined the design. People were shoving Tyra, making it difficult to stand still. They were shouting to get the worker's attention, but she was focused on Tyra now, finally. 'Who made it?'

'The best dressmaker in all of Midgard,' Tyra replied.

She had been at the market with her mother enough times to know that the truth was not what anyone wanted, when they were out to buy clothes or beads or combs.

'Midgard,' mused the woman, and looked up at Tyra's face, studying it more closely. 'Did you get it from the Yule offerings?'

Not knowing how else to respond, Tyra nodded.

The worker flattened the skirt of Tyra's dress where she had touched it. Staring at the vivid colours of the fabric, she asked: 'Why do you want to exchange it?'

Tyra had not thought that far. She just had to, and she couldn't say why.

'Honestly...' Tyra said to gain time and think up a clever answer—the sort of answer that Siv might have come up with—and then she had it. Flattery was always the way. 'I've always really wanted to buy a dress from here.'

It was the truth, as well. As a girl in Midgard, Tyra had always wanted to look pretty, like a goddess.

'You'll have to talk to the owner,' the worker said. 'Come.'

Tyra did her best to slip out of the crowd and follow the aesir worker.

There was a door at the far back of the room, and Tyra was pushed through. The door kept opening and closing as workers came in and out. The room was filled with shelves all the way to the top, each shelf full of folded dresses that the workers continued coming back to fetch. At the back of the store room was another door.

The worker who had led Tyra away from the shouting crowd inside the shop knocked on the door and entered. 'There's a girl here with a dress from Midgard that she wants to trade.'

'We don't do trades,' came the answer. It was a voice that sounded like feet crunching over gravel.

'She received it as Yule offering.'

'A famed aesir, then,' remarked the earthy voice. 'Let me look at it.'

'She is wearing it.'

'Then send her in.'

The worker retreated back into the storage room and nodded Tyra towards the door.

With a deep breath for strength, Tyra walked into the room. It was lit by candlelight, and dark in the corners. There were heaps of fabric all around. Bundles of thread, secured with long needles. Tyra had never before seen such riches, even in her sister Ingrid's family house; and Ingrid had married a jarl, so she had the most expensive dresses out of anyone Tyra knew.

The fabrics were dyed in colours she had never seen and never could have imagined. Some looked like sunsets, and some like sunrises. Others moved like water rustling in a stream.

At the back of the room stood four great looms and by one of them sat a woman, weaving.

'Approach,' said the woman. Her voice reminded Tyra of the time in the cave when she had met Buntrugg and Alvis's kinsman.

Tyra followed orders and walked to the looms. The woman's face looked as if it had been cut from rock, it was so sharp, and when she rose from her chair, she barely reached Tyra's shoulder, though Tyra felt small in her presence. She was a dwarf, like Alvis's kinsman.

'I've never seen a dress quite like this,' muttered the owner, and touched the skirt of Tyra's dress like the worker had done. 'So simple in design, but...'

'All of the famed goddesses received similar offerings for Yule,' Tyra said, eager to impress.

'Goddesses?'

'All the aesir *and* vanir,' Tyra corrected, realising that aesir probably didn't call themselves goddesses.

'The vanir too...' the owner mused. 'Then that's all anyone will buy this winter.'

Her slender fingers rubbed the fabric of Tyra's dress. Her eyes didn't look at the fabric that she was touching. She seemed to instead be imagining ideas for dresses to make and fabrics to weave.

'I'll agree to a trade. You can pick a dress in the store,' she said and sat back down by her loom to resume her weaving.

Tyra was about to nod her agreement, but then she remembered what her mother had once taught her about markets: *always ask for more than you want and more than you need*.

'There is another reason that I came to you,' said Tyra, trying to keep the steady voice Siv always used. 'I'm looking for Alvis's kinsman.' Tyra was owed a favour, and alone as she was, in another of the nine worlds with no way to get home, she *needed* a favour.

'Alvis's kinsman?' The store owner's hand stopped moving across the loom. 'You mean, Bafir the Unstoned?' She didn't turn to look at Tyra. 'It's just rumours, that started when his stone disappeared. He died centuries ago.'

Her hand began to move across the loom again.

'It's not rumours,' Tyra assured. 'Alvis's kinsman is alive, and I have unfinished business with him.'

The dwarf laughed. 'Don't we all?'

'So...' Tyra said, as she thought Siv would have. 'Can you get me to him, or is your influence mere rumours too?'

HILDA

Chapter One Hundred and Twelve

THE WIND BLEW silently at Hilda's back. At last she saw it. Down the hill was a large building made from both iron and wood.

'Behold Valhalla,' Hilda muttered to herself and strode towards the grand hall.

The iron and wooden beams that made up the walls were shaped like weapons. Swords with names, sharpened axes, and long spears planted in the earth like trees. Iron swords were thrust point down into the ground. Their pommels, inlaid with shining gold and silver, lined the roof. Their grips were wrapped with silk that flowed softly in the night breeze. Axe heads had been forged atop trees that grew thick as walls, the bark stripped from the trunks. Each tree was carved with different images, like the wooden handles of expensive spears and axes. At the top of the wall, the trees leaned over the hall. Their branches twisted under and over the intricate sword pommels, and their leaves formed a green roof over the enormous hall.

Valhalla was so much more than she could ever have

imagined. Hilda's snow fox yelped at the sight of it and dashed down the hill. The great hall was so grand and so large that Hilda couldn't see the end of it. It stretched both to the right and to her left, as far as she could see. There were mountains in the distance, and at her back was the faint shadow of the tree of life, large as a mountain.

Hilda rushed towards Valhalla. Close up, it looked even more impressive. The swords were spread arm-lengths wide and the tree trunks were huge. Old trees grown hundreds, perhaps thousands of summers ago.

It began to rain as she walked beside the huge outer walls of Valhalla. Though the rain obscured everything, Hilda couldn't tear her eyes away from the gold pommels at the top. The horizon darkened the further she walked, and the rain soaked her clothes. The last evening sunlight glinted off the wet sword pommels as she reached the first entrance.

A spear with two sharp ends was twisted into a troll knot that made up the huge frame of a gate. The gate was as long as six longhouses. Shoulder to shoulder, eight hundred warriors could march through it. Hilda gaped up at it. Nine wavy steps of twisted arm-rings rolled flat, led up to the open gate.

Finally, she was a warrior of Valhalla. Hilda approached the arm-ring steps, and waited at the bottom for Odin to come and greet her as he had promised. The hall was dark and barely allowed her to see inside, but the heat poured from it with the pleasing smell of freshly cooked boar and the strong honeyed scent of expensive mead. The best was provided for Valhalla's warriors, and soon Hilda would be among them. All of her wishes were coming true.

No one came to greet her, and Hilda decided that it was silly to wait.

She took the first step up the silver arm-ring stairs. Her snow fox hopped ahead of her, but Hilda walked slowly, savoured every splashing step through the rain. Finally, she would gain her rightful place among the greatest warriors of all time.

One more step and she would enter the glory of Valhalla. She unhooked the Ulfberht axe. She wanted the moment to be perfect. Both of her feet splashed onto the top step, and like that the moment passed. No one cheered for her, as she had always imagined. No one invited her inside. No one even greeted her at the door, as Einer had promised he would.

It wasn't the arrival at Valhalla that Hilda had spent a lifetime dreaming about. There ought to have been a loud feast inside. Drunk warriors singing for her as she entered. Odin ought to be there holding a speech and welcoming her into the warm hall.

Hilda knew she was worthy of all of that. Time after time she had proven herself. She had shown wit and she had shown ruse. Had shown strength and loyalty to the Alfather, and the Alfather had wanted her and invited her.

Yet no one was there to greet her.

'I'm here,' she yelled into the hall, hoping that someone would hear and come out to greet her. 'Hilda Ragnardóttir of Ash-hill.' Her voice echoed emptily back towards her from the hall.

No one was there.

Hilda took a cautious step through the open gate and into the hall. There were no shields in the ceiling, just great oak branches and leaves that barely shielded the hall from the rain. There were great puddles on the floor, raindrops hung onto the perfect food and the mead-filled horns and cups. The entire hall was empty. Ready for a feast, but empty.

Her snow fox leapt onto a table and dug its snout into pink boar meat. Frigg had told Hilda to wait for her, but there was no reason to wait alone in the rainy hall. If the warriors weren't inside, and their shields didn't line the roof, then they were fighting on Ida's plain. Odin would be there, watching over his warriors, and he would be glad to see her. He had invited her, after all.

The clouds were almost black, above the oak tree over

Valhalla. Ida's plain had to be beyond the hall. With a sigh, Hilda began to trail along the endless rows of empty tables and benches.

The night came and went as she walked, and even then, when Odin's warriors were supposed to sit in his hall and feast, no one came inside.

It seemed like she trailed through the hall all night and for a full day too. Evening approached by the time she caught the first glint of light off the copper gate at the other end of the hall. The rain had stopped sometime during the day. A breeze entered the hall, carrying with it the stench of blood and shit and rot. She thought of the Runes.

At Valhalla's gates she saw Ida's plain. Mountains of corpses stretched as far as she could see. A quiet battlefield. They had long been dead. All the warriors in the hall. They had been lying there at least one night and two full days.

Thousands and thousands of warriors had killed each other and died, transforming Ida's plain into valleys to train for the final battle. Ragnarok would be fierce and worse. There would be giants among the slain, and wolves.

No black wings flew over the battlefield. No valkyries healed the broken warriors. Odin was nowhere, and the battlefield stretched on as far as Valhalla had, and further yet—as far as Hilda could see in the evening light.

Wherever Odin was, it wasn't here.

The snow fox whimpered. Hilda snapped around. The red fox from a few days ago was there, and between its deadly teeth dangled Hilda's snow fox.

Quick as a sparrow, Hilda reached for her axe, but a huge hand grabbed her tunic and cast her backwards. Hilda was thrown onto her stomach. Her chin knocked against Valhalla's hard floor, making her head ring.

A foot stepped on her right hand, locking away her axe. Hilda heard her bones crunch. Hot pain shot up from her broken fingers. She tried to release her right hand. Her fingers dug into the worn leather shoe that held her down. The foot was giant; it pressed her forearm too.

'I've got you now,' said a man she couldn't see. He snickered as he crushed her fingers.

With a grunt to suppress the pain in her hand, Hilda twisted to glare at her capturer.

He was a real giant. The dark of the hall obscured his face, but it was pale, and she could see the smart cut of his beard, and the twinkle of his teeth. A broad smile looked down at her. A sharp chin. Hair cut to the shoulders.

'A pleasure to meet you again, Hilda,' said the trickster Loki.

For a heartbeat, Hilda allowed herself to panic. The most dangerous giant in all the nine worlds had her locked. She had stolen from him, and he had caught her. Worse; he knew her name.

The heartbeat was over.

Hilda locked away both panic and fear and focused back on the task ahead. Her hand was locked away. She prepared her feet to kick Loki away. Her left hand reached for the dagger at her back. She could free herself from the giant's grip. She knew that she could.

The pressure on her broken fingers eased. Loki stepped off her hand and arm and freed her willingly. He didn't bend down to take the axe from her.

Before he could change his mind Hilda got to her feet. She sheathed her dagger and picked up the axe in her left hand. Three of the fingers on her right dangled loose like seaweed. She tested her new grip on the axe. It was awkward to hold in her left hand. By the time she was ready to use it, Loki was gone.

The giant had turned his back to her and walked away, down the steps outside Valhalla's gates, along the bloody battlefield on Ida's plain. Calm, like both Freya and Odin had walked, but with the long strides of a giant.

'Hei, stop there!' Hilda bellowed after him. 'Don't you walk away from a fight!'

Her voice echoed along the empty hall.

Her white snow fox barked after Loki. The red fox had released it, like Loki had released Hilda.

Loki's heels dug into the blood-coloured grass as he elegantly turned to her. His smile was broader than before.

'I'm not walking away. I'm simply waiting for you to catch up,' he said in a superior tone. His posture and calm reminded Hilda of where she was. Asgard, where no worthy goddess or god ran. Asgard, where battles weren't fought with axes and swords, but with words.

She weighed the axe. She had learned to throw with her left hand, but not nearly as accurately as with her right, and she didn't fight well with the weapon in her left hand. In a battle of iron, she couldn't win.

She leaned down to pet the snow fox, and assure herself that it was well. A battle of words was risky against a giant with as sharp a tongue as Loki. Word-battles was a game at which Loki was skilled, and Hilda knew that she was not at his level.

'Freya nearly iced me to death, thinking I was you,' she said and secured her axe back into her belt.

Loki tilted his head to the side, clearly surprised that Hilda gave up arms so quickly. She had an advantage on him. He knew that she could fight with strengths and weapons, but he didn't know her skill with words. Not that the knowledge had served her with the goddess, but every defeat paved a way for future success. That was what her brother had said. On his death-bed.

'I'm sure Freya would be interested to learn that you are here, now,' she said. If Hilda found Freya or Frigg or any of her goddesses, Loki would be doomed. 'All the goddesses are eager to see you.'

'I *am* irresistible,' Loki laughed. His tone bore a hint of surprise at Hilda's decision to set aside her axe. 'Don't steal from Freya, like you stole from me, though,' he advised in a light tone as if he and Hilda were old friends. 'She is quick to scream for murder.'

The wound in Hilda's chest ached at the thought of it.

Loki pretended to leave again, but he didn't. He swayed and stepped this way and that, slowly. Waited for Hilda to stop him from leaving again. The red fox that had to be his fylgja dug its snout into the dead corpses outside Valhalla's gates. Hilda's snow fox followed its lead.

Hilda just stared at Loki. 'Why are you here?' she eventually asked. 'The bird skin is gone. It's in Freya's hall, and ruined. It won't be flying again.' She wasn't exactly sure why she'd help Loki by saying it, but it felt right.

'I'm not here for the skin. I'm here for you.'

'So you can try to kill me too?'

Loki snickered again and hummed his little song. 'Always killings.' He seemed completely undaunted by the fact that they were standing here, at the gate to Odin's hall, and that the Alfather and his valkyries could come home any moment and capture him. 'Nej. I'm not the Alfather, and I'm not an aesir. I don't make boring plans.'

His eyes shone. It was tempting to ask what his plan was, if it wasn't boring. Yet, coming from Loki, everything seemed like a trap. Even more so than it had with the goddesses. But Loki had cornered her. There was nothing to do other than ask for the truth.

'What do you want with me?' Hilda asked.

She had stolen from him, but he'd seemed to speak the truth when he said that he had no intention of killing her for it. It would have been so easy to kill her. But if her father's stories were true, Loki never took the easy and obvious road.

'I want the exact opposite of what loyal Frigg and old Odin want. I want you to find your Runes.'

Hilda's heart raced as if she were in battle. Worse than what Loki had said, worse than the thought that the Alfather and Frigg weren't going to help her, was the realisation that she believed him when he said it.

The wind howled in agreement, and brought with it the

horrid stench of iron and puke from the battlefield.

'The Runes... That is what you call them, isn't it? The whispers in the wind,' he asked, though his expression made it clear that he already knew. Things he shouldn't have any chance of knowing.

'How do you know about that? And how do you know my name?'

'You think I arrived in Asgard today?' Loki's broadening smile was provoking. 'I saw you at the bath-house.' His calm made it difficult for Hilda to stay expressionless as her father had taught her to be during a duel. 'At Yggdrasil. I saw what you did.'

The two foxes were playing on top of rotting corpses, and Hilda winced at the sight of them. She didn't like that her snow fox trusted Loki's fylgja. Especially not when the red fox had bitten it earlier. They must have met elsewhere, while Hilda was with the goddesses, for the foxes looked almost like friends, teasing each other.

'What do you know about the Runes?' Hilda asked, ignoring Loki's subtle threat. 'Why would *you* want to help me get them back?'

'What do I know of the Runes?' Loki scoffed. 'I gave them a name. I gave them purpose. I taught Odin how to bind them.' He shook his head in disbelief. '*What do I know of the Runes?*' He spoke as if he were reciting a song.

Hilda reciprocated in the same fashion. 'Your tongue is a famous flatterer. But there's one other trait it's famous for in all of Midgard. Dishonesty.' She glared up at Loki, unimpressed. He could kill her, but he wouldn't. He must have followed her all day without revealing himself.

Even if he did kill her, Odin still wanted her. Odin wasn't here, now, but he *would* be. He would find her among his dead warriors and his valkyries would wake her. He had nothing to threaten her with. Not even death.

'You won't find a more honest man than me in all of Asgard,'

Loki eventually felt the need to say, and despite herself, Hilda feared it to be true.

Hilda didn't know her gods as well as she had thought she did. Freya had stabbed her and she didn't know what Frigg and Odin had planned. She didn't know her gods at all. So, maybe she didn't know Loki as well as she thought either. 'Then answer me this, honestly: did you come to Asgard for me?'

Though Loki had nothing to threaten Hilda with, she had a lot to threaten him with. It was a dangerous thing for him to reveal himself. None in Asgard would spare him. They all wanted him dead or captured, and if Hilda as much as hinted that she knew where slippery Loki was hiding, all of Asgard would be combed to search for the giant. A hunt of such scale that not even a flea would escape. 'Why risk so much to come here?'

'Because staying away, hiding, would be boring. That's what they expect.'

Hilda sighed, like she was as bored with Loki as he claimed to be of everyone else. She descended the twisted steps from Valhalla and walked onto the bloody mud outside. The sun had set and the sky was gradually darkening, rendering the corpse-infested battlefield a much scarier sight. 'And what prevents me from alerting all the aesir to your presence in Asgard?'

If she went back to tell Frigg, Loki wouldn't have a chance of escaping. They would catch him in less than nine heartbeats. He would be thrown back into his cave of punishment, or worse.

'Nothing,' Loki said and walked closer to Hilda, and as he did, he became smaller in size. He should have been less frightening in a smaller size, but the fact that he could change his appearance so seamlessly was more frightening than his giant height and strength.

He was barely half a head taller than Hilda when he spoke again. 'You can go back and tell Frigg that I'm here, if you want. You know exactly what she has planned for me. She would be thrilled, and you would be rewarded. You could help your goddess. You could even tell the old man, my blood-brother, and witness my eternal punishment.'

He hummed his song as he walked closer to Hilda. Despite how dangerous she knew Loki was, despite everything he could do, Hilda held her ground.

With a smile, he leaned in. Their faces nearly touched. He smelled of smoke, and of sweet honey too. 'But I don't think you will. I don't think you're boring like them. I think you're like me.'

'I'm *nothing* like you,' Hilda snarled

'Then walk back and tell your goddess that she has a visit from an old friend,' he provoked.

It wasn't what she had expected him to say. Loki never said what anyone expected of him. He was fickle and slippery. Distant like ice.

'I could, and I might,' Hilda threatened. He had crushed her hand. He was a violent giant, not a god. But his talk was as enthralling as one of her father's stories. 'How will you help me regain the Runes?'

'You already have found them,' he said.

Freya and Frigg had told her that too.

Loki leaned away from her but still spoke in whispers. 'The wind is always with you.' It felt like the wind was whispering to her again, though it wasn't. It was just Loki. 'It whispers to you.'

'The wind is silent. I thought you knew something, but obviously you don't,' Hilda said in return. She was set on finding out what he really wanted. If whatever he wanted didn't please her, she would slay him and hand his corpse over to the goddesses, she decided. Earn her rightful passage to Valhalla with a blood offering.

Her attempt to anger him only made Loki snicker. 'Have you ever searched and searched through your longhouse, looking for your keys?' he asked. 'Pulled out drawers and emptied barrels and chests, only to find that you were holding the keys in your hand the entire time?'

She had. Last winter the stable keys had been attached to her left dress brooch, but she had searched for them half a day before she had realised where they were. She had felt stupid spending the day searching for something that had never been lost. 'Are you saying that I never lost the Runes?'

Silently she cursed herself for having called them the Runes instead of the whispers, but unlike the goddesses, Loki didn't bother to correct her. 'I'm saying that sometimes you've already found what you're looking for,' he said instead. 'Although you might not realise it.'

The wind pushed around and around Hilda, as if it wanted to be heard. It caressed her calves and swept through her legs. It slithered up her arms and kissed the back of her neck. Reminded her of its presence and told her that Loki spoke the truth. The wind had never left.

'Then why can't I hear them?'

'Because right now, the whispers aren't in your wind.'

He walked away from her then, but Hilda wasn't yet done. The pain from her crushed hand shot up her arm and mixed with the ache in her chest, but she pushed both to the back of her mind. Reminded herself that it was nothing compared to how much it had hurt when her eyes had burned in the forge.

She skipped over the cold corpses of Odin's warriors that littered the battlefield to follow Loki.

'When did your Runes disappear, daughter of Ragnar?' he casually asked.

'Why would I tell you such things?'

Hilda knew she couldn't trust Loki. She knew the stories. Loki always has a secret motive behind actions, and she feared to think of what Loki had planned. All the same, she followed him across Valhalla's corpses as the night fell across Asgard, hoping for answers.

'I suppose you stopped hearing the Runes about two weeks ago,' Loki guessed.

Hilda thought back. It felt exactly like two weeks ago that

they had stopped whispering to her. Though at the same time, it felt like a lifetime, because much had happened.

'Just about,' Hilda answered in disbelief.

'Two weeks and one day, to be exact,' Loki said.

She believed him when he said it. 'How would you know when I stopped hearing the Runes?'

He looked at her expectantly, waiting for her to tie together some invisible threads. His short hair played in the night breeze. It looked like the Runes were ruffling it, as they had used to play with Hilda's hair when they teased her.

'*You* hear them?' Her breath caught in her throat at the thought.

He hummed a little song, a pleasant song that Hilda had definitely heard before. When she was little. A song sung to her as she had grown up.

'*The Hanged God will abandon you,*' Loki whispered. '*In the river, your corpse will rot.*'

The goddesses too had known those words, but they hadn't said them in the same rhythm.

'*It has passed through. We cannot heal you.*'

He did. He heard her Runes. That was exactly what the Runes had whispered to her when her eyes had been burned. The goddesses hadn't known about that. At least, they hadn't mentioned it. Maybe that was why he thought that they were alike. Maybe they could both hear the Runes. 'How?' she asked. 'How could you have them?'

'How can *you?*' he asked.

Until she had arrived in Asgard, she had never quite thought of the why of it all. She had always heard whispers in the wind. Even before she had called them Runes. Before the slaughter of Ash-hill, and before midsummer when her father had died.

The goddess had told her it was her blood lineage that stemmed from the nornir and made it possible for her to hear the whispers. So, there was only one explanation as to how Loki might hear them.

Hilda balanced on the cold thighs of a dead warrior. She remembered what Frigg had asked of her and set the same question to Loki: 'Mother or father?'

She didn't truly need his answer to know. Her father had told more stories about Loki than about anyone else. She knew his lineage. Loki's father was a strong giant, but Loki always introduced himself using his mother's name, Laufey. Throughout Midgard, folk called her Needle. The bloodline that made him hear the whispers had to stem from her.

The three famed nornir in the cave of fates spun threads of destiny, but none truly knew what all the other nornir in the nine worlds were up to. Maybe they threaded destinies with needles and sewed them together. Laufey had to be a norn. There was no other explanation.

Loki stood over her. A patient shadow with the night at his back. She could just about see the shine of a smile and the outline of his crooked nose. He was only part giant. Unless he was merely making her believe that he could hear the Runes.

'You are not boring, Hilda,' he whispered to her when she finally looked up into his eyes. 'You are not stupid. So, I think you already know that I do a lot more than just *hear* those whispers in the wind.'

Hilda's heart nearly stopped at what he suggested. The wind pushed teasingly at her back. Loki's smile broadened. Then, his stare lifted to look at something behind Hilda.

Her heart leapt again. Hilda spun back to Valhalla's great hall, expecting to see the Alfather, Frigg, or a valkyrie or a conjuring of runes, but there was nothing.

She turned back to Loki, but the giant was gone.

As suddenly as he had appeared. Hilda was left alone outside Valhalla's gates, surrounded by the stench of thousands of rotting bodies. A soft wind howled. Loki had disappeared with the breeze as if he was the wind itself. But he couldn't be…

Hilda's snow fox came running down a hill of corpses. Its puffy white fur was red with blood. Her fylgja looked as confused as Hilda. The red fox, too, was gone, then.

She was alone, on the battlefield outside Valhalla and at any moment her gods might come home. After what had happened it felt wrong to stay by Valhalla and wait for Frigg and the Alfather. Because though she had found Loki—or rather, though he had revealed himself to her—she had no intention of telling her gods. If the goddess or the Alfather reached Loki before Hilda regained her Runes, she would remain Rune-less all the way to Ragnarok. They would never help her then.

Hilda turned away from Valhalla and the glory she had dreamt of for a lifetime. Back towards the cold, bloody corpses and onto the battlefield, after Loki.

Somehow, he had been right. They were more alike than Hilda wanted to admit. They both heard the Runes and had norn blood. And he seemed to know what the Runes meant, what they were, and what they would do and say. He seemed to know everything about them.

The wind pushed at her back like an embrace and whispered in her ears. *The Hanged God has abandoned you. Wise are those who change their destinies.* The Runes were back. They flew in with mysterious whispers and advice as if they had never left at all.

Her snow fox barked at the wind, and once the relief had passed, the worry came. The Runes had arrived just when Hilda had decided to follow Loki and not betray him.

A crushed hand to remind you of owed promises, the wind whispered, as if it was the Runes who had crushed her hand, and not Loki's foot.

Loki did a lot more than just *listen* to the wind.

DARKNESS

RAGNAR'S ATTEMPTS TO right his wrongs at Ragnarok were futile. His daughter was out there, somewhere. Through the hole in the Darkness he had seen her, and if Ragnar could not right his wrongs and prevent Ragnarok, it was Hilda who would suffer.

The small dot of a light was still out in the distance. Sometimes Ragnar could see it. Sometimes he couldn't; when the shadowed warriors gathered, scrambling over each other to have a good look. Hilda was out there somewhere, but Ragnar didn't know where it was, or why she was there, or what he could do. For now, he had to right his wrongs and capture Loki. That was his only hope of preventing Ragnarok and keeping his daughter safe.

With thoughts of Loki in mind, Ragnar tapped the distaff. A thread surged from the hollow top. A shriek of a thousand knives sharpened on glass squeaked, but the shriek no longer surprised nor disturbed Ragnar as it had used to do.

Ragnar passed through the veil into another world.

Birdsong and grass with clover grown to perfection greeted

him. His distaff made the Darkness pulsate away in the rhythm of his heartbeat. Ragnar closed his eyes and concentrated on seeing more, and as he opened his eyes again, the Darkness retreated further and further with every breath he took.

The perfect grass made it clear that he was in Asgard. Ahead of him was what appeared to be a valley bathed in mist, and as more of the Darkness was pushed back, Ragnar saw people, each and every one as perfect as the next. Gods and goddesses, he was sure, for their perfection was so complete.

The Darkness retreated further. The gods and goddesses were assembled by a great pyre, greater than any Ragnar had ever laid eyes on before. It was tall and wide and filled with presents for whoever had died. It was a funeral worthy of a powerful god. Perhaps it was that of Odin's son, Baldur, Ragnar thought, but Baldur's corpse had been sent on its way in a burning ship, so it could not be.

Ragnar twirled around in search of Loki in the crowd. He had thought and demanded to be taken to a time after that in the cave where he had freed Loki from his bonds of punishment. After that, Loki would not easily seek the company of gods and goddesses. He had to be hiding somewhere.

There were tables and trees on the plain, but there were gods and goddesses close to all of them, and Loki would not have gone unnoticed. At Ragnar's back was the cliff-side of a mountain, with a large, open gate that led inside. The hall would be a good place to hide, but three shadowed figures stood outside and guarded it.

Ragnar moved away from the crowd, up the hill towards the open gates. By the gates, he moved along the cliff-side, searching for a good hiding spot. His guess was correct. He found Loki huddled behind a large boulder along the cliff-side, humming his usual song.

Now, all Ragnar had to do was capture the giant and make certain he be put back in chains, never to be liberated.

A nagging voice at the back of Ragnar's head, told him that it would not be so simple, and of course, Ragnar knew it to be true.

Just as he had found Loki, and just as he was ready to act, Ragnar heard someone speak.

The voices echoed around him. They did not originate from the mountainside, but from the Darkness.

Ragnar listened with more care, but he could not make out the words. The speech was muffled, and he could not hear how many voices there were.

Something appeared at the edge of the Darkness his distaff pushed away: shadow warriors, like the ones he had seen crowding the hole in the Darkness. The same shadow warriors who killed Ragnar whenever he made a sound.

Ragnar retreated a few steps and cowered behind the boulder, as Loki did. Despite the fact that the boulder was merely a vision, and that, truly, he was not cowering behind anything, it made him feel safer.

Shadow warriors continued to advance, and Ragnar's heartbeat sped up. They were coming for him, although he had not spoken and had not done anything. They advanced across the plain, across the Darkness, straight towards him.

There were so many of them, but only one of them seemed to speak. As they approached, he could hear that it was a woman, and although her voice was muffled by the presence of many, he could hear what she said: 'Here, of all places.'

Ragnar knew her voice. The sound of it sparked some half-forgotten memory of a past life in Midgard, when he had been a father and a skald and an important man, but he could not place it.

The shadowed warriors came closer. Their hands were on their weapons and shields. Across the plain they advanced, and it felt and looked like the beginning of Ragnarok, although he knew that it was not.

Ragnar could hardly hear his own thoughts for the pounding of his heart as he searched the warriors for the familiar voice that he could not place.

And then he saw her.

In the midst of shadowed warriors was a woman, leading the crowd. A shadowed warrior, like the rest, but not dressed in armour like them, and not quite as faded of a shadow.

Her long blonde hair was braided in the old style. She was larger than he remembered her. Straight at him she stared, through shadow warriors and their weapons, and through the boulder behind which Ragnar cowered, and then she smiled.

'Long time, Ragnar,' said Siv.

FINN

Chapter One Hundred and Thirteen

'BLOODY SPEAR, FINN,' said Harald. 'What happened to that sweet Christian priest?' For now, he was being polite.

Finn licked his filed teeth and smiled with his mouth closed so as not to reveal the new marks. His eyes darted around the room to find Siv. Thralls and guards were inside, but no freemen and certainly no woman. Siv must have heard that he had arrived, but she had not come to greet him.

'What happened to your beautiful wife?' Finn asked, careful not to show his teeth. He laughed to release the tension in the air.

Laughter and light-hearted talk were always the best ways to get information, but apparently not when facing Harald Gormsson. King Harald no longer appeared amused. His mouth fell to a pout.

'What have I said?' Finn asked, keeping his tone cheerful. 'Has she left you for a younger man?'

'She is gone,' Harald said and rose from his chair. Slowly, he walked to the wine bucket that stood on a table at the far corner of the room. 'For good, I fear.'

The thralls eagerly tried to take his cup to refill it for him, but Harald paid them no attention and plunged his own cup into the bucket. The wine dripped over his hands and the cup and the floor as he walked back to his seat.

'She disappeared,' he said. 'Weeks ago. She went to Ribe and never came back.'

'Alone?' Finn asked. He could not imagine Harald sending off his new bride on her own, especially not one as beautiful and precious as Siv.

'They disappeared. Both her and the girl,' Harald said, staring into his cup.

It was a bad surprise to receive in Harald's presence, and Finn did not know what to do about it. Finn was well aware that without Siv to protect and defend him, his position as Harald's thrall was dire. Without her protection, he might never leave Jelling alive.

For all of his pride, Harald would not look past Finn's filed teeth. They marked him as a man of Odin, and that made it clear how the priest who had been sent to Ash-hill had died. None of it would be forgiven, Finn had known that all along, but he had counted on Siv to be there to soften the punishment and make Finn look strong, as she had always made Vigmer look strong.

Harald must have been eager to talk about his wife's disappearance, for although he did not need to, and the situation already seemed perilous enough to Finn, Harald continued to explain. 'They were taken from their sleeping furs in the night. She had told me that they were out there, those people who attacked, but I didn't believe her.'

The filed teeth, the killing of the Christian priest: all of it pointed to Finn's disloyalty. There had to be a way to make Harald believe that Finn was loyal to him, and gain his trust for another season. Finn just had not thought of it yet.

'I sent everyone I trust to look for her,' Harald continued. 'But whoever took her, they're long gone by now.'

Finn should have known that Siv was not there. Last time he had been to Jelling, there had been so many hired warriors guarding Harald's town. Today there had been nothing more than one shabby guard looking over the Oxen Road.

He had known that something was strange. He should have paid attention to the signs and asked a guard, or anyone at all, before coming in. Now he was here and it was too late to leave.

'So she is gone.' Harald stared blankly into his wine cup. He came to his senses then and took a deep drink, before his sight settled back on Finn.

No matter what Harald said, Finn knew that Siv had not been captured and taken away. She was a proud woman, always had been, and would rather have been killed. If she was gone without a trace, then she had left at her own will. Maybe Harald was not powerful enough to protect her anymore, although if that was the case, Finn would have expected her to come home to Ash-hill.

In any case, it was bad news that did not help him on a rainy day. He had counted on her being there, but he should not have. If anything had become clear to him after being reduced to a nameless thrall, it was that there was only one person in all the nine worlds that Finn could trust, and that was himself.

'I tried to introduce the idea of keeping our Christian church, but given everything that has happened up north... Ash-hill's warriors are ready for many things, but not another Christian priest.'

'Quite a coincidence.' Harald gained a chilling smile that only a man truly superior could flaunt. 'When he returned from Ash-hill, Thorbjorn told me exactly the same thing. "They are ready for many things, but not a Christian priest," he told me.'

Perhaps the wise thing to do was to claim that it truly was a coincidence, but although Harald was not the most intelligent man Finn had ever met, he was a man with a lot of pride. He wanted to be taken seriously, so the last thing he would reward was a blatant lie. It needed to be a good one.

'That is no coincidence at all,' Finn said. 'We talked of it often, after it happened. I can't say that I was sad to see the man bleed, but I had not wished for it to come to such an end. It made everything much more difficult.'

Harald leaned back in his seat and listened to Finn explain.

'As you might have heard, I have been elected as their chieftain and they have accepted your terms, but more change will need patience. It will take time to convert such heathens to the ways of Christianity.'

'Not as long as it will take to convert you, Finn the Nameless, or perhaps you've changed your calling name. Is it Finn the Liar, now?'

Finn closed his mouth, and immediately, he knew his mistake. Eager to solve the issue of the murder of the Christian priest, he had spoken without thinking. He had opened his mouth and showed his filed teeth without realising.

'Smile,' Harald coldly ordered. 'Show me your betrayal.'

'It's not a betrayal,' Finn said, careful when he spoke this time not to show his teeth.

He could not tell Harald that the warriors had done this to him without his consent or it would make him appear weak and untrustworthy, which was the last thing he wanted.

There were no freemen in the hall for Harald to impress, only thralls and four loyal guards. Harald had already invested so much in Finn. His explanations would be believed, because Harald wanted to believe them. Harald wanted to believe that he had made a good investment by buying Finn.

'I had to show myself as someone they could trust with their beliefs, or they never would have elected me as their chieftain.'

'Finn the Liar, that truly is your name now,' Harald said.

Finn knew better than to argue.

Harald pushed up from his chair and stepped down from the raised floor, towards Finn. For four entire heartbeats they stared at each other, then Harald seemed to make up his mind about something. He downed his drink, flung his empty cup at the floor, and walked to Finn. He rubbed his curled beard as he approached.

Finn stood with his arms behind his back and stared as Harald walked to him, although he knew that he should be afraid of Harald for his wealth and influence. He was not called Bluetan for his kindness. He had a hunger for the expensive colour of blue and a greed for all of that which came with wealth. He commanded a great army of warriors and he was a king with strong ties in the southern lands.

Harald stopped half an arm-length away. His rounder build reminded Finn of how Vigmer had looked in his younger days. Vigmer had been a better chief than Harald, though.

Harald grabbed Finn's chin and held him still.

'I told you to show me,' hissed the king.

He pressed his round fingers into Finn's cheeks to force his mouth open.

Reluctantly, Finn lifted his lips to show off his filed teeth. They still ached whenever he remembered Thorgal's cold file scraping against his teeth.

Harald examined the teeth as he would have examined those of a horse before a purchase. He licked his own teeth and grimaced as if imagining the pain Finn had gone through.

'Not a betrayal, you say,' Harald muttered in disapproval. His gaze flashed up to Finn's eyes, but he did not remove his thick fingers from Finn's bearded chin. 'You should know your place, Finn the Liar.'

Finn lifted his hands to forcibly remove Harald's grip on his chin, but his fingers only grazed the king's expensive tunic before Harald's left fist hammered against Finn's face.

Teeth shattered and rung. The pain made Finn's eyes bulge. The surprise made him stagger and his skull rung and rung like a Christian bell.

Finn struggled to stand up, but Harald's hold on his chin was stable and hard.

'You—' Again Harald punched Finn. His jaw crunched under

Harald's knuckles. 'Are—' Another punch, right on the nose. Pain shot through Finn's head. Tears were forced into his eyes. Pain wrenched into his cheeks and down to his jaw and teeth.

Harald let go of his hold on Finn's chin, and lifted his arm.

Finn cowered to protect himself from the next blow. He could easily have given back twice as hard, but Harald was a king and to hit him was to agree to one's own execution.

'A thrall,' Harald spat.

Another punch pounded against the side of his head. Finn was cast to the floor. His left shoulder took the fall. His head dunked with pain.

'Nothing but a *thrall!*' Harald yelled over him. His voice was a distant echo. 'You do what I tell you and nothing more.'

Finn spat out blood and a filed tooth with it. A tooth so painfully filed and marked lay in his spit and blood. The wooden floor was cold against his cheek. Finn tried to lift himself up.

'Stay down!' Harald kicked him in the stomach.

Finn curled up. His lunch crawled up from his stomach. Another kick stabbed into his chest. His arms, his shins, his back. His teeth and face hurt more and more with every kick. Finn closed his eyes, tightened his muscles and prepared for the next kick, and the next.

If he wanted, Finn could grab Harald's foot and bring him to the floor. The knowledge made it easier to sustain the pain. He was in control. At any moment, he could stop it. If it got too much, he could slam Harald to the ground and beat him to death.

Instead, Finn clenched his filed teeth and took the beating. They were not alone in the longhouse. There were four warriors as well, standing back, but who would protect Harald, and if Finn fought back, he would have to be certain he could kill everyone in the room, or he never would survive. He didn't have a weapon. He didn't have a shield. His vision was blurred and his head rung. He might be able to kill Harald, but not all four of the warriors. They would get him, and then Finn would die. If he wanted any chance of survival, he had to take the beating. Even from a coward like Harald.

At last the kicks stopped.

Harald puffed for breath. His steps were loud as he walked over Finn. The floor planks creaked and bent under his weight.

Eyes closed, Finn assessed his pain. His stomach and chest were crying out, but this was one of those rare times when pain was better than no pain. He felt capable of moving, although he did not possess the strength to try, yet. His face had taken the most, and he had lost a tooth. Others were loose when he glided a tongue over them, like the rocking teeth of a child.

Wet and slimy spit landed on Finn's cheek. 'Now, you listen to orders,' Harald snarled.

Finn lay still. At this point any movement might provoke another burst of anger from Harald. Any provocation may get him killed, even rolling around may get him killed, and more than anything, Finn wanted to survive. He was not yet done with life in Midgard. He had not yet regained his name and lineage.

Steps shambled over the wooden floor, followed by a door slamming shut. The room was quiet. Finn was alone. Even the four warriors had left.

Despite all of his anger, Harald had not killed Finn, though he could easily have ordered it. As disobedient as Finn had been and as disappointed as Harald must have been, the king too knew that he gained nothing from Finn's death. He had spent too much money buying Finn and Ash-hill. To kill him now would be a waste of effort. But Finn had not been certain that Harald always allowed reason to make decisions for him.

He rolled to his back. Harald's spit ran hot along the side of his cheek. It tickled over his swollen jawline and into his beard. Finn took a few ragged breaths before he could convince himself to lift his sore arm and swipe the spit away.

The room was empty. They had all left him, but they would be back, and Finn needed to be gone by then. He had been granted life, and he needed to keep it.

The door to the back room in the longhouse opened and a head popped out: a young boy with long curly hair and a patchwork of single hairs on the chin that was probably supposed to look like a beard.

'It's Svend, right?' Finn called to the boy. His voice was mumbled and all wrong from the pain. His cheeks were hot and swelling up, and the rest of him was too.

The boy did not leave. Finn was right. It was Harald's eldest son and heir.

Finn waved him over.

Siv had been right. She was always right. Someday, someone would have to overthrow Harald, and as Siv had told Finn the last time he had been in Jelling, the only one who could do that was Harald's eldest son.

The time to begin was now. Finn's opportunity had come.

'Do you know my name?' he asked the boy who was reluctant both to approach and to leave.

'Finn the Nameless,' said the boy, finally deciding to enter the room.

Everyone knew Finn the Nameless. Soon everyone in Jutland would know who he was. He was the first thrall turned chieftain, after all, and that was no little matter. It was a threat to all chiefs and freemen. Especially those who claimed to have been chosen by a god.

Finn pushed himself up to sit, wincing at the pain in his stomach as he did and waved the boy over again. This time the young man listened and crouched down next to Finn.

Finn ruffled the boy's curly hair. 'Smart boy. Especially for a king's son.'

Svend frowned. 'Sons of kings are supposed to be clever.'

'And thralls are supposed to be obedient.' Finn reached for the filed tooth he had spat out and put it into his pouch.

'You're not supposed to be a chieftain, either,' Svend said. He was smiling now.

'We're not supposed to be anything.' Finn reached a hand out to Svend to be helped to his feet.

'I thought he was going to kill you,' Svend said without taking Finn's hands. He must have been watching from the corner of the room while his father had beaten Finn.

Finn tried to sit comfortably, although nothing was comfortable and everything hurt, especially his face. He felt the broken bridge of his nose. 'At first, so did I,' he said. 'But you don't waste a good beating on a dead man. A beating is a lesson, and dead men don't learn.'

Finn reached a hand out again. This time Svend took it and helped him to his feet.

With the longhouse empty of people, it looked different. Finn should have noticed right away. There were fewer guards and warriors in Jelling than usual, but something else also seemed to be missing from Harald's hall. Up by Harald's raised chair, there had used to be a hawk cage, he recalled.

'Where is the hawk?'

'My father is taking it with him,' Svend said. 'It's his favourite hunting bird.'

'Taking it with him where?'

'As soon as the weather is in favour, he will travel north to Vik.'

Vik was far north. Not as far as Frey's-fiord, but far from Jutland and the Dane lands, and if Harald was leaving so soon after Yule, in the middle of the winter, then it was no simple visit. The self-proclaimed king of the Danes was fleeing the lands, and there could only be one explanation for it.

Their attack on Magadoborg had brought the fury of southern kings to Harald's doorstep, and he had been too weak to withstand it all. He feared for his life and his rule, so he fled his lands to spare his own life.

That was why he had beaten Finn and not killed him. Harald

had not been thinking about his expensive investment, or Finn's worth; he had been pressed for time. He did not have time to search for anyone to fill Finn's role in northern Jutland. He had hoped that a beating would be enough to blind Finn to the truth that the king of the Danes was fleeing because he was done, but although Finn's right cheek bulged up to shield half of his sight, he was far from blind to the truth.

'So, he is going to Vik,' Finn mused aloud. He humped towards the door. At every small step, he winced. His ribs hurt more than after a proper fight.

'Is it far away? I've never been up there,' Svend said. He was a young boy full of curiosity at the worlds.

'Far, but not so far again. Last summer, I raided with people from up there. They're nice,' Finn said to reassure, though he didn't know why he bothered. He supposed he did it because he felt some sympathy for the boy. Finn was a man of Odin, and the Alfather stated that those who gave kindness would receive it in turn.

'They do speak rather funny though,' Finn added. In truth, Finn didn't really know them. Although they had raided with Frey's-fiord on the way to Magadoborg, he hadn't talked to many of Sigismund's warriors, but what he said was the truth about most northerners, no matter where they came from.

'That's what I heard too,' Svend said. 'Someday I'll go.'

'You aren't going with him?'

Svend stalled for a moment and stared down as if he had not thought before that he was, perhaps, supposed to go as well. 'That's fine,' he decided. 'There is nowhere like home. It's just a small trip for raids and bargaining. They will be back soon.'

Svend too had to know that was a lie.

Standing by the door, gathering forces for the trek outside, Finn glanced at the room. More than the hawk was missing. Furs had used to line Harald's chair and the shelves that had been full of things were now as good as empty. No one packed that much for a small trip.

'You're always welcome in Ash-hill, if things get boring here in Jelling,' Finn said with a welcoming smile that showed off his filed teeth and allegiance to the Alfather.

The sight did not intimidate Svend. He knew as well as everyone what filed teeth meant, but unlike his father, he was not an angry Christian, just a regular one.

'I have to stay here for when they come back.' Svend said it in a sad tone, and they both knew that he was not talking about his father's return.

'Your mother?' Finn asked, although he knew well that Siv was not Svend's mother.

'Tove isn't my mother. But when she and Tyra return, I have to be here to welcome them home.'

Then Svend could wait here his entire life, because Siv had left by her own will, and she was not coming back. She had left Ash-hill the same way. Without warning or trace, she had disappeared, making them believe that she was dead.

'*If* they come back,' Svend realised on his own.

Unlike his father, he was a smart and kind boy, and Siv was right in thinking that with the right push, he might someday possess the will to kill his coward father and take over rule of the Dane and Jute lands.

'If they don't come back with your Christian prayers,' Finn said, giving his first push. 'You will simply have to be a man of Odin, Svend, and go to bring them back.'

HILDA

Chapter One Hundred and Fourteen

THE HANGED GOD *has abandoned you,* the Runes whispered.

'That's what you want me to believe,' Hilda whispered back. Everything the Runes had said to her had come true. There had been no false whispers; not any that she could recall, anyways. But knowing what the Runes really were changed everything.

Now Hilda knew why the Runes whispered what they did. Loki wanted to stain her view of the Alfather and to trust him instead. Loki, Frigg, Freya, *all* of the goddesses, and even Odin—every one of them was eager to sway her, and Hilda didn't know who to trust. Or if she could trust anyone. She had known them through her father's stories, but they were different in person.

A mist had settled on the battlefield between mountains of corpses, and Hilda no longer knew where she was headed. Valhalla had long disappeared at her back. It felt like she was walking in circles. Hilda's snow fox darted out from the field of corpses. Its tongue hung out far and it waited for her to catch up. The fox seemed to know where they were going, and had taken the lead.

A crushed hand to remind you of owed promises, the Runes repeated.

'I do owe you a promise, so come out and let me repay it.' She was tired of endlessly walking across this stinking battlefield.

The mist became thicker the further into the battlefield she moved. It was like walking through a dream, with everything blurry and distant and unimportant. She heard the caw of birds and then that too faded away. Left was only the sound of her own steps.

Her snow fox moved quietly. Its white fur was easy to see in the dark. Hilda followed it up and down hills and mountains of corpses. The wind swirled around her, forcing the harsh sting of blood into her nose. Rot made her stomach turn.

'I waited centuries for someone like you,' Loki whispered in the mist. Not a wind moved. There were no other whispers, just one. He was here in person. 'I waited centuries for someone to hear my distant song and come to free me.'

It had truly been Loki whispering to her all along. She hadn't wanted to believe it, but with the certain knowledge rose so many questions, and she had to ask them.

'The axe wasn't a gift meant for gods,' Hilda realised. 'Not in the way you had me believe. It was meant to set you free.'

'I knew you weren't boring. Or you wouldn't have heard my call through the nornir's song.'

Loki appeared out of the mist with his usual large smile. His nostrils alone were as large as Hilda's face. He was crouched over to be hidden in the mist. His large size was not awkward on him as it would have been on most.

'An axe meant to free you,' Hilda thought aloud to have her thoughts confirmed. 'But I didn't free you. You stopped whispering before I arrived in Asgard.'

His sharp chin shot forward as his smile widened. 'Someone else heard my song. Like you, they heard, and they came.'

A chill crawled up Hilda's calves and thighs. The Runes were not hers alone. Loki had stopped whispering to her because someone else had been listening. 'Who?'

Loki snickered and leaned away from her. 'That is a mystery that we shall have to uncover.' His whispered voice rung over the battlefield with a giant's strength. He wasn't scared of being heard or seen. Hilda didn't think he was scared of anything.

His tone was inviting. Though Loki could easily make her bend to his wishes, if he wanted. She had heard his whispers for so long, and he knew so much about her. Her darkest secrets were all his. Loki could force her, but he didn't need to. She knew of what he was capable. Her broken right hand was a good reminder of his physical strength, as was the size of him. More important, he had been her whispers. He had helped her countless times. It didn't seem like the sort of thing Loki would do.

'Why do you need me?' she asked.

'Alone I don't have everything I need to get my answers,' he said.

Her fox returned out of the mist, tongue hanging out, waiting for Hilda to follow, or make up her mind about what to do. Loki raised his eyebrows at her, challenging her to accept his quest.

'Why would I help you get answers?'

'You've come here, all this way, thanks to my whispers.'

'That was before I knew what the whispers in the wind were.'

'You followed me from Valhalla,' he reminded her. 'Knowing hasn't changed your position. Do you think old Odin would be interested in you if you didn't hear my whispers in the wind? Do you think Frigg would? Freya? How about Idun or Sif?'

His questions rung emptily out over the rotting battlefield.

'Even without your whispers, I'm a skilled warrior.' Her snow fox leapt to her side and growled up at Loki to confirm.

The giant stared down at it with mistrust. 'Skilled enough to be noticed?' His tone was steady, but his gaze stayed firm on the growling fox. 'If the seating ranks in Odin's hall were truly decided by skill and abilities, are you still so blind to believe he would seat you at his high table?'

He smiled from his large height and waited for her to make her choice: her gods, or him. Her choice would change everything. Either way she would gain enemies and she didn't know who was more terrible to face: Loki or the Alfather.

Always, she had wanted to follow the Alfather and sit in his hall, but Loki had something else. Something that she had always searched for, but never known what it was. He was the answer to an unspoken question burning in her mind. He was her whispers.

Her snow fox took a step towards Loki. Again it growled, reminding Hilda not to trust him, not entirely. But Hilda had always trusted her Runes. 'Who freed you?' she asked, her choice made. 'It wasn't me, so who was it?'

Her snow fox stopped growling and looked at her for guidance. It trusted Hilda to decide their path.

'I don't know,' Loki easily admitted, and the mystery of it seemed to intrigue him as much as it intrigued Hilda. 'Fate itself. Whoever or whatever is hiding where no one should be able to survive.'

'Hiding where?'

He glanced through the mist, licked his lips, and readied to tell her the biggest secret in the nine worlds. 'In the Ginnungagap,' he whispered. 'In the Darkness.' His whisper slithered dangerously over the battlefield. There was no one but Hilda alive to hear him, but his voice carried far and made Hilda uneasy. At any moment Frigg, Odin or his valkyries might return home and overhear.

'The Darkness inside Yggdrasil,' said Hilda. Her axe had cut straight to it, and there had been someone there, inside the tree, staring out at her.

Loki flashed a triumphant smile. He was always smiling 'And how do we find someone hidden in darkness?'

'We ask the Darkness whom it hides.'

He set off through the mist again with giant steps up a hill made of corpses. Hilda's snow fox scurried after him, eager to be off again. Hilda followed. Her mind raced with questions and she struggled to follow Loki's swift pace up the hill of sticky corpses. Her snow fox leapt far ahead.

'How do we ask the Darkness whom it hides?' Hilda said at Loki's heels. 'Through your whispers?'

'Our whispers don't reach into the world of nothing and nowhere,' he replied.

Our whispers, he had said. The thought of it made Hilda feel like she was soaring through the skies in the falcon skin again. In Loki's presence she felt as worthy as a goddess. Then it occurred to her: 'If our whispers don't reach into the Darkness, how could someone in there hear?'

'Didn't your goddesses, too, know about the whispers?' Loki asked, although he had been listening to the conversation in the bath-house, and definitely knew the answer.

Freya had quoted the Runes, and when Hilda had told Frigg what the Runes had whispered to her, the other goddesses had recognised the phrases. Even Idun and Sif had reacted to it, although none of them heard the whispers in the wind. None of the goddesses had norn blood, or they wouldn't have needed Hilda. 'How did they know?'

Loki didn't avoid the question as the goddesses had, but instead he answered with a story. 'For centuries I was tied in a cave…' He inhaled the stench of the battlefield as if the smell of rotting corpses was the same as fresh air to him. 'Norn visions kept me aware and gave me hope. Terrible hope of being freed someday. Eager to hold onto that hope I began to whisper. Through the visions I whispered. Loud enough for anyone inside the cave to hear.'

'They visited you,' Hilda realised. The goddesses must have come to the cave to ensure that Loki was still chained. There they must have heard his whispers. 'And someone else did too.'

'Someone hidden in Darkness,' Loki confirmed.

In the not so far distance, the first light of morning outlined Yggdrasil in all of its glory.

'Is that why we're heading back towards Yggdrasil?' asked Hilda. First her fox and now Loki had steered them across the battlefield, but not in a straight line; in circles almost. Yggdrasil was in front of them, and somewhere down there was a hole into Darkness that Hilda had accidentally cut into one of the ash's great roots. 'To look into the Darkness?'

Loki chuckled at her question. 'I doubt we would see much. But no matter where you're headed in Asgard, you're always headed towards Yggdrasil in the end.'

A new grand quest unfolded in front of Hilda. The Runes had always led her ahead. They had given her a reason to keep going and they had brought her to a destiny she never could have imagined. They had brought her into a dwarf forge and given her a godly axe. They had lured her to Asgard. While Loki had allowed her to believe that the axe was meant as an offering to the gods, he had never specifically said so. The journey his whispers had pushed her along was unlike any destiny Hilda might have fought for in Midgard. Thanks to him, she had seen the nine worlds and had come into the presence of her goddesses. If Loki hadn't whispered to her through the wind, Hilda would never have accomplished everything she had.

'So, how do we find out who hides in the darkness?' she asked as they scaled the last of the corpse mountain, leaving the morning mist behind.

'We ask a slain giant.'

Hilda stared down at the murder that had been done on this plain. She doubted a dead giant would be more talkative than the dead warriors at their feet. 'Corpses tell no tales.'

'Says the dead girl.' Loki looked at her over his shoulder with a smile.

Hilda too smiled. Being around Loki was easy, like being with an old friend. In a way, she supposed that Loki *was* an old friend. He had whispered to her since she had been a child. It felt like Loki pushed her to always learn more and become better. Like a true friend did. Einer had done that too.

In the presence of her goddesses, she hadn't felt smart or capable. Not as she did now, walking across dead bodies with Loki. At the top of the mountain he let Hilda catch up. Her snow fox stood at his side with his red fylgja. They both looked at Hilda, bloody snouts and tongues hanging out. As soon as she reached them the two foxes darted away, racing each other down the mountainside.

Hilda continued a few strides past Loki to get a head start. He walked much faster than she did. 'To Jotunheim, then,' she decided, and set a steady pace that she could hold.

Loki and she would have great adventures together, like she and Einer would have had if the three nornir had spun a longer fate for Hilda in Midgard.

Hilda's eyes dropped to the gold arm-ring Frigg had given her. She remembered what Frigg had told her about the whispers in the wind. She only walked the edge of her abilities by listening to Loki's whispers. She needed to learn how to conjure visions. 'Can you teach me how to see visions?' she asked of Loki.

He didn't bother to answer. If he could have taught her, he probably would have already. The goddesses seemed confident that she could learn to see visions. The reason Loki hadn't taught her had to be because he didn't know how to teach someone how to do it. Hilda looked over her shoulder to confirm her thoughts.

The wind swept around her. Loki had vanished. Again.

Hilda let out a frustrated scream. During all of that time without the Runes, she had almost forgotten how annoying they had been. How they had repeated the same things over and over, and rarely ever answered her questions. How they had always abandoned her when she most needed them. Exactly like Loki. They truly were one and the same, he and the Runes.

Her snow fox came hurtling out of a pile of corpses, startled by her yell. The red fox didn't come. Hilda waved her fylgja off, and it leapt away into the morning.

The true identity of the Runes ought to scare her, but it didn't. She had her Runes back, and she knew what they were now. She was worthier than she had ever been. The thought gave her strength to speed up towards Yggdrasil. The Alfather and Frigg and Freya should have offered more. As Loki had. She liked the way that he said *we*, and that he had referred to the whispers in the wind as *ours*. With Loki, she didn't so much feel like a girl in the presence of her gods. He treated her like an equal.

The wind was silent, but Loki was there, steering the wind's hand. She knew that he was. He had never abandoned her. While the wind had been silent, Loki had followed her in Asgard.

'So can you teach me or not?' Hilda asked of the gust that swirled around her and lifted her hair.

The wind gave no answers.

Hilda broke into a smile. She hadn't really expected an answer. She already knew where she was headed. If she was to help Loki in any way, she needed to learn how to see norn visions. Loki had already given her the direction she needed. *No matter where you're headed in Asgard, you're always headed towards Yggdrasil,* he had said. Yggdrasil's shadow became longer as the sun rose. Hilda made certain her heading was true and began her long trail towards the ash.

In Midgard she had been forced to find her own way more than once, and she had succeeded. Many times over she had proven her worth to Loki. As he had proven his worth to her. They could trust each other. She would seek out the three nornir to learn visions, and then she and Loki would storm Jotunheim, together, to get answers to their questions. A worthy path for a true warrior.

RUNEMISTRESS

Chapter One Hundred and Fifteen

A FRESH RUNE was undone. Tress traced the bark where it had been. Not five heartbeats earlier she had carved it there. The sight brought her out of her hard-earnt trance.

At last, the skald's daughter was using the runes.

Madness had long taken over Tress' mind, but the realisation brought clarity to her thoughts and made her cackle with age-old laughter. Her voice had been worn, not by age but by her many visions.

Her mind was full of visions seen, most of them showing the skald's daughter, and that was why she carved her runes. So that, someday, when need be, the great Hilda Ragnardóttir could use her runes and listen to the whispers in the wind, and help set them all free.

Tress lowered her knife from the tree, and began the short trek home to her warm hut.

In her rune-carving trance, she had been vision-less. A bliss she had long forgotten; ever since she had taken on the name of Runemistress, the visions never ceased to flood her mind.

In her trance she had focused merely on her task, and who had given it to her. The great Alfather had granted her a visit, and an unspoken task to carve runes for Hilda of Ash-hill. Ever since the Alfather had touched Tress' hands and her task had been given to her, Tress had wondered why the Alfather had honoured her with a visit, and why this young girl was so important. Every day, she had wondered, until her carved and coloured runes began to disappear, and she had known then that Hilda Ragnardóttir was not just the daughter of a skald, but a norn.

Even so, it had not been by his own will that the Alfather had come to Tress. Fate was the one who had sent the god to make Tress watch over Hilda. No matter if the Alfather—who neither saw visions nor heard the wind's whispers—knew or not that he had not come at his will, it was the truth. The story-maker had sent him.

Why the story-maker had chosen *her*, Tress, for the task, among all runemistresses, she knew not. She supposed that the norn blood in her veins was thick enough for one as powerful as the Alfather to acknowledge her worth in the nine worlds.

Some were runemistresses only in name, a profession chosen and fulfilled. For Tress, there had been no choice. Her visions were a gift passed down her bloodline for generations. It carried with it a duty to connect the people of Midgard to the gods and the life beyond this one. It carried with it a duty to procreate and extend the bloodline: a duty Tress had not fulfilled. But the time of runemistresses was coming to an end. All over Norse lands, runemistresses were being killed. Besides, Tress was not as powerful as her mother had been, and her mother was not as powerful as her grandmother had been, and none of them had been as powerful as Hilda Ragnardóttir of Ash-hill.

Hilda's father, too, had been powerful. His story-telling had enchanted all who listened, but neither Ragnar nor Hilda carried Tress' burden. Neither of them had been trained in visions. Hilda knew not her bloodline, as Tress knew hers, nor the burdens with which it came, and so she needed guidance.

Hilda knew only how to use the runes to listen to the whispers in the wind, whispers too faint for Tress to ever hear—though, as a child, her grandmother had heard them. Tress' blood was too thin and too weak for such things.

From mother to child, the gift and burden of visions was passed, sometimes strong, and sometimes faint. Usually the gift was passed from the mother to her first child, although Tress' older brother had not had the gift. Already during early pregnancy, her mother had realised it, so when at last the child had been born, she never gave him teat and instead she had let him cry himself to eternal sleep. On the beach he had lain until the waves had washed him away, and the gods had taken the blood offering.

Her mother had often told Tress of the sacrifices to be made. When again she had been pregnant, it had been with Tress; a child who could one day take over the burden of a runemistress. The blood sacrifice had been accepted.

Tress entered her carved hut and put her knife onto the table. Her hand was red with blisters from her constant carving. The entire hut was full of runes, both thick and thin. The woods, too, were full of them, all the way to Horn-hill's remains. Enough runes for a lifetime of use.

Tress' carved runes would carry Hilda until Ragnarok, and once Ragnarok was upon the nine worlds, no one in Midgard would need Tress anymore, not even Hilda Ragnardóttir.

Staring at the dancing warm fire, Tress sat on her sleeping bench and rocked back and forth on her pillows, waiting to die, at last.

She knew her mother had not gone to Helheim. She knew that Valhalla did not wait for her in the afterlife. What happened to nornir when they died? Whatever it was, if there was anything at all but the black void she saw when she closed her eyes, Tress supposed that death came with peace.

In her life she had lived as a servant to her linage. She had seen fates, she had told futures and uncovered pasts long forgotten. Most of all she had carved runes for another, as the Alfather—or rather, the story-maker—had demanded of her. In death she would be lifted from the burden of her blood. Death would free her.

Staring into the flames, Tress resigned herself to die, and that is when her last vision came to flood her mind.

A motherly hand caressed the blooded face of her child. In the sand he lay, bright blue eyes staring up at the woman who had birthed him. She rose from his side. Although she saw little and although it had been many winters ago, Tress immediately recognised her own mother from the ragged dress to her elegant steps.

The child screamed for her attention. It squealed for life and touch, but the woman gave it neither. Her steps crunched over the sand as she left. The beach rang loud with an infant's cries. Waves crashed in and with every crash the baby cried louder. No one picked it up, no one held it. No one soothed it nor fed it. The infant knew its fate. Its cries halted. Its breaths were ragged. On this beach it would die.

It should have been over, but the vision lingered.

Waves continued to crash onto the beach. A rhythm that lulled the infant to sleep, and then the rhythm was disrupted by the crunch of steps on sand.

Someone was coming. The baby cried anew, but when hands reached for the kid, the crying stopped at once. It was not motherly hands that reached for the blooded infant. Large, rough hands held the baby, and lifted him up. Tears streamed down the man's face as he held the abandoned child in his arms and sat on the sand.

'You're god-given,' whispered the man as he stroked the baby's soft cheeks. He balanced the child on his knee, and declared it his. 'Ragnar Erikson.'

The vision dissolved.

At last, right before the bliss of death took her, Tress

understood why the Alfather had selected her for this task. Once more, her bloodline had dictated her destiny. She had not spent all the days of her life carving runes for a stranger.

She had carved them for her niece.

Tress used her last moment to smile. Fate was kind to tell her the truth, before the final end.

The story-maker was her brother. He had sent the Alfather to Tress to save his own daughter. Ragnar could free them all; everyone imprisoned by invisible bonds sealed in blood. Only he could free them, and if their mother had been wrong, and he had even one drop of blood-given talent, he would.

DARKNESS

Ragnar stared at Siv with mistrust.

Hundreds of shadow warriors stood at her back, and although she had spoken, they had not killed her as they always killed Ragnar. They stood behind her, weapons and shields in hand, as if they were *her* warriors.

'You don't know me, Ragnar?' Siv asked.

Of course he recognised her, but the more he stared at her, the more he realised that she was also different from how he had known her. She wore an expensive, glittering gown. Her hair was braided perfectly, like that of a god or goddess. She had all the attributes that belonged in Asgard.

She was not the Siv that he had known. Her face was riddled with shadows.

The Darkness was playing tricks on him. Now that Ragnar had finally begun to master silence to stay alive, the Darkness threw a new challenge at him.

Although the woman before him looked like Siv, she could not be. She was too different, and when she spoke, the shadow warriors did not attack her.

'Have you forgotten Ash-hill? Have you forgotten your life in Midgard?' Siv asked.

She wanted him to speak. The Darkness wanted him to speak, so that it could send its shadow warriors to kill him. But Ragnar had an uncontrollable lust to answer Siv. He had not seen a familiar face for an eternity. He had seen his daughter, and he had seen the gods, but none of them had seen him, or acknowledged him, until now. They had been in the visions his distaff conjured. This was different.

Even if the Darkness was tricking him into being killed, Ragnar had been killed so many times before. It was just one more death, he told himself, but the thought of dying still made him tremble with fear.

The shadow warriors crowded at the edge of the Darkness his distaff pushed away. They were standing in the grass down the hill, and, at Ragnar's back, their shadow torsos stuck out from the cliff-side. They were everywhere.

Siv waited for his answer. She had stopped twenty arm-lengths from him and tilted her head to the side, waiting for him to speak.

Ragnar finally found the courage to face one more death.

'How are you here?' he asked aloud.

A spear was hurled at him.

Siv leapt to block the flying spear, grabbed it and spun in front of Ragnar to block the blows.

Warriors attacked from the back. A sword broke through Siv's defence and carved through Ragnar's shoulder. Ragnar cried out and clasped his arm. He fell to his knees.

'Why don't you fight back?' Siv yelled at him. Her spear clashed against the weapons of the shadow warriors.

Ragnar knew he could not survive. He knew he should not have spoken, but Siv looked at him with surprise. She had not expected him to die. He had thought she was a vision conjured by the Darkness to tempt Ragnar into making a mistake, but she was not. That much was clear to him now.

Another sword broke through Siv's defence. A blade carved through his neck.

Death, pain, and fear.

HE WOKE TO the Darkness exactly where he had died. Everything was black. Ragnar tapped his distaff so the thread and veil appeared and the staff pushed the Darkness away. To the shrieks of weapons sharpened on glass, Ragnar passed through the veil.

Loki was still hiding behind a large boulder next to Ragnar. The meadow was empty, but out of the Darkness came figures. The shadow warriors were there, again.

'You can speak now,' Siv said.

She stood behind him, down the hillside.

Ragnar faced her, but he knew better than to speak. The shadow warriors surrounded him and they would kill him again.

Siv sighed and walked up the sunny hill to Ragnar. No matter how she made herself known and heard, the warriors did not attack and kill her as they did Ragnar.

It put everything into question. Everything that Ragnar thought he knew about the Darkness seemed wrong. 'What is this place?'

As Siv had promised, the shadow warriors did not attack him.

'My afterlife,' she answered, although this place was neither Helheim nor Valhalla.

Siv's smile told him everything he needed to know. She was not like him. She was not supposed to go to Valhalla or Helheim like all freemen from Midgard, and somewhere deep down Ragnar had always known that Siv was different from others, god-like, almost, but that did not explain why they were both trapped in this black darkness. 'Then why am I here?'

'It would appear that it's your afterlife too, story-maker.'

EINER

Chapter One Hundred and Sixteen

'YOU'RE NOT LISTENING,' Einer's grandmother's voice made him tremble.

Einer released his hand from the enormous door. 'She could be out there,' he said to convince. 'She wasn't in Valhalla, as she should have been. She's either out there, in the ice, or in Helheim.'

'It doesn't matter where she is,' his grandmother insisted. Her sharp teeth didn't part as she spoke. Her already high eyebrows were raised at him. 'The forefathers don't care where she is. They care where *you* are.'

Einer took a step back into the house. He knew better than to incite the fury of a jotun. She clenched her fists to supress the rising anger for both of them.

A lot of praise could be sung about Einer's giant grandmother, but she did not possess his mother's elegance, and from what Einer had seen, she was not anything like his uncle, Buntrugg, either.

She did look like his mother, though, or at least she had

the same long golden hair, plaited into a braid of braids that reached her hips. Her anger appeared to calm as she watched him back away from the door and walk towards the longtable.

'That ice is as venomous as the waters. It might kill you before you can free anyone from there.'

'I just want to find Hilda again,' he insisted. Reluctantly, he climbed onto the chair by the huge table, as his grandmother demanded of him. His mother's commands too had used to be impossible to ignore.

'Death isn't the solution,' his grandmother reasoned. She sat in a chair across from him. 'You won't find her in your afterlife.'

He felt like a child again, as he often did these days, sitting at this giant table in this giant home being scolded over his recklessness. He recalled how everything had looked big as child, and how the rules of the world of adults had been a mystery to him, as the rules of Jotunheim and giants was a mystery to him now.

'I wasn't trying to die,' he said, for he hadn't been.

'No one is trying to die.' She sighed. 'But we all are anyways. All we can do is keep ourselves alive another day. Keep each other alive another day. But you, Einer Glumbruckson, are difficult to keep alive. Like your mother. She used to scurry off onto the ice. No thoughts of the consequences.'

Two nights Einer had spent in his grandparents' house, and although his grandfather was rarely home, his grandmother always was, and all day she talked and talked, but this was the first time she had mentioned his mother.

'Who was my mother searching for in the ice?' he asked.

His grandmother pressed her thin lips together. Even a talkative woman like her would rather stay silent than tell Einer anything about his mother. 'You better not go there again,' she told him without looking at him. 'All that waits on that ice and ocean is more death, and we have seen enough of that here.'

She tapped her hand on the table to mean that was that and they would not talk of it again, but Einer was not yet done.

'Why don't you talk about her? I ask, but you never say anything.'

She hesitated, but her thin lips were eager to speak and she couldn't keep them closed any longer. 'There is nothing to say about Glumbruck.'

Everyone else had talked about his mother with admiration. 'But all other giants talk about her.'

'All other giants?' his grandmother scoffed at the suggestion. 'What giants do *you* know?'

'I know your son,' Einer said.

She shook her head, pursed her lips together again, and sighed deeply. 'Buntrugg doesn't know her. She left long before he was born. He doesn't know anything.'

She walked away from him to the shelves at the back of the room to get out her knife and the unfinished bone comb that she carved every night.

Einer did not give up. His uncle had not been the only one who had spoken fondly of his mother.

'Skadi too spoke of her like she was a great warrior. They all did.' All of the giant warriors he had travelled away from Ida's plain with had spoken of his mother with respect and a certain fear.

'Skadi,' his grandmother grumbled.

'Now you're insulting our reputation,' rung his grandfather's icy voice.

Had Einer known that his grandfather had arrived, he wouldn't have said anything else. His grandfather had not spoken much during the evenings when he had been home, and no conversation of any importance had been had in his presence.

Now he knew why his grandmother had evaded his questions.

'You're mistaken,' grunted his grandfather. 'My wife is the last person who would talk to you about Glumbruck.'

His grandmother stood with her back to Einer so he could not see on her face if it was the truth or not.

'But you're going to keep asking,' his grandfather correctly guessed. 'So I will tell you why you shouldn't, and let this be your last warning.'

He walked to the table. He was so large, and his strong shoulders and cold eyes, hidden under bushy eyebrows, made him seem larger. His movements were slow and calculated, like those of an old warrior.

He placed his closed fists onto the table and leaned against them. Fists as big as Einer's head. They looked like they could punch through stone, perhaps even a mountain.

'Glumbruck was never an obedient daughter. Even as a young jotun she caused trouble.' He lifted one fist and hit it hard against the table. 'She got my brother killed. I had to hack his head off with my own iron.' His grumble of a voice was sharp as a snake's hiss. His fists were clenched white from the anger of the forefathers. 'But Glumbruck did much worse than that. She destined her life to dishonour our family; our heritage. All through the nine worlds she raged her destruction over us.'

Einer couldn't imagine his mother destroying anything, certainly not her own family. More than anything, during all the summers and winters he had known her, she had always stood up to protect Einer, and in such a way that others would not think that he had called on her to do it.

Nothing that his grandfather said or described sounded remotely like Einer's mother. She had been elegant and proud and protective and kind. He couldn't imagine her wanting to hurt anyone, least of all her family.

'At last, she was captured, and taken to the high courts of Jotunheim,' his grandfather continued. 'They exiled her, but before she could be taken to the black forests, she had disappeared. Again.'

That Einer could imagine. His mother had always been good at disappearing and then coming back at the exact right time.

'She is a thief and an outlaw. Our boy was ripped from us because of Glumbruck. She destroyed us, and her reputation destroys us still.'

His grandfather left the table at that and walked to the back room, where only he was allowed inside. He locked the door after himself.

Einer's grandmother sat back in her chair at the opposite side of the table from Einer. Her hands were busy with knife and bone and her eyes were fixed on the work.

Einer wanted to ask her more about his mother, because none of it made sense to him. But he also knew that he should not ask, because he was certain that his grandfather could hear through walls.

For many heartbeats, they sat there in silence before his grandmother resumed talking. 'How old are you?' she asked.

'Twenty-four winters,' Einer replied.

She smiled warmly. 'So young. I had thought you were older. At least fifty, since you already know how to stave runes.'

'Fifty winters is a long time to learn things like that.'

She nodded and looked down at his small figure. The sight of him seemed to remind her that he was no giant. 'I suppose it is for you,' she admitted. 'How long do short-lived usually live?'

'Fifty winters is not a bad life.'

The shock was clear in her gaze. To her fifty winters did not even make a jotun old enough to know the runes or travel alone.

'What can you possibly accomplish in fifty winters?' she asked. It was a heartfelt question. She had stopped carving to gape at Einer. Her face was marked by wrinkles and age spots, but she often had a young way about her. 'You aren't old enough to work, or *do* anything.'

'I've worked,' Einer responded. 'I have been working for almost a decade.'

His bragging did not impress her. In Midgard, ten summers of work was not nothing, but to his grandmother, he had barely begun.

'Work,' she said and chuckled. 'Ten winters. So, you're still in training, after all.'

'I have commanded my own ship for several summers. I've been a warrior and sailor and a farmer, and I was a chieftain before I came here.'

As he said it, he could see her piece the information together, but their worlds were so different and she knew nothing whatsoever about Midgard.

'And what do you know of Jotunheim, Einer?' she asked.

He knew less than she knew about Midgard, that much was clear. Although he was supposedly half jotun, Einer didn't know what it meant to be a jotun, and until recently he hadn't known anything about the forefathers or their anger. He didn't know how to conjure fire or warmth and he didn't know how to survive in the cold frost as his grandparents had done for hundreds of summers and winters.

'Hundreds!' his grandmother laughed. 'Oh, to be that young.' She sighed longingly. 'In our first hundreds, we travelled through Jotunheim. In my youth I travelled all the way to Skrymir's fortress...'

'In Utgard?'

'You know Utgard?' she asked, surprised that he knew something about giants after all.

'There are famous stories of Skrymir in Midgard.'

'So he is famous in Midgard. I hope no one ever told him. He would be too pleased. What other jotnar do you know?'

'Skadi,' Einer said, still unable to comprehend that he had met her and had dined in her house and fought her on Ida's plain. 'Surt,' he said, continuing his list.

'Barely a jotun anymore, that one,' his grandmother commented. She was back to carving her bone comb as she listened.

'Thrym, Geirröd, Hrungnir, Tiazzi, Bestla, Jarnseaxa, Borr, and Aegir and Ran. And Loki, of course. There are many.'

His grandmother acknowledged each name and commented on each one with either a surprised hum or a disapproving scoff.

'And Bergelmir, do you know of him?' she asked.

Einer thought back to the stories Ragnar had used to tell. He had certainly heard the name before and it was a famous story too, as far as he could remember, but he couldn't place it with certainty. 'Wasn't he one of those who survived the flood of Ymir's blood?'

'Not just. After the Alfather and his brothers murdered the first being in the nine worlds—after they murdered great Ymir, and his blood flooded the nine worlds—Bergelmir and his wife were the only jotnar to survive.'

'Right,' Einer said, remembering the old story of creation Ragnar had used to tell around the fire during the cold winters. *The blood gurgled like a stream and roared like the sea. Red waves crashed across the worlds*, he had used to say. Einer sighed longingly. He missed old Ragnar's stories and those cosy nights huddled close by the fire.

'Bergelmir is your kin,' said his grandmother. 'Your grandfather is his ninth son.'

'So that makes Ymir my great-great-great-grandfather,' Einer mused. His bloodline went straight back to the oldest being in the nine worlds, and he had not known. Now he understood why his mother had often asked Ragnar to tell the story of Ymir's death and the creation of the worlds. It hadn't merely been because all the children loved to hear how Ymir's blood flooded the worlds, and how the Alfather and his brothers had used Ymir's corpse to shape the nine worlds. It had been because of Bergelmir and her blood relation to Ymir. To his mother it must have been a piece of her past.

'So, she *did* teach you something...' his grandmother said.

Despite what his grandfather had claimed, she *did* refer to Einer's mother from time to time, even if she refused to speak of her with her husband near.

'So, what does Midgard look like?' she asked him.

Einer smiled as he thought of home and described the soft hills of Jutland, and their harbour and inlet, and life in Ash-hill, and as they talked about Midgard, the evening turned to night and then his grandfather returned from the back room and, with a grunt, declared it bed time.

A regular bench had been pushed up against the wall by the warm oven and made into a sleeping bench for Einer. It was as wide as any good sleeping bench and much longer. One giant blanket had been folded in half so that he could both lie on it and wriggle into it with his feet sticking out by the warm oven.

Einer lay and waited until he could hear his grandfather snore. He waited until he could hear his grandmother breathe deeply too and knew that they were both asleep, and still he waited, rolled up in his blanket and warming his feet, while he could.

After he was certain that they were asleep, he got up, slipped on his shoes, strapped on his weapon belt and found a coat to keep warm. He took the sleeping blanket with him too. It would be cold on the ice, and the last thing he wanted was to freeze to death.

After he had strapped on everything and was prepared, he waited for a while, by the door, listening to his grandparents breathe as they slept. They were far away in mumbled dreams when he reached for the door and opened it.

He was careful with it, and it did not creak, but the cold wind outside howled so he made his exit quickly, careful not to step onto the crunchy snow until after the door was closed behind him.

The night was lit by snow and ice. Einer began his long trek through the cold towards the beach of corpses. He had rolled up the sleeves of the large coat he had taken and although it had been the shortest on the rack, the ends of it trailed behind him in the snow.

The wind howled and froze him. Every step was difficult. His shoes were slippery in the deep snow and his legs cooled from the ice.

'I told you not to go.'

Einer halted his trail through the snow.

'Come back with me,' said his grandmother. She had not been sleeping after all. Or perhaps she had woken and knew where he was headed. She was so much larger than him; catching up to him would not have taken her long.

Einer faced her.

Unlike when he had first seen her on the beach, she was not covered up in warm clothes. She stood behind him with a simple blanket thrown over her. It was her coat that he had taken, but she did not ask for it back. She didn't say anything more.

'I have no choice,' he told her. 'I have to try.'

She smiled bitterly. 'There is always a choice. You're the only one who is saying that there is none.'

'I'm supposed to stay here and just wait?'

'Do you truly think that's all you're doing? Just waiting? Aren't you learning too? I thought you were. Perhaps I was wrong.'

She knew that she was not, and Einer knew it too, but he had to try. Even in the company of the Alfather, all he had wanted was to find Hilda.

'And how do you know that choosing to stay here won't lead you to your girl faster than risking your life to find her in the ice or trying to cross those waters into Hel's world? You certainly won't find her in your afterlife.'

'I am not going to my afterlife,' he said. 'I just need to look for her.'

'Then you must go search. But if you do find your short-lived girl in the ice, don't be foolish enough to try to free her.'

'Why not?'

'If the ice is broken, you risk us all. It might not be time yet, but they will come searching. And they will find you.'

'Who are *they*?'

'Don't do it, Einer.'

'I wish I could say that I wouldn't, but I can't. The anger

might take me, if I do find her trapped in ice. I *will* free her.'

The forefathers had taken over for him in Magadoborg when she had died. Whenever Hilda's safety was in question, the anger had full course.

'The forefathers will be the least of your problems out there,' his grandmother said, to Einer's surprise. 'Listen to my warning, Einer. If you disturb the ice and force them to come for you, the forefathers' anger won't help you escape.'

TYRA

Chapter One Hundred and Seventeen

THE CORRIDOR WAS long and crowded. Tyra tiptoed out of the way of the long row of dwarfs.

'Eh, aesir, no cheating,' a dwarf grumbled at her back. 'Get in the queue.'

Tyra started to a stop. 'Forgive,' she blurted and turned to him.

He was half a head shorter than most of the others, and his rock-hard stare was fixed on Tyra. Other queuing dwarfs watched her too, but they looked worried, afraid almost. They looked at her like people had used to look at Siv. And Siv wouldn't have minded this dwarf. Despite his confident stance and hard stare, he never would have dared address Siv, if she had been there.

'Are you talking to me?' Tyra asked the dwarf. She kept a cold tone and her head high, as if she couldn't believe that anyone had dared address her. As Siv would have done.

The queue was long, hundreds of dwarfs, and Tyra didn't have the time to stand and wait. It could take days and weeks to get to the front, and she needed to get back to Svend, and quickly, before Odin and his valkyries found her.

'Do you see any other aesir skipping the queue?' He narrowed his eyes at her. Everyone else diverted their stares when Tyra looked at them, but they were watching. They were scared of her.

'I asked for *your* sake,' she told the dwarf.

'What are you going to do, aesir?'

Tyra didn't know what she would do. She didn't think there was anything *to* do. Siv could draw her seax and kill or silence someone with a stare. For Tyra things were different. She didn't have Siv's strength or confidence.

Her breath trembled when she exhaled. 'What am I going to do?' she repeated, slowly.

Tyra's eyes darted to those standing in front. Her stare matched that of a dwarf who hadn't diverted his eyes in time. The surprise made him hiccup. They stared at each other and Tyra imagined how Siv would have looked at him, as if he was nothing.

'You... you can go in front of me,' the man stammered.

Tyra smiled in such a way that her teeth didn't show, so she looked elegant, like Siv. 'I thought so,' she replied. She swallowed her worries and continued walking. Soft as silk, her new dress ruffled at her calves as she walked. She focused on pushing her shoulders back as she walked.

No one else stopped her. They had all heard the exchange.

As long as the corridor was, and as far as Tyra could see, there was a queue of dwarfs, waiting. A few other beings too, but mainly dwarfs. There were many doors along the hallways, but no one went through any of them. They all waited to enter the same room. Tyra passed them all, and at a faster pace than earlier. She gave no one else time or opportunity to stop her, until she saw the closed door at the end of the corridor.

In there, in that room, was Tyra's only chance to go home. If this didn't work, she didn't know what else to do.

The door at the end of the hallway opened. A dwarf left with a satisfied grin and the next one in line stepped inside. Tyra advanced steadily. Her arm brushed against the satisfied dwarf as she passed him in the hallway. The door at the end of the hallway shut.

Tyra made her way to the very front. The first dwarf in the queue stared up at her in disbelief. She couldn't wait in the hallway or she would be forced away. In a moment's decision, Tyra opened the door and stepped inside. Dwarfs who had diligently waited their turn loudly complained. Tyra shut the door in their faces and let it drown out their protests.

The room was brightly lit by candlelight and gold. There were great bundles of things. Two dwarfs stood bent over a mountainous pile of iron.

One of them clawed through cast bowls and cups and weapons, while the other picked the items up and placed them carefully on the ground. Tyra recognised the back of the second dwarf's chestnut hair and let out a relieved sigh. It was him.

The first man swung to her. 'It's *my* turn,' he complained. 'I waited six days for my turn!'

'Not another one,' grumbled the other—the one she knew. 'Damned dwarfs. Wait your turn!' His back was turned to Tyra as he yelled, and he didn't face her. He just assumed that she would go away, as the others must have, but Tyra didn't have time to wait in the hallway. She had come this far, and if she went back outside, she would have to go to the very back of the queue and she didn't have days to waste waiting for her turn.

'I am not a kinsman of yours, kinsman of Alvis,' she said.

He stopped his doing, and with two axes in hand, he turned to look at her. He smiled when he saw that it was her, but quickly the smile faded with the realisation of why she was there. 'You've come to rob me too.'

'Merely to ask for a favour, as I'm owed.'

'And I am owed my grandfather's silver ring,' complained the other dwarf. 'Wait your turn, aesir.'

They all thought that she was an aesir, except for Alvis's kinsman who had met her in Midgard and knew who she really was.

'Come in,' he said. 'Sit down, and wait your turn.'

He pointed to an armchair in the corner of the room. It didn't look like anyone had ever sat in it, but Tyra walked to it and sat with crossed legs, as she imagined an aesir might have.

The dwarf who was searching for his grandmother's ring glanced at her and felt the pressure of her stare, as Tyra had used to feel Siv's stare. His search was hurried by her presence.

Alvis's kinsman stood back, and watched, and waited.

Finally, the other dwarf got his hands on a silver arm-ring. 'Now you just owe me the interest,' he said.

'I don't,' replied Alvis's kinsman. 'My brother owes you interest, and you can collect from him when he is unstoned.'

'No one comes back from the afterlife,' snarled the dwarf.

'I did.'

'"Bafir the Unstoned." Bafir the *Swindler* would be a more fitting name.'

'Ah…' said Alvis's kinsman, whose name was Bafir. 'But "the Swindler" was your grandfather's calling name. His wife was just as bad. I can't imagine your father was any better. I can't imagine that you are. You should be thankful that I care more about my own reputation than my brothers' thieving treasures.'

'Everyone knew that you were a trio,' said the other, but he closed his hands on the silver arm-ring and left the room anyways.

Another dwarf tried to enter as he left, but Bafir waved them out. 'Wait until you're called,' he said. Reluctantly, the dwarf backed out of the room and closed the door to wait in the corridor.

'Greedy kinsmen,' Bafir said like a curse. 'When I came to the trade house to exchange my petrified brothers' possessions, I had been certain everyone had forgotten our names. Obviously, they haven't. I thought myself clever to come to Asgard instead of trading at home, but even here they found me. I barely came inside before I was ambushed by a dozen people. They line up outside the front door day and night. The backdoor too, now.'

Right at that moment, a knock came from the backdoor of the room. As if someone out there had been waiting to be noticed.

'Give me a chance to catch up!' Alvis's kinsman loudly complained. 'You've waited three hundred and twenty winters, you can wait a day longer!' Bafir combed his smart hair.

All the while, Tyra played Siv. She did her best to sit still and look confident, and she waited for Bafir to speak first.

The dwarf grinned like they were both in on a secret. 'Do you know what happened to our friend?' he whispered to her. His breath smelled of stone dust.

'I don't,' she answered. 'You saw him last.'

'That I did,' sighed Alvis's kinsman, and leaned away from her. 'That I did.'

He walked back to the middle of the room and continued to arrange all of the things the last guest had thrown aside. It was clutter, but it was organised clutter.

'So what do *you* want, short-lived?' he asked. 'You've decided on a favour?'

'I have,' Tyra replied and thought very carefully about how to phrase her request. She didn't want there to be any misunderstandings. Dwarfs could be treacherous and greedy, if the stories were to be believed. And considering what she had seen today, she thought that they were indeed to be believed. So, if there was any way that her request could be misunderstood, it would be.

'So what is it?'

'I want a way for me to safely travel between the nine worlds.'

'Oh... Of course. A short-lived in Asgard, wanting to go home.' He seemed relieved at her request. It had to be an easy one for him to grant. 'Come, I will open a passage grave for you.'

Tyra let out a relieved sigh, finally she would get to go home to Svend and Midgard and all things familiar. And then, in time, Siv would come and find her, like she had promised.

She was about to push off from her chair and follow Bafir out the long hallway again, but then she stopped. Siv wouldn't have been satisfied with that.

'Nej,' Tyra insisted, because Siv would have. 'I need a way to safely travel between the nine worlds.'

'A way to travel between the nine worlds,' Bafir repeated thoughtfully. 'To come and go?'

'To come and go,' Tyra confirmed. If the nornir were right, Siv wouldn't be able to come back for Tyra. And in that case, Tyra needed to be able to get back through the passage graves and search for Siv herself. Sometime when the valkyries were no longer looking for her. Sometime when she knew more than she did now.

Bafir paced around the room as he was thinking. 'A short-lived, travelling through the worlds,' he mumbled. An idea seemed to form in his mind. His eyes gained focus and he snapped his head over to look at her. 'Was Gribul out there?' he asked. 'Short, a plaited beard, hair in his eyes, usually. Brown eyes, square chin.'

Tyra didn't know how to answer.

'We all look the same to you,' he concluded in a sigh. 'Sharp and cut from the same stone, each one of us.'

She couldn't deny it. Before Bafir, she had never met a dwarf, and other than him and the owner of the dress shop, she hadn't met another until she had walked through the hallway of the trade house, which was lined with dwarfs.

'I'll have to go and look, then,' Bafir said. He walked to the door and put a hand to it, took a deep breath and left. Dwarfs loudly complained as soon as the door opened. People were yelling and Bafir too was yelling. Then the door slammed shut and swallowed the chaos outside again.

Tyra sat and waited.

There were so many things in the room. She wondered how Bafir had dragged it all inside without being ripped to pieces by the crowd outside.

There was gold and silver, but there were more weapons than anything, both in silver and steel. Anything from axes to daggers was piled in big bundles. There seemed to be no order to the bundles. Gold and silver mixed, drinking cups piled up next to swords. But there clearly had been some order to the mess, once.

Tyra wanted to touch the many items and see what they did, because the stories about dwarfs and their forging told her that the cups were not simple cups and the swords too were special. But had Siv been there, she would have told Tyra to stay still, so that was what she did.

Bafir was gone for a long time. Someone knocked on the back door twice, and once someone came in, and Tyra had to drive them out with a harsh stare.

Suddenly, the front door swung open. Dwarfs were yelling for their possessions. Bafir hurled the door shut. 'I am not going out there again,' he grumbled and laughed to himself. His laughter died when he saw Tyra sitting exactly how he had left her. 'Gribul was there, but I had to negotiate,' Bafir willingly revealed. He was a talkative man.

Tyra had used to be talkative too, at least according to Siv, but she had come to learn that sometimes silence said a lot more than words ever could. People respected silence.

'But I finally got it,' Bafir bragged. 'A way for you to travel through the nine worlds.' He pushed away from the door. He held a weapon in hand. It had been used; the blade was drenched in blood that dripped off the tip onto the floor.

'Did you kill him?' She didn't want to ask, but she felt like she had to.

Bafir laughed at that. His laughter sounded like a stone being scraped along a rock. 'I didn't need to,' he said.

But there was blood dripping from the blade. And his reply

meant that he would have killed Gribul, if he had needed to, but he hadn't. He was not above killing, and he still hadn't handed her the dagger he had fetched.

At the corner of her eyes, Tyra searched the nearest pile of items without moving her eyes away from Bafir. She searched for the nearest weapon without raising suspicion, as Hilda had taught her to do when danger was near.

An axe stuck out of the nearest pile. She would have to stretch to reach it, and it was in the middle of the pile. She would have to pull back hard to free the axe. It would take her a lot longer than it would take Bafir to come at her with the bloody dagger.

She tried to calm her racing heart. If Bafir intended to kill her, he would have had no reason to leave the room. He could have used any of the weapons in here to do it.

But the dagger made her uneasy.

'If you didn't kill him, then why is there blood dripping off the edge of the blade?'

It was a slow drip; an entrancing one too. Tyra could hardly pull her eyes away from it.

'It was soaked on Ragnarok's bloody plains. It was soaked so well and deeply that the blood is still dripping off.'

It couldn't be the truth. 'Ragnarok hasn't happened yet,' she said. If he had told her that it had been recovered after the war between aesir and vanir, she might have believed him, but Ragnarok was a step too far.

'Not yet,' Bafir replied. 'But this dagger is proof that it *will* happen.'

'How can it be here, soaked in blood, if the blood on it hasn't been spilled yet?'

'Gribul's great grandfather used to say that the Ginnungagap must have sent it. It came from the place of nowhere with no time and nothing.'

A place of nothing and a place that was nowhere.

'The ash,' Tyra muttered.

Siv had hidden her away inside the darkness of the ash tree

during the battle in Ash-hill.

'How did you know that?' Bafir breathed. 'How did you know it was found by the root of the ash tree? I didn't know until Gribul told me, out there.'

Tyra swallowed her thoughts. She hadn't known, but she wasn't surprised to hear it. Siv had told her that the Ginnungagap belonged inside ash trees.

It was one of many things that Tyra had discovered and learned while travelling with Siv. Siv had told her that there was no time in there, and if there was no time, then a dagger soaked in the blood of Ragnarok wasn't impossible.

'How does the dagger work?' Tyra asked to change the topic. The dwarf was watching her with mistrust. 'Do I have to cut myself with it?'

Bafir laughed. 'You could,' he said. 'But it's soaked in the blood of long-lived, so you don't have to.'

'I just let it drip onto the stone,' Tyra knew. She had seen Siv do it. Spill her own blood over the stones to open passage graves. 'And if the blood dries out?'

'It's been dripping for hundreds of summers,' the dwarf said. 'It won't dry up until Ragnarok comes.'

She knew what his phrasing meant. Someday it might dry out, but hopefully, it would be after Tyra was done with it. But it was more than she had hoped for. It was her way home, and it was hope to find Siv again. It was a lot of things.

Tyra got up, ready to get the dagger and leave Bafir to trade with the many dwarfs outside. But though she stood over him, looking down at him, Bafir didn't give her the dagger. He was reluctant to hand it over.

'This dagger is not for free,' he said in a whisper. 'It's going to cost you.'

'You owed me a favour,' Tyra said. 'That is your payment.'

'That's not what I mean.' Bafir looked up at her. He wet his lips and seemed to hesitate to speak, but he was talkative and he couldn't keep the information to himself. 'The price this dagger demands won't be paid to me, and it won't be paid to Gribul or his kinsmen either.'

'Then to whom?' Tyra asked. She wasn't sure what he meant, or what he wanted, but there was fear in his eyes.

'You don't have to pay it to anyone. Carrying this dagger will be a punishment in itself.'

'Why?'

'It has pierced through thousands of beings, collected their screams and tears. It has reaped Ida's plain. It has seen the worst of days. Carry it and it will bring you to demons and it will bring you to the worst of days.'

'I'm not scared.' Tyra said.

She had already seen the worst of days. She had seen her parents and sisters die and her town burn. She had been separated from Siv, and the longer she was away, the more Tyra feared that they might never meet again. The dagger couldn't bring her to days worse than those.

Tyra reached for the dagger. Her hand closed around the guard. Bafir stared up at her with an open mouth. His hand was still on the hilt of the dagger.

'Tak,' Tyra said. 'Your debt to me is paid.'

'Tak,' he said in response. 'And I hope, that in return, I will never see you and that dagger again, short-lived. Not until Ragnarok lies in the past.'

HILDA

Chapter One Hundred and Eighteen

AESIR SHOW NO *mercy to foxes,* Loki whispered in the soft wind.

The Runes had always been cheeky, but now Hilda felt like she too was meant to understand what was funny. All day he had warned her to be careful of Frigg and Odin and the other gods. In Asgard she supposed that there was always a danger of running into a god, but Loki whispered to her as if he knew something was coming and didn't want to tell her what.

She had left the corpse mountains and valleys behind. Hilda's snow fox ran back towards her to make sure she was following. When it saw her, it stood there for a few moments. Then it shot away again, into the forest. Hilda walked in the warm sunlight. The days had turned colder. The nights were freezing, and Hilda knew that she was supposed to be cold but she wasn't. Her snow fox kept warm for the both of them, running around until it could hardly breathe anymore.

Aesir show no mercy to foxes, whispered Loki again. It sounded like he was reminding himself. His whispers made

Hilda reach for her axe. Her fingers fondled the sharp end of the weapon.

Asgard was nothing like home. The trees had no stray branches for pigs and sheep to nibble on. The grass looked like a trimmed beard, not a goat's proud patchwork. There were snow-tipped mountains in the distance. Real ones, not just dead corpses. That too didn't feel like home. Asgard's perfection made Hilda walk faster.

She almost never rested. She no longer needed to scour for food, for she was never hungry and the snow fox was a skilled hunter. It ate for them both. She no longer needed sleep either, but her fylgja did. So while the fox slept, Hilda had made a fire and stared at the flames until they had gone out and left an ember stain on Asgard's perfect plain. Then she had lain back and stared up at the stars Freya said she didn't know. Fondling Frigg's gold arm-ring, she had relived her conversations with the goddesses.

'When I was in the bath-house, Idun conjured ice,' she told the wind. She had been thinking a lot about that moment. The goddess had named the rune of ice and real ice had appeared under Hilda's feet to make her trip. 'Can you teach me that?'

Kauna, may my heat be yours. Naudir, you shall eat in my stead.

Hilda nodded along. 'I know their names,' she said. 'How do I conjure them? Use them?'

It had to be possible for her. In Midgard, she had blessed the rope for the Holmgang. She had switched places with her snow fox to bring it back to life. Besides, the goddesses had said that the whispers in the wind came to her through the runes. She used runes to listen to the whispers. So she had to be able to conjure them like the goddesses.

She didn't know what to picture with all of the runes, but a few were obvious. Like the rune of fire and the rune of ice. 'Isa,' she tried. Nothing happened.

Kauna, may my heat be yours. Naudir, you shall eat in my

stead, was all Loki said. Maybe he was pointing her to an easier beginning.

'Kauna,' Hilda muttered. The rune of fire had to be a good place to start. Besides, conjuring fire seemed useful. 'Kauna,' she said aloud. All Idun had done was name the rune. But nothing happened.

'Kauna,' Hilda said, thinking of the shape of the runic staves and the heat of fire. 'Kauna,' she tried again. Louder this time. There had to be something more to it.

Her snow fox had come out of the forest and stood watching her. It tilted its head to the side. She probably looked mad, shouting for fire.

'Kauna,' she said again. Nothing happened, except that her snow fox darted back into the forest.

Whatever she needed to do, naming the rune obviously wasn't enough.

Kauna, may my heat be yours. Kauna, may my heat be yours. Kauna, may my heat be yours. The Runes wouldn't shut up. Loki was doing it just to annoy her. Hilda was certain of it.

'Let me concentrate,' she snapped.

Hilda stopped walking, closed her eyes and focused. She knew that it was possible to conjure ice, so she went back to that rune. She pictured the stave of ice. One straight stave. She imagined ice crystals forming on the grass on front of her. 'Isa,' she said and opened her eyes.

Frost tinted the tips of the grass at her feet. An arm-length wide around Hilda, the perfect warm grass had been dipped in ice from her use of the rune.

'Ja!' Hilda yelled. She hopped around and punched the air.

Kauna, may my heat be yours. Naudir, you shall eat in my stead, the Runes repeated in celebration.

With a growl ready to defend, her snow fox tumbled out of the woods. It fell silent when it saw that Hilda was alone. Cocked its head at her.

'Watch this,' she told it. Again she closed her eyes. She

imagined ice on the grass exactly one foot in front of her, each strand enclosed in thickening ice. When it was all she could think about, she named the rune: 'Isa!'

Fresh ice had formed atop the grass. The coat of frost was neither as large nor thick as she had imagined it to be, but it was there.

Hilda glanced up at her snow fox. It stood back, tongue hanging out. It watched her, seemingly confused.

'Come here,' Hilda told it and pointed to the ice she had conjured almost as seamlessly as a goddess. 'Come and see.'

Hilda crouched and brought a hand over the ice, feeling her palm cool. She had succeeded. Loki whispered in excitement. The wind tickled up her neck and praised her.

Her snow fox made a wary approach. Stretching far it sniffed the ice. Bounced backwards and approached cautiously again.

The ice melted under her touch. She held her hand out to the cautious fox. It came closer and licked her hand. Twisting its neck from one side to the other, it lowered its snout to the melting ice and licked that too.

'You made me recite runes,' Hilda said to the wind as she watched her snow fox.

Her voice wasn't much louder than a whisper, but Loki would be listening. He listened to even her most quiet words. Sometimes she even though he heard her thoughts.

'Back in Magadoborg. You made me recite runes to save my fox. Those were blood promises.'

Frigg had been surprised to hear Hilda list the runes with their properties.

'What exactly did it do?' she asked of Loki. She had done it without questioning the price, but she had always known there was a price and that death was not all of it. Reviving her fox had been expensive, and Hilda knew that everything had changed.

The fox sustained both of them, but she didn't truly understand what that meant.

Two parts of one, and never alone, Loki whispered in the wind. Eager, as ever, to explain, and probably proud that he could. *Two parts of one, and never alone.* That had been one of the runic promises she had made. The oath for Odal, the rune of home: *Tied in life, tied in death.*

Hilda understood what he meant. When one of them passed on, the other would too. The fox and she shared a life. By saying runic promises, she had bound the two of them together. Both in life and in death. 'So, if my fox dies...' she said to make certain.

Aesir show no mercy to foxes, the Runes repeated. Loki had known what she had been thinking about. He had known she would ask. *Aesir show no mercy to foxes.*

Her gods would kill her without hesitation.

BUNTRUGG

Chapter One Hundred and Nineteen

FEW BEINGS IN the nine worlds knew how to create passage graves. Fewer knew how to undo them. Only a skilled svartalf would be able to help Buntrugg, but that was not an easy encounter. Svartalvar induced fear and trauma. His mind needed to be strong.

The sun had set as Buntrugg stood at the edge of the bare fields that separated the dwarf dwellings from the obscure land of the svartalvar. There was no moon tonight. Precious rain fell over the desert and obscured the night. Buntrugg's mind was full of thoughts as he looked ahead at what he could not see but knew was svartalvar ground.

The forefathers stirred strangely in the place by his heart where he often felt them. They knew where he was, and they would not test their anger on him until he had left Svartalfheim. The stakes were too high here.

The rain slashed over him. Buntrugg took one last deep breath to swallow his fears and then dragged his boots through the splash of rain. The dry ground cracked under his weight. It had been a long time since it had rained in Svartalfheim.

His crunching steps echoed and it sounded and felt like there was someone following him.

Buntrugg looked over his shoulders, despite knowing that he would not see anything and that, most likely, there was no one. He had been alone at sunset when he had arrived outside the last dwarf home and waited for night to fall and for the invisible gates to svartalvar territory to open.

There had been no one behind him. Yet it felt like there was someone. It sounded like there was. Buntrugg sped up his pace.

Heavy raindrops dripped from the edge of his hood. They flicked his nose as they fell. *Too* heavy: it was blood dripping over him.

The sky thundered. Buntrugg ducked and ran, frightened that lightning might strike where he stood. A giant alone on the deserted land was an easy target for Thor's rage.

Before he knew it, he was racing through the pouring rain, puffing in fear of the unknown.

The dark made him stumble over his own feet. His palms smacked against the hard ground and stung. Buntrugg scrambled to his feet and kept running. His hood fell and rain poured over him. Without the hood, the sound of drums seemed louder.

There *was* someone following him. It was not just rain. It sounded like a dozen people chasing him through the downpour.

The wind howled and Buntrugg thought that he heard screams in the winds, and the howl of wolves. His palms itched and stung from his fall. They were bleeding, and his legs were shaking from uncertainty at every leap forward, but stopping was more terrifying.

With every gasp, Buntrugg's heartbeat hastened. His fears crept up his back like a spider. They slithered up his legs like snakes and made the hairs at the back of his wet neck rise.

Buntrugg stopped running. He had gone far enough into svartalvar land for someone to find him and come for him.

His eyes searched through the pitch-black night. The rain slammed over his bare head. The sound of the rain hitting him, and the sting of the drops as they touched his skin, made Buntrugg think of the fires of Muspelheim. The cackles of demons. He thought he could hear them in the wind. They were chasing him. Even in the rain he would never be safe from Muspel's children. They were coming to burn him again. His scars itched. His flesh remembered the heat. It felt like he was burning again.

A thought crept up Buntrugg's spine and cooled his memories of Muspel's fires.

His fears were not real.

Perhaps the thunder too had not been real. His emotions were heightened and his fears worsened by the presence of the svartalvar. That ought to have been a heartening thought; it was anything but.

He was already standing in the presence of svartalvar, and there was no being more unpredictable and frightening than a svartalf at night.

Buntrugg itched his scarred arms. Something nipped at his fingers, like flames and the lick of demons. 'I know you are out there!' Buntrugg's voice did not carry through the rain, but they would hear his loud thoughts.

His body was shaking. The rain poured over him.

He closed his eyes to the dark that surrounded him. He clenched his fists and concentrated on his breathing. His skin was being melted by fires that rose up his arms, or so it felt. He could smell his skin burning.

But he knew that it was not real. It was just a svartalf, standing in the dark of night, making Buntrugg's fears rise so the sweat rolled off his forehead with the rain.

His hands were shaking from fear and terror as he reached for his hood and pulled it over his head again. The thick hood dulled the sound of the rain and thunder and the visions of fires retreated to the back of his mind where they were tolerable.

Somewhere in the dark, a svartalf was revelling in Buntrugg's fears.

In the dark, they lived; any dark, anywhere. They never spoke, and never made themselves noticed. They only ever revealed themselves through visions of fear provoked by the night in which they hid.

With that knowledge, Buntrugg slowed his heartbeat. His fears retreated.

'I come to seek the council of your elders,' Buntrugg shouted, through the rain and in his mind—loud enough for the svartalf to hear, he hoped.

No one had ever seen a svartalf, not even Buntrugg, who had been in their presence many times before. He did not know if they had eyes to see or ears to hear, or if they were short or tall. His fears told him that they were great shadows that could bend over even a giant like himself and suffocate him, and Buntrugg believed his fears.

No answer came, not in whispers and not in visions.

His fears were not reinforced and given purpose. Perhaps the svartalf had left. Perhaps Buntrugg stood alone in the dark downpour.

There was no way to know.

If he was all alone on this empty plain, no one would come to guide him back to the candle-lit dwarf dwellings. No one would hear him scream in the night. It was a much more frightening thought than being followed.

Buntrugg swung back to stare through the dark where there was no one and nothing, and then he knew.

There *was* someone. A svartalf, preventing him from venturing further into the sacred land of svartalvar. Someone who wanted him to turn back before he could reach the black forest and be lost to its eternal darkness.

'You will die before the war of gods and giants even begins,' Buntrugg said. 'We will all die, unless you allow me to speak to your elders.'

All long-lived feared the end of their long life. There was nothing more frightening. Most long-lived did not have a wonderful afterlife to look forward to.

An eternity of anger waited for all giants. Few destinies were as grim as that, and Buntrugg trembled at the thought of becoming a forefather. A giant lost to rage, doomed to haunt and curse all descendants of Ymir's bloodline. As his sister was now.

His thoughts were reinforced by the svartalvar's visions.

The afterlife of all beings flashed before Buntrugg's eyes.

Screams full of jotun anger. Muspelheim's flames flicker and fade to ash. Dwarfs turn back to stone, and watch the worlds spin by. Aesir and vanir sail to Helheim. Short-lived flood into Niflheim. Most are picked up before they reach the shores. A song calls them to Helheim, Ran's net catches them on their descent to the depths and Odin hauls them through Valhalla's gates. Alvar dance with their backs turned to the dark. They sing and dance, until the dark calls them. Alvar turn their back to the light and step into the night.

'You are already dead,' Buntrugg muttered with newfound understanding. 'You are alvar who have been consumed by the dark. This is where dead alvar go. Into the night.'

That changed everything. Svartalvar were not long-lived after all, they were in their afterlife. He had not known, and Buntrugg doubted that the alvar themselves knew what they became in their afterlife.

If the svartalvar were not long-lived, then their priorities were different from that of other beings, but there had to be something that would make them act on Buntrugg's behalf. All beings wanted something, even if it was to be left alone.

'You move in the night and in the dark. You follow creatures and short-lived. When you go through...' Buntrugg's words faltered to a stop.

He did not know if svartalvar used the passage graves to travel between the worlds. He did not know if they could walk through the tunnel, or if they had blood to offer for passage. No one had ever laid eyes on a svartalf and the longer Buntrugg stood in the presence of one, the clearer it became that he knew near to nothing about them.

The rain splashed over his hood and his hands were cold and wet. His palms throbbed from his fall earlier.

The svartalvar were dangerous. He might be surrounded in this very moment and he would not know it. They could kill him—they could do worse—and no one would ever know. Buntrugg calmed his fears and focused again. To talk in the presence of a svartalf was a difficult task.

'Surt sends me.' He started simple, and focused on what he knew. 'Centuries ago, your elders built a passageway to a dwarf forge. The passage is leaking. It leaks Ginnungagap, and that leak is spreading through all passage graves. The worlds are drifting apart. Soon they will run out of Ginnungagap. And you will be stuck here.'

A loud crash came down right next to Buntrugg. He started away from it and spun around. The rain fell harder. The dark was obsolete. Clicks and crashes rung loud around Buntrugg. They came from everywhere in the dark. He had nowhere to run to for safety.

Buntrugg did his best not to move. Perhaps the svartalvar were trying to tell him something. He did not know if they were capable of speech anymore.

You gave us fear, came the answer. No voice uttered the phrase. The svartalvar borrowed Buntrugg's thoughts and voice to speak through.

We have never known fear before.

Buntrugg was stunned into silence. It had never occurred to him that beings like the svartalvar, who inspired so much fear in others, could not feel it themselves.

Give us more, Buntrugg's loud thoughts demanded.

'I will give you more fear, if you help me.'

Thunder ripped through the world. Buntrugg shivered from

worry that the next crash would hit him, whatever it was, but he stood his ground and mustered all of his courage. He would not allow the svartalvar to intimidate him into retreat. He would not give into their threats.

'The nine worlds will fall to ruin,' Buntrugg said, to make them understand and listen, and to escape his own fears. 'Time shall be undone, and this world will be undone with it.'

Buntrugg closed his eyes. The crashes and the rain made everything sound like Muspel's children. He was transported back to the forge where Muspelheim's demons had melted his skin. The scars on his arms and legs and head itched as if they were burning all over again.

'Unless you come with me and undo the harm you have done... If you don't undo the passage graves that you and my ancestors built, the nine worlds will be undone; and you and I, and all beings in all the nine worlds, will never have existed.' He shouted to the rain. His fists were clenched tight to keep from itching his skin and from running away from the fear of it all.

Give us more, Buntrugg's thoughts loudly demanded.

The svartalvar were listening, but Buntrugg did not think that they truly heard what he meant and understood. Perhaps they did not care, but the thought of being undone had given them fear, and they wanted more. They wanted *something* after all.

'Answer me this,' Buntrugg yelled to the rain. 'If I give you fear, will you come with me and close the passage graves?'

Give us first, and then we will, his thoughts answered. If they truly wanted fear, Buntrugg would give them the biggest fright in all the nine worlds.

'Then open a door into Muspelheim and I shall give you fear to dwell on for centuries to come.'

TYRA

Chapter One Hundred and Twenty

IT WAS A relief to see Svend again. Being home in Midgard was a true relief, but that was not why Tyra cried. They were real tears, too. Because Siv wasn't around any longer, and she no longer would be. Their destinies had been spun and they no longer spun together.

Tyra tried to make the tears stop. She knew that Svend worried and Harald could only look at her with disgust and anger, and she didn't want to cry in front of him.

She was alone now—she had to be brave. She was older than Svend, so she would need to set the example and show him the way, like Siv and Hilda and Einer and Ragnar and her sisters and her parents had done for Tyra. She was the one who had to lead now.

'I was taken in the night,' Tyra sniffled and explained. 'I didn't see who it was. I got away, but I didn't know they had Tove. Not until I came home.'

'And why did it take you so long?' Harald asked. He didn't speak kindly or try to console her, as her father would have done. Harald was leaving town, and he neither wanted nor had the time to speak to Tyra.

'I was scared. They were after me,' Tyra babbled. 'I travelled off the roads, and then I got lost...' She started crying again, this time on purpose, so he would stop asking her questions she would have to lie her way through.

'So you came alone?' he asked again, to confirm.

Tyra just nodded.

'Styrbjorn thought you dead,' Harald announced.

Barely had Tyra trailed home through the gates before he was trying to marry her off again.

'I will send word to him and arrange transportation for you to Jomsborg.'

Tyra nodded again and looked at her feet, avoiding the talk and saving her complaints for later.

It worked. Harald went on his way. He left them standing there: Tyra, Svend and half a dozen guards.

Tyra didn't know where Harald was going, if he was really riding off now, like he said he was, but she didn't much care either. She was just happy that he was gone and no longer asking questions she couldn't answer.

Svend scowled after his father. 'Come,' he told Tyra and gestured towards the inner courts like he was its owner and she the guest. She supposed it wasn't entirely wrong. She hadn't lived here for as long as he had, but it had become her home too.

Tyra dried her tears with a backhand as they walked past Svend's grandfather's huge gravemound.

When they were far enough away from the guards, Svend glanced over his shoulder to them, and then he leaned close to Tyra. 'I prayed to the gods,' he whispered. 'For your safe return.' With a satisfied grin he leaned away again.

'And they listened.' Tyra didn't at all think the gods had helped her, with the valkyries chasing her like that, but Svend wouldn't understand.

'I was preparing to go after you as soon as my father left.'

'Where is he going?'

'Up to Vik.'

'What about Hakon? And Sigrid and Gunhild?'

'Hakon and Sigrid are going with him. Gunhild is supposed to go too, but she is fighting it and saying she wants to stay.'

Svend and Tyra walked in silence for a little while. Tyra smiled at the thought of Gunhild fighting with Harald. Gunhild reminded Tyra a little of Hilda. They didn't fight in the same way, but they both fought for their own destinies. Hilda too would have hated Ragnar if he had abandoned the gods and prepared to flee from his lands.

'Then you will be all alone here,' Tyra sadly said.

'The two of us,' Svend corrected and smiled.

At the corner of her eye, Tyra saw his smile fade when he looked at her and saw that she wasn't smiling, like him.

'You won't really go to Jomsborg, will you?'

'I have to,' she said quite simply. 'You think that your father will let me stay here, if I don't? I don't hold any value for him, unless I marry.'

'He is your father too, now.'

'Exactly.'

Harald was not a kind father, and he had never shown any care for Tyra, but now that he was her legal guardian, he could do as he pleased. She had no real choice. She had to go to Jomsborg, as he told her to do. At least now she knew what to expect from her future husband. Siv had made certain she knew the dangers.

'No matter what, I can't stay here in Jelling,' Tyra said.

It was not just a question of what Harald wanted. Everything was safe in Jelling, but there was nothing there that Tyra could do to save the nine worlds as she had sworn to do. Without Siv she could not make Harald see the truth of the nine worlds. She and Svend shared their belief, but it was not enough. The runes were still disappearing, and the nine worlds were drifting apart, like Siv had told her. With Siv gone, it fell to Tyra to save the nine worlds, like they had planned to do together.

'It was never the plan to stay,' Tyra mumbled.

Siv always had bigger plans, and this could not be it. Tyra would not save the nine worlds by staying in Jelling with Svend, where everything felt safe even when it wasn't.

Harald had become Christian and it had changed everything, but there were other Christian kings in the Norse lands, and from what Tyra had heard in Harald's house during the past few moons, there were more and more. Jutland was not the only place where Runemistresses were killed for speaking the words of the gods. If she wanted to save the nine worlds, she needed to do something about all of the kings and their attacks on the old traditions, and she couldn't do that from Jelling.

Besides, if Siv wasn't around, only Tyra knew that Styrbjorn of Jomsborg was chaos and fire and dangerous. He needed to be eradicated, and that task fell to Tyra.

'You'll really leave...?'

'Come with me,' she offered Svend. 'You know Jomsborg. Didn't your mentor live there?'

'Palnatoke?' Svend's interest peaked at the mention of his mentor, whom he had always talked about with fondness. 'He was chief of Jomsborg before Styrbjorn defeated him.'

He had told her many times, but she did not tell him that. 'They probably kept him locked away as a trophy,' Tyra lured. 'Come with me to search for him.'

'He was like a father to me,' Svend said. He stopped in front the last runestone in the ancient ship formation that surrounded the new Christian church. 'But I can't leave. Father expects you to marry, and he expects me to stay.'

'Don't, Svend,' Tyra begged. He was so close to giving in, and she didn't want to leave him behind. Not again. 'It's not safe for you to stay here.'

'Why?' he asked, but his voice was flat because he already

knew the answer to his own question. He was not stupid like other boys.

'Your father leaving like this. In the winter. You know what it means.'

Guests had come from far away for Harald's wedding, but they had travelled over land with expensive retinues. No one set sail in this sort of winter, unless they were fleeing from something, and considering the raised voices Tyra had often heard from Harald's longhouse, the truth seemed pretty obvious. He was sailing far north.

'He wouldn't leave me if it was dangerous to stay,' Svend muttered.

But that was exactly what Harald would do. If he left his son and heir, it didn't look so much like he was fleeing, though he was. Tyra couldn't tell Svend that, though. But she didn't need to. She knew Svend didn't want to say it aloud, but he knew the truth. He was scratching at the side of the runestone in front of which he had stopped; he didn't want to look at her.

'What do I do?' he asked. 'I can't leave Jelling.'

'You can and you will. We will stay here over winter, you and I, and pray to the gods that no one comes. And when the spring flowers bloom and the ships are at sea again, we will sail to Jomsborg together.' She said it with certainty and strength, like Siv had always spoken.

Svend looked at her surprised and wide eyed. He wanted to go with her, she could see it on his face. He wanted to believe that all would be well, and Tyra did too. From now on it was just the two of them and Tyra was the elder. She had to act the part, and tell him what needed to be done, like Siv had always told Tyra.

'I will stay with you, Svend,' she reassured him, as Siv had reassured her so many times before. 'But then you also have to stay with me.'

He looked into her eyes, and she into his. He studied her face, searched for any uncertainty, but Tyra thought of Siv and showed none. She was certain. She had seen her own fate. The nornir had promised to spin her and Svend's fates together, she knew that he would come, and more than that, she knew that he had to, or he would die in this lonely town.

Svend nodded. 'Over winter we pray, and in spring we leave,' he agreed.

EINER

Chapter One Hundred and Twenty-One

COLD WIND SLAPPED in from the ocean with the early morning light as Einer searched through the frozen corpses for Hilda.

The edge of Niflheim was colder than any winter day Einer had ever known. Wrapped in his blankets, his beard was a block of ice, and his eyebrows and eye lashes were tipped with white.

Einer approached another pillar of ice. They seemed to have been made by waves crushing into shore and spitting out corpses. That was how Einer had arrived on this beach, and it had to be how every frozen corpse here arrived. But these people had not had anyone waiting for them on shore, to warm them and save them from the cold, so they had frozen on the spot, right where the waves had spewed them out.

There were people in the pillars and on the ground. A thin layer of ice and sand covered them and blurred their faces.

Einer stared down at them, hoping not to see Hilda, hoping that she was elsewhere; in Helheim, perhaps. Even a life in Helheim, far away from the gods and fights that Hilda craved to see was better than a frozen eternity on these shores. There were few things in the nine worlds that were not better than the frozen shores of Niflheim.

Some of the corpses breathed. The fresh ones, Einer assumed. The ice creaked with their breaths. Sometimes, their eyes were open, too.

Einer swept a foot over the sand to expose the next corpse. The ice creaked beneath his feet. A man's ragged tunic was blurred by the thin cover of ice, and the chest moved with faint breaths.

There were many corpses, but few women. Einer was about to move along to the next one when the edge of the man's tunic caught his eye. He had studied that detailed embroidery before.

He stopped his hasty search and leaned in to better see.

The embroidered band at the edge of the tunic was thick, and Einer definitely knew that pattern of arrows and trees. With his palm, he swept away the cold hard sand, and peered at the face of the corpse trapped in ice under his feet. A blonde beard edged a face half-hidden by long wavy curls of hair that had been frozen into place.

'Sigismund,' Einer muttered. His breath turned to ice in the air.

Sigismund's head was turned to the side, and his eyes were closed. His face was bloated. He must have drowned, and Einer shuddered to think how he had ended up here. Sigismund's chest moved, barely, but enough for the ice to creak and for Einer to notice. He looked deep asleep.

Einer turned his gaze to the beach. He had walked along much of it, staring down at dead faces and searching for Hilda, as he had once searched for her in Ash-hill. He could not leave his best friend stuck in the ice for all eternity, but his grandmother's warning was vivid in his mind.

Despite her warnings, he had to do something. He reached for the dagger in his weapon belt. His fingers were stiff. It hurt to clasp the dagger. Ice and sand creaked under the dagger's touch.

The beach stretched on as far as Einer could see. There were so many corpses left to search through. He had barely begun.

If he freed Sigismund from the ice, or attempted to, someone would come, as his grandmother had warned him. He did not expect to be able to continue his search for Hilda then; but he could not leave a friend to a doomed eternity in the ice. Certainly not as good a friend as Sigismund.

There was no question in his mind that he had to do this, even if it meant giving up his search for Hilda. His destiny had led him here, and be it in this life or the next, he would find Hilda again. If she truly was stuck in the ice, like Sigismund, then she would stay there until Einer could come back and find her. Like the corpses on Odin's battlefield, she would likely never know how long it had taken him. A day made no difference, nor a week or however long it would take Einer to come back.

He raised his dagger and prepared to strike the ice. It would take many hacks to free Sigismund entirely, and Einer did not know if his friend would wake once his body was clear of the ice, or if he was so close to death that only a valkyrie could wake him.

Whoever it was Einer's grandmother had talked about, they would come if he freed Sigismund, and Einer did not know how long he would have. He hoped that it would be long enough.

It didn't matter, he decided. None of it mattered. He could not leave Sigismund. No matter if monsters came for him, or if Sigismund didn't wake, he had to try to save his old friend.

He plunged down the blade, and the ice chipped away. He hacked again, brushing away the big pieces of ice as he cut them up. He started by freeing Sigismund's shoulder, so that if his strike was off, it would not leave a fatal injury.

The ice was new and cracked away more easily than he had feared. Hardly had Einer begun before he touched Sigismund's wet, stiff woollen tunic when he brushed the ice chunks away. The wind picked up the ice shards and scattered them.

After each blow Einer glared along the beach, worried that

someone was coming for him, as his grandmother said they would.

By the time he had cleared Sigismund's ears and cheek and chin, there was yet no one, but a fierce wind of ice had begun to rise.

Curly hair got stuck and chipped away with the ice. Einer worked as quickly as he dared to free his friend. The face was delicate, but Einer did not have long.

Sigismund's skin was soft and bloated, and ice cold to the touch. Einer took the blanket off his own shoulders and put it over Sigismund's shoulders and face, though he was sure it made no difference.

Sigismund's chest moved ever so slightly, but Einer could not make his friend warm, as his grandmother had done with him. He could not somehow make a fire burn within Sigismund to make him wake from the cold. The ice had already claimed him.

Yet Einer continued to hack into the ice. His grandmother had warned him against it, but the damage was already done.

Without the blanket on his shoulders, the cold wind went straight through his wool jacket, and Einer shivered. The bracteate hammered and burned against his skin. It kept him warm and aware, and suddenly Einer knew there was only one way to help his friend.

With newfound hope, Einer freed the back of Sigismund's head. He took three short breaths and embraced the burning warmth on his chest.

The bracteate had melted into his skin. His mother had instructed him never to remove it, to always wear it and keep it close. Bad things happened when he took it off. He had nearly died when he had last parted with it. It had woken him from death and kept him alive more than once. But despite his mother's warnings, Einer could no longer keep it.

He made the decision.

Well aware that it meant that he would be defenceless, Einer removed his neck-ring. The bracteate didn't come off. It had burned into his skin.

If there was any chance that it would do for Sigismund what it had done for Einer...

He ripped the bracteate off his chest, and his skin tore off with it. Einer shrieked with pain and placed the bracteate on Sigismund's chest. He stuffed it under his friend's tunic.

Not a heartbeat of rest he gave himself before he returned to cutting the ice.

The cold enveloped him and the northern wind blew around him. His fingers became white with ice. He was freezing like any other corpse on the beach, but he kept moving and scratching at the ice that trapped his friend.

The more of him Einer freed, the warmer Sigismund's skin got, and Einer knew that it was the bracteate trying to wake Sigismund with a fever, as it had once woken Einer and kept him alive.

Einer worked as quickly as an old carver with chisel and hammer. The ice became easier to free. It seemed to melt away at Sigismund's touch.

'When we promised to meet each other in the afterlife, this is not how I imagined it,' Einer said to the warming corpse.

'Valhalla?' Sigismund's voice was a weak whisper. His eyelids batted with activity.

Einer glanced to the surroundings. 'It's good to see you again. Good to hear you.'

Sigismund said nothing more as Einer freed his chest. His breaths deepened. His arms were next.

With every crack that echoed along the beach over the crash of waves, Einer became more worried that someone would arrive. His grandmother had sounded serious; whoever or whatever was coming for him would not be pleasant.

Einer tugged the blanket around Sigismund again.

'Valhalla,' Sigismund muttered once more. His eyelids fluttered, but he kept his eyes closed. It was too cold.

'Is this truly how you imagined Valhalla?' Einer asked and had it not hurt to move his lips, he might have laughed.

Sigismund's teeth clattered from the cold, but he smiled. The bracteate was helping him. 'Then why are you here and not there?'

'I left,' Einer said, not quite willing to explain how or why, but thankfully Sigismund did not ask for an explanation.

'How did you find me?' was his next question.

'I was looking for Hilda,' he said.

Sigismund smiled again. On a warmer day, he would have laughed. 'I thought you were just determined to keep your promises. To round up old bench-mates.'

Sigismund's legs came free of the ice easily. Einer glanced along the frozen beach, looking for shadows and people and monsters.

'The Midgard Worm came for us,' Sigismund said. Although the bracteate gave him heat to survive, his entire body still shivered from the cold. His lips were blue, but the conversation seemed to give him strength and to wake him.

At last, Einer freed Sigismund's feet, and pushed him up to sit. 'You're free. Go now,' he urged. 'Go, before they come.'

Sigismund's eyes widened in surprise and he stared at Einer for an explanation that was difficult to give.

Einer put an arm around his friend's shoulder and helped him to his feet. Sigismund could hardly stand, let alone walk, and there was nowhere to walk to at any rate. There was only one way to go.

Einer pointed to the shore on the other side of the ocean that his grandmother had showed him, when he had first arrived. The shore was far away and the waves swept up tall and hid it from view. A blizzard was coming.

'Helheim is over there,' he told Sigismund. He could not see the shore for the grim weather, but he had seen it the other day and he knew it was there.

'Einer... Before *who* arrives?'

'It doesn't matter,' Einer said, although he did not know either.

He did not need to know who they were, to know that he should be afraid. His grandmother, a powerful giant who knew how to keep warm in Niflheim's cold and knew much more than that besides, had been scared, and that was reason enough.

'Keep the neck-ring on, always,' he instructed, like his mother had once instructed him. 'The bracteate will keep you safe and alive.'

Ice cracked somewhere in the distance. Not just the crash of waves, but the crunch of ice. Monsters were coming.

'They are already on their way.'

Whoever they were, they could not find Sigismund here. They could not find either of them.

'You can't stay here. Swimming is the only way to escape these shores,' Einer said, guiding Sigismund towards the cold sand. 'The water will be treacherous, and burn your skin, but the bracteate will keep you safe. Keep swimming. Make it to Helheim.'

Sigismund looked Einer in the eyes. What remained of his curly hair flapped in the wind. His stare was hard and precise. Then he nodded and approached the sea without any questions. Sigismund knew that Einer had his best interest in mind, and if Einer said that he could not stay, then he could not, and if Einer said that there was no time to explain, then there was not.

They were loyal friends to each other.

'You're the one in a hurry,' Sigismund said by the water front and looked over his shoulder to Einer. 'Coming?'

'I'm not going,' Einer said and matched Sigismund's gaze.

They knew each other so well. Einer did not regret his decision to give Sigismund the bracteate. It would allow Sigismund to survive, and Einer still had the deep dark anger to sustain him, for now.

Sigismund smiled, accepting Einer's decision to sacrifice himself for his friend. It was a worthy sacrifice, but only if Sigismund accepted the terms.

'Tak,' Sigismund told Einer and faced the sea.

'Sigis!' Einer called to him before he could launch away into the waters. 'Say "hei" to Ragnar for me. And to Hilda, if you find her.'

'I will, old friend,' Sigismund said. A wave crushed like thunder at his feet and made him stagger. Sigismund turned his gaze to the roaring sea and gulped.

Einer's swim had been hazardous and he had thought he would die, but Sigismund's swim would take much longer and be much worse.

A wave retreated, and Einer watched Sigismund run at the sea. Another wave crashed over him, and when it flowed back to sea, Sigismund was gone, taken by the waves and the ocean. Einer hoped that he had done the right thing by freeing Sigismund and pointing him to the venomous sea, where the Midgard Worm bit its own tail.

There was no time to regret his choice. Sigismund was gone, and loud roars approached. *They* were coming.

Einer unsheathed his two swords. The Ulfberht rose ready to attack in his right hand, while his old sword scraped along the sand, ready to defend.

With a deep breath, he steadied his heart. He did not know much about this world, but he knew how to fight. He had fought his way across Ida's plain and survived. He had faced giants and he had slain warriors who had done nothing but fight for thousands of winters. Whatever came his way could not be worse than Ida's plain.

That was what Einer told himself, to calm his beating heart, although he knew that he was wrong. Something was coming for him, and without the bracteate hanging from his neck and protecting him, it would be much worse than Ida's plain.

BUNTRUGG

Chapter One Hundred and Twenty-Two

RAINWATER DRIPPED FROM Buntrugg's coat onto the sleek stone floor. The drips echoed in the large hall. The svartalvar had left, but there was light inside the room into which they had lured him. Enough to see the outline of a single metal door in the middle of the room, and enough to see that there were no svartalvar.

The light came from the door's keyhole. Fires flickered beyond. The closer Buntrugg walked, the more clearly he heard the crack of fire and screech of demons.

The door led to Muspelheim.

The mere thought of opening the door made Buntrugg sweat. The heat he would face would be as bad as the heat in the dwarf forge when he had been burned. His skin itched at the thought. The forefathers cowered inside him with the memory. He did not think that he would be hauled from danger and healed by the Alfather again. Nor would his forefathers save him. Since he had heard their individual voices, he felt like he knew them, and the forefathers were not a shield that would save him every time he was in trouble. They served only themselves, as all giants did.

Reluctantly Buntrugg approached the door and his worst fears. There was only this metal door between him and the fire demons who had nearly killed him.

His wet hood was up as he stared at the metal door. He hoped that the door would not melt when he opened it and exposed it to the heat of Muspelheim.

He touched a hand to it. It was cold, at least on this side. Dwarf-forged. The door was simple and bore no carvings. It had been conjured in a rush. The keyhole was small and the key in it was simple.

Buntrugg removed the key and crouched to look through the keyhole. Light flashed in all the colours of fire. Heat waved through the keyhole and dried his eyes, and fear crept up inside him.

He put his ear against the keyhole, and heard the panicked shouts of demons muffled by the whip of their flames so he could not hear what they said, but their voices were enough to make a chill travel up from his ankles to the back of his head.

The svartalvar would not help him unless he gave them fear, and Buntrugg knew only one thing that all beings in the nine worlds feared: the sons of Muspel. Only one being in all the nine worlds could walk through Muspelheim without harm, and that was Surt himself.

In the early days of the nine worlds, Surt had tamed fire, and since then Muspel did not dare to attack the ancient giant. Despite having lived at Surt's side for many winters and summers, and learned his ways, Buntrugg could not step foot into the world of fire.

He examined the conjured door. It was not meant to let anything through until it was used, but if Buntrugg went over the threshold and into Muspelheim, he would melt faster than he could scream. The forge where he had burned had been heated through an open furnace; it was nothing compared to the heat of Muspelheim itself. But Surt, who was a jotun like Buntrugg, had tamed fire, and so, in theory, survival was possible.

Buntrugg tried to convince himself of that, but he knew that this was different. Surt had been stronger than Buntrugg was now and he was an old being. He had conquered fire back when fire did not know other beings than its own demons. It did now. Like giants knew about fire, fire knew about giants. It had killed many, and it would kill many more. To Muspel and his demons, Buntrugg was just another giant to devour in their flames.

Buntrugg clenched his hand tight around the key. His fears gave him goosebumps and his doubts made him retreat away from the door, into the dark of the room.

The echo of his retreating steps made him stop. His fears were worsening. There were svartalvar in the room. Standing in the shadows where Buntrugg could not see, ready to see the fear he had promised to unleash into their world.

Buntrugg inserted the key back into the keyhole. Opening the metal door was the last thing he wanted, but he had made the svartalvar a promise. One last breath of fresh, cool air he took, and then, he opened the door.

Heat struck his face. Colours too bright to be looked at swished past. Demons screeched. They did not yet know that he was there, watching, but as soon as something stepped across the threshold, they would know and they would burn him as they had done once already.

The fire demons were whispering. Many voices muffled each other, but one stood out to Buntrugg because of what it hissed.

'Five full suns since the lid was closed,' hissed an accusing demon.

'Grow your flames. She will be back,' answered another.

Understanding the language of fire demons was not enough to understand every conversation, but Buntrugg had been given plenty of practice working for Surt.

The demons were talking of an opening out of Muspelheim where other demons had escaped, and there was only one of those: the forge that Buntrugg had closed. That had been a few weeks ago, but the fire demons seemed to think it was five summers in Midgard.

Surt had been right: time in the nine worlds was spinning out of control.

Summers and winters might have passed in Midgard while Buntrugg had been in Svartalfheim, or hardly a day. He needed to hurry and close all of the passageways, as Surt commanded.

The last thing in all the nine worlds Buntrugg wanted was to reach into Muspelheim. Yet, he needed the help of the svartalvar, and he had promised them fear. A fire from Muspelheim blazing through their own world might scare the svartalvar enough to act on Buntrugg's behalf.

If a child of Muspel was brought into Svartalfheim, nothing would keep it from burning the entire world to the ground. Buntrugg needed to control the flame he brought back, and he only had one try. A simple mistake would destroy this world and him with it. It would mean the death of all nine worlds.

Buntrugg's heart pounded with fury, and he was short of breath. He inhaled deeply to overcome his fears. The longer he stood here, the more svartalvar would gather to watch and the more his fears would mount and make the task ahead impossible.

Whatever hand he plunged over the threshold and into the world of fire risked never coming back. At Ragnarok, a battle that had once seemed so far away but now approached at an alarming speed, Buntrugg would need to fight for his kind. His weapon hand was his right hand, but his left was made to carry heavier loads like a metal shield, and a shield could serve as a weapon. His right was the better sacrifice.

'*Isa*,' Buntrugg said aloud, to reinforce his command on the rune of ice. He focused on his right hand. It cooled with his command. His skin stung and his heartbeat slowed as if he stood in Niflheim.

Buntrugg positioned himself dangerously close to the open door and searched the flashes of light.

If he was to succeed, he needed to find a target. A weak flame he could reach and bring back before the demons sensed him and melted his arm off.

His eyes could hardly look at the lights, but he kept staring until his eyeballs turned numb from heat and pain, and the shapes of nearby demons began to emerge.

At the centre of Muspelheim, the demons let their flames roam free. They only assembled into bodies as they left their world. Certain flames belonged to certain demons. Dragging out one part of a demon would drag it out in its entirety, and that could be dangerous. Especially since most of the flames and heat belonged to Muspel himself; to drag Muspel from his home would be to condemn the nine worlds to burn in the time of nine heartbeats.

Buntrugg needed to pick well.

The flames gleamed in specific ways, indicating which belonged to the which demon. There was something about the sound of their cackle and the shape of their flames that marked them and bound them together.

Buntrugg searched for a lone flame. A young flame that had not yet been claimed by a demon.

Finally, his eyes caught sight of it. The perfect little flame. It was within range, but it moved quickly.

Buntrugg swallowed his last fears. He thrust his ice-cold hand into the heat. His arm stretched over the threshold and into the fires. His fingers waved through flame. He struggled to grasp the little one.

The flames sensed the open door and his presence. Demons screeched and jumped at his arm. They clawed into his skin with their flames. His arm unfroze from his rune casting. His skin blackened from their touch. His flesh melted to a crust.

His fingers could not quite grasp the small flame. It kept slipping away, as if it skipped on ice. It was exactly like that, of course. He had frozen his hand to withstand the fire for longer, but he shouldn't have.

'Kauna,' Buntrugg said. Fire demons screeched and cackled so loud that he did not hear his own voice.

The heat of fire erupted up his arm. His fingers became warm and familiar to the small flame. He clasped onto the flame and pulled back.

His arm returned from Muspelheim on fire. Buntrugg pushed the metal door shut and fell onto the hard floor. Flames flared up and lit the dark room. Shadows scurried away. 'Isa! Isa!' Buntrugg screamed. His skin melted away.

Heat was all he felt on his throbbing right hand. The flames were extinguished and his skin cooled with the help of the rune of ice, but Buntrugg hardly felt it. The heat continued to sear into his very bones.

Although this time he had the runes to help him, the pain was as bad as the first time he had been burned. Buntrugg squirmed on the cold floor.

His face was wet from tears, and snot and sweat mingled and stung on his charred skin. Buntrugg breathed through bared teeth, closed his eyes and focused on the rune of ice and the cold of ice.

His arm cooled so that Buntrugg felt the pain of ice instead of fire fill him. His entire body throbbed and his heartbeat skipped out of rhythm. His arm was numb but he no longer felt the fire. The skin on his shoulder was tight and hard.

There were still flames, though. Buntrugg saw it through his closed eyelids. Light flickered in the previously dark room.

Buntrugg opened a cautious eye. The room was bright as if a fire was lit somewhere, although he had closed the metal door. The light came from Buntrugg himself. He glanced down his arm, enrobed in the ice that he had conjured out of desperation. At his wrist, ice tried to form, but it melted right off his hand.

Buntrugg leaned in to better see. A blue glow of light flickered from his hand. A small flame filled his giant palm. A small, warm flame that he had ripped from its home in Muspelheim.

He had conquered fire, like Surt. Granted, Surt had conquered all of Muspelheim, but Buntrugg was well content with the small blue flame in his palm that scared the svartalvar away into their shadows.

Buntrugg punched the ice off his numb right arm, breaking it free. He could move it, but felt nothing. He commanded his arm to move, and it did, but he did not feel it do so. The flame nibbled into the black crusted skin on his palm, but Buntrugg did not feel that either.

Grimacing, he rose from the puddle of melted ice and his own sweat and walked back to the metal door. He locked it, wrenched the key out and threw it into the darkest corners of the room.

'This is a light that you cannot extinguish,' he grunted to the svartalvar. 'It will burn every piece of you and every memory of you, if you even try to extinguish it.'

Buntrugg bent the fingers on his blackened hand. The flame expanded and retracted with his movements. He brought it up to his face to look. It was warm, so much so that he thought it might burn the skin off his face. He opened his palm flat, so the flame rested in the middle, perfect and content, and could stretch its limbs.

The svartalvar had requested fear. He would give it to them.

He filled his lungs, and with all of his power, he blew. The little blue flame stretched its limbs. Red fire raged to the corners of the room.

His lungs were empty. The fires retracted back into the little blue flame.

Buntrugg stared into the pitch-black of the hall. 'A flame from Muspelheim. And it answers to me.' The flame settled into his palm, but Buntrugg clenched his hand shut, so it would learn its place, and always know that it was he who controlled it. 'Is that enough fear for you?'

What do you need? the svartalvar finally responded.

DARKNESS

RAGNAR SHIVERED AND stared into Siv's strong eyes.

'Why do you call me that? Story-maker?'

It was how the veulve had spoken to him, too. Everyone who acknowledged Ragnar since he had passed on called him *the story-maker*, but he was not. He was simply a skald; a story-teller.

'It is what they call you,' Siv answered. She didn't look at him, but at the many shadow warriors who surrounded them. 'It is what you are.'

'Then who are they? Why do they kill me?'

'They must have grown blind from an eternity spent in darkness. But they hear you. They hear us.'

'They don't just hear you.' Ragnar started away from a shadow warrior approaching from behind. 'They listen to you.'

The shadow warriors surrounded Siv and him on a mountainside in Asgard. Unlike before, the shadow warriors no longer attacked when Ragnar spoke. They certainly never attacked Siv. He had never heard *them* speak, but they had kept him from his rightful afterlife. They had killed him when he had first woken up in the dark, riding on horseback following the villagers' singing voices.

'There was a veil into Helheim,' he told Siv 'How do I find it again? How do I find my way into Helheim where I'm expected?'

Siv raised a questioning eyebrow at him. 'Into Helheim? Ragnar...' She said his name in her motherly tone. 'If you are here, you're never going to Helheim.'

All of Ragnar's hope crumbled at once. Wide-eyed, he stared at the many shadowed faces and along the valley where aesir and vanir walked around but didn't see him.

There was no escape from the Darkness. Never would he escape this horrid afterlife. Never would he see his family. He would never embrace Signe again, or kiss her plump lips. Never would he see Leif and her, and live with them, as he had been meant to do in the afterlife. They would wait an eternity for him, and he would never join them.

He clenched the wrung narwhale stave in his hand. With the distaff, he could see their past, but never could he meet them. Never would they know that he was there. He would always be an observer, watching family, gods and giants through the veil of his distaff.

'Why?' Ragnar's voice broke with the thought that he was doomed to be in this Darkness forever. 'Why have the gods doomed me to observe?'

'You're not an observer,' said Siv, so certain. 'You're the story-maker.'

Ragnar swallowed his tears at the face of Siv, who was so much younger than him. He attempted to calm his breathing and make his fear retreat.

'What does that mean?' he asked.

Looking at the scary faces of the shadow warriors helped. They were less terrifying when he could see them and knew that they weren't sneaking up on him to kill him, but still he spoke in fear.

'Why would the gods send me here?' he asked Siv.

'Why do you think it's the gods who sent you?'

Ragnar sniffled and looked into Siv's calm eyes. 'Who else could have?'

Siv nodded to his distaff. 'It gives you influence to sway minds, doesn't it? Even that of gods.'

'I haven't done this to myself,' he hissed at the accusation. Ragnar had made mistakes in his life, and in the Darkness, but never would he do something like that and doom himself to an afterlife in this place.

'Not yet, you haven't.'

'I would never,' he said aloud, but part of him already doubted it. He had done a lot of things in the Darkness that he never thought he would even think to do. Perhaps it would be as it had been with the Alfather's death. Perhaps in trying to prevent himself from entering the Darkness in the afterlife, he would end up dooming himself to this fate.

Perhaps there was time to change it and wake up in Helheim.

'Never...' he repeated, less convinced the more he thought about it.

'You will.' There was no doubt in Siv's voice. 'You are the story-maker, after all.'

Again, that name.

'What does that mean?' Ragnar yelled at Siv, and the shadow warriors, and the Darkness, and his gods. None of this was how it was supposed to be.

'It means that this is *your* story, Ragnar. You decide what happens to all of us. Any time. Past, present, future. You are what we all call *fate*.'

EINER

Chapter One Hundred and Twenty-Three

ICE CRACKED AND crashed. They were coming, whoever they were. Einer was shaking from the knowledge and the cold. His grips on his two swords were so stiff that it felt like his hands had turned to ice. His chest was cold, and Einer felt bare without the bracteate. He hoped that fate would be kind.

Ice clashed at his back, Einer swirled around. A thick mist crept over the coast, and cracking booms echoed through Niflheim.

The Ulfberht sword was raised and ready. Einer's own sword scraped along the ice as he turned and peered into the blizzard that approached like a wave. While he could still orientate himself, Einer planted his feet in the ice so that the wild ocean was at his back.

The blizzard advanced like a monster coming for him. Ice crashed everywhere, and then the ice descended over him; a storm so thick that his feet were hidden by it. It shielded the sunlight from above and enrobed everything in black shadows.

Ice shards slashed across his face.

Something clashed to his left, and a loud bang echoed through the blizzard. Einer flinched away, found his foothold again and steadied himself. He slowed his breaths, and thought of Sigismund getting away, and of Hilda smiling.

A wave splashed at his back. Every sound startled him in the dark of the storm, and then, Einer heard the worst kind of sound. A hiss of a whisper.

'Einer,' said the whisper that seemed to come from within.

He slashed his sword. His weapon swept through the air and hit nothing. Another wave crashed. Salt waters splashed up on his face and Einer staggered backwards not to get caught in the next wave. He had to take a secure stance where he had placed himself before the blizzard had arrived, but he no longer recalled exactly where he had been standing and he could no longer see his feet or even his legs. The dark enclosed him, full of clashes and growls, and the whisper was still there, in his ear. 'Einer... Einer...'

Einer tried to plant his feet securely on the slippery ice. He held his breath and listened to the storm. Some crashes were far away, while others sounded like they were right next to him.

Something whipped past Einer so fast he felt the air on his cheeks. The Ulfberht sword clanged against rock. Far above A creature howled with pain. Einer slashed out again, but his sword found nothing. He held both swords in front of him and waited for the creature to strike. The howl disappeared, and as soon as it was gone more howl rose from all over the stormy world. Howls so loud that Einer heard nothing else. Not even the sweep of air, as he was knocked to the ground.

Giant fingers grabbed him while creatures howled.

'I have him!' yelled a strong voice.

The fingers clenched Einer so he couldn't move. He dangled in the air, held tight in the grip of a frost giant. The cold fingers pressed around him cooled his core, and slowed his heartbeat. His hands were nearly frozen onto the hilts of his swords. Wind ruffled his hair as he swung through the thick blizzard.

Hail was coming down over him.

Though he could barely keep his eyes open and think any longer, from how cold he was and how his blood pulsed through him, Einer considered his next move. He had to get free. Perhaps if he cut the hand that held him, the frost giant would release him. He swung too high in the air to risk it. The fall might kill him, especially if he banged his head on the ice, and he did not have his mother's bracteate to heal him and keep him alive. At least Sigismund was safe.

The giant thumped over the ice. The cold tightened around Einer. His breaths were shallow, his heartbeat slowed, and then his eyes closed to the cold.

EINER'S FINGERTIPS FLUTTERED to life and the rest of him followed. Voices rung in the near distance. His cheek was pressed against a warm stone floor. Einer did not move, and did not open his eyes; merely lay and listened to the voices, hoping to hear what they said.

His swords had been taken from him; his weapon belt removed. He had no means with which to defend himself, and he did not know where he was.

His limbs stirred with gradual heat that felt like an animal nibbling his skin. The voices were muffled, and Einer could not make out what they were saying, but he was pretty certain that they were talking about him.

'Where is she?' asked a voice meant for him.

Einer gulped, involuntarily, and knew that he could no longer pretend to be asleep. 'Who?' he asked. His body was sore and his skin prickled with needles of heat and cold.

The heat rising from the floor had warmed his skin and brought him out of sleep. In the waves of heat sat his grandmother, at a fair distance. Her long hair waved over her shoulders as if she had not had time to braid it. She was crouched down to speak to Einer, and she looked smaller than she had last night.

'Where is she?' his grandmother demanded to know. She truly was smaller than she had been, and she stared at him with kind eyes. 'Where did you hide the corpse?'

'Her...?' Einer muttered trying to come to his senses and understand what was happening.

'You were looking for your girl, out on the ice.'

People talked in the distance, and when Einer looked around, he finally noticed that he was not in his grandparents' home. He sat in a pit of heating stones. The top of the pit had been closed by an iron cage.

His grandmother sat in the pit with him. 'Where did you take her corpse?' she urged.

'I didn't...' he barely muttered before his grandmother flooded him with more questions.

'If it wasn't the girl, then who did you free?' she asked before Einer could say anything. 'Why were you so insistent on being out on the ice? How did you know where to look?'

She asked so much and did not give Einer any opportunity to answer.

The voices in the distance above the pit faded; whoever they belonged to were walking away. The iron restraints above were bright like heated metal. Trapped in the pit, Einer had already begun to sweat.

His grandmother leaned in and his attention snapped back to her. 'Don't tell them I tried to stop you and told you this would happen,' she warned in a whisper. 'I will protect you, as I should have protected Glumbruck, but don't make it any harder for me.'

Einer frowned at her. She had told him that *someone* would come, but not who or what, so while she had told him not to go, she had not told him why he should stay away from the ice.

Finally, what his grandmother had said fully settled in his mind. 'Protected my mother...?' The name Glumbruck still sounded awkward to him, and it did not sound like a name that belonged to an elegant woman like his mother.

Einer's grandmother nodded wisely, and leaned in. 'She sat in this same pit for two weeks, on trial for freeing a corpse from the ice. She was burning the corpse on the frozen beach as the blizzard came. Flames and smoke protected her from the ice, but not us.'

Einer could not quite decide if she meant that the smoke had not protected his mother from her parents or if the smoke had not protected his grandparents from the ice, and his grandmother did not tell him which one was right, only frowned like it hurt to think about.

'What is this place?' he asked.

The distant talk he had heard earlier had faded.

'The town hall,' his grandmother answered, as eager as ever to teach him. 'The court room. It has many functions. By tomorrow the pit will be too hot for you to survive. A jotun might survive another week, but you're not a full jotun.'

Yet his mother had sat in the pit for two weeks. There was much that he did not know about his mother, and Einer still struggled to believe it all, because she was not there to confirm any of it, and it was strange to be told that his mother had led such a different life before Einer had been born. And besides, the more he learned about his mother's past, the more he missed her.

'You should have listened to me,' his grandmother sighed. She rocked uncomfortably on the hot stone floor. 'Tell them where you hid the corpse,' she begged of Einer in a whisper. 'They won't be harsh on you if they can return the body to the ice.'

'They? Is that who you meant were coming?'

'You should have listened. The blizzard and ice nearly took you, and us with it.'

'I don't regret my actions,' Einer said. 'He was a friend and he is free now.'

'Why does it matter where this body rots? In the ice or elsewhere?'

Einer did not answer, for he thought it wise to keep to himself that Sigismund was not just a corpse, but a walking corpse, thanks to the bracteate Einer had parted with to save Sigismund. He did not know if giants had any claim in Helheim, but he intended to give Sigismund the best chance possible of a clear escape.

The iron cage above them swung open and his grandmother rose to her feet. Her size increased as she did, and then she lifted herself out of the pit.

'The corpse's name is Sigismund and he is not yet dead,' he heard her say as the cage shut behind her. 'A gold neck-ring keeps him alive and awake.'

Einer cursed his own loud thoughts. His uncle had warned him. Njord had warned him. His grandmother too. They had all warned Einer that his thoughts were loud, and now it had gotten his friend into trouble.

As he looked up at the hot bars above him, Einer feared that he would not survive this place and that even in the afterlife, he might never see Hilda again.

HILDA

Chapter One Hundred and Twenty-Four

'KAUNA,' HILDA WHISPERED. No matter how carefully she imagined fire, she couldn't conjure it. Ice was all she had succeeded in conquering. For most of the runes, she didn't even know how they could be used. Fire ought to be as easy as ice, but she hadn't succeeded in conjuring any flames.

Her fox waited for her to catch up. The mist by Yggdrasil's root was thick. Hilda could hardly see five arm-lengths ahead. Her fylgja no longer ran off. Not further than Hilda could see through the mist. Sometimes her fox dashed back and forth. This time it looked like it sighed at how slow Hilda was being.

'Kauna,' Hilda said again. If she kept trying, she would eventually succeed. Even though Loki was no longer waiting for her.

The wind had stopped whispering sometime during the night, after telling her that she was close to the nornir's cave. Occasionally Hilda thought she heard a faint whisper of their last words of warning. *Aesir show no mercy to foxes.* Maybe she was imagining it.

Her snow fox snapped its attention to a hill that led out of the mist. Its front paw lifted. It was ready to dart into action. In a heartbeat, Hilda's hand was on her Ulfberht axe.

A woman giggled and Hilda recognised the giggle as Idun's. Without removing her hand from her axe, Hilda walked ahead through the mist. Up the hill, and out of the shadows. Her snow fox fell in at Hilda's side. The mist lifted as they approached the quiet voices and Idun's youthful humour.

Up on the hill was a great pyre, taller than any Hilda had ever seen before. Her father's funeral pyre had been built from nine different woods, but this was something else. Worthy of the presence of gods. A ninety-nine wooded pyre—or more—taller than a tower. It looked like it was touching the clouds. Still, at Hilda's back, beyond the misty valley, Yggdrasil rose higher yet.

She wondered what the pyre was for. Midsummer was far away, and Winter Nights had come and passed. It didn't look like Yule celebrations, either. Winter hadn't truly begun in Asgard yet, though the nights had cooled. Whatever the pyre was for, something was definitely being celebrated.

The further up the hill Hilda walked, the more voices she heard. Until, finally, she saw Idun. The plump goddess waved to Hilda like she had been expecting her. A basket of gold apples hung from her arm, and she walked with a slender man. He said something to Idun. As his lips parted Hilda saw runes graven into his tongue. Bragi, first maker of poetry and the greatest skald of all. A real rival to her father's skills.

'Freya said you'd come,' Idun said in delight. Her squirrel fylgja dived out of the basket of apples to look at Hilda.

'Freya...?' Hilda didn't understand how they could have known she would come. She hadn't been looking for the goddesses or expected to see them, although Loki had warned her.

'Verthandi told her you'd be here,' Idun explained.

'But I thought the three nornir are loyal to Odin,' Hilda

said. That was what Frigg had told her, and why the goddesses couldn't ask the nornir to point them to Loki. It was why they needed Hilda.

'Ja, but you're just a short-lived.' The answer came not from Idun but her gold-haired rival. To Hilda's left Sif walked up the hill and out of the mist. Her long gold hair had been braided neatly and she bore a weapon belt with two daggers and an axe much prettier than Hilda's own. Sif looked ready for a duel. The wolf who was her fylgja growled at Hilda's snow fox.

'Just in time,' said another goddess, Freya this time. Her lips were painted a dark red that reminded Hilda of blood. She too had a weapon belt strapped around her waist, but her dress was long and flowing and certainly not meant for a fight. 'We'll be ready to go, then,' she said as her cat elegantly walked in front of her, stroking her leg with its long puffy tail.

'Go?' Hilda asked. 'Go where?'

None of the goddesses answered her. Even Bragi, the greatest story-teller in the nine worlds, had fallen silent with them all there. Next to them, he was just some long-bearded man Idun wore on her arm, as casually as an arm-ring.

The fylgjur watched Hilda like they were ready to attack. Hilda's snow fox retreated carefully to hide behind her legs. The wind was silent and Hilda tapped her fingers on her axe-head. This was dangerous company, especially given what Hilda knew.

'So, where is he?' asked a husky voice that belonged to Frigg. As suddenly as Sif and Freya had made their appearances, the Alfather's wife arrived at Hilda's side. As suddenly as she had shifted to sit next to Hilda in the bath-house.

Hilda started away from Frigg. The goddess was dressed not for war, but something similar. Not for a feast, but for something between the two. Two axes, a sword and a dagger hung from her waist. Each as golden as the many rings that clinked on her wrists. Her viper fylgja was slung around her neck. It hissed to Hilda for an answer.

'Where is he?' Frigg repeated.

Loki. They were asking about Loki. They thought that was why Hilda was there: because she had found Loki and had come to tell them where he was. She *had* found him, but that wasn't why she had come.

'I don't know,' she said aloud, but none of the goddesses seemed to believe her. Her heart was beating fast at the thought of lying to her own gods. Their fylgjur were agitated at her answer. Sif's wolf stepped forward with a growl. Frigg's viper leaned away from the goddess, towards Hilda with a hiss. They knew she was lying, of course they knew. They were gods.

Hilda tried to calm herself. Her father had used to say that all lies were discovered. At the very least she had to tell a version of the truth. So Hilda lifted her eyes from the many fylgjur to look directly into Frigg's cold eyes. 'I don't know where he is now. That's not why I came here.'

Frigg's viper ceased hissing. Its tongue showed but it slithered back to Frigg's shoulder. Sif's wolf let out a whimper and lay down on the grass. It seemed obvious to her, now, that the goddesses couldn't see their own fylgjur, like the warriors in Midgard didn't know their fylgjur until they were in mortal danger. But Hilda saw them. Always. Thanks to them she knew who the goddesses were inside, and could guess what they were thinking.

They knew she had spoken the truth this time. She hadn't come to deliver Loki to them.

'How did you come here?' Freya asked.

'The whispers in the wind came back,' Hilda admitted. She had to admit something to appease the goddesses and their deadly fylgjur. Even Idun's red squirrel looked ready to kill. 'Did you know all along who whispered to me through the wind?' Hilda asked. 'Why didn't you tell me?'

'Would you have believed us if we had?' answered gold-haired Sif.

'You're my goddesses, I would have believed anything,'

Hilda said, but she knew that it was untrue. She wouldn't have believed it. Not unless she had discovered it for herself.

The goddesses' fylgjur were agitated again. Something was wrong. They were dressed for an occasion. The huge pyre reared above the line of trees at Idun's back.

'Why are you here?' Hilda asked. She hadn't expected to see them on her way to the nornir's cave.

'It's a funeral,' said Freya. 'A funeral we have all waited a long time to celebrate.' She said it like a funeral was a happy occasion.

'Who died?'

'No one important,' said Frigg, but a woman like Frigg would never have attended the funeral if the pyre didn't belong to someone important. The viper slithered down her arm. Frigg lifted the hand out towards Hilda. 'Would you like to meet your gods, Hilda?'

'Everyone is here,' tempted a smooth, manly voice. That of Bragi, the skald above all skalds. Hilda wished he would never stop speaking. The runes on his tongue gave his voice an enthralling ring. His beard was long from a long life full of stories.

Idun and he walked away. Sif and Freya followed to the line of trees and then through them towards the huge pyre.

'You are not unworthy of the company of gods and goddesses, Hilda Ragnardóttir,' said Frigg, but her viper hissed for Hilda to follow so she did.

In the presence of her gods Hilda hardly felt capable of anything. Even if she tried to fight her way out of their midst, she wouldn't succeed. Their weapons were better than hers. Their reflexes sharper. They were better in every way, and they only acknowledged her worth because they wanted something from her. They wanted Loki and there was no way they would let her leave until she delivered him to them.

Frigg walked with Hilda to the tree-line and through it. Aesir and maybe even vanir were assembled with their fylgjur in a large crowd around the enormous pyre, halfway up the hill towards a mountainside with a huge gate leading into it. The nornir's cave. Loki's whispers had led her to it. He never led her astray.

The goddesses brought Hilda closer to the pyre and her gods. Before her were so many famed aesir and vanir, and she could hardly believe that she was there. It felt like a dream.

Most she couldn't name, but some she recognised. There was Freya's brother, Frey, the great farmer everyone prayed to for harvest, with a hog fylgja at his back. He looked exactly as Freya did, with kohl-lined eyes and elegant steps, but his arms were large and his skin was tanned dark from his work in the field. Freya kissed her brother on the cheek as she joined him, and waved Hilda closer. Hilda stood back, with Frigg at her side, and looked out over her gods. They were all there.

Heimdall with almost translucent skin and his great Gjallar-horn, so large that it curved around him like a thick gold robe. Tyr dressed more for war than a funeral. Gold chainmail and more weapons than Hilda could count. There were so many fylgjur around that she couldn't quite tell which one belonged to which god, but there was more variety than any she had seen in Midgard.

There had been many deer, wolves and oxen in Midgard, but in Asgard, no two gods seemed to have the same fylgjur. A reindeer lifted a hoof onto the stomach of a seal. Bird fylgjur circled above. An eagle swept over the crowd. Its huge wings sent shadows over the crowd of gods.

At last Hilda's eyes fell on her hero. Thor's red hair and beard were red as flames in the sunlight. His short-shafted hammer was awkwardly fastened to his strength belt with a buckle as large and round as a shield. The perfect warrior, with muscles the size of tree trunks. He was everything she had ever imagined, and more.

And then there was the Alfather. Closest to the pyre. His two wolves lay at his feet and all three of them stared up at the ninety-nine wooded pyre. Thralls crawled up and down the huge ladder to arrange the top level of wood under the Alfather's watchful eye.

The wind blew at Hilda's back, but carried no whispers.

'I...' Hilda stammered. She hardly knew what to say or do.

'Go to him,' ordered Frigg. Her viper showed its forked tongue.

Hilda complied. In a near trance, she approached the Alfather and the great pyre. Her snow fox walked alongside her, so close that Hilda could feel its fur on her legs.

The Alfather was perfect in his old age, with his long silver hair and his slender build. His clothes looked modest on him. Even the gold bracteate with the motif of Yggdrasil that hung from his neck. It almost looked like the one Einer had worn at her father's funeral.

The Alfather spoke to her before Hilda could figure out how to truly approach him and what to say.

'So, where is he?' asked the Alfather in his comforting voice.

Hilda halted a little in front of him. 'You know?' She hadn't expected him to. She had hoped to be able to gain some time, talk to him of other matters. Of Ash-hill, and Valhalla.

'Everyone knows,' said the Alfather without looking away from the tall pyre. Even his wolves didn't glance at her. 'Why do you think all the aesir have gathered here? For a funeral?' he laughed at that. A gentle laughter, not mocking as it could have been. 'Tonight, the hunt resumes. With her gone, there is only Loki left.'

Hilda didn't want to give up her Runes. Give up Loki.

'He is your blood-brother,' she tried to reason. 'Doesn't that mean something?'

'It's why he isn't dead,' said the Alfather.

'I've come to present a worthy present,' said Hilda before she could change her mind, or forget. Again. 'To ask you to keep my town safe.'

'Ash-hill is safe, I don't need any presents,' the Alfather easily dismissed. 'All I need is my blood-brother. So,' asked Odin in an imposing tone Hilda couldn't ignore. 'Where is he?'

She had to answer.

For a moment she forgot why she had joined hands with Loki. She forgot what he could possibly have told her that could have made her ignore the Alfather. For there, in front of her, stood the great Odin. The man she had spent her entire life wishing to impress. He acknowledged her, and addressed her. He had invited her to Valhalla. She had no reason to protect Loki. So she gave in.

'He was in Asgard,' she said. 'But he went to Jotunheim. To find a giant.'

She felt warm inside as she revealed the truth to the great Alfather.

'Go up to the hall,' said the Alfather. He still did not look at her. One of his two wolves yawned loudly.

As quickly as the warm feeling had arrived, it disappeared. So simply he dismissed her, after what she had told him. After how she had betrayed her own Runes to help him. As easily as that, the Alfather moved on.

'Tell them to bring the body,' he ordered. As if Hilda was nothing but a servant. To the Alfather, naturally, that was all she was.

So, like a good servant, Hilda obeyed. She turned away from her god. With her snow fox she trailed up the mountainside past her gods and goddesses. Away from the Alfather, her mind cleared. She hadn't meant to tell him anything. He had made her. He had used runes on her to get the truth. He had forced it out of her.

Now, Hilda remembered why she had joined Loki. He was right. Loki was always right. Aesir showed no mercy to foxes. In the presence of her gods Hilda was nothing but a servant. With Loki it was different. With Loki she had been an equal, and now, she had doomed him. Doomed them both.

BUNTRUGG

Chapter One Hundred and Twenty-Five

FEELING HAD NOT returned to Buntrugg's arm and hand. Blinding light shone from his palm. The Muspel flame he had captured tamely glittered at him, but it was kin to demons, and Buntrugg was not convinced that any demon could be tamed.

The passage grave smelled of old stones and river and ice. It had been built by Buntrugg's forefathers a long time ago, but it had not been intended as a permanent passage between Midgard and Jotunheim. None of the passage graves had been intended to stand for so many centuries.

'What do you think?' he asked the beings hiding in the dark.

No answer came. None ever did. The svartalvar did not speak willingly.

Buntrugg shone the light of his Muspel flame inside the grave to examine the inner walls. Nights were no longer dark to Buntrugg; evenings no longer cool.

The walls were the same as in any other passage grave. Big stones had been placed upright and the ceiling was no different. After having instructed the svartalvar to close countless of these

494

passage graves, Buntrugg had found only one way to tell if a passage grave was leaking or not: going through twice.

Buntrugg prickled his middle finger on his giant dagger. His belt hung large on him in his reduced size; the buckle alone was as large as his fist.

He pressed the bloody fingertip to the end of the passage grave. The grave rumbled, and Buntrugg closed his right hand to lock away the flame in his palm and not accidentally alert anyone to his presence inside the old grave.

He crawled out of the passage. Buntrugg had made himself as small as a boar, but the passage was narrow even so.

Outside the passage the trees were bare and the forest bed was wet and sleek with fallen brown leaves. The sky was obscured by clouds. Winter had arrived in Midgard.

Buntrugg retreated back into the passage grave, and retreated back into the passage before the stone could roll shut. He watched the opening close entirely. When it was shut and the passage grave was pitch black again, Buntrugg counted ten heartbeats, playing with the bright Muspel flame in his palm. Once more he touched his bleeding finger to the stone and exited the passage grave a second time. Out, he crawled and stared at the treeline he had seen before. Red leaves fell in the breeze as the sun shone over the lands.

Mere moments had passed inside the passage grave, back in Jotunheim where the grave was anchored, but in Midgard at least three seasons had passed, perhaps longer.

Buntrugg sighed. Looking into Midgard made him think of his sister, though he tried not to. Surt had said that she was with the forefathers, but Buntrugg refused to believe it. She had been well, the last time he had seen her. She had been well and she had been cared for and she was so strong; stronger than any other jotun Buntrugg knew. Sometimes he thought that she was as strong as Surt. She couldn't have gone to the afterlife. Not before Buntrugg, and not before lesser jotnar.

Buntrugg shook the thoughts out of his mind, and decided

that Glumbruck was alive somewhere in the nine worlds, and simply wanted everyone to *believe* her dead.

Clenching the bright flame in his palm, Buntrugg shambled back into the grave.

'This one too,' he ordered the svartalvar in the dark of the passage. He knew they were with him, although he could not see them.

They did what he asked and that was what counted.

They worked at night, but they were quick workers; perhaps more so because it was Buntrugg and his Muspel flame who oversaw the progress. They were terrified of him, and their fear kept them working. There were thousands of passage graves in the nine worlds. So far, they had examined half a hundred, but they had closed every single one.

'Time is slipping faster and faster,' Buntrugg observed.

At first it had been harder to tell; the difference had been no more than a few days. But that was no longer true. The nine worlds were being wrenched apart.

TYRA

Chapter One Hundred and Twenty-Six

STYRBJORN'S VOICE RUNG up the stairs to where Tyra stood in the shadows and listened. Her husband was angry, and rightfully so. Seven summers had passed since Harald had last shown his face in Jomsborg. In the end, Harald hadn't dared to stay away any longer, for fear that his alliance with Styrbjorn might fail—and it would, but not without Tyra's help.

'Father,' Tyra said as she slowly descended the steps to the great hall where her husband and Harald were shouting. 'I thought that was your voice.' She spoke cheerfully and kept her tone light, pretending to still be the sweet twelve-summers-old girl whom Harald had married away so many winters ago.

Svend was there too, though she hadn't heard him speak from upstairs. She wished he hadn't been; not today, when she was finally preparing to send her husband and Harald and all of their warriors to their deaths. Svend wasn't supposed to be there.

His caring eyes stared at her as she came into the room. He looked her over, all of the men did—Harald and all of his warriors, and her husband and his warriors—but none of them found her eyes afterwards and smiled, as Svend did. And when their eyes met, it felt as if they had never been apart at all.

Though she wanted to, Tyra didn't smile back to Svend or tell him to leave Jomsborg. That would have to come later.

As soon as she was in the hall, she walked to Harald and took his hands, exactly as she had prepared to do.

'The lands of Uppsala rightfully belong to Styrbjorn,' she said, like a little girl who had been told that horses could talk, and believed it. 'You must help us, father.'

Ten winters of having to defend herself in Jomsborg had hardened her. Ten winters of having to fight off Jomsborg's famed berserkers who all thought they could plant their claws on her hips had taught her how to survive, and how to convince, as once, Siv had taught her too.

'You must, father. I told Styrbjorn he could count on your men and you.'

Standing in the hall with all of his men and surrounded by Jomsborg's famed fighters, Harald couldn't refuse a pleading daughter.

'Of course,' he said with a frown on his face, for he knew that he had been tricked. 'We must.'

Tyra gave off a happy squeal and hugged Harald as she imagined she would have done if he had been her real father granting her something she had always wanted.

His face was flushed when she let go of him, and finally Tyra turned to Svend.

Svend's hug was warm and he posed his bearded chin on her shoulder as he always did and whispered the same words he always whispered when he came back from fights and battles. 'The Alfather offered me a seat, but I asked him to keep it for another day.' He muttered it so that his father would not hear.

'And I am glad you did,' Tyra said, as she always did.

Reluctantly, and only because she knew it was expected of her, Tyra left Svend and marched down the hall to her husband, lounging on his seat by the hall's largest feasting table. She gave him a kiss on the cheek, sat at his side and reached for an apple from the fruit bowl on the otherwise empty table. Feigning happiness and excitement, she munched on her apple as the war chiefs discussed tactics and as her husband, Styrbjorn, basked in the pride of it all.

They would die, all of those who would march on Eric in Uppsala; Tyra was certain of it. It was why she had instigated the fight, and whispered into her husband's ears until he thought that the idea to go to war was his own. Or maybe that of the fire demon that lived inside him. It was why she had tricked Harald into finally coming to Jomsborg to stay true to his family pledge. Svend hadn't been supposed to be there. He had come although she had told him to stay away. But Tyra would not let him die like the rest of them. The nine worlds needed Svend to rule after his father died. He had to survive. Somehow, Tyra would make it so.

'We shall come home victorious,' Styrbjorn assured Tyra after the rough terms of their warfare had been agreed upon.

He was pleased with his success, but it was not his alone, and all the men in the hall watched Tyra, for they knew that it was she who decided. Hungrily, Styrbjorn grabbed the back of her head and forced her lips to his and his tongue down her throat while his other hand rubbed the curve of her hip for them all to see that the woman they stared at was his.

'We shall,' Tyra told Styrbjorn when he was done. 'My treasure.' She had planned it all, carefully, and her plan required her to be there. Especially now that Svend was going. She could save him, but only him, and only if she went with them.

The smile on her husband's face faded and before he could question it, and before the fire demon inside his fiery eyes could take over, she told him of her intentions but addressed the crowd as if it was to them that she announced her sudden decision—as if Styrbjorn already knew, so that he couldn't decide that she had to stay behind in Jomsborg.

'We shall take what is rightfully yours. I shall proudly stand at your side and watch you win the biggest battle of your life,' she announced.

Her husband had no choice but to agree and pretend that it had been his idea. Besides, it looked good to the warriors. It looked like he was so certain of his victory that he had the leisure to bring his wife.

They feasted together, all of the warriors who belonged to Jomsborg and to Harald and Svend. Tyra said flattering words and laughed and giggled as she knew they expected of her. A few more weeks of lies and they would all be dead, everyone in this hall. And Tyra would finally have saved the nine worlds by relieving them of King Harald, and by seeing her husband off to his death.

It would not be the first time Tyra had plotted with war heroes to kill her fire demon of a husband and Harald, but this would be the time she succeeded. Winters of planning made her certain.

Eric of Uppsala was a big chieftain and Tyra had made certain he knew of the attack and how to counter it. She had planned it all so well. And then Harald had brought Svend with him to Jomsborg and ruined all of Tyra's careful plans.

She knew that Svend would be reluctant to go with her on the battle night and leave his men to die, but Tyra would find a way to save him.

With the good excuse of being on her blood moon and tired, Tyra left her husband and the many warriors in his halls. She gave Svend a secret smile as she passed him by and went upstairs to her room.

Behind her, she closed the door, lit the candle on her shelf and released a long sigh. She unhooked her right brooch to remove the string of glass beads that hung on the front of her dress.

Someone sniffed at her back. The door hadn't opened; it was neither her husband nor Svend.

Tyra whirled around, the glass beads clattering to the floor.

Her hand flew to the blooded dagger a dwarf had given her ten winters ago. She drew it quick, ready to defend herself as she had done a thousand times over, though it had been winters since anyone had dared come into her bedroom.

The man was robed in shadows. All she could see of him was his bright silver mane of a beard and long wavy hair. He wasn't one of her husband's warriors. She would have noticed someone of his size and slim built if he was a Jomsborg warrior. In that case, he must have come with Svend and Harald, but she hadn't noticed him in the hall downstairs.

The glass beads rolled across the floor.

The man sniffed again. 'It *is* you,' he said in a soothing voice. 'You've grown.'

'You're not from Midgard,' she knew at once. The giants she had met on her travels with Siv so many winters ago had sniffed the air when they had met her. They had smelled her and known who she was, as this man did.

'For days, I've tracked you across Asgard. You threw me off the scent.'

Tyra hadn't stayed long in Asgard, not since Siv and she had parted ways. She had been back through the passage graves to search for Siv since, but she had never stayed long enough to be noticed or tracked, and the last time had been three moons ago. He wasn't talking about then, and suddenly she knew who he was, although she couldn't see his face. To Tyra's knowledge only one man in all of Asgard had chased her.

'How are my parents?' she asked her Alfather.

Knowing who he was made her feel smaller in his presence, but Tyra thought of Siv's bravery, put the bleeding dagger back into her belt, pushed her shoulders back, and removed her silver brooches and rings as if she hadn't been interrupted.

'They fight well, but they miss you,' the Alfather eventually said. 'They worry for you.'

Tyra nodded as he talked, but calmly met his gaze as she removed the many rings on her fingers and arms. She did her best to pretend that the Alfather was no different than any other warrior who had ever stood in her presence. 'And my sisters?'

'Eager for you to sit with them.'

She missed them, she truly did, and hearing the Alfather acknowledge that her entire family sat in his hall made her miss them all the more, and made her want to go with Odin to Valhalla, if he would allow her into his hall, but she knew that she was far from done in Midgard. She had not yet saved the nine worlds, as Siv had instructed her to do.

'They will have to wait some more,' Tyra bravely said. Summers and winters of speaking in front of great chiefs and war heroes made it easier to speak in the presence of a god.

'Nej. Tonight, you shall feast together. I've come to collect you,' said the Alfather, tentatively, as if he needed her permission to do so.

'I know,' she said, for she did. 'I've waited many winters for you to show.'

'You truly have grown,' he took a step out of his shadows. The light from the candle Tyra had lit cast new shadows across his face and onto his missing eye.

'I am not the same little girl who ran from you in the Hall of Fates.'

'I can see that,' said the great Alfather. His stare pierced her with a sharpness that rivalled iron spears. 'But *I* am the same man who chased you in that hall, and this time, you have nowhere to run.'

He took another step out of his shadows. His single eye didn't allow her to move. It held her captivated as Siv's stare had used to do, and it made it impossible not to obey his wishes.

'I don't want to run from you. Not anymore.' She meant it. Unafraid, she stared into the Alfather's single eye. 'But I can't leave Midgard. I made promises to Glumbruck.'

The Alfather froze at the mention of Siv. His stance tensed and his eye released Tyra, for a moment, as he stared not at her, but into his own memories.

'I promised her to save the nine worlds,' said Tyra. 'I can't leave until I've tried.'

'The nine worlds have been saved,' the Alfather said in a strange tone that reminded Tyra of Siv and how sometimes she had spoken of her own death, without truly speaking of it.

Runes had stopped being undone from runestones, and runemistresses could freely carve their symbols without fearing their disappearance, but Tyra knew it was not because balance to the nine worlds has been restored. They were still in danger.

'The nine worlds are far from safe. In the hall beneath us sits a fire demon disguised as a chief, with a self-proclaimed king who doesn't follow you. Who no longer listens. Harald is not the only king to have abandoned your ways and made his people do the same. You have lost your hold and influence in Midgard. But Svend can give it back to you. I can chase the fire demon from Midgard. I have made arrangements. I can give you back your influence over Midgard. Svend will listen and follow your wise advice, but only as long as I am with him. That is how the nornir have spun it. I am the one who will keep him true to the faith. Is my death really more precious to you than all of Midgard?'

'It wasn't Glumbruck's task to lock away fire demons and keep the nine worlds from drifting,' mumbled the Alfather without looking at Tyra.

'No one else did it, so she took the task upon herself,' Tyra said, refusing to give in. The Alfather could silence her if he no longer wanted to listen, but he hadn't silenced her yet. Maybe he was looking for a reason to let her go. 'And now that you've taken her, the task falls to me,' Tyra said. 'Let me complete it. Let me do this for you.'

'That's why she took you,' the Alfather muttered barely loud enough for Tyra to hear. 'That's why she was there.' The great Alfather stepped back into his shadows. His leather shoes crunched over one of Tyra's glass beads, but neither of them reacted to the sound.

'Where is she?' asked Tyra. 'Where do you keep Glumbruck?' But the Alfather faded back into the shadows, and when Tyra approached the dark corner of the room, he was gone, although there had been nowhere to go.

Tyra stared emptily into the dark where Odin had been. The candlelight flickered at her back. It had been so long since Siv's and her paths had parted in the nornir's cave. So many summers had come and gone, but Tyra had never stopped hoping and wishing for Siv to live up to her last promise.

Quietly Tyra muttered, 'She promised she would come back for me.'

FOREFATHERS

Chapter One Hundred and Twenty-Seven

WE TRY TO be rid of her voice, making us search. We try to be one again, but we know her name, and Glumbruck will not be one of us. To her own avail, she uses us. Through us she searched for you. We try to distract her and keep her away. Her insistence overpowers us.

Midgard has bound her to time. The memories are strong within her. Within us too, and with them we search for you. She forgets herself, but she has not forgotten you. Our insistence makes her forget her own name, but we cannot forget yours.

Einer Glumbruckson. She searches for you.

Your name gives her strength. Her persistence threatens our unity. We will give her peace so she will accept her fate and join us. We let her find what she searches for. Through us, she surges into you. Through our rage she takes over.

Her eyes peer through yours. In a pit of heated rocks, you sit. We know the pit. Many before you have sat in it, and Glumbruck knows the pit, for she was one of the many. The iron gate is shut above, but Glumbruck uses our anger and tries to pry it open. She knows, as we do, that it is pointless. Still she tries to free you.

She is your forefather and she has found you, Einer Glumbruckson.

EINER

Chapter One Hundred and Twenty-Eight

DEEP RUNES HAD been carved into the stone floor in front of Einer. His fingers were bloody. His inner berserker must have done it, during the time that he could not recall.

The runes spelled his name. *Einer Glumbruckson.* They were deep and beautiful and despite the evidence of blood on his fingers, the runes did not appear to have been carved by Einer's own hands. The staves were too evenly dispersed and too perfectly straight. Einer's writing had always been crooked, particularly when he carved in stone, but he knew the shape of these staves well, and he was not in doubt about who had written them.

His mother had been there.

There was light outside the pit, but there was nothing for Einer to see other than long shadows over his mother's staves that had been carved into the burning hot rock at his feet. Muttered voices approached.

'Don't repeat the same mistakes,' Einer heard his grandmother beg.

'I won't,' replied his grandfather. 'I shouldn't have protected her.'

Einer looked up and out of the cage, but neither his grandmother nor grandfather approached enough for him to see them, and then their muttered voices faded, and their shadows disappeared.

The blooded runes were so perfect. Einer brushed his hands over them and thought of his mother. He knew that she was not in Jotunheim, or his grandmother would have said something, but he also knew that the staves were her doing, although his bloody fingertips told him that he was the one who had carved them, in his rage.

The forefathers, as all the giants called their rage, had done it and Einer did not like the thought that his mother was a forefather. His uncle had said that she was well. Einer had believed it, and he had thought that she had survived the attack in Ash-hill and made a new life for herself; one that Einer could come back to after he found Hilda. He had counted on it, he realised. It had been reassuring to know that there was a safe place somewhere in Midgard where his mother waited for him with a hot pot of stew and hugs and ears eager for him to tell his adventures. If she was a forefather, then there was nowhere safe to call home for Einer any longer.

The realisation dawned on him as he sat in silence and stared at his mother's runes. His throat was dry and the sweat leaked down his arms and hands and along his fingers, until they dripped and evaporated above the hot stones.

HE HAD NEARLY managed to fall sleep again, despite his grief and the heat of the pit, when a commotion rose. Voices and laughter echoed down to him. Shadows flickered across the open pit, and then, the hot iron cage above creaked open. A giant hand reached into the pit and grabbed Einer.

He was lifted out with a firm finger on his chest and another on his back, and he wished and wished that the giant who held him would be careful and not squeeze him to death.

Giants filled the hall above the pit. They stared at him with delight and talked and whispered and laughed at him and other things. They were seated by tables that edged the outer walls of the large hall, and they were feasting on meat and stews and bread. Their drinking horns were so big that Einer could drown inside one, and he hoped that was not the intended outcome of this—whatever *this* was.

The fingers released him. Einer plummeted to the ground. His feet crashed against the floor, and his palms slapped flat onto the stone. The fall rang through him, but he was not injured by it. The floor was not as hot as the stones in the pit.

Einer felt something creep through him. He recognised the anger as the forefathers, and he felt like his mother was watching over him and giving him strength.

The giants were talking and feasting and enjoying themselves, while watching him as they might watch a child who was about to launch into song. They were seated in a long row on the single side of a table filled with all sorts of huge fruits and meats. There had to be close to a hundred of them.

'Not just a loud thinker, he is a fast counter too,' one of the giants said and then they all howled with laughter.

Einer rose to his shaking feet and tried to repress the anger of the forefathers. All of the giants were laughing at him, or almost all of them. His eyes fell on his grandmother and grandfather in the crowd. They did not laugh like most of the others, and Einer hoped that his grandfather had changed his mind and would help him out of this mess, and that his grandmother would make good on her promise to try and free him.

His grandmother looked nervous. Although she had told the others who Einer had freed, he did not believe that she had been put into the pit to spy on him. She cared about him, and if his thoughts truly were as loud as everyone claimed, then the giants could have heard it outside the pit. His grandmother gestured down the table, and Einer followed her gaze.

It was all just more jotnar feasting, but then he noticed that many of the jotnar were looking to one particular giantess. She did not stand out from the crowd. Her clothes were elegant and formal, but so were those of all the giants in the room. Her posture was straight, but again, that did not set her apart from the others, but her face, half buried in a huge chicken leg, bore a slim burn and her skin looked like it had been smoked. She finished her meal in her own time, as more and more jotnar turned to look at her.

'Einer son of Glumbruck,' said the great judge as she wiped her mouth.

Giants all over the courtroom gossiped at the mention of the name. 'Like his mother,' they whispered at the corner of the hall. 'Like mother, like son.'

The forefathers were filled with rage at the sight of the judge and urged Einer to launch forward and kill the giantess, but Einer restrained himself.

'He is charged with treason,' announced the giantess.

If jotun courtrooms were anything like the Tings at home, being sentenced with treason would either see Einer stripped of all he owned, or outlawed, but Einer was not certain that Jotunheim and Midgard dealt with crimes in the same way, and he feared that his punishment here might be death by crushing.

The forefathers loudly reminded him of their presence, and it felt like they wanted him to know that they would not allow that to happen.

'I demand to see a lawspeaker,' Einer said, for there had to be a way for him to save himself.

The fire-smoked judge sighed. 'Then we shall call on a lawspeaker and review your case in a fortnight.'

It was neither the answer Einer had expected, nor hoped to get. His grandmother had been quite specific about how quickly the hot pit would kill him. 'You might as well execute me.'

'We aren't passing hasty judgement,' said the giantess in charge with a bored yawn. She smacked her lips after her yawn and looked at Einer. 'Put him back. We will review the case in a fortnight.'

'And in a fortnight, I shall be dead in that pit. That *is* a hasty judgement.'

The forefathers were rooting for a different kind of hasty judgement, and Einer struggled to keep them calm.

'We can't let you free in our hall, or you would run away.' The giantess's voice was coarse. 'Like your mother did.'

'Then review my case tomorrow and not in a fortnight.'

The giantess yawned again. 'Court... every fortnight. Everyone knows that. You can't expect Ygovir and her five kids to travel over here from Muspel's mountain every day.'

'Trial by single combat, then,' Einer shouted. 'Give me single combat now, and then Ygovir and her five kids won't have to travel back here in a fortnight. The case will be settled.'

The giants laughed at him. He was proving to be good entertainment for their meal.

'Single combat? You're charged with treason, not murder. Your sentence is either death or outlawry to my iron-woods.'

'I didn't commit treason,' Einer said in a loud voice, angry from the forefathers' insistence, but his protest was ignored by the jotnar, who ate their meals and laughed and talked and chatted in anticipation of something big.

'Do you want the trial now, or in a fortnight?' asked the giantess.

'Now,' Einer reluctantly chose.

'Time for the vote,' said the giantess, although nothing else had been established and Einer had been given no opportunity to present his case. 'All of those who believe Einer, son of Glumbruck, to be free of charge, make it known.'

Einer sighed with relief when he saw many hands shoot up

in the air. His grandmother had made good on her promise to help him. He need never go back into the hot pit, or fear death by crushing.

The judge was counting the show of hands as a formality, but the vote was clearly in Einer's favour. Only his grandfather and four other men did not vote for his innocence, and Einer felt a lump in his throat at the thought of what he would face back in his grandparents' home.

'With ninety-four jotnar voting to find him innocent and five guilty, Einer Glumbruckson is found guilty of all crimes.'

Most of the giants in the room had voted for his innocence. No case had been presented and no opportunity given for him to prove his innocence to the stubborn few who had voted against him. If only he were given a chance.

'I am not a jotun,' Einer desperately yelled. 'I didn't grow up in these lands. I can't be guilty of treason when I don't belong in Jotunheim.' The forefathers nearly escaped his hold and took over, but he calmed them in time. Even if the forefathers could get him free of the situation, he refused to let them.

The excited chatter among the giants died down at Einer's protests.

So far, the judge had been speaking in a bored but amused way, but her expression hardened now, and the words that followed were sharp as the snap of wolves. 'You didn't betray Jotunheim, you betrayed all the nine worlds. Are you claiming that you are not a being of the nine worlds?'

'I didn't commit treason,' Einer repeated.

'Do you deny disturbing the ice to free a short-lived corpse?'

'I don't, but I did *not* commit treason.'

The talking in the hall ceased completely.

The giantess set down her meat and dried her hands, all the while glaring at Einer from across the table. The silence in the hall was complete, as if all the giants were holding their breath, and Einer too. They all listened when she spoke.

'I know what sort of stories they tell of jotnar in Midgard.

You must look at us and think that we are stupid, but I assure you that this is not a court of dumb valley giants. We live on the edge of Jotunheim, where the frost of Nifl seeps through and snows over our lands. The Midgard Worm lashes its tail and spreads its venom over our lands, and we defend all of Jotunheim against the ice storm and the end of times. You may have dined with the Alfather, but you have never stood in more capable company.'

She made Einer feel smaller than he was. Not even a short-lived in the presence of giants, but an ant under their feet. The giantess who was his judge had a larger presence than any of the others in the hall, and as Einer looked at her smoke-stained skin and the burn scar across her face, he realised that he knew who she was. She had referred to the terrible forest of Iron-woods as her own. Her hands were dotted with what Einer had first thought to be age marks, but now, as he examined her closer, was convinced were snake bites.

His judge was the famed Hyrrokin, who rode a wolf as if it were a horse, taming it with snakes as her whip and reins. A giantess so strong that with a single hand she had pushed Baldur's gigantic funeral ship out to sea, although none of the gods had been able to rock the ship for it was weighed with funerary gifts. Hyrrokin who had mothered the wolves Skoll and Hati, who would swallow the sun and moon at Ragnarok.

Einer had never been in more dangerous company.

'I did not intend any harm,' Einer maintained all the same. He was determined to protect himself through law and reason, not through the strength of the forefathers. 'I wasn't born here, and I didn't know what would happen. I still don't. Nothing *did* happen.'

'Stealing without knowing it's a crime is still stealing.'

The logic of Jotunheim was not one that Einer readily understood, and he took a deep breath to calm his racing heart. 'I just want to know why freeing a friend from the ice gets me charged with treason.'

Hyrrokin leaned forward in her chair and whispered her answer. 'What do you know of Ragnarok, Einer, son of Glumbruck?'

The words were dragged out of Einer. 'It will be the end of all living giants and gods.'

'And how does it start? Do you know?' Hyrrokin treated him like a child, but Einer supposed that his requests seemed stupid to them—and his size did not help him to look like an adult either.

'It starts with Loki being freed from his chains. Wolves howling, roosters calling, your sons swallowing the moon and sun.' Einer began to recite all of the signs of Ragnarok that he could recall, and then he remembered what the very first sign of Ragnarok was. 'A winter that lasts three years,' he solemnly said.

'So, you *do* know why you are here,' said Hyrrokin and leaned back in her chair.

'I did not know,' Einer muttered. He had thought that perhaps if he knew why the blizzard was so dangerous he could express his regret and ask to be forgiven and for his sentence to be lessened due to his ignorance, but if the ice storm was what started the three years of winter, then he had just started Ragnarok and that was not something that could be forgiven by any one person. 'My mother disturbed the ice knowingly?'

No matter how he tried, Einer could not reconcile the woman that he knew and loved with the stories he had heard of his mother since leaving Midgard. She had never done anything for him to question her motives, not during the time of her life when he had known her.

'Glumbruck disturbed the ice, hoping for Ragnarok. She was lucky that time was on our side and we could quell the ice storm then. As long as she lives, we can quell the blizzard.'

'My mother is dead,' said Einer before he could stop himself. His entire being blazed with the knowledge, and the forefathers reminded him. There was no other explanation to how his

mother's runic staves had appeared on the stone in the pit. 'She is a forefather now.'

Bones clanged against plates, and a clay pot crashed onto the floor into a hundred and twenty pieces. Every last giant in the hall stopped in their tracks. Mead splashed over the stone floor where a giant dropped his horn. The jotun did not move to clean up the mess or dry his own tunic.

Hyrrokin was the first to regain her composure and close her gaping mouth. 'She should have come to Iron-woods with me,' she sighed. Her eyes settled on Einer and demanded the truth from him. 'This is not a time for lies to get you out of trouble, Einer.' Her speech was painfully slow. Each word was followed by a long silence that almost made Einer forget what had come before. 'The nine worlds depend on your honesty. Are you certain of what you say?'

'I know my mother's writing,' Einer said and then he explained about the forefathers taking over and about the writing in the pit, and showed off his bloody fingers to prove it.

At his tale, his grandmother rushed from her seat into the burning hot pit, where she crouched by the staves the forefathers had carved last night, and although Einer could not see her, he thought that he heard her sob.

Hyrrokin was quick to take charge. 'Release my sons, sound the horns and light the fires. We move tonight.'

Giants lifted from their seats and rushed out of the hall without a single protest or question. They moved quickly, and the giant who had spilled mead all over his shirt did not dry himself before he put on his coat and left the hall with the others.

Left inside was Einer, his grandmother sobbing in the pit, the judge, and his grandfather who sat motionless as a stone statue of the south.

None of them said anything and Einer did not dare ask what had happened, for he feared that he had brought on Ragnarok and the end of the worlds.

'You think you could conjure Ragnarok on your own? You are simply one of Ragnarok's many tafl pieces,' said Hyrrokin in a tone that was almost kind. Her blood-strained eyes were fixed on Einer. 'You should have made certain he stayed away,' she finally said, not to Einer, but to his grandfather. 'Deal with him as you dealt with your brother.'

Einer's grandmother sobbed all the harder down in the hot pit.

After a long stare, Hyrrokin rose from the table. Unlike all the other jotnar, she took the time to wipe her mouth and dust off her jacket before she left the room with a lingering stare on Einer.

A threat hung in the air of the quiet court room. Einer's grandfather was ordered to deal with Einer as he had his brother, and Einer had heard the story. It ended with a cloven head.

Einer would like to think that he would not have freed Sigismund from the ice if he had known that the act could lead to the beginning of Ragnarok and the end of gods and giants, but even now that he knew, he did not regret his decision.

He wondered if Sigismund had at least escaped safely, and he wondered where Hilda was, if she was not in the ice. He supposed that he would never know, for he knew now what fate waited for him in the afterlife. He clenched his fists and felt the forefathers' rage.

Einer faced his grandfather, but he did not know what to say, and he supposed his thoughts had said it all. 'I was just helping a friend,' he muttered in one last plea to be understood. 'Making good on old promises.'

'So were the nine worlds,' his grandfather replied. 'Making good on old promises.'

'Why did you condemn me?' He had been five votes away from innocence. 'Do you hate my mother so much?'

His grandfather did not answer the accusations, and Einer suddenly felt stupid for voicing them. Although his grandfather had condemned him to death, Einer had condemned them all to the same fate. Hyrrokin had been right; it did not matter that it had not been his intention, for they would all die for his mistake.

'There has to be a way to stop the blizzard,' Einer said. 'My mother disturbed the ice, and the ice storm came, but you quelled it. It didn't start Ragnarok then. So there has to be a way to stop it.'

His grandfather sighed. 'It was different for your mother.'

'How so?' Einer demanded to know. He had never felt so hopeless before. He had always known what he needed to do, and when he had not known, he had looked at what Hilda was doing and copied her, but now he had no idea what to do and Hilda was not there to show him the way. 'Why was it different for her? Why can't it be different for me too?'

The end of the world approached, but all Einer could think about was that he still had not found Hilda and he still had not made good on his promises to her; and worst of all, he knew now that she was no longer safe. No one in the nine worlds was safe anymore.

'The nine worlds lost a lot because of her.' It was his grandmother who answered his questions. She had lifted herself out of the warm pit, and sat now on the edge, her feet dangling over the heat. She was still crying, but no longer sobbing. The tears ran down her cheeks and shook up her voice. 'So her destiny was tied to the blizzard. She became its guardian, and we became the guardians of Niflheim to ensure that she would never return. We all paid a lot for her mistakes, Hyrrokin and the Alfather included.'

'The Alfather?' Einer asked, and suddenly he understood that it was not his skill in fighting that had made the Alfather seat him at the high table in Valhalla. It had been his mother. She always watched over him, and always carved a way for him. Whatever it was that Einer wanted, his mother had always made certain that he had it. 'What happened?' he asked.

'*To begin with, the beginning had not begun,*' answered his grandmother cheerfully, as if reciting a famous song. Einer took it to mean that he would not get an answer, and perhaps he was not entitled to ask.

He supposed that he could ask his mother in death. As a forefather he would greet her, and then he could lean into her warm embrace again, and she could tell him that all was well, and that it was not his fault, although he knew that it was.

'There is nothing any of us can do to stop the blizzard with her gone,' said his grandmother, to bring an end to the discussion. Their fates were set.

'So, I will die an early death,' said Einer. 'And Sigismund, and my friends and family, and all of my loved ones, and even my gods, and Hilda... They will march to war and die one last time, never to be woken again, and I can do nothing to stop it.'

'It is not your fault, Einer,' said his grandfather unexpectedly. It was the first kind thing his grandfather had told him.

'It wasn't your mother's fault, and it isn't yours. Remember what Hyrrokin said.'

Much had been said, and Einer did not know which part of it he was supposed to remember, but as ever, his grandfather heard his thoughts.

'We are all mere tafl pieces to Ragnarok,' he reminded Einer. 'No one calls upon the war between giants and gods. Ragnarok calls upon itself.'

HILDA

Chapter One Hundred and Twenty-Nine

THE RUNES REFUSED to talk to Hilda.

Her snow fox followed her up the mountainside with a bark. It jumped all around, as agitated as Hilda. She hoped that Loki was smart enough to hide, because she had given him up to the Alfather, though she hadn't wanted to.

'Answer,' Hilda pleaded with the wind. 'They're coming for you. They know where you are.'

Thralls were moving up and down the mountainside to prepare. Hilda followed four of them to the huge gate that opened up into the mountainside. She didn't know how the thralls would be able to lift a body up to the top of the huge pyre. She supposed there was a way. In Asgard, anything was possible.

Three women stood in front of the gate: the nornir. Hilda stared at them as she approached. She sensed a sort of hum of mumbled thoughts from them. She fondled the gold arm-ring Frigg had given her. The three nornir would be able to help her unlock her full potential, Frigg said. Show her how to use the runes and see visions. Their faces were hidden by capes. Not one of them moved.

They didn't look like they wanted to be disturbed. She would wait behind after the funeral, Hilda decided as she came closer. Odin had dragged the truth out of her. The gods and goddesses no longer needed her. Loki was right: they'd only wanted her because of her whispers. They didn't care that she was a good fighter and worthy of Valhalla.

Hilda followed the thralls past the statue-still nornir into the Hall of Fates.

The hall was dark. Only a little sunlight, which came through the open gate, lit the hall. Threads were spun between pillars, deep into the shadows.

As soon as they were inside, Hilda's snow fox raced off into the hall. Hilda let it; it deserved to roam free. Besides, she knew it would come back to her. They were bound to each other in blood.

The wind came strong at her back. It didn't whisper, but the Runes were there. Loki was listening. 'Leave,' Hilda whispered to the wind. 'Thor, the goddesses, the Alfather, they're coming for you. They will catch you.'

The wind gave no answer. No indication that Loki had heard her warnings. She didn't want him to be caught. Loki's whispers had helped her more than once, and Hilda didn't like how the Alfather had addressed her after she had told him where Loki was. Nor how he had used runes on her.

In the hall, thralls were gathered by a corpse. They had cleaned the corpse's skin, and braided her long golden hair. Despite the perfect clothes and how docile and quiet she lay, Hilda recognised Einer's mother at once.

'What is she doing here?' she muttered to the breeze that blew in through the open doors.

The enormous pyre outside the Hall of Fates had been made for Siv. The corpse that the Alfather, Frigg, Thor and all of the important gods and goddesses had gathered to watch burn was that of Siv.

She looked different, but it was definitely her. Her blood had dried into the stone floor. Her skin was blue and red from a thousand cuts. Her nose was different, her hair a brighter shade, but it was Siv. There was no doubt.

The thralls looked up at Hilda and stopped their work. They knew that she mingled with the goddesses and that she hadn't come to help them.

'The pyre is finished,' said Hilda, remembering why she had been sent there. 'They're ready for the corpse to be brought out.' Her voice rung emptily into the hall.

Hilda stared at Siv's corpse as the thralls hurried at their tasks. Finished braiding Siv's hair, arranging her jewelled clothes, and cleaning her nails and skin. They applied kohl to her eyelids and coloured her lips with raspberries.

Finally, they hauled her out of the hall. Ten thralls it took to lift her and carry her away.

Hilda backed into the shadows, away from the open gate where Siv was being carried out. A giant hand folded over her shoulder. Loki.

'You need to go,' Hilda said without turning to look at him. If she laid eyes on Loki, it would be more difficult to hide the fact that he was here from her gods and goddesses. Here, in the Hall of Fates. Right next to them.

'Why?' asked Loki in a whisper.

'They're looking for you. They'll catch you. Thor is here.'

'Thor,' Loki repeated and laughed a little. 'Don't worry about them. They won't look in here. They can't.' For some strange reason, that put Hilda's worries to rest. She believed him, she realised. She believed everything he said.

'Why is Siv out there?' Hilda asked him in a whisper. She worried that her question would be heard by the nornir outside the open gate. They had to be the reason Loki had stopped whispering through the wind; they too could hear him.

'Siv?' asked Loki in turn. 'I don't know who that is.'

'Her,' Hilda said and nodded after Siv and the thralls carrying her down the mountain slope. 'The dead woman. Her name is Siv.'

'Is it now?' asked Loki with a snicker. His hand lifted from her shoulder.

'Why is she here?' A large funeral in Asgard was not where Hilda had expected to see Einer's mother.

'I suppose she died here,' said Loki, unconcerned.

'How?'

'Axes and spears,' Loki said. 'Cut to pieces, it would appear.'

'I can't believe she's here.' Siv had survived the slaughter in Ash-hill and she had survived many other things no one ought to have survived. She had seemed like she could never die. She had seemed like a constant in Hilda's life. Einer's mother had always been there, to welcome her and Einer home with warm cups of brew and the best rabbit stew in all of Ash-hill.

She couldn't be dead. She couldn't be here. Maybe it hadn't been Siv at all, maybe Hilda had seen wrong, but she knew she hadn't. 'I can't believe she's dead.'

'Not dead. In her afterlife,' Loki corrected. 'And all beings can be pulled back from their afterlife.' He thought about that for a little moment and then he corrected himself. 'Almost all beings can be pulled back from the afterlife.'

'Are you going to revive her?'

'I'm not,' he answered simply.

Hilda frowned and looked up at him for the first time since she had entered the hall. 'But you could. She doesn't need to stay dead.'

'You think I'm a god?' said Loki from his grand height. And in that moment, he looked like one.

'As good as,' she said.

The thought of it seemed to please him. Then he sighed. 'If reviving someone was an easy thing to do, everyone would do it.'

'Then why are you here?' Hilda challenged. 'It's too dangerous. They're all looking for you. Waiting to hunt for you through the nine worlds.'

'You and I are here for very different reasons.'

'What reasons?'

'You will see,' Loki answered and then he began to walk into the dark hall. 'Kauna, may my heat be yours,' he said in the sing-song voice of the wind's whispers and there, right in front of them, a pale flame flickered into being and lit the way.

So it *was* possible to conjure a flame with runes.

Hilda followed him. Her heart raced with worry. Loki was a dangerous man and she didn't like the thought of following him into the hall without knowing his motives. Especially not with the gods outside, looking for him.

Loki had to have a reason for guiding her here. He had to have a reason not to kill her for having stolen his bird skin when they had first met. Or for having revealed their plans to the Alfather. He hadn't mentioned it, but she was certain he knew.

With Loki there was always a bigger plan.

'Do you know why giants go to war at Ragnarok?' he asked.

Hilda shook her head, and wondered why Loki asked, or bothered to talk to her at all. Idun and Frigg and the other goddesses hadn't bothered to explain much to her. She supposed that was why he did it. Loki was nothing like any aesir or vanir Hilda had met. It felt like he wanted to teach her something. Looking at the shadows his small flame cast over his face, Hilda was reminded of her father's stories about Loki. Suddenly she wasn't sure she wanted to learn whatever it was Loki wanted to teach her.

Even so, she welcomed the conversation. It stopped her head from going in circles. Stopped her worrying about the gods outside. Stopped her wondering why Siv was there. Her head spun with questions she supposed would never be answered.

'At Ragnarok, giants go to war to alienate the afterlife,' Loki told her.

His conjured flame was lowered close to the floor. They were following a trail of blood into the dark. A trail of blood that had to have come from Siv.

'Not just their own afterlife,' said Loki. 'But those of the gods and the short-lived, and all those my blood-brother decided were worthy of an afterlife. They wage war for equality.'

'Equality?' Hilda asked and hurried to catch up with Loki's giant steps. 'What do you mean?'

Both of their voices rung through the hall, and Hilda glared over her shoulder to the three nornir standing outside. She didn't think they were allowed to walk further into the hall, but the nornir didn't stop them. The gods weren't coming either. Somehow, they didn't know that Loki was there. He must have used runes to shield himself.

'You know... the Alfather is the first murderer in the nine worlds,' said Loki suddenly. He walked fast, and Hilda struggled to follow.

'I know,' Hilda said. Everyone knew. It was why Odin had gained such repute. For with the corpse of the first being, Ymir, Odin and his brothers had created the nine worlds. 'What does that have to do with equality?'

'Back when Ymir lived, the nine worlds were mere tangles of worlds, none of them quite as defined as they are now, none of them named.'

To listen to Loki talk felt a little like listening to her father when he had been alive. Hilda smiled at the thought.

'Back then, when nothing was as it is now, we all invented games and created worlds, until Odin invented a new game. The last game. We called it death.'

He held a pause and slowed his walk so Hilda could follow more easily.

'It took care of the boredom, killing each other. Creating mountains out of teeth, seeing rivers of blood form the oceans. It was truly a beautiful game, but Odin kept adding more rules. He decided that he and all those he deemed worthy could be revived to live again.'

Loki was a skilled story-teller, and half of the time Hilda didn't know if he was telling the truth or some obscure, poetic version of it. It sounded like a pretty version of *some* truth. A lot of it was difficult for her to imagine. Yet, Hilda knew that the nine worlds had been different at the beginning, before the worlds had truly been formed. Back during the time Loki told her about. A time that she supposed he remembered.

'The Alfather, he called himself, and pretended that it wasn't cheating to change the rules. He said that it was his game and he could do what he wanted, but it wasn't just his. We all played his game. You either played or became its victim, dead at the hands of its creator.'

Something felt odd about the tale. Something always did with Loki. As far as Hilda knew, he always spoke the truth, but he liked to twist the truth in his favour. He was doing it again.

'That game of death,' Hilda interjected. 'It's called life. Cattle die and kinsmen die. Death is the natural end.'

'It is *now*,' Loki agreed. 'But we don't die likewise.'

She wasn't sure what he meant by that. Everyone died, eventually. All the same.

'What happens to you short-lived when you die?' Loki asked. He answered his own question before Hilda could. 'You go to Valhalla, or you go to Helheim, because Odin is your Alfather, and you are his cattle.'

He stepped over a tangled web of threads, and helped Hilda cross it. They walked into the hall in strange patterns, avoiding the biggest tangles of destinies. Hilda knew she would never find her own way back as readily.

'What do you suppose happens to aesir and vanir when they die?' Loki asked, holding a thread up and out of Hilda's way. This time he expected an answer.

'They go to Helheim,' Hilda said. That was what the story of Baldur's death told.

'And dwarfs?'

'Turn to stone.'

'And that seems fair to you?' he asked as they circled a pillar.

'One kind of long-lived get to live again, among people who worship them, while another is returned to that from which they came?'

'Dwarfs aren't the ones fighting at Ragnarok,' Hilda answered instead. 'Jotnar are.'

'You are right. So, I riddle you this: what happens to giants when they die?'

Hilda didn't know the answer to that one. Her father had told her all of the stories in Midgard. He had told her about the famed jotnar who often perished on Thor's great quests of blood in Jotunheim, but none of the stories mentioned what happened to the giants once they were dead.

'If we die, then we're dead. Does that seem fair to you? Like dwarfs, we are returned to that which made us; retrieved by the Darkness that created us. Does that seem fair to you? Does that seem fair to you?' he repeated the last sentence like a verse in a song.

'It doesn't have to be fair,' said Hilda. 'The Alfather is a god. He can do what he wants.'

'And that he does, but what makes him any more of a god than me? Or even you?'

'He created the worlds,' Hilda said without so much as a heartbeat of hesitation. 'That makes him a god.'

'We all created the worlds. Only Odin took the credit.'

'As you said, he invented the game,' Hilda replied. 'So, he is its god.'

'Well soon this game will come to an end,' Loki said. He almost seemed to relish Ragnarok, and savour the thought of it, but Hilda still couldn't understand why. Everyone feared Ragnarok and the end of all things, except for Loki. The gods chased Loki to chain him up to prevent Ragnarok. But even if they caught him, Hilda didn't think it would change much. Loki seemed set on making the great war happen.

'But why go to war?' she asked to understand. 'Why not just change the rules too?'

Loki laughed at the suggestion. 'Ragnarok *is* to change the rules.'

'But why kill everyone and everything?'

'*Because change changes and does not change back, and in the end the ending will not come to an end,*' Loki said. There were those phrases again. The runemistress had said the same thing when Hilda has asked about her future. Freya had said it too. So they had been speaking about Ragnarok, then.

'But no one survives Ragnarok. And if there is no afterlife after the battlefield either, then... Why fight a pointless war?'

'Because for once, on the battlefield, we will all be equal again. Everyone dies and everyone stays dead.' Loki's chin shot forward in a wicked smile as he said it. 'The old man's refusal to let us die and stay dead will be his undoing.'

'What's so good about staying dead? Why not find another way?'

'We've been searching for another way for centuries and centuries. There is none, and we're tired, Hilda. We're angry.'

Right then, he stopped walking. A dried puddle of blood was at his feet. A spider-web of a grey thread trailed along the floor and soaked up the blood.

'It's her fate,' he said. 'Your Siv.'

Hilda frowned at the faded thread. It was grey and dead, and it seemed strange that Loki had brought her so far into the hall, in such a complicated manner, just for her to see Siv's severed destiny. Unless he had something more in mind.

'You said you weren't going to revive her—' Hilda mused. She didn't know why else they would be there.

Loki smiled, and it felt like a compliment. Like Hilda had said or done something out of the ordinary. Something to be praised. 'I also said that we are here for different reasons.'

'You want *me* to do it,' Hilda realised. She didn't think she could. She didn't know how to start. But she supposed that Loki would lead her hand as the Runes had always done.

The Runes had blessed the ropes of the holmgang for her.

They had revived her snow fox, and bound it to her with runes and chants. That feat had cost Hilda her life, and Loki hadn't bothered to warn her how much it would cost. She couldn't imagine that reviving Siv would cost any less.

'I'm already dead,' said Hilda. 'You can't take my life to give to her.'

Loki hummed contentedly. 'To revive a long-lived will be a lot more expensive than death,' he said. 'But with the right ingredients, it's possible.'

'Why her?' Hilda asked. 'You said we needed a giant. To ask the Darkness whom it hides. To find out who freed you.'

'And out there she lies, our giant,' said Loki. 'My kinsman.'

'Siv isn't a giant,' Hilda said, but she wasn't entirely convinced. Siv had always been different. She had always been *more*. The Alfather felt fuller than most people and Siv was like that too. Better, stronger, different.

'You know her as Siv. I know her by another name,' said Loki, and once more, Hilda believed him. 'My dear old friend. Once upon a time, I brought her to Asgard.'

It had been a trap. All of it. Some wicked revenge he had planned for Hilda because she had stolen from him and told the Alfather where he was. Hilda didn't think Loki did anything if it wasn't part of a bigger scheme. He must have known who Siv was to Hilda. It *was* a trap, and finally Hilda realised what it was all for.

'This is why you don't fear Ragnarok,' she said.

If all beings could be returned to life after they died with the right tools, death was not so scary, even a death on the battlefield of Ragnarok. If Loki could be brought back to life after Ragnarok, then the great war was nothing to be feared. 'That's the second thing I owe you, isn't it? You brought me here to show me how to revive a giant, and then, after Ragnarok, you want me to bring you back.'

'That would be nice,' Loki said and his smile widened. 'Things will be different after Ragnarok. You don't have to do it if you don't want to,' he said, but he was still smiling, and Hilda knew that she had been right. Loki expected her to revive him after the battle at Ragnarok. He expected to die, but not to stay dead as the others would.

The Alfather and Loki were blood brothers. Tied together as surely as Hilda and the snow fox. When one died, the other did too. But if only one of them could be brought back, then Loki might assume the Alfather's place and rule over the nine worlds undisturbed.

Hilda's heart raced as she looked back at Siv's faded thread of destiny. 'How do we do this?'

'Painfully,' answered Loki.

'You're going to kill me, aren't you?' Hilda realised. She reached for her axe, ready to defend herself.

'Death is just a little pain,' Loki snickered. 'And nothing to be feared.'

Hilda backed away, her axe drawn in her left hand. She wouldn't go down without a fight, though she knew that Loki was powerful enough to kill her in a heartbeat, if he truly wanted. 'You won't kill me.'

'Nej. I won't,' Loki agreed, but he had used this trick before. Just because Loki wouldn't kill her, didn't mean that Hilda wouldn't die in this hall, by someone's hand.

'I'm not giving my life,' she insisted.

'You're dead already.'

'That's a different matter. What's a bigger sacrifice than death?'

Loki smiled all the brighter at her question, though for once, he didn't answer it. He was humming a song. A song that Hilda was certain she had heard a thousand times before. The wind blew strong through the hall. It shook the many fates so they sung like a harp, and the Runes whispered in her ears.

Jotnar die,
Aesir die,

We must die likewise.
Only one thing never dies.
Destinies spun by the wise.

DARKNESS

RAGNAR STARED AT Siv's glossy eyes, too scared to speak. The shadow warriors looked ready for a fight, and Ragnar had no particular wish to die. Siv stared off into the darkness, a world away.

Of course, Ragnar too was a world away. His distaff pulsated to push the Darkness away and allow him to look into Asgard. He looked down at the gods and goddesses surrounding a grand funeral pyre. Loki had been crouched beside Ragnar, but while Siv and he were talking, the giant had snuck away, and Ragnar had not noted where Loki had gone. He had been so shaken by Siv's insistence that he was the story-maker—was fate itself—and that he could decide the outcome of everything.

Siv was still staring off in the distance. The shadow warriors were starting to grow visible through Siv's body. She was beginning to become one of them. She was fading.

Ragnar turned his attention back to Asgard. He had conjured an opening into the world of the gods in the hope of finding out where Loki had gone after Ragnar had accidentally released him from the chains that bound him in the cave. But it made no sense for Loki to come to Asgard after having been released. If the gods discovered him there, they would hunt him and tie him back up in the cave, or do much worse. Of all the places in the nine worlds, Asgard was the last place Ragnar expected to find Loki.

Least of all in such close company to the gods, and at a funeral.

Ragnar wondered whose funeral it was. He walked down the hillside, away from Siv who was far away in thought, towards the aesir at the edge of the Darkness his distaff pushed away. There were so many gods and goddesses.

All of the famed aesir and vanir were there, and it was not the funeral of Odin's beloved son Baldur, for Baldur had been sent off to the afterlife aboard a huge ship that the giantess Hyrrokin, had pushed out.

At the foot of the stacked wood stood the Alfather, looking up at the pyre. A young man stood at his side, and they were talking in quiet voices. Ragnar approached and focused his hearing.

'This is what we all wanted. Her too,' the young man told Odin. 'She chose this.'

'I had it all planned. It could have been perfect,' said the Alfather, simple as that. He stared up at the pyre as if he could see through the wood to the woman who lay up there.

Ragnar followed the Alfather's gaze. It couldn't be the Alfather's wife Frigg. She was foretold to survive Ragnarok. The Alfather's death at Ragnarok was often referred to as Frigg's second grief.

'She didn't want to be perfect. Not with you, Father,' mumbled the young man, and walked away.

It had to be Frigg's funeral, after all. That explained why all of the gods had assembled.

Ragnar stared after the young man to find out which one of Odin's famed sons he was. He wasn't Thor; he neither had the red hair nor the strong built. And he couldn't be Baldur or Höd, because they were both dead. Their deaths had been the reason Loki had been imprisoned in the cave.

A hand grabbed Ragnar's shoulder. He startled away, out of the grip.

Behind him stood Siv. She was no longer in her trance, staring off in the distance.

'Where'd you go?' Ragnar asked, his heartbeat racing.

'Where are you?' she asked in return. 'What are you looking at, Ragnar?' She stared up, trying to see what he did, although she didn't appear to see anything. 'You are not in the Ginnungagap, are you? Your runic distaff pushes the dark away for you. What do you see?'

'A funeral, in Asgard.'

'Whose funeral?' asked Siv.

Ragnar stared up to the top of the funeral pyre. A ladder was placed against the pyre for people to climb and say goodbye, but the pyre was too tall for Ragnar to see whose corpse was to be honoured. 'Someone important,' he said.

He wanted to confirm his doubts. The Alfather's conversation had intrigued him. So he approached the ladder, and urged by Siv's question, he climbed up.

The ladder shook as he climbed and climbed. Ragnar stared at the ground. Already the ground was so far down that Siv and the shadow warriors and gods were mere dots on the perfect grass. The funeral pyre was so tall, and Ragnar did not understand why it had to be so tall. A nine-wooded pyre was impressive too, but no one needed a ladder to climb it. This looked like a ninety-nine-wooded pyre. The gods never did anything the modest way.

A wind blew in and shook the ladder.

Ragnar froze, his hands tight on the ladder. *Don't fall, don't fall, don't fall*, he chanted to the ladder in the same way he had asked the Alfather to run at Ragnarok. Trusting his own power of persuasion, Ragnar crawled the last few steps to the top of the funeral pyre.

The bright gown the dead woman wore nearly blinded Ragnar. It reflected the sunshine and blinked with colours Ragnar had never seen before. There were no grave gifts for the corpse, no sacrificed animals or thralls or expensive drinks or weapons, just the gown that glittered like it had been fashioned by dwarfs.

Her skin was full of cuts and scars and her long hair was braided perfectly in the same manner as those of the many gods and goddesses who had assembled by the pyre, and then Ragnar saw her face.

'Who is it?' asked Siv from the bottom of the ladder.

'It's... you,' answered Ragnar as he stared at Siv's corpse.

TYRA

Chapter One Hundred and Thirty

'WE SHALL CONTINUE on foot in the morning!' Styrbjorn bellowed to his warriors, though there were thousands of them. His commands were passed down the ranks, but not quickly enough for an impatient fire demon.

Styrbjorn grabbed Tyra's wrist and dragged her through the crowd to a tired old gravemound from where they could see all of the ships and all of the commotion. Things were being carried inland. Mostly from Styrbjorn's crew and ship, whose sailors had already been given confirmation that they would travel on land from now on, though they hadn't taken down the sail, merely turned it so as not to catch wind.

The crowd of sailors focused on Tyra and Styrbjorn and approached the gravemound to better hear what their chief and leader had to say.

Styrbjorn grabbed Tyra by the waist. He had been glad to have her along, for his certainty of victory sounded less mad with her at his side, and Tyra had made certain that Styrbjorn knew it.

Their ships had been spotted downriver, but thanks to Tyra's continued whispers, Styrbjorn was still certain of his victory. He didn't know what Tyra did. He didn't know why the river had been blocked outside the forest of Fyris, and he didn't know what waited for them in the forest and further inland. He didn't know that thanks to Tyra's plans, chief Eric had gathered and trained warriors all winter. He didn't know that he and all his men would die in these lands.

'Look at our number, look at our strength!' Styrbjorn gestured to the large crowds streaming off the hundreds of ships in confusion. No one knew why the first of the ships had docked here—away from towns or proper camp grounds—when the wind was favourable. 'Our path has been blocked with river traps,' Styrbjorn explained. 'But if we could sail all the way to the gates of our enemies, we would hardly get to taste battle before we took these lands. Our gods have gifted us war and a chance to prove ourselves.'

Thousands of warriors drew closer as Styrbjorn repeated his shouts. They wore their armour and weapon belts, and their shields hung on their backs, but none of them seemed eager to walk the last way to Uppsala. They would have to walk around Fyris, along marshland which would mean chief Eric would have longer to mount his defence. There they would be met with warriors who intended to defend their lands.

Tyra searched for Svend in the crowd. His ships sailed at the back of the hundreds of Dane ships which followed Styrbjorn's own fleet. During the entire trip, Tyra had only seen Svend once, in a busy tent while fifteen war strategists had gathered.

There were too many warriors to find anyone in a crowd, but Tyra kept looking, until she saw Svend's war strategist, Sibba. He was an easy man to spot, for he was both thick and bald. At his back came more of Svend's men. Tyra recognised them, now that she had spotted them. They were yet far away, coming up the way from some of the last ships where Tyra knew that both Harald and Svend sailed, and then in the midst of the gathering warriors, she saw her Svend, laughing at the company he kept. Older men walked at his side and made him laugh, and though it had been many winters since she had last seen him, Tyra recognised the man who walked at Svend's side.

Many winters ago, Siv had given him his famed calling name; Finn the Nameless. Now, his hair and beard had begun to grey. His arms were wrapped in jewellery. He was a trusted and famed chieftain now, but to Tyra he still looked like he had at home, during her last midsummer in Ash-hill.

It was not just him either; there were other faces that she remembered from her old life. They hadn't been supposed to come on the raid. She hadn't expected to see any familiar faces other than those of Harald and his warriors.

Suddenly, Tyra felt compelled not only to save herself and Svend, which she knew she could do, but also to save all of Ash-hill's warriors, and to stand up for her town as she once had.

Her eyes darted over the Dane and Jute crowd that walked inland from the ships behind Svend and Finn. Memories of her old life that she had forced herself to forget for so many winters and summers flooded back to her.

So desperately Tyra had come up with excuses and stayed away whenever Svend went to visit Finn the Nameless in Ash-hill. Once or twice in both winter and summer he went, and always he invited her. They had travelled many other places together, and Tyra encouraged Svend to go but always found an excuse for her to stay away from Ash-hill. Ten winters had passed and she still wasn't ready to face northern Jutland in the flesh. She didn't think that she could ever go back there.

When she thought of Ash-hill, she still thought of the hundreds of torches in the night. The yells as the southerners ran up the hill. The banging on the gates. She remembered each person she saw die that night. She remembered the screams and grunts, and the smell of blood and smoke as everything burned. She remembered trampling over her mother's dead body. Never could she forget.

'Let's hurry and leave the river,' she hissed to her husband, exactly as she had planned it, but with a newfound desperation. She shifted so her back was to Ash-hill's warriors, in the hope that none of them would recognise her.

The plan had been for her and Svend to escape while the rest of them marched to war. With the blood dagger from Ragnarok's plains she had been given by a dwarf many winters ago, Tyra could open a passageway. Svend and she could walk into another world and take another passage grave home, to somewhere safe. It had been a good plan, but they could not escape with all of Ash-hill's warriors that way. There were too many of them, and Tyra couldn't leave them to die.

Tyra spat on the holy ground where she stood, clenched her teeth and gripped the dagger like a true warrior. Her shoes felt sticky with blood. The blood of the hundreds who had died in Ash-hill. Merchants, farmers, children. Her knuckles were white with the force with which she clenched her sheathed dagger that always dripped blood down her dresses.

'Look at their faces. They believe me mad,' her husband said.

The quicker Styrbjorn ordered them to move out, the quicker Tyra could find Svend and urge him to gather up Ash-hill's warriors and sail away.

'Then let's hurry to leave before they let fear take them and try to flee,' she urged.

'Oh, they won't flee,' said Styrbjorn. 'I will make certain of it.'

Goosebumps rose up Tyra's arms at the chill in his voice, and when she stared into his eyes, she recognised the look of destruction there. The same look he had in the torture chamber, and after he came home from battle. The same look that had terrified her for the last ten winters. He had made plans without her.

'Burn the ships!' Styrbjorn ordered.

The sail on his own ship shot up in flames. A fire climbed up the rigging and shot across the sail. The wind blew in. Fire leapt from Styrbjorn's ship to the next. Smoke rose from further down the row of ships. The rigging on another vessel smoked and flamed, and down the row, torches flickered. Hundreds of them. Fire was thrown onto the ships. It caught the rigging and the lowered sails.

The warriors were too stunned to say anything, but then one of them shouted, and chaos followed. Sailors threw themselves at the waters. They splashed water on decks and yelled for help.

This was why Styrbjorn's men had begun to light the fires as soon as they had stepped into land. This was what he had conferred about with them two nights earlier. They were so well organised. Calmly, her husband's men continued down the row of ships with their deadly fire, and there were enough of them to keep the protesting warriors away.

All of the ships Tyra could see were in flames. Their rigging was ruined. Fire spread from ship to ship, flames tall as a mountain. Sailors squealed and burned, desperate to put out the fires.

In the chaos, Tyra had lost track of Svend. He and Finn had both been close by, making their way to the gravemound. Tyra should be able to catch up, towards the Dane ships down the river. The fires hadn't started down there yet. She was small enough to slip past the big warriors. She set off, but didn't get far. Her husband clenched her arm and forced her back up to the top of the gravemound.

'It's safer up here,' he said and proudly watched the chaos erupt.

Sailors tried to rescue their ships and their belongings. They yelled and jumped into the waters. Spent their efforts to put out the fires. A useless task. Styrbjorn growled with laughter at his own success.

A few of his sailors surrounded the gravemound with shields and weapons ready. Clearly, they had known what was coming. They would protect him when the sailors' despair turned to anger.

Styrbjorn kept her close. Tyra searched through the tangle of tunics to spot Svend and Finn again. There were so many heads bopping away in the distance, by the last row of ships. Sailors who were desperate to salvage their own ships, and warriors who were desperate to escape the clutches of mad Styrbjorn.

They were all moving away. Except for one head. One person looked not to the ships, but inland, to the gravemound on top of which Styrbjorn and Tyra stood. Svend wasn't moving to the ships.

'Go on, go on,' Tyra mouthed, and wished and wished that Svend would hear, but Svend wasn't leaving. He wouldn't leave without her. She wouldn't have left without him either.

Four dozen ships were already in flames. The Dane ships had sailed at the back, but the fire setters were on their way, and Svend didn't budge. He stared at her from afar.

Somehow, she had to get to him. She had to get away from Styrbjorn, and past his armed warriors, gathering in a larger and larger mass around the gravemound. If she could get past them, she could get lost in the chaos. Svend would find her there.

Tyra felt the blood soak her dress at the hip where she carried the Ragnarok dagger. It was the only weapon she carried, and she did so in an almost religious manner, which was why Styrbjorn allowed it. Besides, the blade was no longer sharp.

But it was all she had to defend herself with.

Tyra jerked her head at the forest. She tried to make it seem like she was shaking her hair out of her face, so that Styrbjorn wouldn't think twice on it. Svend glanced to the forest on his right. From afar, he gave her a nod.

She had to break free from Styrbjorn and the warriors by the gravemound. Svend was clever enough to know that if he approached and tried to free her from the outside, they would both be killed. Styrbjorn might acknowledge Tyra's worth at his side, but he had never been beyond the idea of killing her. The first winter he had come close twice, before Tyra had found a way to remind him of her usefulness.

Tyra fumbled with her left hand on the worn hilt of the dagger. If she acted quickly, she might get away into the crowd before the fully-clad warriors realised what had happened and before Styrbjorn could order them to stop her.

Her fingers were awkward on the bone handle of the Ragnarok dagger now that she intended to use it for war. Although it was the wrong hand for a weapon, she grabbed it like a seax, and she felt like she was back in Ash-hill with the life and death of everyone she cared about at stake.

Styrbjorn chuckled at the fiery scene of warriors pouring water over ships that blazed like funeral pyres. The sailors refused to give up, though anyone could see that it was hopeless. Those ships would never again sail.

Tyra drew the dagger. The warriors around the gravemound had their backs to her and Styrbjorn. They didn't expect the attempt on Styrbjorn's life to come from Tyra.

Tyra clenched the dagger tight and considered her options. Styrbjorn held her close, and he was a lot stronger than she would ever be. She couldn't twist far, and her reach was not as wide as his. If he saw the dagger coming before she could strike, he would stop her. His reflexes were sharp and Tyra's dagger wasn't. He would see the dagger if she lifted it to strike his heart or throat.

Svend was gone from the crowd, hiding in the forest, as she had asked, or so she hoped.

Tyra smiled, for she knew that at the corner of his burning eyes, Styrbjorn was watching her reaction to his display of fire, and she knew that he expected her to enjoy it. His hand on her waist tightened at her smile and proved that she was right.

She knew what needed to be done. She remembered her father's lessons, and those of her mother and sisters and Hilda. She remembered everyone who had fought and died before her. She remembered Siv most of all, and she willed herself to survive in honour of their sacrifices.

She plunged the dagger into Styrbjorn's thigh. He growled,

and his grip on her waist hardened. Tyra slid the knife out and stabbed Styrbjorn's hand on her waist. So hard that the dull knife penetrated her stomach and clanged into her own rib.

Styrbjorn yelled and screamed. Tyra retrieved her dull knife. Her head spun with pain and blood, but she had to move. Styrbjorn wrung forward. Tyra wriggled free of his grip. She kicked him on the shin and darted down the gravemound.

The warriors turned to her and she lifted her bloody knife quick to slice the nearest one in the neck, as once her father had taught her. Often, she had practised it in her mind, and she knew herself capable of it, but her knife was dull. It barely grazed the warrior's neck before he was out of her reach, and swung with shield and weapon ready.

Tyra ducked under his blow but his shield slammed her backwards. Styrbjorn was yelling incoherently. A few more heartbeats and he would come for her, and he would kill her, at last.

Another warrior turned to Tyra, raising his axe. As he did, Tyra saw an opening. Right under his axe-arm. She could duck through. She would likely take an axe to the hip, but she had taken worse. She slid under his arm. Tyra turned to face the warriors and backed away. She knew better than to show her back to an armed man. Her only defence was to hope to find sympathy. She made certain that they could see her frightened face. She made her right hand, the one with the dagger, shudder and shake so they would think her weak.

More warriors assembled as Tyra stumbled backwards away from them, hoping for a moment to break and run, but she found none. They liked her too much to kill her, but they also wouldn't let her disappear into the crowd.

A spear was thrust at the warriors.

'Run,' ordered Svend. Without looking, Tyra spun and ran, for she trusted Svend with her life.

She didn't stop to check if Svend came with her. But she heard the steps of someone following, and she knew that it was him.

The crowd was thick and wrung like serpents intertwined. Tyra struggled to push through arms and legs of warriors yelling over their flaming ships. She carved the way through the crowd for her and Svend.

Before long, they were far enough away that Tyra dared to look back, and see him. Svend had left his spear behind, but carried his mail and sword, and with a nod he urged her on.

They had not yet lost their trail, and Tyra was easy to spot. She stood out in her dress and pretty jewellery. If they broke away from the crowd to run into the forest, they would be seen immediately, and they would be easy to track.

The stab wound at her lower rib began to ache, and it hurt more and more as they moved. Tyra kept a hand on it, so that she would not accidentally get hurt bumping into another warrior.

Svend offered her his outer tunic. Tyra slipped it on discreetly, over her dress and brooches. She untied her hair and let it fall at her back so she looked no different from any short warrior. Under sweaty armpits and past mead bellies, Tyra slipped with a hand over her bleeding wound. Svend followed at her back, until finally, he put a hand on Tyra's shoulder and told her that they had successfully disappeared into the crowd.

For a while longer they walked, before Svend stopped to examine her wound. He told her what she already knew: it would heal, but she needed to go slower or it would keep bleeding. She had blood all the way down her legs already.

They shielded themselves in large groups of warriors who were in high discussion about what to do now that their ships were gone. A few ships had made it away, and the sailors all talked of it. Twelve ships, some said; six, said others; but everyone agreed that it had been the last few ships in the long row. Harald was named, and although she looked out for them, Tyra could not see his berserkers in the crowd. She hoped that the sailors were merely confused and the crowd too large and thick for her to see Harald, but she feared that he had gotten away and her big plan would go to ruin. At least Styrbjorn was there. The coming battle *would* kill him.

When the sun began to set, Svend and Tyra finally judged it safe enough to disappear into the forest.

The long row of ships was still a wall of flames. The fires lit the evening far into the forest. Svend and Tyra rushed further and further away from the river, in search of a passage grave. Their hope shot up every time they found a mound, but every time, it proved to be a simple gravemound with no passage, and their search resumed.

So far into the forest they went that the sounds of life from the ships disappeared and the flames no longer shone any light, and the needle trees were too thick to let any light through. Tyra stumbled over roots and thickets, and clenched Svend's hand. Her other hand was pressed against her lower rib where she had stabbed herself. The wound didn't bleed as much as earlier, but it had begun to sting, and her skin was warm.

Tyra and Svend searched gravemound after gravemound, and tirelessly trailed through the forest, and over fields, until finally, they found a gravemound with the dark hole of a passage.

Tyra let out a relieved sight, and crawled to the slim opening, her heart racing in the dark. Her knees were mudded and there was hardly enough room for her and Svend both.

When they were both inside, and ready, Tyra brought forth her dagger. It dripped with blood—not from when she had stabbed Styrbjorn, and herself, but from Ragnarok. Tyra let the blood drip onto the rock at the end of the passage as she had done so many times before.

The passage didn't open. The rock didn't shake and roll away. It didn't react to the blood she had dripped onto it, and it wasn't because there was other blood on the blade. It hadn't been the first time she had cut someone with the blunt blade. And it wasn't because Svend had come with her. Either the dagger had stopped working, as the dwarf Bafir had once warned her that it might, or the passageway was sealed.

'We can't go through,' Tyra had to admit. She sheathed the dagger.

'What do we do?'

'We won't find another. It's too dark, and it's too dangerous,' Tyra decided. 'We should stay here.'

As ever, Svend agreed with her. 'We will get some sleep and head out at first light tomorrow.'

The grave was tight and small, but they could lie next to each other, shoulders touching, and with their legs curled up they wouldn't be visible from outside.

The earth was cold at Tyra's back, and she kept a hand on her stab wound. Her other held onto Svend's warm hand, and she lay still, listening to the both of them breathe.

The pain in her lower rib reminded her of the battle in Ash-hill and the arrows she had pulled out of Siv's shoulders. It was a long time ago, and she hadn't expected to see Finn again, or any of the other warriors from Ash-hill. Tyra hoped that they had managed to escape, and wouldn't march to battle with her husband and be slaughtered.

'At least Finn and his warriors escaped,' said Svend as if he had been thinking the same as her.

'How do you know?' asked Tyra. All she had heard when they had hidden in the crowd was that the last few ships in the row had managed to sail away while others had blazed with flames.

'Ash-hill sailed last,' Svend explained, and then he took a shaky breath. 'I told them of your plan. They had guards, and they were all ready to bolt at Finn's command.'

'So, they knew...?' Tyra asked, allowing herself to hope that the last people she knew from home had managed to escape the slaughter she had brought upon them all.

'They did,' he confirmed. 'Finn insisted on coming, even after I told him the plan. His way to show his loyalty to me, he said.'

Tyra's eyes teared with relief. She no longer minded the thought that Harald had managed to escape. As long as Ash-hill's warriors were safe. She blinked the tears away from her eyes and sniffed to keep her nose from running.

'Are you alright?' asked Svend. He must have heard her breaths quicken with the tears and relief.

'It doesn't hurt that much,' Tyra answered.

Svend said nothing, but Tyra knew he had not been asking about her wound. He had examined it already and he had to know that was not what she had been thinking about, for he knew her better than anyone.

Tyra pressed her lips together, a decision forming in her mind. 'You know me better than anyone in the nine worlds, Svend,' she finally said. 'But there is one thing I have never told you.'

'I know you lived in Ash-hill before you came to Jelling,' he said, before she could tell him. He let out a relieved sigh. 'Tak.'

'What for?' asked Tyra.

'For finally telling me. Finn told me. Many summers ago, now, but I wanted *you* to tell me. I guessed that when you were ready to face it again, you would come to Ash-hill with me.'

Always Svend had asked Tyra to join him when he journeyed to Ash-hill. He didn't always ask her to come when he went elsewhere in the Jute or Dane lands, but he had always offered to take her to Ash-hill, when he went.

'That's why you kept asking me to come,' Tyra realised. 'You never said that you knew.'

'I didn't think you wanted to be reminded.'

Svend was more than patient. For ten summers he had waited for Tyra to tell him about her past. For ten summers he had known that she kept secrets while he had shared everything with her, and for ten summers he had been convinced that someday she *would* tell him, though even Tyra hadn't thought that she ever would.

'How did you know?' she asked despite herself. Svend had more faith in her than she had in herself but she supposed that she also had more faith in Svend than he had in himself.

'Back when you first arrived in Jelling, you told me of the

battle you fought,' Svend said in a distant voice, and Tyra remembered how they had been sitting on his favourite gravemound. 'You told me that your parents passed away in the fight. I knew it would take time before you could talk about them, but I also knew that since you told me of the battle, then, someday, you would tell me the rest.'

Tyra didn't think she could answer without her voice cracking so she just clenched Svend's hand. 'Tak,' she finally said.

'What for?' he asked, as she had.

She clenched his hand a little warmer and tilted her head to rest against his shoulder. 'For waiting.'

Svend clenched her hand back, and for a while they just lay there, staring up at the dark ceiling of the passage, holding each other's warm hands and listening to their own breathing.

'Would you...' Svend began, after such a long while that Tyra had thought him asleep. 'Would you tell me about them? Your family?'

Tyra nodded against his shoulder. 'I'll tell you anything you want to know.'

HILDA

Chapter One Hundred and Thirty-One

LOKI HUMMED. THE strings of destinies drummed.

Only one thing never dies: destinies spun by the wise. Loki said through the whisper of the wind. The hall darkened around them. His conjured flame died out. His face faded into shadows, and then the shadows faded into pitch-black dark.

'Kauna,' Hilda said to conjure a fire of her own. Her heartbeat was so hurried that she felt it in her ears. 'Kauna!' No flames appeared at her commands. She brought out her axe and clenched it hard in her left hand.

Hilda swirled around to more pitch-black dark.

The outer gates had been shut. There was no light in the hall. No candles, no fires. She couldn't see Loki. She couldn't see anything.

'Your blood soothed the pain of fire's touch,' said a voice that didn't belong to Loki. A voice from the dark of the hall. Hilda swung around, careful not to trip on destinies. Her axe swished through the air, but hit nothing.

'It makes you see fylgjur and hear whispers,' said another voice.

'Someday, it might make you see the future too,' said a third.

Destinies spun by the wise. Wind whisked around Hilda, struck the strings of a thousand destinies.

Hilda held her axe in front of her to defend. Ready to attack, too. She concentrated, to hear beyond the thrumming strings. To hear steps on the stone floor. There were none. Whoever the three voices belonged to, they were silent walkers, as was Loki.

'Change the future,' three voices said as one.

Hilda wished she could see who they were. Wished she could see where Loki was too. Where her axe ought to strike.

'Kauna,' she said, desperate to see. Candles at the top of the pillars flickered alight. Hilda's commands had been heard.

The destiny threads shone in a dozen different colours under the candle-light. Loki stood in front of Hilda. Her axe was within reach of him, but she didn't strike. Her axe could do damage, but not in the way Loki could. He could crush her, even in his reduced height.

Three hooded figures circled Hilda and Loki. Locks of long hair escaped their hoods. Though their faces were hidden, Hilda knew who they were: the nornir.

They had been standing outside their hall when Hilda had entered. She had wondered then, why they let her enter and now she knew. They had known, of course, that she was there and who she was. They had wanted her to enter and get lost in their webs.

'Delivered and ready for use, as promised,' Loki proudly said. He rubbed his smartly cut beard, and smiled so his chin almost seemed to pop out.

Loki had planned it all. From the start. He had strung Hilda along, and she hadn't realised. She had thought it her own idea to protect him from Freya and the gods and come to find the nornir to learn from them. She had wanted to warn him and save him.

'All of it was just to get me here,' Hilda muttered. 'Some grand scheme. How far back?' she asked. Had he whispered to her in Midgard to get her here? Had he whispered to her all her life to serve her up to the nornir?

'I had different plans for you,' Loki admitted. 'But then someone else freed me from my chains, and you found me in Midgard and ruined my plans.'

He was like a skald acting the part of a character from his story. He raised his eyebrows high in exaggeration to tell and sell his tale. He was a skilled story-teller, and she had trusted him because of it. Because his storytelling reminded Hilda of her father.

'This...'—Loki tilted his head at one of the three nornir—'is a much more recent plan. An alternate route,' he revealed. He seemed entertained by Hilda's questions. Answered only because they amused him. 'I am not like the Alfather, stuck on my initial plan. Because *change changes and does not change back*, and here we are, all the same.'

'Why?' Hilda asked. Loki's betrayal made her chest feel tight. Her cheeks flushed in embarrassment. It was Loki, yet she had trusted him. The giant who cheated everyone.

'I've told you why,' Loki said, blinking his eyes in exaggerated surprise at the idea that Hilda didn't remember. 'I told you that it's possible to bring a giant back from their afterlife... provided one has the right ingredients.'

With one phrase, Loki reduced Hilda's entire existence to a tool for the nornir to use.

'I am not an ingredient,' Hilda snarled. The gods and goddesses had treated her like a sock to be tossed from hand to hand and now Loki reduced her to even less.

She turned the axe in her hand obviously enough for Loki to notice. He knew her skill with it. He knew that it was no ordinary axe either. It had been forged to free Loki from his chains of eternity. Hilda suspected that it could cut anything. Even the bones of a giant.

Loki matched her stare. He expected her to strike, and he would stop her before she could. He wasn't a stupid giant like the ones from her father's stories. Despite how little she liked it, Hilda lowered her axe. Loki held her gaze and examined her for a few heartbeats longer, and then he leaned away.

'I've delivered her now,' said Loki, his eyes still fixed on Hilda. 'How about a little reward?'

He had betrayed her. He had dragged her along her entire life, and now he betrayed her.

'You didn't do it for the reward,' answered the norn to Hilda's right. A red lock escaped her hood. Loki smiled without moving away from Hilda.

'Doesn't mean I can't use one,' said Loki, and as ever, he was ready to charm his way to what he wanted. A large smile creased his face. He turned his back on Hilda. Moved towards the nornir. Not fast enough.

Hilda saw her chance. Her axe swished through the air and struck. Even delivered with her left hand, the blow was hard. The cut went deep. As far as the axe-head could go in. All the way to the bone.

Loki roared in pain and pulled away. The handle slipped from Hilda's grip. The axe-head was stuck firmly in Loki's arm. His scream stopped when he laid eyes on the axe in his arm. His eyebrows furrowed in anger. Hilda had no more weapons. She lifted her fists. If she had to, she would defend herself with her knuckles.

Her eyes were fixed on his. Watched every movement. Every twitch. His mouth rippled to the edges, and his frown flattened out. His tense muscles relaxed. His posture too. He stood straight and proud again, axe still stuck in his forearm.

He wouldn't kill her. He had handed her over for the nornir to use, and Hilda was pretty certain that she needed to be alive for the nornir to use her.

'Did you think killing a giant was so easy?' he hissed at her. 'This is useless.' He flicked her axe away with a finger. Easily, as if it were nothing more than a fly on his arm. The iron clattered onto the stone floor.

Despite what he said, Loki clutched his arm where the Ulfberht axe had struck.

'One blow has to be the first,' said Hilda. She bent over three fates and picked up her bloody axe. Her eyes never left Loki. Her body was tense and prepared for anything. He might not kill her, but he could still break her left hand, as he had broken her right. Her right hand ached all the more, when she remembered how he had crushed it.

'I could really use that reward, now,' said Loki. His harsh stare was fixed on Hilda as he backed out of her reach.

He retreated to stand next to the red-haired norn to Hilda's right. Out of her robes she drew a neck-ring with a gold bracteate. The flat coin attached to the neck-ring glistened under the dim candlelight. It bore the image of Yggdrasil.

Hilda had seen the pattern before. She knew the gold bracteate. It was like Einer's. The one his mother had given him. The one that had saved his life over summer. The same as the one Hilda had seen Odin wear.

'Einer?' Loki asked, hearing Hilda's thoughts. His fingers closed over the cold coined neck-ring 'Einer has one,' he mumbled. 'Your Einer.'

For a moment, Hilda had forgotten that he was the Runes and had always been able to hear her thoughts. She shouldn't have.

Loki's attention snapped to the norn to Hilda's left. 'And where is her Einer now?'

The norn didn't reply, but Loki would charm his way to what he wanted. He always did.

'Don't tell him,' Hilda pleaded.

'You want me to succeed as much as I want to,' said Loki, ignoring Hilda and her plea to the norn. 'One final battle and you will be free of the chains that tie you to this place, to these fates. One battle and all of your people will be free. You won't be the old man's favourite thralls anymore. You will be whatever it is you want to be.'

'He only cares about himself!' Hilda shouted, desperate to be heard over Loki's words. She was convinced that he could sway the three nornir. He was a good speaker, a brilliant one, and besides, Loki always spoke the truth. At least, a version of it.

'Home,' said the norn with blonde hair. 'He is home.'

With a smile of triumph, Loki pocketed the gold bracteate. 'Have you told the Alfather?' he asked, casually. He stared past Hilda, down the hall, to the closed gate.

Outside, aesir had been assembling when Hilda had entered the Hall of Fates. The Alfather was out there. Maybe he would capture Loki or come to Hilda's rescue so she could warn Einer that Loki was after him. Warn him not to trust Loki, despite how convincing he was. It would end in betrayal. All Loki's stories did.

'Told him? Before we had her?' asked the red-haired norn. Her black hood turned to Hilda. 'He would have expected one of us to pay the price. What are we? Mad?'

Loki smiled. 'In the best of ways.' In the distance, she heard his fox laugh. At that, he strolled further into the hall, hopping over some threads, ducking under others, spinning as he did. Without disturbing a single fate, he danced into the shadow of a pillar, and in a blink, he was gone.

The wind struck the many destinies. Whispered into Hilda's ear. *The Hanged God will abandon you.* It had been Loki's first warning to Hilda, and it felt like it would be his last too. Though it was *he* who abandoned her.

'She wants to kill us,' said the first norn, reminding Hilda of their presence.

'She will try,' said the red-haired one.

'She knew Glumbruck,' said the third.

Hilda brought her axe up. Ready to strike. 'I won't just try this time,' she said. 'The first blow is the hardest. This time I will succeed.'

'And leave Glumbruck to die?'

Hilda positioned herself so that she could see all three nornir at the same time, and could easily strike any one of them. 'I won't let you kill me.'

'We won't,' said the first norn, as if it were that simple. At least Loki had warned her that what was to come was worse than death. At least she knew. She wouldn't be fooled again.

'I'm not a thing, to be used to revive anyone.' Even for Siv. Whatever Loki had meant by a larger sacrifice than death, it wasn't worth it. 'I have sacrificed enough. I won't sacrifice anything more.'

'It's not up to you,' said the first norn.

'Not anymore.'

'You are here now.'

They came closer. Hilda struck out after them. Her axe swung through the air, and then it stopped. Mid-swing, her arm stopped moving. She was frozen in place. Couldn't even blink.

Two of the nornir advanced closer. The third one stood back, as frozen as Hilda. It had to be her who commanded Hilda to stay still. The other two came ever closer until they stood mere fingertips from Hilda, and she could see the shine of their eyes from the dim candle light.

The first raised a distaff, with a sharp point, at the top, where the wool was supposed to go. The other readied her spindle.

Hilda couldn't blink. Her eyes began to tear up from the effort of holding them open. The tears spilled over, dripped onto her cheeks and ran down to her chin. She tried to move her left arm, to swing the axe at the two of them. Her hand didn't move a fingertip.

The third norn relaxed. She was tense and frozen, but not like Hilda.

The two other nornir seemed ready. The first lifted her sharp distaff over her head. It was made of metal and she held it like a spear. Ready to thrust it at the enemy.

Hilda would have cowered if she could have. Would have protected herself. She focused on her axe. Tried to make her hand move. She couldn't and there was no time.

The nornir stabbed Hilda's right hand. The metal distaff penetrated her palm and shot out the other side.

The pain tore through Hilda's very being. A shriek of pain rung in her head, but only in her head. No scream came out of her mouth. She couldn't part her lips to scream, couldn't move. Her hand burned with pain. It shot through her like Thor's lightning.

Then, as if the pain of the distaff through her hand was not great enough, the nornir turned the distaff. Hilda's blood pooled out of her hand and ran along the metal distaff. The third norn collected the blood with her spindle, as if it were wool, and spun and spun, as she hummed.

Hilda wanted to scream and hit back. She wanted to strike and kill and get away, but she couldn't move. The distaff ground through her finger bones, tore at her flesh. Blood dripped red from her hand and distaff onto the floor. It trickled along the metal distaff and onto the other norn's spindle.

The pain shot through Hilda, and she could do nothing to stop it.

The nornir continued to spin and spin, as the blood drained from Hilda's body and her mind turned weary. All the while, Hilda tried to stay awake and alive. All the while, she wondered what could possibly be worse than death. What price she would have to pay.

'Life,' said the frozen norn who stood apart, in response to Hilda's thoughts. 'Life is a higher price than death.'

So, it was as she had thought. Eternal death. No one would revive her, after this. Not Loki, not her gods, not anyone. She would die and she would be dead. No afterlife to live. Like the future Loki dreamt about.

'You won't die,' said another of the nornir, the one who pressed the blooded distaff deep into Hilda's flesh. 'You will live. Probably. It is your life that we take.'

'Every memory, every trace,' said the spinning norn. 'No one will know who you are. Your existence will be undone. You alone will bear its mark.'

Loki was right. Life was a bigger price. There was no bigger price than to be undone.

Unforgivingly, the nornir continued their task. They drew the life from Hilda. Didn't respond to anymore of her thoughts. Not that her thoughts were truly thoughts. She didn't have the strength to finish a single one. The pain drummed through her. Her heart pumped blood to her bleeding hand.

A pool had formed at her feet and around her, a pool of her own blood, and she was drenched from it. The distaff scraped into her wound. A big gaping hole in her right hand. Her weapon hand. The metal distaff turned in the wound. Constantly, making new pains. Pains that stabbed and pains that numbed.

Suddenly, she was released from her frozen stance.

Her axe clonked onto the floor. Her own blood splashed up her calves. Her legs wobbled. There was no strength there. As if all the blood in her legs had been drawn out and used.

Hilda fell. Her knees knocked against the floor, drenched in her own blood. The rest of her followed. Her left arm landed first and took the worst of the fall. Her chest slumped and her head slammed onto the floor. Her nose broke with a loud crack, and Hilda felt warmth spread over her face.

Her right hand was still held up by the norn with the distaff. They continued to spin away. Taking her blood, and her life.

Hilda wanted to wrench away. Wanted to release herself from the distaff and the pain, but there was no relief. She had no strength.

The nornir continued to spin and hum. Lulled Hilda further into her weariness.

Before she knew it, it was finished. Not the pain. Never the pain, but everything else. The humming stopped. The spinning too. The distaff wasn't being wrenched around the wound in her palm to draw blood anymore.

Hilda blinked herself awake and aware. Blinked up until she saw the three nornir hover over her.

'Who is she?' asked the first.

'I don't know,' said the second, narrowing her eyes at Hilda. 'She doesn't exist.'

The third sniffed the air. 'Norn,' she said. 'One of us.'

Hilda blinked her eyes furiously to stay awake. To tell them who she was and what they had done to her. The blood seeped out of her hand. She had spilled so much; everything was bright red with her blood. There couldn't possibly be any more blood left in her veins. It had all dripped onto the floor.

Her body felt weak. She couldn't get any words out. Didn't think she could move either. The candle light was so bright. Hanging far up on the pillars.

Hilda fought to keep blinking, to keep her eyes open, but some fights couldn't be won. Her mind drifted. Her eyes shut, and her blood continued to run hot over the stone floor.

DARKNESS

'It's me?' asked Siv from the bottom of the funeral pyre. She was wearing the same shimmering clothes; her hair was braided in the same fashion. There was no doubt that it was her on the pyre, as it was her at the bottom of it, but Ragnar didn't understand how he could be standing over her funeral pyre and why she was there.

'How can it be *your* funeral? In Asgard,' Ragnar muttered and looked back at Siv's corpse. Her eyes were closed. Her eyelids had been coloured with kohl and her lips were bright red. For a dead woman, she looked perfect. As perfect as the gods and goddesses assembled for her funeral.

Ragnar looked down over the perfect crowd of aesir that surrounded the pyre. They wore sparkling clothes and the perfect grass at their feet was covered in flowers. They looked up at the pyre, and Ragnar was somewhat relieved that they could not see him standing on the ladder at the very top. All of the famed gods and goddesses were there.

Red-haired Thor with his great hammer secured in his

large belt. His arm was slung around the waist of his wife, the gold-haired Sif. Their children surrounded them, most of them grown adults. To their right was a young woman with a basket of gold apples: Idun, who cared for the gold apple tree of youth, and with her was her husband the great skald Bragi. His beard was long and Idun giggled as she braided flowers into it, and placed them in his long hair too.

Next was Freya whose steps left behind new flowers for Idun to pluck. Her daughters linked arms with her, each of them more beautiful than the next. Naturally, the Alfather was there. He stood out because of his age; the only aesir with long grey hair and a beard to match. His wife, Frigg, had joined him and she had streaks of grey in her hair too, but she still somehow looked young.

So many more gods and goddesses circled the famed ones. Only Höd and Baldur were missing, but they were dead already, for Loki had already been punished for the crime of their murder.

Everyone else was there, or so Ragnar thought.

Surrounding it all, the gods and goddesses and the perfection, stood the shadow warriors of the Darkness. Always Ragnar was reminded of his predicament.

He looked back over his shoulder, down to Siv, for he felt that he had to say something, and tell her what he saw, and how she was being honoured in death.

He could not find her.

Siv was not there, although she had been. Again, she was gone, but this time, it felt different, and looking at all the shadow warriors who surrounded the pyre, Ragnar did not dare to shout her name, or say anything at all.

Siv found him before he found her.

'Ragnar.' His name was a hiss. 'I know you're there.'

Ragnar startled at the voice. His heart raced, searching for the owner of the voice. It had sounded like Siv, but she lay dead on her pyre, and she was not with the other shadow warriors either.

He turned back to the pyre and looked down at Siv's corpse. Her eyes had opened wide. It had been Siv who had spoken his name. Not the Siv in the Darkness, but the corpse in Asgard.

The sheer shock of it made Ragnar stagger on the ladder. A wind blew in and threatened to throw him off. Siv reached a hand up and grabbed his wrist. She held him steady. Her muscles visibly tightened. Her face crumbled from the strain. Her grip went straight through Ragnar's arm, but she held him in place with runes as, once, the veulve had.

Her skin was nearly transparent. She was dead, but alive. She was exactly as she had been at the bottom of the ladder when Ragnar had last seen her. A fading shadow, except that she was no longer in the Darkness.

The wind calmed. The ladder rested securely on the pyre again. Siv didn't move.

'Ragnar,' she said. He looked back down at her. Her grey eyes stared off into the distance, and not at him. Like the gods, she could not see him, but unlike them, she knew that he was there. 'Unshackle me,' she commanded. 'Unshackle us all.'

EINER

Chapter One Hundred and Thirty-Two

THE ANGER STIRRED inside Einer and reminded him of his mother, and that she was gone. He bore a certain sadness too. A pain in his chest, like he was searching for someone, or something, although he did not know what it was that he searched for.

'Why haven't you killed me yet?' he asked his grandfather.

The storm was growing thicker as they tracked through it. His grandfather was leading the way, although only his heel was visible through the snow. Einer's grandmother trailed behind, and Einer could not see her, but he heard the loud crunch of her steps.

Neither of them had said anything since they had left the hall.

The wind howled loudly past Einer, and he did not know if his grandfather had heard his question. It did not seem to matter; he was pretty certain that his thoughts were loud enough for his grandfather to know what he had wanted to ask.

His grandfather gave no answer. In silence they trailed through the snow. Already they had marched half a day.

At any moment, Einer feared his grandfather's axe may

slam down over him and slice him to pieces. His breaths were shallow with the thought. He did not want to die.

Equally, he no longer knew why he had gone to the frozen beach and looked at the corpses. He had not been looking for anyone. He had thought everyone he knew was in Valhalla, except for Ragnar and his son Leif. He missed Leif. It had been so long since he had a friend like that. Sigismund had lived too far away to truly count. Since Leif had passed on, Einer had always played alone in Ash-hill.

The memories made Einer shudder from loneliness.

His chest felt cold and bare where the bracteate had used to hang, but his grandmother had wrapped him in blankets and muttered a rune to heat Einer from within. A biting sort of heat tingled at his bare fingertips and melted the snow off his beard.

The snow reached Einer's thighs and he had to move in the trampled snow of his grandfather's footsteps so as not to fall in deeper. From the edge of one footstep he could jump to the next, and he was aware that his grandparents moved slower because of him.

They had been ordered to kill him, and the blizzard would have served as a suitable death, if they had not given him blankets and heat and if they did not walk slow enough for him to follow, but they had and they did.

'Won't Hyrrokin punish you if you don't kill me?' Einer asked, uncertain that any of his previous questions had been heard. He did not want to die, but he also did not want any more trouble to be caused on his behalf.

The blizzard was so thick that it felt like he was swimming through snow and not walking at all. Einer stared up at where his grandfather was, hidden behind the icy wind. Up there somewhere was the axe that would end his life.

He supposed they were walking to his place of execution. He was not large as a giant, but his blood would have stained their proud hall, had he been killed there. Perhaps there was a ritual to it all. Words to be exchanged and a special place for it to be done. At home there would have been, but at home he would have known what to expect, and here he did not. Instead his breaths were shallow and he looked at his grandfather's heel without truly seeing it, and instead imagined how the axe would swing out of the ice storm and cleave him. His blood would splash over the snow and within a few heartbeats it would be covered by the storm.

His grandfather's heel stood still in the snow.

Einer rushed ahead, seizing the chance to finally catch up. He wriggled through the snow and made it all the way to his grandfather's foot. He tried to see through the blizzard.

A door creaked open, and then his grandfather's heel moved and Einer struggled through the cold snow to follow. Ice and snow dropped off him when he stepped onto the threshold and into the room. Snow was blown at his back and forced Einer further into the room. The blizzard entered with the wind and blurred the room.

His grandfather removed his coat. Einer stared up at the large room. They had arrived at his grandparents' home, but he did not understand why they had come here if it was to kill Einer. There had to be some kind of ritual then, but Einer did not know what it was or why he had not been killed yet.

'Do you *want* me to kill you?' grumbled his grandfather.

Einer shook his head. 'I don't want to die.'

As long as he was alive, he felt a sliver of hope that he could change what had been decided and push back the ice storm and keep Ragnarok away.

He had not meant any harm. He did not know why he had gone to the frozen beach in the first place, but he had found a friend, and he could not leave him there. Einer had just wanted to help a friend, and his heart felt heavy that the nine worlds would have to suffer for his kindness.

'Then be grateful that you're yet alive,' said his grandmother. Her face was red, both from the cold and from crying. She closed the door behind her and removed her cloak to hang it up. Einer was still standing by the coat rack, staring at his grandfather who had already made his way to a chair to sit and remove his shoes.

'But Hyrrokin said—' Einer stuttered. 'Won't you get into trouble? She told you to kill me.'

'She did,' his grandmother said, eager to talk, again, finally. 'But had she deemed it important, she would have dragged you by the tunic, crushed your bones, and tossed you aside.'

The truth was difficult to accept. Despite everything he had done, and despite what had been said at Einer's trial in the hall, Hyrrokin had let him live.

'She didn't let you live,' his grandfather grumbled in a tone that meant that he had heard enough nonsense for one day. 'Neither did I. The nine worlds let you live, and unlike your Alfather, we don't contradict the will of the nine worlds here in Jotunheim.'

He rose from his chair, dropped his big boots to rest under his coat on the rack, and walked away from Einer, to retreat into his bedroom. By the door to the room, he looked over his shoulder. Einer felt tiny at his stare. He *was* tiny—easily he could be crushed under his grandfather's boot—but at his grandfather's stare he felt smaller than that. Whenever he looked into his grandfather's grey eyes, Einer's thoughts were stolen away so he forgot that he wanted to say anything at all, so much so that he almost forgot who he was. It reminded him of the loneliness in his heart. Sometimes, it felt as if he were missing a part.

'The nine worlds may have let you live,' said his grandfather. 'But Ragnarok will not be as kind.'

NORNIR

Chapter One Hundred and Thirty-Three

THE THREE NORNIR stood over the blonde girl in her blood puddle. Verthandi knew not what her name was. Urd knew not where she had come from, and Skuld saw no future for the girl at their feet.

She was dressed as a warrior, in a blooded tunic and weapon belt. An axe lay in the blood, barely out of her reach.

'She doesn't exist,' said Verthandi.

'She never did,' added Urd.

'And she never will,' Skuld completed.

Right as the words had been uttered, the girl's eyes flashed open. Her deep blue eyes stared up at them, and past them, into the distance. Her eyelids squeezed shut, and opened again. She was alive, but she couldn't be. The nornir knew nothing of her. Not who she had been, not who she was, and not who she would be. She didn't exist, and yet she was there.

Two black streaks lined her cheeks, from her eyes to her chin: bloody tears that had long dried into her skin, and stayed there. Her hand was bleeding. The pool of blood was entirely hers.

Urd's metal distaff went through the girl's hand. Urd wrenched it free. They had been spinning Glumbruck's thread with the blonde girl's blood.

Verthandi admired the work her spindle had produced. Skuld held the blood red thread in her hands. It had not been tied up in the hall. It had no bonds or knots, but those the three nornir would soon tie for it.

They had been spinning with blood to revive Glumbruck and please the Alfather, and they had succeeded. The blood-red thread sang Glumbruck's life song. A new life for Glumbruck. Exactly as she had always wished. With this the nornir's debt to Glumbruck was paid.

They would tie Glumbruck to her *old* destiny, not the one the Alfather had chosen for her.

The blonde girl at their feet twitched. She struggled to stay alive.

Urd tried to think back to how the girl had arrived in their hall, but she could not remember. She could not find the girl in any past. Loki had come and gone. They had talked and they had rewarded him, but for what Urd could not see. Perhaps he had brought the girl. They had agreed to Loki's plan because only with Loki free would Ragnarok begin and free the three nornir from the confinement of their Hall of Fates. Finally, someday soon, they would be unshackled, free to travel the worlds and not slave in these halls, spinning until their sight was gone.

'Loki brought her,' said Urd, for there was no other explanation. 'A norn, as we asked of him.'

'We succeeded,' said Verthandi. Her eyes were resting on the red thread in Skuld's hands that was ready to be bound up in their hall. 'That is why she no longer exists, whoever she used to be.'

'Glumbruck will wake on her pyre,' said Skuld. 'We must stop the torches before they burn it.' She set Glumbruck's long thread of new life down onto the stone floor. They would tie it up later.

The three sisters all rushed down the dark hall.

Urd feared their hard work would be lost if they were too late to stop the funeral. Verthandi knew that the torches were being lit outside. Skuld knew that they were not running fast enough.

They glided down the hall, over the smooth stones their feet had trod on for thousands of summers and winters. The huge gate opened at their approach.

Verthandi let out a sob before they were even at the gates. They were too late. Flames climbed up the ninety-nine wooded pyre.

The three nornir ran into the midday breeze. The pyre was burning.

Aesir and vanir surrounded the large pyre outside. They were singing. Not Glumbruck's own song—only nornir knew Glumbruck's song—but they sang for her nonetheless. Sang her into the next life.

Skuld cried. She searched the future. Searched what was to come, but she could not see Glumbruck's future. It was muffled by darkness, muffled by death. They were too late.

'Loki's doing,' Urd decided. Loki always cheated. He delivered what he said he would, but he always had other plans. He had stayed too long on purpose. He had been following the funeral while they had been talking. He had slowed their work and now they were too late and Glumbruck was gone forever.

Verthandi looked away from the flames of the ninety-nine wooded pyre, and over her shoulder, into the dark of the hall.

Glumbruck was gone, but there was still the mystery girl, bleeding out in their hall. Something to care for. Someone to protect.

Skuld was the first to look to the future and hope for more. She left the murder of Glumbruck's funeral. She walked back into the dark of the Hall of Fates. Behind her came Verthandi, eager to do something to shadow her unrelenting vision of the present, where aesir and vanir and giants alike mourned Glumbruck's final moments.

Urd lingered outside, remembering Glumbruck's life. All that had been accomplished and all that should have been and never would. Finally, she trailed after her sisters back into the hall and closed the large gates after herself.

A brilliant white snow fox had appeared inside their hall. It licked the bleeding hand of the blooded girl. Its white fur was stained red with blood. It had scars up its legs. It had been in battle.

As the three nornir approached, the snow fox scurried further into their hall.

Over the body of the girl, the three sisters loomed. Again, they stared down at her, and wondered what to do now. How to help a dying girl who did not exist. They could not reach for her thread and attempt to mend it when she had no thread. They could not look into the future and see if she would survive. They could not search the present and find out where she was hurting and what she needed. They looked everywhere, to the past, present and future, and saw nothing.

'She is strong. Like me. Like you. Like us,' said Urd. 'Or she wouldn't have survived.' She crouched down by the girl's bleeding hand and with a thread she conjured from her robes, she bound the hand as through visions she had seen countless of short-lived do with wounds.

'She has our blood,' said Verthandi, watching Urd's skilled work. 'She is our kin.'

'A little sister,' said Skuld, hopeful that, finally, she would no longer be the youngest.

Her eyes trailed to the blood on the floor and then along to catch the last glimpses of Glumbruck's burning thread, but she couldn't find it. Likely, the thread had already burned. Their debt to Glumbruck would never be paid in full. They had freed her two living children as much as they could to allow them to make their own choices, but it was not enough. They had robbed Glumbruck of too many sons already.

Blood dripped down onto Skuld's shoulder.

She touched a finger to it and sniffed. The blood of a norn, and a short-lived. The blood of the blonde girl on the floor.

Skuld tilted her head back and looked up to the many threads bound up in the hall.

While the three sisters had been outside, watching Glumbruck's pyre burn, the blooded thread of destiny had begun to tie itself into the hall.

Dead giants needed no destinies. A burned corpse meant a burned thread. Instead, Glumbruck's thread was tied up in the hall by an invisible force that was not the nornir and their sight. The blood-red thread swirled around pillars, without needing the three nornir's help. Fate itself tied up Glumbruck's thread.

A new future was forming, and the three nornir were not its story-maker.

Their shackles were lifting.

ACKNOWLEDGEMENTS

ALLOW ME TO begin this feast of thanks by filling Odin's wisdom mead into the drinking horns of my parents who ensured that I could walk shackle-free into the nine worlds. You encouraged me to find my own path, and when I fell down, as all children inevitably do, you did not sweep in to pick me up, you taught me to get up on my own and keep fighting. As long as I had something worth fighting for. That is the true spirit of a Viking, and I have it from you.

Let us raise our horns to my agent, Jamie Cowen, who told me to keep writing Shackled Fates although, at the time, we still hadn't sold the first book. Your assurance and belief that the Hanged God Trilogy would sell made it possible for me to write on. Thank you for giving me the dream.

Now, brave warriors, join me in a roar for my editor, David Moore, thanks to whom I had an amazing time as a debut author. As a young writer, one hears many stories about the mysterious publishing world, so when it was my turn, I did not know what to expect. With David and the team at Rebellion, my suggestions were valued and I felt like we were all part of a crew. There to brace against the treacherous seas together and fight the Midgard Worm, if it came to it.

Speaking of crews, let me turn your attention to the crew of the *Sea Stallion*, alongside whom I've faced monstrous waves and perilous harbour runs to the local pubs. Whenever I catch a whiff of tar, I'm right back on our ship, hearing the water rush in through the oar holes. Such times we have lived.

My grandfather, Arthur, passed away before he could see me sail with the *Sea Stallion*. He would have loved to see me sail with the warship, and would probably also have loved to sail along too. One day, grandpa, in Ran's and Aegir's hall. I'd like to drink another hornful at the memory of my grandmother, Else, who yearned to see me find my place in the nine worlds. I've found it now. It was here all along.

In the gaping absence of Arthur and Else, Ane and Lau swept in with unconditional support, so I urge you, dear warriors, let's have a drink in their honour too.

Another one for Sif who was born when I first began work on this novel. It is in large part thanks to Sif that the goddesses made such crucial appearances. For small Viking girls need big Viking girls to look up to and dream about.

Before the end of this feast, I'd like to raise a horn to my friends who endured rambling messages about my debut, and who calmly waited when I disappeared for weeks at a time to bury myself in edits. Thank you for your patience and support.

Last, but not least, thank you to all of the reviewers and readers who read and loved *Northern Wrath*. Thanks to you brave warriors, the experience of debuting during a pandemic was not lonesome, as one might expect. Whenever you tagged me in photos or wrote to me to share your excitement I gained the same wonderful rush as when I first held the book in hand.

Thank you all for championing this story!

ABOUT THE AUTHOR

Thilde Kold Holdt is a Viking, traveller and a polygot fluent in Danish, French, English and Korean. As a writer, she is an avid researcher. This is how she first came to row for hours upon hours on a Viking warship. She loved the experience so much that she has sailed with the Viking ship the *Sea Stallion* ever since. Another research trip brought her to all corners of South Korea where she also learnt the art of traditional Korean archery. Born in Denmark, Thilde has lived in many places and countries, taking a bit of each culture with her. This is why she regards herself as simply being from planet Earth, as she has yet to set foot on Mars...

Thilde is currently based in Southern France where she writes full-time.

FIND US ONLINE!

www.rebellionpublishing.com

/rebellionpub /rebellionpublishing /rebellionpublishing

SIGN UP TO OUR NEWSLETTER!

rebellionpublishing.com/newsletter

YOUR REVIEWS MATTER!

Enjoy this book? Got something to say?

Leave a review on Amazon, GoodReads or with your
favourite bookseller and let the world know!